PRAISE FOR
ANGEL OF CHAOS

"Literate... intelligent... a pleasure to read."
—Barbara Rogan, author of *Suspicion*

"A very realistic world full of interesting people and enough political twists to keep everyone reading."
—Clelie Rich

PRAISE FOR
DARWIN'S PARADOX
SEQUEL TO ANGEL OF CHAOS

"A thrill ride that makes you think and tugs the heart."
—Robert J. Sawyer, Hugo and Nebula Award-winning author of *Rollback*

"Perfect for any collection appealing to avid science fiction readers. "
—Midwest Book Review (Reviewer's Choice)

"The story is intricate... imaginative, and intelligent... The medical and scientific [premise is] completely plausible and perhaps our fate." —Rhonda Low, CTV News, and Clinical Associate Professor in the Dept. of Family & Community Medicine, University of British Columbia

"Munteanu [has] created an inventive and exciting future... a mystery virus... unsettling artificial intelligences... and an indomitable hero."
—Kay Kenyon, SF author of *Bright of the Sky*

"Munteanu is clearly a writer with big ideas."
—C. Gilbert (Top 500 Amazon Reviewer)

"I easily recommend this book to anyone who enjoys a nice mix of science fiction, political intrigue and some big scientific concepts. Go pick it up!"
—Brian Brown, Dragon Page

ANGEL OF CHAOS

NINA MUNTEANU

ANGEL OF CHAOS

NINA MUNTEANU

Angel of Chaos

Copyright © 2010 Nina Munteanu

All rights reserved. Reproduction or utilization of this work in any form, by any means now known or hereinafter invented, including, but not limited to, xerography, photocopying and recording, and in any known storage and retrieval system, is forbidden without permission from the copyright holder.

pISBN 978-1-897492-12-3

Dragon Moon Press
www.dragonmoonpress.com

Printed and bound in the United States of America

This is a work of fiction. Names, characters, places, and incidents are the products of the author's imagination or are used fictitiously and are not to be construed as real. Any resemblance to actual events, locales, organizations, or persons, living or dead, is entirely coincidental.

DEDICATION

For Kevin with everlasting love

ACKNOWLEDGEMENTS

I thank Dr. Michio Kaku for discussions on the evolution of Artificial Intelligence. Janine Benyus provided diverting conversations on *biomimicry* and nature's 'intelligence'. I acknowledge the wisdom of many additional scientists whose works in chaos theory, neural science, epidemiology, co-evolution and ecology I consulted. A complete bibliography of works consulted can be found in the sequel to this book, Darwin's Paradox.

Special gratitude goes to my editor, Gabrielle Harbowy, whose quiet grace with words and cadence transformed song into symphony. I thank Dragon Moon Publisher Gwen Gades for her faith in this project, her unending energy, vision, support, and friendship.

This book and its sequel were written listening to Enya, Dido and Pat Methany's *Off Ramp*. I thank them for their inspiration.

BOOK ONE:

A BUTTERFLY IN PEKING

Then I saw a new heaven and a new earth; for the first heaven and the first earth had passed away, and the sea was no more. And I saw the Holy City, new Jerusalem, coming down out of heaven from God... its radiance like a most rare jewel, like jasper, clear as crystal... and the street of the city was pure gold, transparent as glass... By its light shall the nations walk; and the kings of the earth shall bring their glory into it.

~~ The Book of Revelation

1

JULIE Crane slunk out of Kraken's office in the Pol Station feeling like a five-year-old caught lying. She jammed a hand in her trouser pocket and stroked the smooth clean surface of her Level 1 card. Would she lose it and its associated privileges now?

A Pol dressed in beetle-black, eyes and nose obscured by the dark visor of his shiny helmet, swaggered past her, boots clacking. He slowed and turned his head, lips sliding into an oily smirk. Julie forced a tight smile and picked up her pace. She smoothed her red tunic and commanded her steps to keep from careering toward the exit. *Vee, I hate this place.*

Julie shifted her mind to veemeld with SAM, her AI companion. *Sam, are you still there?* She sent her thought over the low random chatter of a million machine voices in her mind.

Where else would I be? SAM's pleasant male voice quipped in her head. The moon? Have you noticed that no one goes there for a vacation? That's because it lacks atmosphere...

SAM followed with its annoying tinny laugh. Julie grimaced. Terrific. There was something almost unsavory about a machine that laughed at its own jokes—and usually at her expense.

Well, that went well, SAM added.

Julie shot her gaze to the vaulted ceiling. It wasn't her fault that she'd missed her deadline. The model she'd promised the Head Pol today was far more complicated than he'd let on.

Perhaps you should reconsider making promises that you can't keep.

Park the advice, SAM, she snapped and left the station to enter the crowded mall.
Your naked face is showing.

Thanks. Julie tidied her unruly hair and put her vee-set on. She felt a shivering tickle as the set shifted like a gangly spider getting comfortable on her head. It molded itself to her scalp, coiling its four metalloid legs to poise over right eye, ear and mouth with fourth counter-balancing leg nestling snugly through her thick curls. It was like wearing a vee-com on your head. Icarians relied on them. But she had SAM, Julie thought smugly, stepping into the swells of people and robots.

Sunlight from the mall's transparent ceiling filtered through the tall trees, dappling the store windows and glinting in the pools below. Her gaze drifted to two Enviro-workers washing off a recent act of vandalism on a storefront wall. She could still read the blood red smear: "Darwin's Evolution Kills! We KNOW Who's to Blame!" Distopians were getting brash these days, blaming the government—

She stopped mid-stride to stare at an old woman. Jostled by impatient Icarians, Julie wrenched off the shiny claws of her vee-set to get a better look. Apart from not wearing a vee-set, the woman was outer-city enough: purple hair and hoary skin stretched from neurgery and nuyu treatments. But her sad expression came from another world. Julie knew that look. It stirred feelings of shame and fear that she thought she'd safely buried.

Julie, what're you doing?

As if drawn to her, the stranger turned and they locked eyes. Julie looked away, pulse racing. When she glanced back the old woman was gone. Feeling an inexplicable compulsion to find her, Julie searched the milling crowd. *Where'd she go, SAM?*

I don't know, but I suggest you put your vee-set back on.

A tube-jet approached the mall station. Clutching her vee-set, Julie wandered toward it, gaze sweeping the crowd. At the sound of a sudden shriek and men's yells, she picked up her pace and shoved her way to the platform edge. The old woman stood on the track, smiling smugly at the oncoming tube-jet.

Not again! Julie, don't—

Mind snapping out of veemeld, Julie leapt down and pushed the woman aside onto the adjoining empty track. Instead of sprinting to safety, Julie stumbled back and froze. She saw the driver scream. The tube-jet jerked to a stop less than a meter from her. The flood of noise from the people crying out in relief and the smell of spent tube-jet fuel brought her down to the anticlimax of reality. A hysterical laugh escaped her lips.

Julie fumbled to replace the vee-set on her head while the murmuring crowd pressed forward on the platform. She felt their eyes on her and the set's metalloid legs slipped in her clammy hands. Once she got it on, Julie turned to the old woman who lay sobbing in a heap on the side of the rail. The intro-mode default on Julie's vee-set displayed the woman's identity on her eye-com: "Isabella Lippi, just retired dental hygienist, recently demoted to Level 8 privileges." Which meant a mandatory move to the inner-city. She obviously hadn't earned enough merits to keep her Level 5 privileges past her useful working years. Was that why the woman had tried to kill herself? Offering her hand to the old woman, Julie noted from her blotched face and pale lips that the woman's nuyu treatments were wearing off—

Julie started back as a violent spasm slithered up the old woman's face. Vee! She had Darwin Disease! Julie's stomach clenched. Her face tightened to hide the revulsion and she forced herself from instinctively retracting her hand. But Isabella caught it and glared at Julie.

"Bitch!" she yelled, face still convulsing.

Julie winced.

"Self-serving bitch!" Isabella snarled over her shoulder at Julie and clamored up the platform. The crowd stepped back and waited dutifully for the AI20 robots. Isabella shook her fist as Julie climbed up. "You robbed me!" she yelled from the midst of four brightly colored AI20s that closed in around her, clucking obsequiously to her supposed aid. She burst into howling sobs and Julie fled without a backward look.

"Move along, move along," droned the AI20s, pushing people from the platform with their iridescent arms.

Julie turned and glimpsed a black Pol loping toward the old woman. Not far behind, a second followed, adjusting his beetle-like helmet. Julie froze, certain that he looked right at her. Then he turned his head to the first Pol, who had already seized the crying woman. "Shut up, parasite!" the first Pol yelled. He yanked Isabella to her feet. "Who's your rescuer, eh? Tell us, virus!" He shook her.

Julie winced and quickened her pace.

"So she's a bitch, is she?" Julie heard him shout. "We'll throw her in with you for interfering. Two bitches in a cell is better than one."

Julie ducked through an exit and tore down several flights of stairs to the lower levels. She raced down a dim corridor until she felt alone then stopped and bent down, hands on knees, to catch her breath. The smell of hot metal and sewage reminded her of the inner-city slums. She slipped back into veemeld and SAM's matrix washed in. What happened! You almost got us crushed!

Us? Me, you mean. You'd just have to find a new interface.

Your heart rate and breathing are elevated due to activation of the sympathetic division of your autonomic nervous system. Your blood pressure and blood sugar levels have increased to—

You sound like my PCU. Give it a rest. She straightened up to get her bearings. The overhead light cast her gloomy shadow down the gaping corridor and she smelled organic waste and vented hot air. Machines sighed in the distance. Why did she always take herself down here?

Julie, remember that my advice is for your own good.

Yes, SAM. I know. Sometimes SAM was like an overbearing parent. *Let's skip the yak for now. I need to think.* She pulled off the vee-set, its claws raking through her hair, and strode down the graffiti-littered corridor toward the stairs to the next tube-jet station.

Why do you always rush into trouble without a second thought? It's frightening.

As if SAM could get frightened.

And for what? To save someone who's already dying from Darwin Disease... After a pause SAM continued, What's bothering you? Why'd you freeze in front of the tube-jet?

If I knew that, I probably wouldn't have done it. She saw the entrance door to Odum Mall and quickened her steps.

This can't be about what Kraken said. That's no reason to exterminate yourself.

I wasn't trying to exterminate myself! Why did she keep saving people who didn't want to be saved? She vaulted the steps two at a time to the entrance door and emerged in a tide of rushing people and robots. Julie fumbled to replace the vee-set on her head, then turned it off.

The musky perfume of the mall's vast indoor park beckoned. But she was in a hurry. Avoiding the park and ignoring the holo-ads blaring overhead, she surfed the metal-human sea past the glittering shops of the mall toward the waiting tube-jet. *What if Kraken knows about us? Already plans to send me to the DP?*

You have to start trusting people. Of course he doesn't know about us. Nobody knows—

—That I'm a freak?

You're not a freak. Strange, maybe—

SAM, I'm the only Icarian—the only veemeld who can veemeld whenever, wherever with an AI—with you. No one else has you in their head all the time, do they?

No; you are unique that way.

And who else hears the whole machine world in their head?

Very unique.

Ever since she'd fallen ill at age five, the "voices" had crept uninvited into her head: constant machine droning interspersed with distinct phrase, like pieces of a conversation from another room. At first she thought that she'd gone insane, but when she eventually realized that they weren't the ghosts of dead Icarians haunting her soul, she relegated their constant drone to the back of her mind—

Her shoulder collided into an AI20 traffic droid and she instinctively grabbed its smooth rainbow torso for balance.

"Watch where you're going!" It jerked out of her grasp and disappeared into the crowd before she could apologize.

You sound angry. Don't you enjoy having me—us—around all the time?

Had she imagined a plaintive note in SAM's voice? Julie swerved just in time to get around a stout litter droid picking up a discarded wrapper. *Yes, of course I do.* She wasn't sure about the dull machine chatter in her head, but she couldn't imagine not having SAM there. She reached the tube-jet door and hesitated at the wall of blank one-eyed faces, entertained by their vee-sets.

"Move along... move along..." a traffic robot droned. Julie let the droid push her into the packed car. The door slid shut. The smell of old shoes and foul breath engulfed her as the tube-jet plunged into the dark tunnel. She grabbed a rail by the door for balance and stared at her own reflection in the window.

Noticing an empty seat mirrored in the window, she pushed through the standing passengers and sat, glancing furtively at the young man next to her. He caught her glance and smiled. Julie fought her instinct to grimace, realizing why the seat had been empty. His face and hands convulsed with the early signs of Darwin Disease. The Med-Center would pick him up soon. Julie shifted in her seat and leaned into the rail, trying to put some distance between them. Vee, that was two Darwin victims she'd run into in the last hour! *He's got it bad, doesn't he, SAM?*

People may express a certain genetic predisposition to this neural disease. Several scientists now think that it is environmentally-induced. However, most information relating to Darwin is now classified. CDC revealed an alarming 60% increase in the rate of transmission...

For distraction she gazed at the holo-ad above her. It displayed two young men with fake smiles, seated in a cafe. They were comparing acquisitions. The one dressed in Trans-Center blue boasted of his quantum vee-com and his Senscape 3000; the other in Law-Center purple grinned and winked at her. He flashed his Level 1 card and said, "Good work gets you toys; hard work gets you *everything...* Aspire to Level 1!"

She stroked her Level 1 card in her pocket and imagined Kraken's smirking face. His parting remark had triggered her alarm. "It'd be a shame to see you go the way of the others before you," he'd said, hiking up his brows for punctuation. She squirmed at the words. What had happened to the others?

Sam appeared to read her mind: Kraken chose you for your unique veemeld skills. You're extremely gifted.

Julie stifled a nervous laugh. If she was so extremely gifted, why had her boss pulled her off the Darwin project and thrown her to Kraken? She looked down at her scuffed boots and buffed them on her pant legs. *Maybe I don't want to be unique.*

If you weren't unique you'd probably still be in the inner-city.

Julie's lips tightened. She'd left Neo behind and lost her sister in the inner-city. Were they still alive? Darwin Disease raged there like an open wound. With no Center for Disease Control, no screening or pick-up program, inner-city families abandoned Darwin victims and left them to aimlessly wander the halls.

Besides, Kraken's the Head Pol. Intelligent.

Julie frowned. SAM still had a lot to learn about people—and intelligence.

You need to trust people, Julie.

SAM lecturing her about trust; now *that* was a joke. SAM trusted everyone.

Find your ecological niche in the outer-city. Use nature's heuristic process and complete the link in your community-web.

Julie couldn't help a smile at SAM's recent fascination with ecology. She wasn't sure she understood exactly what SAM was after. Did AIs have hopes and dreams too?

She remembered the first time she'd snuck outside Icaria on her own—not completely alone, SAM was already in her head by then. She'd scrambled up a small hill to gaze at the sun trembling over the horizon. A summer breeze stirred the rioting blossoms and brought with it their heavy perfume, coaxing vivid memories of walks with her father when she was a child. He'd explained how the heath had sprung up from climatological change and replaced the mixed oak-hickory woodland. According to the Ecologists, the heath's unruly bog and scrub exploited disturbed environments. Normally, longer-lived plants succeeded the pioneer community. But the heath refused to abdicate. Julie remembered glancing back at the glittering towers of Icaria-5 and picturing it an island of harnessed order that floated on a rough sea of entropy like Jupiter's Red Spot, drifting steadily and unperturbed by the chaos around it. The heath neither ended nor began. It simply existed, like the universe, and undulated toward infinity—

You've reached your destination, Julie.

Thanks, SAM. Julie elbowed her way off the tube-jet into Pielou Mall, feeling an impending darkness she couldn't shake. It was her birthday today. Why did it feel like her last? Between the rising threat of Darwin Disease and the increase in subversives, Icaria was in a mess—and she had stopped to save an old woman who was dying of the plague. No, Julie thought again, *I'm* the one in a mess.

2

DANIEL Woods tinkered with the vee-com console of his tube-jet and squinted at the growing light of Darwin Station. His head throbbed from last night's party. Needing distraction, he switched off AI-pilot and let his fingers play over the manual controls. He closed his eyes to the drumming ache. I should stay away from those drug parties. But, vee, Colleen was beautiful!

His face reddened at the memory. He'd watched her for half an hour, rehearsing his opening line. She kept artfully flicking her flaming hair behind her mahogany face, like she knew someone was watching her. No one there knew his inner city background, much less his decrepit techno-slummer history, but his heart still thundered when he finally made his move across the room, noting from her earrings that she was a healthy bisexual and that she wore no rings of committed attachment. He straightened his blue uniform, pushed his blue hair back with both hands, picked up a glass of *delilah* from a tray and sauntered toward her. She smiled at him. He tripped. The drug flew out of his hand and splashed her face and the front of her tunic. She shrieked—

An old woman stood on the track meters in front of his tube-jet. She glared at him with a familiar defiance. Chaos! Another suicide. Daniel grabbed for the emergency stop. The brakes squealed. His knuckles turned white. He was going too fast. Fool! She smiled in malicious victory. Daniel felt his dinner coming up.

A girl leapt down from the ramp and pushed the old woman violently aside, throwing her onto the empty track. The girl stumbled back a few steps, then froze like a startled deer, her wide eyes meeting his. He screamed some expletive. In a second the train would hit her and drag her underneath like a rag doll. The steel guide wheels would slice her up like bread.

The train jerked to a stop less than a meter from her, throwing him forward. The girl burst into a crazy laugh. She followed the old woman onto the platform and stepped coolly away without a backward look. Daniel let go of the brake handle and leaned back in his chair, waiting for the AI20s and the Pols to arrive. His schedule was ruined. Craste would recycle him; put him back on the fringe lines. He smelled the cloying stench of unspent tube-jet fuel and gagged at the dizzy memory of fumes and vomit that had almost consumed him. Reminded of his headache, Daniel cradled his head in his hands and rocked slowly.

The old woman was screaming at her rescuer. Daniel peered out his window and saw no sign of the girl. The crowd and the AI20s drew back for a Pol. Where was the second one? They always travelled in pairs. Then Daniel spotted him, not far behind, adjusting his helmet.

Daniel felt his stomach churn as he prepared for one of them to board his tube-jet. He started to shiver with fear, or anger—he wasn't sure which it was. He despised Pols. Hated their cruel precision, their faceless arrogance. Machine-men, predators feared for their silent death-strikes. Pols *always* got their prey. They were almost as bad as veemelds. At least Pols didn't pretend to be human. Veemelds lured you into thinking they cared, then turned their backs on you. They'd sold their souls for knowledge, speed and status. They were worse than Darwin plague. *They* were a plague. Damn them all. Especially that veemeld, Angel, the first girl who'd kissed him, then deserted him.

Daniel watched the Pol drag the old woman away to the Pol Station. *Where she'll rot*, he thought. The car door creaked open and he jumped. The second Pol stepped inside. Daniel felt his breaths come in shallow spurts. He could only make out the Pol's small but strongly set jaw beneath his helmet and mask. Then the Pol did the unthinkable: he removed his helmet, revealing a young wolfish face under a mat of dark gold-tipped brown hair. Daniel had expected something else: metal, luster and corrugation.

Thin lips formed a tight, straight line as falcon-eyes appraised Daniel. "Submit your vee-disk," the Pol said with a reedy tenor voice.

Daniel sprang up and stabbed the console button several times before the disk ejected. It slipped from his hands and clattered to the floor. He scrambled for it and handed the surveillance disk to the Pol, stuttering, "I had it on m-m-manual, so you won't get anything—"

"Why is that?" The Pol's blue eyes narrowed. "Were you experiencing difficulties?"

Daniel squirmed. Sweat tickled the back of his neck. "No, n-n-not exactly." His stammer always returned when he was nervous. He knew he'd breached a serious protocol by switching to manual. Craste was definitely going to deep seven him. Wall art.

To his amazement, the Pol didn't pursue the matter. Daniel thought he recognized a faint smirk as the Pol downloaded the disk in the mini-vee that hung on his belt. After studying the readout, he handed the disk back to Daniel. "Can you describe the woman who intervened?"

"No," Daniel said. He'd be damned if he was going to tell the Pol anything. "I guess I was t-too s-startled." His hands clenched and unclenched.

The Pol pulled out a portable vee-pad and laser pen from his pocket and scrawled something. "So, you can't remember anything? Not even what she wore?"

"No."

There was that smirk again. Daniel's heart throbbed harder than his head. I'm in trouble. He doesn't believe me.

"You may proceed. You're behind schedule." The Pol turned and left the train.

Daniel slumped in his seat and let his breaths return to their normal rhythm. Of course he remembered what she wore. And everything else about her. How could he forget the snug fit of the Com-Center's bright red tunic on her slender body. Her flaxen hair, flared nose, brilliant green eyes. He thought her extraordinary looking. Not beautiful—she looked too much like a wild animal, hair akimbo, wearing a savage expression. Her lips seemed made for kissing, but her feral eyes warned of danger. He suspected she was a natural—no nuyu—not that she needed any. She'd worn no earrings either. Was she a deviant? More like crazy. The plague was killing so many, yet she was saving someone who didn't want to be saved. Something about her sparked dark memories of the inner-city. Images of rusty shacks, slimy with stale refuse. And love's first kiss slipping through his fingers.

Daniel stretched his neck. He felt strangely used and abandoned. He longed to see the girl again. As he eased the tube-jet out of the station, Daniel realized with sullen humor that the incident probably shook him more than it had the girl he'd come so close to killing. He frowned at his own reflection in the window and began to wonder if he'd been driving the tube-jets for too long.

3

WITH a brisk nod at the security droid, Julie hurried down the main hall of the Com-Center, toward the Department of Information Control. The "big dick," Nancy called it. Julie yanked off her vee-set, folded it and hooked it on her belt. Shaking her curls loose, she entered her dark workstation with a sigh. "HAL, configure," she instructed her office vee-com and sank into her chair. The holo-console appeared in front of her and a 5-metre square holograph of swirling blue light sprang to life to the strains of Beethoven's Moonlight Sonata.

Her fingers glided furiously on the console that threw data pertaining to her predecessors into the holo-image while she adjusted her mind to veemeld with SAM. It took longer than usual to reach the critical tension point. She took in a deep breath to help her mind relax and finally found the sweet spot. Like a space traveler freed from gravity, she floated into SAM's world of abstract imagery and felt the colors and textures of logic caress her mind. *Hey, SAM.*

Hey, Julie. Happy birthday.

She slumped in her chair. *Thanks. Great start...*

You need the bad moments to appreciate the good ones.

Now, there's a cheerful thought.

The data on the holo-image made her jump. Her fingers had been independently researching her two DIC predecessors as if in a dream. The data turned into a nightmare. Soon after each had been assigned to model Renegade Pols for the Head Pol, they'd met with some kind of accidental death and their data had conveniently gone with them. Julie pressed her hands against her temples. She didn't believe in accidents. The *Moonlight Sonata* moaned like a dirge. *This is worse than I thought. I'm Pol meat, SAM! Getting Kraken's assignment is like a death sentence. I'll get the deep seven. Wall art.*

Really, Julie, no one's going to recycle you into wall art. You need to get past this inordinate fear of AI07s. They're not such a bad lot. A little primitive, with absolutely no humor, but they do—

Is this what Kraken meant? Someone didn't want the Renegade model to be completed. And it didn't take a rocket scientist to figure out who that might be. *Is Kraken suggesting that my best chance to survive is to finish the model as quickly as possible, before the Renegades figure out I'm the new modeler and toast me?*

Julie, I can't make conclusive comments at this time.

Wonderful. Spoken like a machine.

It wouldn't hurt to follow that advice even though your assignment for Kraken is classified. No one knows—

Yet. She snatched a vee-book from the pile on the desk beside her and searched the drawers, stuffed with info-cubes, for a laser pen to record the victims' names. She'd seen it a moment ago. Frustrated, she abandoned the search and stared at the holo-image, sucking in shallow breaths as she read the gruesome details. Thirty-one-year-old Carol Hudson had worked seven months on Kraken's project until she became the victim of a crowd-pushing incident. She fell on the tracks in front of an oncoming tube-jet. Unlike the old woman Julie had just saved, the Pols removed Hudson in pieces. Ted Blake, Julie's immediate predecessor, had worked in Icaria-9 for 15 years before transferring here to work on Kraken's project. He only lasted three months before getting caught in the crossfire of a Pol and a supposed Distopian. The Pol, obviously a Renegade, shot Blake in the back, killing him instantly.

How could she veemeld herself out of this one? She recalled the mixed feelings of elation and disappointment she'd felt when her boss, Fitch, had assigned her to the Head Pol's project three months ago. She'd marked a milestone as the youngest DIC handler and the first veemeld to work for Kraken. But that assignment had come on the heels of her sloppy loss of that Darwin cube and her prompt removal from the Darwin project. Julie couldn't help thinking that chasing subversives wasn't nearly as important as saving lives. It was turning out to be far more dangerous also. It was obvious that Fitch didn't trust her anymore; he'd tossed her to the Head Pol, who's project was likely to get her pushed in front of a tube-jet "by accident"—

"Boo!" said a low voice.

Julie gasped and jumped in her seat. The holo-image broke up into a cube of liquid color. Laughter erupted behind her and Julie turned.

Nancy's stout body jiggled with laughter under her tight yellow and black uniform. "Are you ever jumpy." Hazel eyes sparkled like an elf's. "So, who peed on your vee-com? You should've seen yourself!" She mimicked Julie's face a little too well for Julie's taste.

"How'd you get in here without my seeing you?"

"You've got to get a life, Ju." Nancy wore no earrings and hadn't used nuyu to treat her fly-away brown hair or improve her pocked face. She was always making a statement, even with her looks, Julie thought. "You still listen to that ancient stuff. What is it with you and old people? That Beethoven dude's been dead a thousand years."

It's actually two hundred and sixty-eight.

"Two hundred and sixty-eight, actually," Julie corrected her.

Nancy wrinkled her pug nose. "You sound like you've swallowed a vee-com. I just walked in while you were gaping at that big holo-cube in front of you. You married to that thing or something?" She pointed to the holo. "If it ever crashes, you'll be so lost."

Julie felt her face burn. "And no one stopped you?"

"Your fancy security system's a joke."

Julie, she's a security risk—and a bad influence. Remember, the last demerit you got was because of her. It was her idea to take that short cut—

"Just because you were able to come in doesn't mean that you're allowed, Nancy. You'll get a demerit. They don't like people from the Ed-Center in here."

Especially little snoops. She'll get you in trouble again. Do you remember how embarrassed you were last month when you saw your picture in the mall for a demerit?

Be quiet, SAM.

"Well, what about my freedom to come and go as I please?" Nancy pouted.

"There's always the vee-com," Julie suggested.

"It's so impersonal! Don't you think? No, you don't," Nancy snorted. "Let me answer for you." She mimicked Julie's voice, "It's more efficient. No one asking you embarrassing questions or asking you for a date while transferring data."

Julie squirmed in her chair. "I don't sound like that."

Yes, you do, Julie.

Julie rolled her eyes.

"I came to take you out for a birthday lunch and to get tanked again."

"Using my card, I suppose." Paying for her birthday present again.

"Well, my card wouldn't work. Come on, you introduced me to tanking, remember?"

That's against the Icarian code. I advise against it.

Nancy mimicked Julie's tilting her head, as if she were listening to a distant sound. "It's restricted to Level 1 users."

"Who cares! Icaria has too many restrictions and rules. It's driving me mad!"

"It'll drive you—us—to the Pol Station," Julie said quietly.

That's right, Julie. Common sense is best.

"Come on, Ju. You're working too hard. Give yourself a break. You need me to save you from your dull life and your dull friends."

Julie knew who she meant. "Brenda isn't dull." Offended at being called dull herself, she couldn't help returning Nancy's barb. "Brenda just follows the code, not like some people I know."

Nancy snorted. "That's what I'm here for. To put some excitement back into your life."

Julie picked up her vee-book and searched for her laser pen, mumbling, "My pen..."

Nancy grinned in sudden amusement. "Stay still." Reaching past Julie's shoulder, she pulled out the pen that Julie had earlier inserted to bind her thick curls. They tumbled down her shoulders as Nancy held the missing laser pen in front of Julie's nose. "Like I said, you've got to get a life. You get along better with that AI than you do with people!"

Julie snatched the pen. She knew what Nancy thought of veemelding.

"Lately all I've heard you say is: 'SAM said this' or 'SAM said that'. Chaos, what are you? Lovers?"

Julie blushed.

"You use Interact-SYM like an umbilical cord. You might as well be attached!"

If Nancy only knew how far beyond that she and SAM had progressed. She hadn't used Interact-SYM for a year. She didn't need to.

"They're already calling you cyborgs, machine-people."

"I'm not a machine," Julie muttered under her breath.

Nancy raised a brow. "When was the last time you went out with someone?" She paused to remember, gazing into space. Julie frowned. She didn't want to think about it. Nancy's eyes lit up. "Oh, yeah, it was three months ago with that geek from the Vid-Department. What's his name? Paul something... Getz!" She grinned, pleased with herself.

Julie cringed. Her mind involuntarily summoned his nervous eyes, seamed forehead and shuffling gait. "Yeah, Paul Getz."

Nancy snorted. "Chaos, Jules. Why d'you always hook up with such losers?"

Julie was reminded of the ungainly but sweet face of Neo, the first boy she'd kissed—certainly not a loser, but irreparably lost. That was a long time ago and he'd no doubt forgotten about her¾and her broken promise—by now.

"Remember how Getz dumped you at Benny's, then had the nerve to ask you out again—"

"Yes, yes, I remember." She was trying to forget. "Not everyone likes veemelds—"

"Oh, for vee's sake, Ju!" Nancy scoffed, slapping her own head. "Then don't tell them. Chaos, you do a great job keeping it a secret from everyone else. The only reason you even told me was because I guessed."

Julie dropped her gaze and shifted her mouth with unspoken words.

"And what about that guy before him?" Nancy persisted. "Lester..."

"Alex," Julie corrected. Nancy didn't know when to quit. "All right, all right." She slumped in her chair. "Let's get tanked."

Julie! Why did you agree? It's dangerous.

Julie's mouth grew taut. "Let's meet at Pepper's in the Rec-Center at 1200."

This isn't the time to be careless, after what we've just learned about those previous data handlers.

I know, SAM. I know. Why did she always let Nancy bulldoze her like that?

Nancy was the only person she knew who'd managed to collect more demerits than she did. Nancy should have gone to the Shame Court long ago for the pranks she'd already played.

Nancy beamed. "You won't regret this, Jules!"

"I just might," Julie muttered and turned back to her holo. "HAL, reconfigure Icaria-5's population demography." Her console returned and the holo displayed a three-dimensional graph.

Nancy draped her arm over Julie's shoulder and turned with more than passing curiosity to the 3D-graphs embedded in the holo-cube. "Still working on Kraken's project?"

"Yes, still." She played the unclassified data with her console, waiting for Nancy to leave so she could do her real work.

"The Distopian movement is part of it, isn't it?"

Careful, Julie, SAM cautioned. That's classified information.

Julie's mouth tightened. She remembered to nod to Nancy and slid her fingers along her holo-console.

"Information pirates, huh?"

More like information terrorists, Julie thought, not answering. Distopians blamed the government for Darwin Disease. They even accused them of willfully spreading it. Distopians claimed to have created their own virus, INV, which would destroy the entire cyber-network, and threatened to use it if the government didn't do something about the disease.

"I guess you guys don't like that wild bunch and their fight against info-privileges and favoritism to machines over humans. Sort of like freedom fighters, wouldn't you say?"

"No, I wouldn't." Total anarchy and blind prejudice wasn't her idea of freedom. Distopians hated veemelds and their privileges.

Nancy leaned over Julie's shoulder. "Yeah, I'm not sure I agree with them insisting that the government put *everything* on the vee-set intro, even your demerits." And whether you were a veemeld, thought Julie. So far, for better or worse, that was still privileged information. "Guess it depends on what side of the scan you're on," Nancy went on with a smirk.

And whether you were clean, thought Julie. Distopians were usually clean. She continued her work in silence and glanced at the ancient analog watch strapped to her wrist. A present from her eccentric uncle. Hoping Nancy would take the hint.

"Hey! Weren't the Distopians responsible for the big Com-Center leak three months ago?" Nancy went on. "The same time you got into trouble for losing those data-cubes?"

Julie felt her face redden. "It's just a rumor."

"The ultimate irony for the Com-Center, huh? Communicating a little too much?"

Julie grunted.

She's treading on dangerous ground, teasing you out—

I can figure that out for myself, SAM!

"And what about those fascist Renegade Pols? They sacked that AI Human Vector lab, the place that tests for veemelding, six months ago. I think they hate you guys—Hey! You're doing it again! Looking all goofy like you've got a vee-com in your head."

Julie glared at Nancy. Didn't she have some work to do?

Nancy chuckled. "Okay, I'll let you get back to your secret stuff. Guess that's why you can use the tanks and us Level 4 plebes can't. See you at Pepper's." She squeezed Julie's shoulder. "Happy Birthday, Jules!"

"Thanks. Bye, Nan." Julie wondered how Nancy kept her job in the Ed-Center. One day she'd wind up in the Pol Station, Julie thought as she copied the confidential data on her predecessors to a coded cube. After a swift cast around to make sure she was still alone, she transferred it to a cap on her back molar.

4

WITH a touch of his wrist-vee, Victor Burke opaqued the windows of his house and watched the distant towers of Icaria-5 disappear. He forced a smile at Gaia, seated next to him. Light from the fire across the room fluttered over her porcelain face like the hands of an unsure lover.

Victor absently patted the old golden retriever reclining at his feet and cleared his throat. Gaia had come for his progress report and he didn't want to disappoint her. Facing the 3D-image on the wall, he said, "Vee-com, find Julie Crane and display her." Julie's face appeared. Her tongue comically stuck out the side of her mouth as she, unaware that eyes probed her, stared straight at her hidden observers.

"You place your cameras creatively," said Gaia, her lips curling in amusement. After studying Julie's face for a moment, she leaned forward with a frown. "Is she a *natural*?"

Victor bit back a smile. Did his superior disapprove? Had she spoken out of female jealousy? Gaia herself looked two decades younger than her 59 years thanks to neurgery, healthy doses of nuyu and impeccable grooming—not one hair or piece of clothing was out of place. A thick curtain of midnight-colored hair framed a regal face of classic splendor. Exterior beauty was obviously important to Gaia. Victor turned from the artificial beauty to the natural and his gaze swept over Julie's sea-green eyes, rosy skin and lips, and golden hair. No nuyu treatment could recreate those flecks of sun trapped in liquid shades of honey. He loved watching her like this, in the vacant contentment of veemeld. Her full lips curled on one side in a wonderful expression of dazed pleasure. A girl's eyes peered out from a woman's face, her beauty unfurling like the bud of a flower, ready to be picked.

"Ms. Crane's working on her vee-com in her DIC office," he said, ignoring Gaia's question.

"So, she's the modeler you described. Not a Distopian?"

"Of course not!" His eyes darted to Gaia. She arched a brow and he found her vague smile unnerving. Victor pulled at the collar that cut into his throat and rested his eyes on the holo-image again. "But she is a wild card." Julie's curls were tied back, emphasizing her softly angled face and full lips. Her mouth was too large, he thought, except when she smiled. "As a minus, she has a dirty record," he continued, keeping his gaze on the girl. "Two demerits in '94 and already two this year. One for taking a short-cut through a restricted area and the other for helping an old woman who'd fallen by blocking an AI20. Her uncle's a Luddite—peddles peripheral literature, some of it Distopian. She has questionable friends. As a plus, she's one of the best database modelers in Icaria." He leaned eagerly toward Gaia, aware that his voice had risen an octave. "She's a hard worker, usually on time, and often stays into the late hours: a vee-cube to her core. She's done this type of modeling before with great success. Fitch has lent her to almost every Center. Her defragmentation and data-link probes have given her an uncanny ability to piece together entire data sets from just a few key points—"

"Isn't that illegal?" Gaia interrupted.

"Of course it is." He smirked, self-pleased. "She's already applying her illegal research to the Project. She's very clever."

"Maybe too clever," Gaia raised an eyebrow. She crossed her legs and leaned toward him, almost touching. "You're certainly impressed with this girl, Victor," she said archly.

He felt his face redden.

Gaia reached for the pocket e-file that Victor had given her earlier and slid her fingers on the grid, coaxing out information. She glanced from the data readout to Julie, looking back at her from the holo-image. Right then Julie's face frowned and puckered in a struggle for composure. Then she leaned back, clapped her hands to her mouth and broke into a wild laugh.

"I don't like all her demerits," Gaia frowned, distracted by the laughter. It looked as though Julie was laughing at *her*. "Shows disrespect for Icaria." She pointed to Julie with the e-file. "Does she take her work seriously? Look at her. She can't be more than eighteen."

"She just turned twenty today," Victor said, thinking that he was twice her age. He enjoyed Julie's open-mouthed laugh.

"Her two predecessors were clever and far more experienced. They were only working on the Renegade model and look where they ended up. And your Head Pol has given her Distopians to model as well. We're running out of time, Victor." She tapped the e-file against her leg. "I think she's dangerous."

Victor stiffened and broke into a sweat. Did Gaia know the girl's dubious history after all? Julie had settled back into a studious expression. She couldn't possibly hurt anyone, he thought, watching her bite her lower lip in concentration.

"We can't afford to lose another data manipulator," Gaia said. "We need answers *now*." She smacked the e-file for emphasis.

Victor winced and snapped his head to face Gaia. He straightened up and wrung his hands. "She'll save us the time we've lost, because she's very fast and a divergent thinker." He heard his voice go shrill and tried to calm it. "You should see the inventive way she models. Both her predecessors scored as Type 1 intelligence on the Isabo ITT: logical-mathematical. She's a Type 3 combination of spatial-linguistic. She looks at things differently. She's the only one interviewed who achieved 100% on the SPAT-LOG exams." He paused and licked his lips. "And she's a veemeld."

"Ah," Gaia said, putting the e-file down beside her and placing her hands quietly on her lap. "Our first."

Victor expected her to say more, but she smoothed her dress in silence. Disappointed with her lack of enthusiasm, he cleared his throat. "I think veemelding will make the difference to the Project because—"

"—of its versatility and speed. You see, I'm also familiar with the hype those AI-Human Vector people promoted." She half-smiled. "The girl's certainly good at it. One of the best."

Victor tried not to look surprised. Gaia spoke like she knew the girl!

"She's even personalized her AI-entity."

Victor stared at Gaia. "Her *entity*?"

Gaia smiled, flicking back her raven hair. "Yes, Victor. The place that she goes when she veemelds." She glanced at Julie's image. "The part of the central AI-core that communicates with her. It's most fascinating. A collaboration of her mind and the AI core's collective consciousness. She's unique, Victor. Of the thousands of veemelds we know about in Icaria-5, she's the only one who's achieved this personal kind of communication."

Damn Gaia, Victor thought, fighting down a flush of anger. She had feigned ignorance about the girl to draw him out: *Not a Distopian?... Ah, our first... You're certainly impressed with this girl, Victor...* Damn, damn, damn her!

"The others are certainly talented and competent," Gaia continued. "Some better than she technically, though I grant you, none as imaginative. They use their AI-component successfully. But their interaction remains self-limited. She's gone beyond *use*. She's *melded*. Her melding with the central AI has spawned an independent entity—a product of the AI and her mind."

Victor realized his jaw had dropped and closed his mouth, blinking hard.

"Yes, Victor." She let her smile linger and raised a brow. "The thinking machine and the evolving brain. Remarkable, isn't it? She calls her entity SAM: Smart Analog Mind. It's an odd liaison. Almost like a lover's," she mused, glancing back at Julie's face, which seemed to half-smile back at her. Gaia killed her own smile and gazed hard at the girl's image. "I wonder if this is a function of her individual genetic makeup or something to do with her unique environmental background. I believe she spent several of her formative years in the inner-city." She turned back to Victor with that hard look. "This is something we must elucidate, Victor. Are we looking at a unique phenomenon? You should research your other veemelds for this potential. I can't do all your work for you."

"How do you know all this?" he blurted out. She knew more about one of his own Icarians than he did.

Gaia raised a brow enigmatically. "I know *everything*, Victor."

He frowned and bent to pat his dog. It responded by rolling over on its back. Victor ruffled the dog's fur with nervous strokes. Six months ago he had surrendered to Gaia the only proto-type veemeld vector developed by the now defunct AIHV. At her insistence, he'd also given her a list of his 160,000 veemelds. The vector was originally designed to permit any non-veemeld to tap into an AI. Instead, whether by clever design or by fluke, the vector allowed its user to eavesdrop on someone who was veemelding. Gaia had obviously gotten a lot out of the vector, he thought, suspecting that she had eavesdropped on all his veemelds, not just on this girl. Realizing that she was not going to elaborate, he nodded to himself and muttered, "The veemeld vector."

Without turning to face him, she curled her beautiful lips in a cryptic smile.

"Then you know all about her," he said, trying not to sound peevish. And about all my other veemelds, he thought.

She broke her gaze from the holo and turned to him without a smile. "Only about her thoughts. Not about her numerous demerits. Or her history. I can't spend all day on your vector, listening to her veemeld and hoping for a gem in the midst of all that data handling. I depend on you for that kind of information. Where's all this research you promised me?"

He took in a deep breath. "Her parents might have had her veemelding ability, but they were both dead or missing when the veemeld technology emerged. We'll never know. We have no records because they had their children before the DP offspring-potential scans became part of our protocol."

She pursed her lips. "Who were her parents?"

Glad for a diversion from her stare, Victor glanced down at Julie's data displayed on the e-file on his lap and pretended to read. Vee, hadn't Julie's thoughts revealed anything to Gaia? He drew in a breath and plunged in. "Father's Leonard Crane."

Her eyebrows rose. "The same Crane who—"

"Murdered your colleague in '87." He swallowed, trying to sound casual, eyes flickering over her face but never quite meeting hers. "Of course you recall the history."

Gaia looked through him with icy blue eyes. "Not the background details."

She's toying with me, drawing me out again, he thought. So she can reject the girl and embarrass me. Averting her cold stare, he pretended to consult his e-file for the information he knew too well. "Crane was a promising scientist at the Department of Industrial Ecology until he disgraced himself by developing the inverted loop model and allying himself with the *stable chaos* theorists."

She narrowed her eyes. "Fairweather's theory defies the second law of thermodynamics. Our revolution should have put an end to that heretical distopian ecology."

Victor shrugged. "It's seen a resurgence with the inverted loop model. Using six case studies, including Icaria-11, Crane's controversial paper in the *Icarian Scientist* predicted the spread of Icaria-specific diseases like Darwin and the collapse of Icaria-11 as the first of many."

Gaia waved her hand as if to dismiss the remark. Victor thought he recognized defensiveness in her annoyingly calm face. Darwin Disease was gaining unprecedented momentum throughout the Icarias. He thought it definitely a thorn in her side and she obviously didn't have the answers he did. Keeping a straight face, he continued, "As for Crane, the conservative scientific community soon humiliated and ostracized him. It must have broken him. He went on a rampage. Destroyed his office. Killed the head of government and his own DIE supervisor who'd ironically been a supporter of *stable chaos* theory—"

"Yes, yes," she waved him on impatiently. "I know all this. What about the family? The girl, her mother. What about them? Where's all the background research you've conducted?"

Victor pulled at his collar and focused back on his e-file. "The mother, Deborah Lerner, abused drugs and was reclassified to the inner-city with her two children—"

"The girl has a sibling?"

Victor straightened. He swallowed down the commotion rising up to choke him. "A younger sister." His voice cracked. "Not a veemeld. I'm trying to trace her."

Gaia watched him askance. Her eyes swept down his body appraisingly. "The girl probably ended up in an inner-city Care-Center. Miserable places." She shook her head and focused past his shoulder as if musing to herself. "Most of the children were raped by the Care-workers."

He stiffened and focused on her blood-red lips.

"I wonder if they've abolished that abhorrent practice of wiring the seducer and having new Care-workers virtually experience an enhanced version as initiation," she continued her absent muse. Then her eyes caught his and gripped. He felt he was being strangled. Gaia narrowed her eyes briefly as if aiming for his heart. He felt its spasms as though she'd reached in and was firmly squeezing. "Didn't you work there for a while, Victor?"

His chest tightened and he fought down a gasp, ears ringing. He lowered his gaze and furiously ran his fingers on his vee-pad, pretending to search the database. "Yes," he said. "I did, for a short while, a long time ago."

"That system's a little reminiscent of the innovative surveillance technology you use with your wired Pols, isn't it?" She half-smiled, a brow arching.

Heart slamming, Victor avoided her eyes and felt his face burn under her intense gaze. Did she know about his little *faux pas* and his connection with the sister? He threw up his hands in mock frustration. They were sweating. "I can't find her," he lied. "They keep terrible records in the inner-city. People disappear there. It's full of chaos."

Gaia waved her hand casually. "Never mind the sister." She released him. "Go on with Ms. Crane's history."

"The mother disappeared, leaving the children to fend for themselves in the inner-city." He looked up from the e-file. "This girl didn't have a pleasant past. Not that it prevented her from success. When the Pols found her she tested positive for veemelding, and was returned to the outer-city." He hoped Gaia wouldn't notice that he'd purposefully skipped Julie's troublesome years as a techno-slummer in the inner-city. "She lived with her uncle, Robert Crane, until she was fifteen, then took her own flat. She'd already shown an interest in communications and her talents in that field were recognized and encouraged by the Ed-Center. The DIC hired her before she finished out her semester. At fourteen, she became the youngest person there. They gave her an Interact-SYM and no one's been able to touch her since. By eighteen, she'd made her boss, Fitch, the most efficient and sought after DIC manager in North-Am. He's lent her to Kraken for the Project." Victor checked his wrist-vee. "Kraken's just met with her. He's very pleased with what she's done so far."

Gaia nodded. "Yes, but what about all these demerits of hers?"

They'd come full circle. Victor gazed at Julie's placid face and forced himself to unclench his teeth. "Simply the hallmark of impetuous youth," he said. Julie Crane was one of his most productive citizens. By placing her on Kraken's Project, Victor had narrowed her future down to only two possible paths: if she proved worthy, she might find her way in with the Ecologists, perhaps even the *Circle*; if she proved unworthy, she'd have to be disposed. He'd fausted himself, given Gaia one of his best again. Hoping to convince her, he said, "The girl's actually quite tame. Avoids the drug party scene. She's only brash in her data modeling—"

"Not with two demerits already this year. You dwell on surfaces, Victor. She may demonstrate a meager intent toward convention, but her actions betray her. Her illegal info tampering supports irreverence for Icaria's rules. Dangerous behavior and dangerous thoughts. Just like her father. You're taking an awful chance with this one, Victor, veemelding aside," Gaia frowned. "What are the odds of her sabotaging the project, getting herself killed like the others, or turning into a Distopian like her father?"

"She's far too dedicated." He bridled in a surge of anxiety.

"I agree, she is certainly dedicated. But is she dedicated for the right reason?" Gaia raised a brow. "Whose wild card is she?"

How could he answer her? Victor shifted in his chair, thinking of the girl's father, and tugged at his sweater. Gaia probably knew the answer better than he did. Meeting her stare evenly, he saw himself at a disadvantage despite his superior surveillance system: unlike Gaia, he hadn't been reading the girl's thoughts for six months.

5

THE stairway door to the lowest level opened with a bang. Two Pols burst into the dark service corridor, heads sweeping the area for a signal. Only the constant chatter of the public vees lining the walls broke the silence and added staccato light. Sensual images swam in rapid succession on the multi-vee screens to the visceral rhythm of synthetic music. Close-ups of giant red lips and pearly white teeth... cheeks... toes... a shoulder... side of a breast... genitals... flowed from one to the other like the shades of a watercolor painting. Frank Langor glanced back at his partner who'd hesitated, caught by the tantalizing imagery. "Ron! You virus!" Frank sent his thought over the helmet mind-link. "This is no time to watch tits!"

Frank continued down the corridor into darkness, past piles of discarded food wrappers, rotten food, and sundry maintenance objects. Frank glanced from the garbage to the broken service lights then to the yawning blackness ahead. Damn Enviro-Centre. They weren't doing their job.

Frank directed them to stop in front of a pitch dark aisle. He swept his head slowly from side to side to allow the tracker beam of his helmet to home in on the signal he was following. "Come on, find their freaking cards..." A signal beeped in his head, indicating a fit to one, followed by a second beep: the other. Two runners crouched behind a debris pile at the end of the aisle, several meters down. A brief description of each runner appeared on the translucent inner surface of Frank's visor. The first man, Leon Barbieri, was a microbiologist with the Neurology Unit in the Med-Center of Icaria-11: an illegal visitor. A translucent image of Barbieri's face with relevant background information flashed in front of Frank's visor. Barbieri was 34 years old, a father of two girls, and held a clean record. The second runner was 19-year-old Fritz Riedl, a local student of Biomimicry in Icaria-5's Department of Industrial Ecology. He, too, was clean. Only the clean ones got to pursue an education in DIE. A clever kid, Frank thought as he surveyed the boy's latest transcript. A pity he was going to be dead soon.

"Shit! Barbieri's from Icaria-11!" Ron's thoughts came through clearly on the helmet mind-link. "What's his interest in a CDC data-cube? And how'd he fucking get here? I thought Icaria-11 was still on quarantine—no one in and no one out—"

"The cube holds top-secret information on Darwin Disease, moron," Frank thought back. "Chaos, Ron, do I have to spell it out for you? The Distopians think this whole Darwin thing is some government plot and they need data to prove it. Our CDC and Com-Center are renowned for their research. The Distopians in Icaria-11 would probably pay droves for the gems in this cube. As for travel, the Trans-Center doesn't have the monopoly on travel. Biologists at DIE have their own ways of getting around."

"How do you know all that?"

"Because I keep track," Frank replied. "Don't you read the reports? There's a major leak—like, of waterfall proportions—out of the Com-Center these days. Worse than when the CDC cube leaked out three months ago. But never mind. He's a Distopian; that's all you need to know." What a techno-slummer! he thought to himself. Ron didn't think beyond his nose. "Anyway," Frank's thoughts resumed on the helmet mind-link, "we want Barbieri alive for mind-scan. He's mine. You take the kid now. Leave Barbieri to me."

"What if they have weapons?"

"Negative. I already scanned and they're both clean. Take Riedl now."

"Okay." Ron punched the familiar sequence on his wrist vee-com that set his visor sensor on high. Frank did the same. The darkness disappeared and the locator grid appeared in front of him, marking Riedl's position. He could see both runners as clearly as if it were daylight. He enhanced sound by 30%, and he could hear the rustle of debris under the runners' nervous feet and their still-panting breaths. He watched Ron creep forward on silent feet.

Riedl was crouched to the right of Barbieri. He looked straight at Ron without seeing him in the darkness. Ron stopped, raised his laser pistol and aimed straight at the target on the grid. He shot once. The high-pitched squeal of the laser drummed Frank's ears. Riedl thudded to the ground. He'd hit his target. Now there was only Barbieri.

"Duck!" Frank thought. Ron dropped to the pavement as several shots from Barbieri's primitive ballistic weapon flew overhead. Their enhanced explosions hammered his ears.

"What the fucking inner-city happened?" Ron's mind screamed.

"Sorry. I wasn't sure about the weapon on Barbieri—my scan wasn't clean. But I needed Riedl out of the way."

"Shit! You're the only Pol I know who can lie in your thoughts! You're a real virus!" thought Ron, shivering adrenaline.

"Listen, I'll buy you a couple of *gomorrahs* when we get off."

"Make it five, chiphead."

Frank sneered. Ron could always be bought, he thought to himself. "I'm going in," Frank thought. "Cover me." He crept forward in the dark. He saw Barbieri clearly, sweat beading on his forehead and blinking hard. Muscles pulled in an ugly tug-o-war on his face and his mouth twitched wildly. Chaos! The asshole had brought Darwin Disease from Icaria-11 with him.

He removed his helmet and shone its light in Barbieri's face. Barbieri shot blindly. Frank leaned close, knowing Barbieri couldn't see him. "Give up, Leon," he said. Barbieri visibly jumped. "Put the gun down now and we won't kill you." He had a mind to kill the bastard anyway for bringing Darwin here. The Distopian stared at him, eyes not daring to stray. Was he wondering if Frank was holding a laser pistol? Frank saw Barbieri lower the gun slightly. "Do it!"

The weapon dropped from Barbieri's hand. Frank watched Barbieri's expression change from fear to dismayed surprise as his eyes adjusted and he saw that Frank's pistol sat snugly in the holster strapped to his thigh. Just as a hysterical laugh escaped Barbieri's lips, several shafts of blue light screamed past them both. One caught Barbieri in the chest and drove him stumbling backwards. Frank felt his thigh burn and dropped to the ground. His helmet slid out of his hand, clattering to the floor, and rolled out of his reach to rest up against Barbieri's crumpled form, casting a shaft of dim light across the aisle.

He watched Ron scramble behind some debris to his left, then squinted beyond the beam. He thought he could make out two shadowy forms drawing near. Frank sprang up, ignoring the stab of pain, took aim and shot twice. Two figures crumpled to the ground. He'd shot blindly. On gestalt energy.

Still crouching behind the debris pile, Ron surveyed the scene with his scanning device. Obviously detecting no one else in the area, he stood up. Then he turned to Frank and shook his head slowly. "Show off," he said out loud.

Frank smiled faintly as he bent to pick up his helmet. He was the best shot in the Pol fleet. He hadn't missed yet. He reached down and put the helmet on, secured his chinstrap and locked down the visor, which triggered the ear probe and bathed the hall in light again. Once the probe reached its destination, the implant in his brain, Ron's telepathic babble came through. "—You son of an inner-city slut! Why d'you always pull that mind-game shit? Chaos, they think we're machines and you go and take your fucking helmet off. You didn't even have your weapon drawn. I know you're good, but one of these days your fucking Pit-Ball game tactics are going to get you killed. Or worse still, get *me* killed. Why d'you do that shit? You son of an—"

He was beginning to repeat himself. Frank wiped Ron's thoughts out of his brain. Good partners were hard to find. He remembered when the helmet had effectively ended the life of James Golding, Frank's first partner on the D-Unit, a month ago. Used in conjunction with the vee-implant, the helmet could enhance almost every possible skill. Indispensable as it was, though, the helmet was also a Pol's Achilles heel. But only Pols were supposed to know this weakness in helmet design. Obviously some Pol-gone-Renegade had known, and Frank's partner had suffered the consequences. One severe turn on a secured helmet and the ear probe tore your brain open; blood and brains gushed out the side of your head in a torrent. It didn't usually kill, but it had left Golding a vegetable, living out his remaining life in oblivion in the Med-Center chronic care unit.

Frank and James had been following up an anonymous tip they'd received during their investigation of the serious information leak in the Com-Center. The suspected cube smuggler was a young olive-skinned razor head with the Vid-Department of the Com-Center. Paul Getz. When they'd reached his flat, Getz, trembling and eyes darting between the two Pols, let them into his place. Images of an open eye and a closed eye were cut on either side of his head. He appeared docile. Their scans had revealed no hidden weapons. The ruse got Getz close enough to James to seize his helmet and twist hard.

It happened so fast that James had no time to cry out. Frank would never forget the insane images that tore into him through his helmet mind-link to James. They brought him to his knees and made him vomit. Getz had slipped away with the cube while Frank retched helplessly. After that, he learned to shut a part of his brain away from the machine and not rely on anything but himself. The razor head was still at large. And Frank knew why. Some Renegade Pol was responsible. But he kept the thoughts to himself.

Frank returned his thoughts to Ron, all business now. "Get four cleaners in here, pronto." He frowned at the garbage. Those slugs at Environment were getting lazy. He had a mind to report them. Recycle droids weren't doing their job.

"The AI07s are on their way," Ron reported through his link.

"Good. I'll tell Headquarters." Frank touched his wrist vee-com. "We lost the cube," he relayed through his mind-link to Pol Station Headquarters. Several meter-high beetle shaped droids scuttled down the hall toward them. "That one's got Darwin Disease," Frank said to the AI07s and pointed to Leon. They'd treat him differently. Frank's eyes narrowed as he watched each droid eject a viscous fluid of recycling digesters. Behaving like an independent entity, the fluid extended pseudopods that engulfed and digested each dead body like an amoeba. He watched the robot suck Riedl into its metallic belly, later to be disgorged into the DIE's main recycling depot. Frank grimaced. He never could quite stomach the stripping of tissue and bone, although he appreciated its elegance. Parts of Riedl might re-emerge tomorrow as part of Frank's nano-prepared breakfast or in the flowing holo-artwork in Darwin Mall. He shivered briefly at the thought.

"Both runners are dead," he continued to headquarters. "We were followed by two other Distopians. They've been dispatched and cleaned—Wait—" His scanner grid revealed an object amid the debris. Leaning on his good leg, Frank bent down and after rummaging in the garbage, found a small flat piece of plastic. "I found something." He smiled and picked up the stolen disk. His visor scanned it. Embedded in the disk was the cube. He read a portion to confirm its content:

Darwin Disease, a neural disorder, named after Darwin Clinic in Icaria-11 where the first diagnosed case occurred in April, 2080. Caused by the retrovirus Pro-V, the disease was initially spread through nosocomial infection and resulted in a major pandemic and the eventual collapse of Icaria-11. Despite full quarantine measures by CDC, the disease rapidly spread to most other Icarias with cases documented as far as Icaria-37. The infection selectively interferes with several neurotransmitters, eventually destroying cholinergic neurons of both peripheral and central nerves. Symptoms develop from simple memory loss, related heart problems and muscle spasms to eventual dementia and death from complications. Duration of the disease from initial symptom presentation to last stages of dementia and loss of critical brain functions varies from a few weeks to five months. Original host and transmission mechanism are not known, although aerosol spread via the respiratory tract has been ruled out. No vaccine available...

A further scan indicated the source of the cube: the vee-com file of Julie Crane! *Her* again! The girl he'd been shadowing for a month. The girl who'd jumped in front of the tube-jet earlier this morning. And the daughter of the man who'd ruined his father years ago. Frank's lips curled into a sneer. Julie Crane had reported a cube stolen by an unknown party three months ago. He felt a surge of pleasure as he gazed at her face and reread the Pol Station's detailed bio on her that included her veemeld status. She would pay for what her father did. But on his terms, not the Pol Station's. She was *his*. His predatory smile broadened as he made the decision to meet her face to face... then quickly buried his thoughts. "We found the cube," he relayed without emotion.

Fluorescent green letters sprang in front of him on his visor screen from Pol Headquarters: "Can you confirm its origin and path?"

"Negative," he lied and set his scanner on erase-mode. "It's damaged. I can't get a fix." He'd probably just saved her from a nasty and embarrassing interrogation.

As he erased Julie's name, headquarters returned. "Okay, Langor. Bring the cube in."

Frank slipped the cube in his pocket. Another Distopian conspiracy thwarted, he thought proudly. As for Julie Crane, he thought with a smirk, he'd be collecting his reward from those inviting lips real soon. And then some.

6

S ETTLED back in his chair after a break for tea, Victor ruffled his dog absently and found himself staring at the scar Gaia had received on her temple during the revolution. The rest of her past was a mystery. Even her name, which she'd appropriated from the Greek goddess of the Earth, veiled her previous identity. All he really knew about her was that she had been Icaria-5's previous mayor, before she had handed him the position so that she could better fulfill her responsibilities in the Circle. Thinking he might draw out her motives, he glanced at Julie's face on the holo-image and said, "Will you be reviewing Ms. Crane as a candidate for the Circle?"

"No, Victor." She eyed him scornfully. "She's too closely affiliated with the Distopians. Perhaps some of your other veemelds. I have great things in mind for them, particularly since most of them are still in school and we are able to oversee their education. You should be grooming them to be Heads of Centers at the very least. Some will eventually be inducted to the *Circle*."

He didn't like the way she kept saying *I* all the time, as if everything was hers. He persisted. "Our remotes show that she's kept excellent records of our climate and seasonal vegetation succession for the past three years. Her uncle gave her an old telescope that she repaired and uses to study the heath as well as to watch the stars. She's accurately charted the constellations."

Gaia leaned toward Victor with an intense look. He quelled the impulse to recoil; he knew that posture. "You mistake a good scientific ecologist with someone who possesses a genuine empathy for deep ecology," she said. Her eyes sparkled like sapphires. "No one enters our elite cadre without having impeccable qualifications and submitting to many more initiations than she is capable of passing. She may be an ecologist but she is not a *deep ecologist*. The science of ecology does not ask what kind of society would be the best suited to maintain a particular ecosystem. Our greater concern is with questions aimed at the level of organic wholeness and 'Earth wisdom'. She knows nothing of these things."

Vee, he hated it when Gaia lectured him like he was an idiot. He wondered what thoughts in the girl's mind Gaia was really objecting to. And 'Earth wisdom'? What in Vee was that? Another obtuse term she'd fabricated to confuse him? He felt responsible for Julie's welfare, especially after what happened to her sister.

"The girl has a far more important use, including as a data modeler," Gaia continued. "I will not permit this pathetic Distopian movement with their twisted ideals of freedom and ignorant thirst for power to spoil the perfectly engineered world we've built. Too much is at stake." Her eyes burned into his. "We're in grave danger, Victor. A danger far greater than Darwin Disease. We've had disease outbreaks before and we'll have them again."

Not like this one, thought Victor, reconstructing the statistics in his mind. He thought her uncharacteristically naïve to dismiss the potential destruction of Darwin on Icaria. Surely she was missing the point. Who cared about a few insurgents if there was no one left alive?

Her voice took on an urgent tone. "They're going outside, Victor." Her eyes sparkled like a rough sea. "And we must stop them. Will this young woman perform for us? Successfully complete the models?"

Victor nodded, hoping he looked confident. "Yes."

"And when she does?"

His lips grew taut and his gaze darted over her face, avoiding her eyes. "She can be taken care of in the usual way," he said, thinking it was what Gaia wanted. He turned away, unable to look directly at her. He knew that he would deny her nothing and fought the resentment boiling inside him. If Gaia hadn't saved his reputation and convinced the *Circle* to appoint him as mayor, he'd probably be rotting in the Pol Station. After a longing glance at Julie's holo-image, he flicked a button and her sweet face disappeared.

"Don't terminate her," Gaia said, surprising him. "Her gift for melding is too valuable to lose. We must study her and preserve the trait for posterity. If she doesn't cooperate we'll just take what we need at the Med-Center's Department of Progenesis. I want her kept safe and out of trouble, Victor. She must finish those models as soon as possible. Then give her to me. Dr. Olafsen is anxious to meet her."

Victor let pity for the girl briefly supplant his anger. He couldn't have wished a worse fate on Ms. Crane than to be left in those crafty hands. Swift termination would have been more merciful. "As you wish," he said. What did Gaia really have in mind for his protégé? It stank of a nasty plan.

He touched his wrist-vee and the windows de-opaqued. Shafts of morning sunlight flooded the room. The dog stirred. It nuzzled Victor's leg and gave him a questioning look. Victor let his gaze stray to the rolling patchwork of purple heather and silver-green shag outside. From his house in the middle of the heath no other building could be seen for kilometers until Icaria-5 itself. He rested his gaze on the self-contained urban center whose towers rose gleaming in the distance and his chest rose with pride and resentment. Icaria-5 was *his* city now. Gaia had given him a city struggling with a disparate, crime-ridden population of 20 million. He'd implemented DIE's latest research to create and manage Icaria-

5's self-sustainable eco-system. He'd selected new Heads and trained them to run Icaria-5 until it shone as an example city. How could Gaia understand his passion, while she flitted across the globe from one Icaria to another as part of her responsibility to the *Circle*?

Gaia sat back and followed his gaze. As if reading his mind, she said, "You've done an admirable job with Icaria-5, Victor."

He shrugged, hoping she wouldn't mention its embarrassing information leak.

"Your achievements in self-sustainability are known to the *Circle*," she said. "Icaria-5 has attracted an impressive list of scientists and ecologists. You appear to have a sharp eye for talent." Although he could not interpret her smile, she seemed sincere enough. "Well, done, Victor," she nodded to him. "I'm relying on you and this gifted veemeld."

Appeased, Victor forced a humorless smile. The victory he'd gained for himself, at the expense of a young innocent girl, cloyed in his stomach.

7

JULIE had just decided to order when Nancy rushed into Pepper's. She hadn't bothered to take off her vee-set and she wasn't wearing her usual smile. "Sorry," she said in a strained, out-of-breath voice. "If you don't mind, let's go to the tanks now."

"Don't you want to eat first?" What about her birthday lunch?

"I'll grab something after. You have to go back soon, don't you?"

"At thirteen."

"Let's go, then." Nancy spun on her heels, already leaving.

Thinking about her growling stomach, Julie pulled on her vee-set and followed Nancy out. The women entered the Leisure Unit of the Rec-Center and stopped in front of a two-person Tank Room. Julie glanced down the hall then turned to Nancy with a conspiratorial grin. "No one around. Here's our chance to sneak you in."

She punched "two" on the pad, pulled out the card from her belt pack and slipped it into the door slot. Once. Then twice. The lock clicked and the door swung open. Julie smiled, bowed graciously for Nancy, then followed her in. They undressed in silence. Turning on the shower, Nancy muttered sullenly, "I hate this place."

Julie stepped under the shower beside her. "What d'you mean?"

Nancy's eyes flashed. "They're turning us into a monoculture. You know that ecology stuff better than I do," she said. Julie glanced at Nancy with concern. She was used to Nancy's rhetoric, but this time Nancy's tone was atypically surly. "Creative individualism is dead in Icaria. And soon *we'll* be dead. There won't be one of us left to fight for nonconformity. And when that happens, we're done for. The whole of humanity'll go down the toilet." Nancy turned off the shower and stormed to the towel rack.

Julie turned off her shower and mutely followed. She jerked to catch a rolled up towel that Nancy flung to her, then stood, dripping, and watched Nancy bend down to dry her body. Pendulous breasts jiggled as she briskly rubbed herself with the towel. Julie unfurled her towel and started to dry her hair in methodical circular motions. "What happened?"

Nancy straightened up. Her eyes sparkled with anger. "My boss fired me."

"What?" Julie stopped drying.

"Just after I got back from seeing you. The virus didn't even have the courage to tell me to my face. He left a note on my vee-com—told me to pack up my stuff and leave."

What would Nancy do now? Julie couldn't imagine losing her job. "Why?"

"For trying to do my job." Nancy smacked the wall with her towel. "Freaking idiots don't want education. Those viruses just want to spread their propaganda. They want us all in a neat little row... and their DPs are up to their in-vitro eyeballs making us into a monoculture so some disease like Darwin can wipe us all out in one fell swoop."

Julie wrapped her towel about herself and watched helplessly as Nancy stomped around the shower room. What had prompted this? Had Nancy called the Head-Educator a "stupid chip-head fascist" again after he'd vetoed one too many of her inventive ideas?

"Well, I've had enough of it." Nancy planted her feet with resolve. She threw the towel into the laundry chute and shook her fist like an amazon warrior, her stout figure striking a threatening pose. "I'm not buying into that crap anymore. The Ed-Center isn't about education; it's about brainwashing. Chaos! They still force the children to recite Isabo's Credo every morning. It's so stupid."

Julie folded her arms around her waist to hold the towel in place. She recalled the lines from her school days: *I obey therefore I am strong; those who disobey are weak.* But everyone liked the credo, she was about to protest. Instead she said, "You didn't suggest they abolish it, did you?"

"No. But it *is* stupid. As for the *Isaboan* technique. It sucks! Isabo is a jerk—"

"*Was*," Julie corrected and quickly added, "He's dead. He *was*, not *is*..."

"Good!" She flung her head back and let out a malicious fake laugh. "He should be. Isabo and his 'community of intelligences.' Behavior engineering, they call it. It's plain indoctrination. All part of their master plan to brainwash us all into being good little cyber pets and not ask freaking questions—"

"Good vee, Nancy!" Julie burst out. Her towel dropped. "Not *everything* is a conspiracy."

"Don't be so naive!" Nancy retorted. Their eyes locked in challenge. Nancy planted her legs apart, hands firm on her hips, mirroring Julie's stance. "Do some sleuthing with SAM. Or are you too frightened of what you might find? You're such an oxymoron, Ju! You work with information every day and still hide from the truth. Get your head out of cyberspace and look around." Nancy waved her arms. Her eyes wandered critically over Julie's body.

Julie appraised Nancy's dimpled body in turn. She could use some nuyu, even neurgery, Julie thought. With the Med-Center's available technology, there was no excuse for her obesity. Nancy had stubbornly clung to her right to remain as she was created: a natural to her core. Julie broke off her fixed stare and bent down to pick up her towel, suddenly self-conscious. She pulled it tightly about herself and tried to change the subject, "So, what're you going to do now?"

"I don't know," Nancy sighed. Her shoulders drooped and her gaze sank to the floor. She looked suddenly very small.

Julie wanted to comfort her with a hug. Instead she found herself asking, "Nancy, are *you* a Distopian?"

Nancy straightened. "Chaos, Jules! You make them seem monstrous." She charged forward and Julie fought to keep from recoiling. "Make up your mind. Do you accept this crazy world the way it is, with Darwin going unchecked? You're too scared to be different. You think you're different but you aren't."

Julie stiffened. Her arms tightened around her body. "That's not true—"

"So, you're a natural. As if that counts with your body and looks," Nancy scowled. "You're a vee-damned phony."

Julie reddened, thinking of the neurgery she'd received when they'd picked her up in the inner-city. She'd never told Nancy that she'd had her teeth straightened. They'd done it without asking her.

"Vee, you're more Icarian than most people I know! And you of all people—with your father—what he did, and what happened to your family..."

Julie bristled. Her father was a brilliant scientist, not an insane killer.

Nancy obviously didn't notice Julie's dark look. Or she ignored it. "I can't believe that you're still so callow and trusting," she railed. "Have you ever thought that your father might have been set up? Framed?"

Suddenly weak-kneed, Julie staggered back as if Nancy had struck her. Her anger drained away. "No, I hadn't thought of it," she breathed.

"Good vee, Jules, you keep insisting he's innocent but you never do anything about it. Your father was a scientist with very unpopular ideas. A perfect target. Wasn't his cousin—the one who committed suicide—a neurologist researching Darwin Disease?" Nancy hiked up her brows. "The two scientists your father supposedly killed were also involved with Darwin: Vogel was his cousin's damn boss, wasn't he? And the other guy, Tsutsumi, was the one who suggested Darwin was linked to Icaria's environment. Maybe they were all on to something, and someone—someone with the government—didn't want them to be. It doesn't take a rocket scientist to figure out that the present government is doing nothing about Darwin." Her finger shot up to prevent Julie from speaking. "Forget the CDC screening and the vee-set tattletale programs. They're just to sweep away the mess so no one sees. The government's covering it up," she ranted on. "You think my being fired is a freak? They don't like people who think and speak up. Just because you work for the big Dick and enjoy Level 1 privileges doesn't mean you're safer than me. They've sucked you right in."

Julie started to feel sick. She grimaced, but Nancy misinterpreted the expression. "You're thinking they won't touch you because you're a freaking veemeld. You're Kraken's darling and you're safe. Well, no one's safe, Ju. Not even *you*." Her finger stabbed at Julie's reddening face. "Kraken won't protect you when it's your turn to get recycled."

Had Nancy read her mind?

"Oh, never mind, Jules. I'm not angry with *you*. Let's get tanked before it's too late." She turned toward the tank room.

They proceeded to the two horizontal tanks. Dropping her towel, Nancy waved at Julie and opened the hatch to one. She stepped inside and pulled the hatch closed behind her. Julie opened her own hatch. She stepped into the warm salt water and climbed inside the dark chamber. Sitting in the shallow water, she pulled the hatch closed over her, extinguishing all light, then reclined and let herself float in the dark silence.

She couldn't relax.

Nancy had no right to make those awful remarks about her work and the Head Pol. She was jealous, Julie concluded. Jealous of her Level 1 privileges, jealous of her abilities, jealous even of her being a veemeld. Damn Nancy. Everything was a conspiracy to her, including the next door neighbor. The CDC was doing the best it could to end Darwin. Icaria's government wasn't perfect, but what government was? Nancy was unfairly playing both sides by blaming others for what she'd done to herself. And she was wrong about Icaria and Darwin.

Julie commanded her mind to think of other things. Nice things. Walking in the heath. The trill of the birds and the rustling vegetation. The sticky-sweet scent of Sweet Gale blossoms. The night sky and the stars. She felt her muscles relax, first aching out their tension then loosening. Eventually she felt like she was floating in space. She imagined herself sailing through the galaxies and nebulae she had charted from her apartment. Her mind drifted into veemeld.

Hi, Julie, SAM's gentle voice wafted in.

Hi, SAM… Mmm, this feels nice. Can you see what I've conjured in my mind?

Yes, your universe is beautiful. Can I show you mine?

Sure.

Her star-studded blackness burst into a kaleidoscope of colors. They flowed and swirled like an evolving watercolor. Liquid images solidified to angular abstract shapes that bled into a sunset sky of purpurin. It darkened to indigo beneath pewter clouds.

SAM, it's beautiful!

Do you really think so? I was hoping it would cheer you up.

SAM, that's sweet of you. Cheerfulness, particularly hers, seemed important to SAM. Warm and comfortable, she eased into a dream.

A hard rap at the door interrupts the argument between her parents. As Julie's father rises hastily from the supper table, her mother commands in a sulky voice, "You're not leaving tonight! No more work!" His finger snaps up to silence her and he quietly urges Julie, her mother and Diana to continue eating, then leaves the dining room to answer the door.

A stern baritone voice says, "You Leonard Crane?"

"Yes," he answers.

"You're to come with us, by order of the Head Pol."

The color drains from her mother's thin face. The three of them creep into the hallway. Two large men shrouded in black clothes and helmets have seized her father. Giant cyber-beetle predators. The officer in charge smirks with his thin, perfectly shaped mouth.

Julie cringes as her mother abandons what little pride she has and lunges for the Pol obviously in charge. "Please don't take him away! He's all I have!" In the struggle she falls to the floor and clings to the Pol's leg. He drags her to the doorway then shakes her loose, smiling with disdain. Julie focuses on the space between his front teeth.

"You're the devil! You're all the devil!" her mother screams.

Julie's eyes fix on her father. His body conveys a strange calm as he lets the Pols jostle him. Held by his gaze, Julie swallows down her fear and refuses to shed any tears while Diana and her mother sob uncontrollably. She doesn't know how to read her father's look. It's strangely peaceful. Julie barely hears the single note of his soft voice over the chorus of wails: "Angel, take care of your mother and sister until I return," he implores.

"I will..." She gags on her promise—

≈

—Julie! You're drowning! Wake up!

Coughing up water, Julie threw out her arms. A loud rap at the hatch startled her upright. She sat up, snapping out of veemeld. The rap came again, more insistent. She fumbled the hatch open. A scowling woman dressed in pink was tapping her foot and holding out a towel. Julie scrambled out too quickly and her foot slipped on the wet floor. She regained her balance and grabbed the towel in the same motion. As she wrapped the towel around her, she glanced at Nancy, dripping beside her tank. Avoiding Julie's eyes, Nancy extended the card that she'd already fetched from the locker. "You don't have authorization in this area," said the woman to Nancy, taking her card. Then she turned to Julie. "You shouldn't have brought her into an access-denied area. I'll need your card too."

Julie thought of SAM's warning as she slunk to her locker. Her wet hand fumbled through her clothes while the other clutched the towel wrapped around her. She retrieved the belt pack and, pulling out her card, found herself thinking of the poor old woman she'd sent to the Pol Station this morning. *So much for my birthday...*

Thank vee birthdays only come once a year.

8

LEFT alone, the women dressed in silence then parted with a terse farewell. Julie wandered back toward the Com-Center through Pielou Mall. Catching the smell of food from a nearby foodstop, she was reminded of the lunch she'd missed. She stopped in and ordered vegetable chowder with gamagrass bread from the attending AI40 droid and sat at a stool by a long counter to bolt her food.

As Julie was about to leave the foodstop, an elderly woman dressed in dull brown entered, walking up to people who were still eating. Someone had taken her card and vee-set two days ago and she had not eaten since then, she claimed. Just a piece of bread, asked the old woman. Patrons ignored her. The droid pushed her out. "We don't serve lazy non-working parasites."

Julie's ire rose at the droid's heartless words. She quickly reminded herself that it wasn't the AI she was angry with but the human who had programmed it. Julie glanced from the old woman to the line up at the till. Impulsively, she sprang from her seat, snatched a bun from the counter, and dashed after the old woman.

What're you doing? You've already got one demerit today—

I'll pay later. She's getting away, SAM!

Julie caught up to the old woman and handed her the bun. The woman's eyes lit up and she accepted it with a cautious smile, then shuffled quickly away. No sooner had she taken several steps and raised the bun to bite into it, when a Pol loomed in front of her, seized her and the bun, and led her gruffly through the crowd.

Julie sprinted toward them to explain, but someone grabbed her arm and pulled her backward. She turned and drew in her breath. Another Pol. His thin, perfectly shaped mouth smirked in amusement. The visor hid the rest of his face. He reached over and pulled off her vee-set with finger and thumb as if it were an insect, so he could get a better look at her. His smile grew. "Where're you going, beauty?"

Oh, dear. This isn't good. Say something, Julie!

"She's innocent. Please, you must let her go," she pleaded.

He looked amused. "Must?"

"*I* took the bun! And I was going to—"

"But *she's* eating it," he said and let go of her arm. He stood a head taller than her, and smelled of smoke and metal. "You both broke the code. You for stealing and she for eating."

"No! It wasn't like that at all!" she objected. "I was going to—"

"It doesn't really matter. Come with me." He turned and limped toward the edge of the mall.

Pay! You were going to pay. Finish your sentence, Julie! You're in danger. Use your head. Reason with him—

Reason with a Pol? She swallowed hard and followed the Pol with a glance in the opposite direction, where the other Pol was taking the old woman. They reached a dark corner of the mall and once in the shadows, he astonished her by taking off his helmet. She'd never seen a Pol without his helmet on before. They weren't half-machines after all. He resembled a young timber wolf, dark brown hair with golden tips swept from the center to either side of his high forehead. A few stubborn strands crept over one eye. His boyish face didn't match the austerity of the uniform, yet in those ocean-blue eyes slumbered something fierce, perhaps even cruel. Why had he done it? To get a better look at her or to show her his face?

I think he's dangerous, Julie.

He's a Pol, SAM. They're supposed to be dangerous.

Taking his helmet off like that. What if he's a Renegade? They hurt people.

As if regular Pols don't?

The Pol watched her and mimicked her tilted head. "So, Julie Crane..." He paused and smirked. If he thought knowing her name would impress her, he was wrong. Any vee-set could do that. She focused on the small space between his front teeth. "You have some very strange habits," he continued, "like saving that hag who threw herself in front of the tube-jet earlier this morning." He laughed at her shocked expression. "You can close your beautiful mouth. I know all about you, Julie Crane. Pols know everything," he said slyly. "We're omnipresent—"

"I think you mean omniscient," she interrupted, then quickly added, "All knowing. It means all knowing..."

His eyes sparkled as if delighted by her impertinence. "Charming," he said. "It's no coincidence I captured you." He paused, giving her a chance to wonder what he would do next. She didn't ask. "And d'you know why I did that?" he said playfully.

She could barely speak. "Why... did you?"

"So I could set you free. But only if you let me kiss you for as long as I want."

She stared. Why would a Pol want to kiss *her*?

I told you he was dangerous! SAM's voice spluttered like a bad channel, cutting through her haze of excitement. Kissing in public's against the code. He doesn't show a recent screen for Darwin and he doesn't look like he has much for brains. Julie, think. Don't let him—

She wrenched out of veemeld and trembled with anticipation. She hadn't thought Pols were exempt from the code and marveled at his brazen request.

"Well?" The Pol raised a brow.

She blinked and fought to keep her breaths even. "But it's against the code—"

"So?"

Confused at her dizzy longing, she clung to her rational mind and drew back. "What about Darwin Disease?"

"No one's proven that it's a kissy disease. Besides, we all die. Live for the moment, my beauty. Take a chance with me." He smiled, showing his teeth.

A Pol who promoted breaking the code? The lingering scent of *hedon* coiled around her in a heady embrace. His lips drew close to hers but she turned her face away. "What about the people?" she said in a voice that quavered beneath a surging throb of desire.

He laughed. "I'm the law. No one gets in my way. Besides, they can't see us."

She trembled as he reached over and swept a rogue strand of hair from her forehead. Before she could speak again his mouth closed on hers, wet and demanding. It sent a charge down her spine, to where she burned. Then he kissed her hard, so hard she was sent reeling backwards and slammed against the wall. Then it was over. He tossed her vee-set to her. "Happy birthday, beauty." As she jerked to catch it, he put his helmet back on and hobbled into the swarming crowd. She was left panting and wondering why he'd stopped so soon. It hadn't seemed so long, like he insinuated. Had he not liked it?

~

Face flushed from exertion, Julie rushed to her workstation, kicked the door shut and strode directly to her chair. She flung her vee-set on the desk beside her with annoyance. *I know Pols are classified information, SAM—*

A vee-set intro-scan would reveal a blank, Julie—

I'm not talking about doing an intro-scan. We have a mental picture of his face. We could simply—

Tap into the Pol Station's confidential files using your new data-link program and abandoned and illegal routes, then crack their codes and drain them of their information.

Julie slid into her chair and smirked. *SAM, I'll turn you into a super sleuth yet.*

It's not sure we should do this, Julie. You're not thinking of getting involved with that wiseguy, are you?

Julie tapped her foot impatiently. She frowned. *I'm not afraid of Pols.*

It's not smart, not with your history and especially now that you're working on this classified project for Kraken. I think you should stay away from Pols, especially this one.

Julie slumped in her chair. SAM had been vindicated in counseling her against going out with Paul Getz. *I know what I'm doing, SAM. I'm just curious.* She hoped her defensive tone didn't show.

I can tell you're attracted to him.

I'm just... well, it's just that he's so...

Intoxicating.

Was she that transparent?

I think you're being illogical again. What if he's a Renegade and he knows that you're the new modeler?

She felt a jerk of alarm and instantly cast it aside. *He's not a Renegade.*

He breaks rules.

Renegades are extreme right-wing types, SAM. So he might break the rules a little. He's breaking the wrong rules to be a Renegade. Julie studied her screen, hoping to discover why he was so different from the other Pols. And why he'd kissed her instead of throwing her in the Pol Station with the old woman. *So tell me what you have?*

If you insist. But I still think you should be working on the project instead of pursuing this. After a pause in which she stubbornly didn't reply, SAM offered, Okay, his name's Frank Langor.

Julie studied Frank's image and the bio SAM had thrown on the holo. Focusing on his intense eyes, she asked, *Does every Pol have a brain implant?*

Yes, all regular Pols do.

The implant lets him access the vee-com database, doesn't it?

In addition to providing enhanced memory, sensory and motor functions and even muscle mass. Together with the helmet-link they have a formidable tool. Did you know, however, that the helmet can be used against the Pol?

No. Really?

Because of the brain-link through the inner ear probe, a sharp pull on the helmet would cause permanent brain damage. Fortunately no one outside the Pol force knows this.

Fortunately, she reiterated absently. *The database,* she hesitated before sending her next thought, *does that include confidential information about a person?*

Do you mean would he know that you're a veemeld?

Yeah. SAM was second-guessing her a lot lately.

Your guess is as good as mine. I don't know whether a regular Pol can access that level of confidentiality. It might only be available to Admin staff.

Frank's father was also a Pol. She skimmed his credentials: *His father was good at his job.*

But at home he beat his wife. She didn't like hearing that. The mother lives with a different man every week, each of them keeping her well stocked in *delilah*. She smokes *hedon* illegally. Gets it smuggled in from the inner-city. She's a drunk.

Oh. She forced down the memory of her own mother's abusive habit and read on. Frank had sped up the ranks from his original placement as traffic controller and risen past the riot-squad and the drug-squad to the special investigations unit, where he now led his four-man team. At 21 years old, Frank Langor appeared to be exactly where every young man wanted to be. She bit down on her lower lip. *Frank Langor isn't a... mean Pol, is he, SAM?*

Like his father before him, he holds the highest score for percent hits on illegals. He never visits his mother, but trades in his merits to maintain her Level 3 lifestyle.

Julie's eyebrows rose and she smiled. Frank Langor had a tender spot in his heart. Then she chided herself: he was still a Pol. The devil, her mother had called them. The "enemy," according to Nancy. Why did she feel so attracted to him? Logic told her to stay away, yet she felt an inexplicable urge to see him again. The chance of that happening was probably as likely as a double eclipse, she thought wearily, scrolling up the file again to the father's bio. Something caught her attention. *It says here that Ed Langor was killed in action in 2091, but the details are unclear.* She noticed that he'd been stamped a Renegade and stiffened with discomfort. *What happened, SAM?*

He'd been investigating a tech-crime he'd uncovered—some guy high up in the Admin-Center was tampering with surveillance. Langor never reported in again. A litter droid found his mangled body in a lower level garbage chute. Soon after, someone gave evidence that he was a Renegade and he was struck from the honor list. As you can see his reputation was spotless up to then.

Julie gripped her lower lip with her teeth, her mind glancing to her own father's humiliating disgrace by the scientific community. She thought of young Frank, how he'd followed in his father's footsteps to become a Pol. Frank was already a crack shot like his father. What else had he inherited from him? Perhaps this explained some of his uncharacteristic behavior for a Pol, like taking his helmet off all the time and his irreverence for some rules.

SAM, what was the evidence against Ed Langor?

Julie, you're not going to like this.

She frowned with determination. *Tell me anyway.*

Ed Langor was the officer who arrested your father.

Julie felt her muscles stiffen. *Are you sure?* Then her memory summoned Langor's stern mouth and build; how he stood with crooked shoulders, like his son, at the door of the apartment the last time she'd seen her father.

It gets worse. Your father's the one who accused Langor of being a Renegade. It's in his interrogation record. Julie, Renegade Pols have sworn to eradicate followers of chaos theory, people like your father...

Her throat went suddenly dry. Maybe Frank *was* a renegade, like his father... and did he knew about what Julie's father had done to his? He couldn't know, she decided. And he couldn't be a Renegade. He'd been far too charming. The way he'd looked at her... Then again, she was already courting fire with Kraken's assignment.

9

CLUTCHING her introductory letter from Fitch, Julie rode the elevator 55 stories up to the top floor of the Pol Station. The door opened to a room that looked more like the leisure room of a home than an office. Decorated with stunning works of three-dimensional art the spacious room rose to a high vaulted ceiling and a spectacular chandelier hung at its centre. She hesitated, quickly scanning for any occupants and found no one. A warm breeze that carried the sweet aroma of honeysuckle and roses rustled through her hair, drawing her attention to the open doorway of a large patio. She gazed past a mahogany table surrounded by comfortable looking leather chairs to the patio behind, intrigued. Julie stepped out of the lift and entered the room, glancing at two photographs on the desk. One portrayed an older woman, about forty, and the other a teenage girl, perhaps thirteen or fourteen. They resembled each other enough for Julie to deduce that they were mother and daughter.

"Well, well." A pleasant voice from her left made her jump. She turned and beheld an older man with strong features, of medium build dressed in a Pol uniform. Although his face was seamed with laugh-lines, she could not gauge his age. Stallion-black hair swept across his wide temple in a thick unruly mane. He gazed at her with probing eyes and a casual smile as he sauntered toward her, hand extended. The Head Pol, she deduced. The man who'd ordered her father's execution; the man she had to impress.

"I'm Wolfgang Kraken," he said with a liquid voice. "You must be Julie..."

"Crane," she finished for him and grasped his hand firmly. "Data Handler for the Head Statistician at the DIC." She handed him Fitch's letter.

"Ah." He accepted it with an amused look. Her cheeks warmed. Of course he knew who she was. His gaze drifted over her in swift appraisal. Undressing her with his eyes.

"Fitch recommended you for this assignment because you're thorough and fast. But also discreet." He tilted his head and frowned. "You're very young to have acquired your present reputation."

She raised her head and set her jaw. "I may be young but I'm not immature. I work hard and apply myself creatively. I enjoy my work and I'm very good at it."

Julie, let's not rile him with your first sentence.

Kraken laughed, booming from the stomach. She cringed. "Excuse me," he said, placing his hand on her shoulder, "but I find your honesty and lack of misplaced humility refreshing, Julie. May I call you that? Come, join me on the patio."

He grasped her elbow and steered her past the glass doors into a huge open deck that overlooked the heath below and seemed to wrap right around the entire building. Julie stared appreciatively at the gardens that included a large assortment of domestic flowers and shrubs, all tastefully arranged into a kind of small park, complete with sculptures and fountains. Julie inhaled the complicated cocktail of flower, vegetation and soil deeply. Kraken led her through one of several walkways and stopped at a table and chairs beside a brilliant red rose bush.

This is spectacular, SAM, isn't it? Few other Icarians have this.

Try 'no other Icarian.'

"My wife persuaded me to make these gardens." Kraken said. "I'm actually the gardener. I quite enjoy it. I find it meditative."

"They're beautiful. I love the smell of flowers." Julie bent to sniff one of the roses.

"So does my daughter," said Kraken. "She's 100% my wife's and mine. No eggs or sperm from the DP. Good genes, eh?" He laughed, then looked pensive for a moment. "Just think, not too long ago it was all left to chance. Anyone could pass on his genes, unfettered." He leaned forward until she felt his warm breath on her and fought the inclination to recoil. "What a disaster, eh? Like broadcasting seed."

Julie nodded politely. *I was born that way,* she thought. *A broadcast seed.*

His eyes swept down her body. "Chaos! You're young enough to be my daughter too!"

I'm not that young!

Yes, you are. Don't get huffy, Julie. I don't think he meant to insult your maturity. You're awfully defensive.

I don't like the way he looks at me, SAM. I'm 55 floors up in the Pol Station Tower and the Head Pol's ogling me. Terrific.

I don't think you know the correct usage of the word 'terrific'. You keep misusing it—

Julie couldn't help a wry smile. *It's called sarcasm. Don't learn it, okay?*

Kraken smiled back at her. "Come." He offered her a chair at the table and she sat down. He reclined on a chair across from her. "What will you drink? *Delilah?* Perhaps you'd like to try our newest *sodom?*"

"Tea would be fine, if you have it."

"Certainly." He pressed a button on the console at his chair side. "A glass of red wine for me—make it a Cabernet—and a tea for the lady," he said to no one in particular. Then he turned to her, "Any preference?" At her puzzled look, he explained, "Darjeeling, chamomile or regular black tea? With honey or milk?"

Trying not to hesitate, she answered, "Darjeeling... with honey. Thank you." *Wonderful. What am I getting?*

Darjeeling with honey.

His vee-com screen slid up from below a panel on the table. She faced the sun and had to squint to look directly at him. "Vee-com, show me Julie Crane's file and scroll at the usual rate," he instructed the com-unit. Several times, he told the vee-com to stop, then started it scrolling again. Julie shifted in her seat. Was he doing this for her benefit? To make her nervous?

Kraken smiled, nodding to himself. Without looking away from the screen he said, "Your credentials are admirable. I see you've got an Interact-SYM." He looked up and his eyes blazed into hers. "So, you're a veemeld." Surely he knew *that*. His smile blossomed into a broad grin. "Part of the new breed, eh?" She couldn't read his smile and felt her chest tighten; was that a good thing or a bad thing? Kraken leaned back and studied the screen again. "Hmm." He tapped his lips with his fingers. "You make very creative use of software." She involuntarily swallowed. Was he being genuine or sarcastic, referring to her off-the-wall programs? Kraken looked up at her. "You take your work seriously: good Icarian. I'll enjoy dialoguing with you."

Julie bit her lower lip to keep from speaking and smiled out of the corner of her mouth. *That's impossible, isn't it, SAM? Dialogue's a noun, not a verb.*

I'm glad you exercised some self control that time.

Kraken raised an eyebrow and grinned. "So, tell me—indulge an old man's curiosity." He leaned forward. "I know that veemelding involves the use of the central AI core—not those limited AIs we meet every day in the hallways. AIHV created the central AI core as an open, bottom-up system, right?"

Relieved that the Head Pol had moved onto a less personal subject, Julie nodded. "Designed to learn and continue to mature."

"Yes. They envisioned a symbiotic relationship between the developing AI core and our veemelding community, which, of course they thought would be every Icarian." He leaned back and shook his head with a bitter laugh. "The idiots at AIHV had no idea that you veemelds were genetically unique and only made up 1% of our population—"

It's actually 0.8%, Julie.

"It's actually 0.8%," Julie corrected. "Eighty million veemelds in Icaria and about one hundred and sixty thousand in Icaria-5."

Kraken smiled, amused. "So you connect with the central AI core by using Interact-SYM on your vee-com. It transmits and receives a quantum corridor beam between the vee-com's holo-receptors and your brain via the retina of your eye, right?"

"Yes," Julie nodded. *Little does he know.* "The theories suggest that the high-frequency signals, called tetanic pulses, can only be received in veemeld brains because their *zif*-268 gene is different from everyone else. The quantum signal produces a long-term potentiation, or LTP, in the hippocampus that's somehow connected to theta rhythms, which are involved in learning—"

"—What I'm really curious about is how it *feels* to veemeld."

Julie blinked. "I beg your pardon?"

Careful, Julie. He thinks you still use Interact-SYM.

"How does it *feel*? What's the sensation?"

How could she divulge just enough to satisfy his curiosity without revealing too much of herself? Kraken appeared genuinely interested and a part of her felt eager to share. "Well, it's like dreaming... perhaps more like self-hypnosis. You need to focus because you're in several places at the same time."

"You mean here and cyberspace or in your mind and outside your mind?"

"Well, both, I guess," she blurted. "It's a little more like an out-of-body experience."

Julie, watch out! Use your brain!

I have it together, SAM... I can do this...

Kraken stroked his chin. "How do you interact with the core's AI? Do you talk to it or feel your way through its variable matrix?"

"Both. At first it was more spatial, mechanical. I found my way. Then we sort of stumbled into interactive communication..."

Good vee, Julie! You're giving away the store.

"...It became less orientation and more relationship," Julie rushed on, unable to stop. "Less place, more emotive. We now have conversations—but not like you and I. It's more intuitive. Like a collaboration of two parts of one mind. A joining of..." of souls, she was going to say, but stopped herself. Thankfully. *Oh, dear... Did I say too much?*

Kraken's eyes sparkled like the sea. "You said *we*. Who—what—do you mean?"

"The entity I communicate with."

Oh, Julie!

His eyes widened. "Entity?"

Oh, oh... I said the wrong thing, didn't I? Her mind raced for an appropriate explanation. "It's an individualized part of the AI core's consciousness. The entity exists as a result of my veemelding."

Don't say any more! Now you've done it.

Kraken looked stunned. She squirmed. *Oh, vee, I blew it, didn't I?*

He can't know the rest. He can only guess.

Kraken gazed at infinity for some moments, then blinked, refocusing his eyes. He smiled like he'd won a prize. A young Pol without a helmet emerged from the suite with a tray of drinks and a plate of small pastries. He placed a cup and saucer, a pot of tea and a container of honey before Julie and a stemmed glass with red wine in front of the Head Pol, then disappeared inside.

Julie poured her tea then dipped the spoon in the honey and transferred it awkwardly to her cup, getting some on her hand. As she licked the honey off her fingers, she felt Kraken's eyes upon her and looked up with a forced smile.

"Help yourself," he said, pointing at the pastries with a sly smile that made her wonder if he knew her penchant for sweets. Julie seized a flaky pastry covered in chocolate and dusted in white sugar. After her bite, Kraken cleared his throat and tapped his own lip. "You have some sugar there," he offered, betraying delight at her vulnerability.

"Thank you." She smiled, embarrassed, and wiped her mouth with a napkin.

Kraken leaned back. He raised his glass to Julie and said, "Here's to beauty. Yours to have and mine to enjoy." His eyes wrinkled with a faint smile. Confused, Julie sipped her tea. She was still waiting for him to get to the business at hand and was just about to ask him when he leaned forward as if to share a confidence. "You know, Julie, I have ultimate power in Icaria-5. The Pol Station really has the final say in everything in Icaria. The other Heads, they listen to me. They don't question me..."

Why share it as though it was news? *SAM, what's he after?*

I don't know, Julie. Stay calm. Your heart's racing.

Kraken pursed his lips and nodded his head slowly to himself. "As for you, young woman, you've already received several demerits. Tsk. Tsk: bad Icarian," he said with emphasis on "bad" and shook his head.

A siren went off in Julie's head. *SAM?*

Julie, be careful. I can't help you.

Oh vee, what's he after?

"I could sentence you to the Pol Station on your dirty record alone or just as easily keep you here as my lover," he said, leaning back in his chair. "No one would be the wiser. No one, I'm afraid, would even care. Except perhaps for your uncle, who has his own troubles; and poor Fitch, who depends on you to keep him competent."

Her pulse raced. She felt the hair on the back of her neck rise and her eyes darted for a possible escape route. The door to his suite, the only way out, was behind him.

"Ever wonder how people with power get to where they are?" he asked casually. "I got here because I recognize the elitist that resides in everyone. Every center harbors an obsession. The Enviro-Center is obsessed with the outside environment, so much so that they don't want Icarians out there messing it up. The Med-Center's obsessed with health, so they've scared off most of the sick people in Icaria. Your Center's obsessed with information, so it refuses to communicate it and wants to hoard it all. The Pol Station's obsessed with order, so some of us consort with our chaotic enemy to achieve it." He paused to sip his wine. "Icaria lies on the edge of a dreadful precipice. It's also on the verge of something wonderful."

What does any of this have to do with me?

Kraken stood up and leaned across the table, blocking the sun from her face. He slid beside her and placed his hand on her shoulder. She felt her own heat rising. His hand traveled down to her breast. She jerked up with enough force to push him off balance. Her chair fell backward and the cup flew off the table, spilling tea on him. It smashed to pieces on the ground. The Pol rushed out, alerted by the sound, but Kraken waved him tersely off. "It's all right, Wayne. Go back inside."

Striving to keep her voice calm, Julie said, "No one touches me like that unless I invite him to. Not even the most powerful man in Icaria-5." Her hands clenched.

Kraken smiled and raised his hands in truce. "Relax, Julie. You have your father's temper. I'm not trying to threaten you or frighten you. I was just illustrating a point."

"What point is that?" She was shaking. She'd lost SAM, unable to hang onto its frequency in her rage. She wanted to wipe Kraken's smile off his face.

"That although I have power, I choose not to exercise it."

"I think you confuse power with tyranny," she said. "The only power you have over me is the power I give you. You can hurt me but you don't have the power of my will unless I sanction it. My soul belongs to *me*." Would he bring up her father's guilt? She couldn't stand the injustice, and she let her outrage release her. "I'll never forget my father's quiet dignity the day he was taken to the Pol Station for a crime he didn't commit." She heard her own voice go shrill and fought the tremor in it. "You executed him but you never got his confession. He didn't kill anyone."

"Bravely spoken." He nodded to her with a half-smile of respect. "I admire your faith in your father's innocence, despite all the evidence against him. Please, sit," he insisted, picking up her chair and placing it before her. She didn't move and he shrugged. "I asked you here because you're one of the best data handlers in Icaria-5, perhaps all of Icaria." Kraken eased into his chair like a cat. "I have an interesting project for you. Icaria, like you, is poised for greatness. If you accept this assignment you may play an important part in defining its future. Whether Icaria flies or falls could depend on you. I need you to help me identify and model two antipodal groups that are giving me and Icaria grief. The first are vigilante Pols—Renegades, impatient with our current justice system. They're a continual embarrassment to me. The second are Distopians, who wish only to tear down the government and cause anarchy. They've made some loose accusations and threats about freedom of information and Darwin Disease. But we don't bargain with terrorists." He waved a hand.

"Recent information has linked these two groups," he continued. "I need you to provide me with a model of both so that I can grasp their motives and deal with them. In repayment, I'll give you the freedom to be exactly who and what you want to be. Your belief that your father was falsely accused of those killings, despite the incriminating vees of him, intrigues me." He tilted his head with an amused smile. "You don't know much about what he was involved in when you were a child, do you?" The patronizing smile slid into something complicated—a chess player's smile. "Remind me to tell you about him some day when we know each other better. And call me Wolfgang."

10

GAIA and Victor rode their horses through the heath. His vast polyculture plots were hard to distinguish from the heath itself. When he found one suitable to show Gaia, Victor reined in and dismounted. He watched Gaia slip off her horse like a petal from a flower. The skirt of her colorful dress swept up as she hopped down, revealing slender but muscular legs. The heath's vibrant thrusts of purple, pink and yellow stirred in the hot summer breeze like waves of a tropical sea. He scanned them as he drew in an appreciative breath, taking in a profusion of scents.

He led her through one of the pioneer heather plots, against the keen, bracing wind, and they picked their way carefully through the diverse plant life. "These are part of our natural-systems perennial domestication," he said, pointing. "They require very little maintenance."

Gaia sniffed the air and smiled, her stern face softening. "Yes, making use of nature's wisdom."

Victor nodded. "The entire thousand hectares is maintained by only five Ecologists and a hundred and fifty eco-droids. This is one of our primary seres. *Calluna vulgaris* makes up the dominant species, along with *Erica cinerea*, *Vaccinium myrtillus* and a few others you might recognize." He squatted down to stroke one of the flowering heather plants. "This plot was altered and seeded two years ago," he said and straightened up. "We take the terminal and unlignified parts of the long-shoots, usually the growth of the current year. Up to 75% of the plant biomass of the young shoots is edible. *Calluna* chips, for instance, provide an excellent source of crude protein, calcium, magnesium and potassium."

Gaia nodded.

"The plot in that hollow there," he pointed to the east, shielding his eyes with his other hand, "was seeded five years ago with grasses in addition to ericaceous plants. It's a more fertile site and can support the higher nutrient grasses like sorghum and gamagrass in the mixed polyculture. Our best yields that combine both quality and quantity come from seven- or eight-year-old stands. But each seral stage provides its own optimum yield. We can provide virtually all our Level 1 and 2 chute services in natural foods with plots like this one. We use nature's own natural succession and maximize our harvests over the long term."

"Marvelous," Gaia said, looking down at him. "Hardy like the heath, yet nurturing like the forest. Your biomimicry practices have surpassed most other

Icarias, even those located in more fertile ecosystems. I'm beginning to see why."

He could not help a victorious smile. "The high diversity of this polyculture serves as its own pest and weed control." Victor stroked a small bush. "This legume acts as a natural fertilizer by fixing nitrogen. Natural selection in action."

Gaia's eyes brightened. "You know, Victor, what you've accomplished here with such aplomb provides a good metaphor for what the *Circle* wishes to accomplish with Icaria, and the planet as a whole," she said. Victor groaned inwardly, steeling himself for another lecture. "We don't believe in forcing artificial traits on people through genetic manipulation. That's what the Technocrats tried to do with their techno-clones and transgenic fiascos, and they failed miserably. The leaders of Icaria don't pretend to be gods, playing with genetic engineering. We're Ecologists. We work with humankind's own natural evolution. Trends based on what is being selected for from the diverse gene pools through chance and heritable variation. All we do is direct an already-existing tendency."

With more than a little help from the DP and the Ed-Center, Victor thought, pulverizing the plant in his hand. Why was she feeding him this rhetoric? He felt his abdomen knot with suspicion.

"Speaking of evolution, your acquisition of veemelds has not gone unnoticed, Victor," Gaia said in a casual tone.

Victor kept his expression deadpan. Had the discovery his microbiologists made leaked out after all? He'd classified all information related to the disease and had removed Julie Crane from the Darwin Disease research project for security reasons. He'd then taken all other veemelds off the project so Gaia could not mind-read the information.

Gaia hiked an eyebrow. "Icaria-5 has the highest percentage of veemelds of all the Icarias on this planet. Hoping for a little competitive edge?" Her lips curled.

She didn't know, he decided. She didn't know that veemelds were immune to the effects of Darwin Disease. She was only teasing him about trying to gain favor for his Icaria based on his population's proven superior intellect. He seized her carrot. Leading her to another plot, he said, "You already had a lot of veemelds in Icaria-5 when you left me the job. They're far more productive and I've encouraged them to stay by giving them Level 1 positions. While other Icarias expel them to keep the peace, I invite them in."

"You may pay with higher disorder, Victor," she warned. Her brows came together, but her lips remained in a dubious smile.

I'll take that risk, he thought, and fought to keep the smugness off his face.

Gaia stopped walking. "Much like this evolving polyculture of yours, Icarians are also evolving through their own natural selection." She swept her hand over the heath as if it were hers. "Survival of the fittest, Victor. Who will emerge from this genetic chaos? Will it be those like your protégé, that young, unusually-gifted veemeld?"

Victor swallowed hard. *Relax. She can't read your mind.* "You mean Ms. Crane?" Shielding his eyes against the sun, he pictured Julie standing where Gaia stood now, smelling like the heath—of honey and spice—regarding him with feral eyes as the breeze teased her wild hair across her face.

"There's no telling what veemelds may eventually achieve, Victor."

And what you might achieve with nothing but veemelds in power, whose minds you can read, Victor thought, fighting down a scowl. Hardly analogous to his polycultures; more like a hegemony of monoculture. He summoned up their earlier conversation at the house, about what Gaia intended to do with Julie Crane. Gaia's intention, if he had surmised correctly, entailed something far removed from natural selection: she meant to devise a way to produce more gifted veemelds. If what mattered for evolution was the contribution of an individual's progeny to the next generation, then Gaia was going to mold this process of adaptation through "Gaia's selection." He fought a frown. He knew more than she did, but she still seemed a step ahead of him.

11

"WHAT'RE you doing?" Julie stood in her leisure room, still in her work clothes. She'd come home from doing laps at the Rec-Center's Level 1 pool to find her uncle Bobby waiting for her inside; he'd let himself in. His gray leisure clothes hung loosely on his small wiry body and his tanned face bore the harsh lines of sunshine: the hallmark of the Enviro-Center worker. He ran his hand along the gray stubble of his chin and coughed. He looked old. Mucous rattled in his throat. Julie cocked her head to one side and remonstrated in a kind voice, "You've got a nasty cold." She studied his thin body, sagging in her couch. His bony face trembled under a labored breath. "You should be resting in bed."

She knew why he had come. When he felt sick he always sought her place. Here on the 30th floor, he could take in her view of the heath, inhale the fresh air from her open windows and sniff genuine leather and wood. His own place was a windowless hovel in the lower outer-city, furnished in nano-technology. He harbored an unnatural fear of closed-in places, which he accommodated by spending most of his day working outside. He had probably caught his cold from working in the rain. When he was sick, he felt the unease more acutely.

"I'm delivering a book," he explained lamely. She watched him caress her genuine leather. No cheap nano-materials in her Level 1 apartment. "Your place was on the way, so I dropped by for one of your herbal teas," Bobby stammered between coughs. "My client's desperate for the book. It took me two months of searching to find it, and Tesla's so anxious to get it he's raised the stakes. If I don't deliver soon, he may change his mind and go with another agent. Vee, I'm getting too old for this sort of thing." He slumped back against the cushions.

"Terrific." She crossed her arms and eyed Bobby with wry cynicism. "What's in it for you this time? A case of the finest scotch? That'll make you better."

"No. Oranges. Something good for this cold."

"Oranges!" A rare find for his Level 5 privileges. Her uncle avoided the Med-Center. He was terrified of the place and she could never convince him to go for medication. She placed her hands on her hips and gave him a hard look. "What's the book? Is it Distopian or just peripheral?"

He sighed, his voice raspy. "It's not on the Icarian reading list. But I don't think it's Distopian." He seemed to shrink further into her couch.

Julie leaned forward. "Don't you know? You should know what you're peddling."

She paced the room, glancing at him periodically. He searched his pocket for a tissue and blew his nose. She finally said, "Where does your client live?"

He avoided her eyes. "District-13."

"Bobby!" She stopped pacing. "That's clear across town! What if someone catches you? The Med-Center's cracking down with this Darwin threat."

He shook his head sheepishly then fell into a hacking fit.

Julie frowned. "What if a Pol stops you for coughing and discovers you peddling books? That's a much more serious offence than being sick in public. It might put you in the Pol Station or even in front of the Shame Court."

He looked down at his hands, then jammed them between his legs like a boy in detention. He pulled them out and wrung them nervously, then stuffed them back between his legs. He was much too old to be publicly shamed. She couldn't bear the possibility. Taming her anger, she exhaled. "Let me take it for you."

He jerked his head up and looked at her with guilty relief. "I've never involved you in my affairs before—"

"And you won't again. But this is different. You're sick. Here's the deal." She pointed her finger at him. "You have a hot bath here, while I deliver this illegal book for you."

"Thank you, honey!" he beamed. A hot bath was a Level 1 treat—something his 30 liters of water a day couldn't provide.

As she drew the bath for him, he hovered over her with instructions. "Remember, accept no less than 22 oranges. Have him count them in front of you. He'll try to reduce the number. Don't let him bamboozle you, Julie. Tesla's a shrewd and stingy old coot. I'm already giving him a good deal. He'll see your innocent face and think he can get away with less than we negotiated."

"I won't let him bamboozle me, Bobby," she reassured him. "Now, promise me you'll relax in your bath and take a nap here before you return home. I'll meet you at your place and make you some supper."

He perked up and smiled like a child. "You're offering to make *me* supper?"

She cocked her head to one side with a crooked smile. "I'm not promising much, but I can cook soup."

"Wonderful," he said and began to unbutton his shirt. "Good luck, child, and be careful!" he added as Julie opened the door to leave.

"I will, Bobby."

≈

Julie rang Tesla's door chime. The door opened and she came face to face with a Pol. She backed in alarm and was about to flee, but he snatched her arm.

"Well, well, what have we here..." He dragged her inside and yanked off her vee-set. The force of his motion pulled her head toward him, hurting her, before the vee-set gave way. The place smelled of oranges and air freshener. She winced at the sound of a hard crack and the wailing of a man in another room. *SAM!*

Keep calm, Julie. Don't show your fear.

How am I supposed to do that?

"What business do you have with Tesla, eh?" His thick wet lips curled up sardonically. They looked obscene somehow, with dried saliva crusted at one corner. "Are you plotting with him?"

"No, no, I—I don't know what you're talking about. I don't know him. I was just—just—" she stammered and decided to save herself from what she instinctively felt was a much more serious offense by admitting to a minor one, "—just delivering this book to him. I've never met him before." She handed the Pol the book as proof.

No, Julie!

The Pol looked down and read the title: *Brave New World Revisited.* After scanning it with his mini-vee, he said in a voice of self-importance, "A fucking illegal book peddler, eh? Sounds a little too convenient. Or is that a disguise so we won't think you're a Distopian, eh? You don't look very prosaic..." He made a churlish smile with those obscene lips as his head swept down her body to take her fully in. She focused on the fresh spittle that bubbled in the corners of his mouth.

"I don't think you know what prosaic means," Julie answered. "It has nothing to do with prose. It means—"

"Shut up!" he snapped. Spit flew from his mouth. "Just shut the fuck up!"

She felt moisture on her face. "Dull... It means dull..." she trailed, wiping her face with a trembling hand.

I don't think you're handling this very well, Julie.

The Pol grunted and dragged her toward the ominous sounds. "Come with me and we'll see if you're telling the fucking truth."

A middle-aged man with curly violet hair and a waxy complexion sat stooped on the bed. Blood dripped from his nose. Probably Tesla. A broken chair lay beside him. Another Pol, his back to them, stood over Tesla. He was biting into a half-peeled orange.

"Look what I found, Frank," said the Pol beside Julie. "A fucking smart-mouth." He pushed her forward.

The other Pol turned. His helmet was unbuckled and his visor was up. Orange juice dripped from his chin. Julie caught up her breath. She was face to face with the Pol who'd kissed her last week.

"Well, well," Frank said. She thought she detected a hint of a smile. Did he know about their respective fathers?

"The bitch is rude and can't shut her fucking yap," the Pol beside her said. "Says she's a book peddler and doesn't know Tesla." Her arm hurt where he gripped her.

"Let her go, Ron," Frank said. "You really need to work on your manners. Finish off here. I'll take care of her." He pulled out several oranges from Tesla's bag, stuffed them in a pocket, and slid beside Julie. Taking her vee-set lightly in one hand and gripping her arm with the other, he led her out of Tesla's apartment.

When they were in the hallway, he let go of her and handed back her vee-set. "Here I am rescuing you again," he said with a triumphant smile as she fumbled with the vee-set. "Seems like you and I are supposed to meet. Our uniforms even match: me in black with red logo and you in red with black logo!" he observed, giving the trite detail an importance it did not deserve. "But this time I better escort you to your destination to keep you out of trouble, my naughty beauty."

As he steered her to the mall, she stole glances at his savage face and wondered what trouble she was getting into. Seeing a waiting tube-jet, he seized her hand and broke into a run with a feral laugh. They slid, panting, into a car before the doors shut. The few people in the car ignored them. Frank sprawled into an empty seat, raised his visor and with a reckless smile invited Julie to sit next to him. She sat down and forced her eyes forward. She'd never felt such giddy excitement with a man before. Certainly not with the men she'd dated—all three of them.

Frank peered out the window, his smoke and metal scent rising in her nostrils. He'd spread his legs apart and brought his knee dangerously close to hers. Her face smoldered as she realized how much she wanted him to touch her. She had a crazy vision of him taking her there and then, in front of all the people, and felt a strange stirring between her legs. If she moved just a few centimeters... He shifted in his seat and touched her with his knee. She felt her heart pulse in her crotch.

The train slowed at the District-7 station and he stirred from his seat. He led her off the tube-jet, through MacArthur Mall and to the dingy Liv-Center. When she saw where they were going, her heart flipped. *He's taking me to Bobby's! How'd he know I was coming here?*

Pols seem to know everything. This isn't smart, Julie. Particularly considering what we know about his father.

When they reached her uncle's door, Frank waited for her to produce her card. With forced calmness she pulled it out of her belt-pack, slipped it in the door slot and they entered together. Bobby wasn't home yet. She pulled off her vee-set. "Thank you," she said evenly, hoping that he would detect the note of finality in her voice and leave. Instead he pulled off his helmet and flung it on a chair, then shut the door. Was he going to kiss her again? Her pulse quickened.

"I'll let you go if..." That pause again.

"Oh, all right," she pushed out her face toward him and demurely dropping her gaze, ready for his lips.

Julie, what're you doing? You need to control your emo—

I'm not a machine! she snapped, and leapt out of veemeld.

"Not that," said Frank. "Something better."

Her gaze jerked up.

"Yes, you know what I mean." He grinned. "I want *all* of you this time."

She stepped back and said with instinctive anger, "You have no right! I'll—"

"Call a Pol?" He smirked. "Go, ahead, report me: Frank Langor, number 2134. But before you do, I should tell you that I know all about your Distopian family: who your father killed and that illegal book smuggling operation your uncle's been involved in since '73. And don't forget where you were only half an hour ago, and with what." He pulled out the illegal book she had surrendered to the other Pol and waved it in front of her.

Instinctively she reached out for it. He snatched it back with a sharp laugh. "Oh, no, you don't. This is my collateral." He stuffed it back into his jacket pocket. "I know everything about you, more than even you know about yourself."

Julie swallowed involuntarily. Did he know about what her father had done to his?

"You and your uncle belong in the Pol Station. I could put you there in a moment." He snapped his fingers. She flinched, thinking of his father. "But I don't want to do that." His voice softened and he moved toward her, eyes intensely appreciating her. "All I want is to make delicious love to you."

A surge of pleasure at his words confused her. She pushed out her chin. "You're just a cheap tyrant, taking liberties—"

He burst into laughter. "And you're just a caged bird hungry for excitement," he said, showing his teeth. "Hungry for *me*!" He seized her wrist. "I saw it in your face. It's there now."

She gazed from the little space between his two front teeth to his eyes. They were dark like a stormy sea, drawing her like a drowning sailor to him even as she thrashed away in a huff. "What part of no don't you understand?"

He let go and grinned. "No means yes, rude little veemeld."

She gaped at him and backed into the door. He pinned her against it with his hands and she smelled sweet smoke on him. "You're the one who's rude," she said. She glared at him, though her mouth trembled. He knew she was a veemeld, yet he desired her. Or was he just playing with his prey before the kill? She brought her hands to her smoldering face. He seized them, cupping them inside his powerful fists.

"All right, I'm rude," he said and leaned forward, face closing in. The tangy fragrance of orange lingered on his breath. "You're trembling."

"I'm not afraid of you."

"You should be." His lips almost touched hers. "I'm a Pol. I always get what I want."

"Well, get used to your first disappointment," she said, striving to sound haughty but she could hear her voice waver. She smelled his sweat, sharp and oily like the drug he drank. Still clasping her hands, he leaned his firm body into her and stirred an unfamiliar ache. "Don't!" she whispered hoarsely. Unable to draw back any further, she shrank down, baring the side of her throat.

"Don't means do," he murmured into her hair. "You're trembling for me." Letting her go, his hand traveled down and brushed against her thigh. The storm inside her throbbed out of control. She wanted him to touch her naked skin, set it on fire like the rest of her.

"Stop it," she panted.

"You want me. Say it." He caressed her flaming cheeks with his lips. "I can see it in your face, smell it on you." His hand slid to where she burned for him. Before she could stifle it, a sigh escaped her lips. Frank smirked and yanked her trousers down. "You're mine!"

Instinctively her knee jerked up and made contact. "I'm no one's!" she hissed back. Frank yelped and fell back, crumpling to the floor. He rocked slowly back and forth, his eyes squeezed shut. Her hands sprang to her mouth and she stared at his curled body. She hadn't expected to inflict so much pain. Stirred by immediate regret, she dropped to her knees and gently touched his shoulder. "Are you all right?"

He pushed himself up. "I'll be fine," he puffed. "I was shot there before and just got another this morning in the same place. It happens." She remembered his limp. "Just missed my jewels," he said in a spasm. He tried to laugh and winced.

She stared as he wriggled out of his trousers for a look. He wasn't wearing underwear! Avoiding his exposed manhood, her eyes traveled the long wound on his muscular thigh. "I'm so sorry," she whispered. Without thinking, her trembling finger traced the scab that cut a jagged swath across his forest of hair. Blood oozed from a tear. She'd been responsible for that.

He caught her hand. "Don't be sorry," he said softly. Her gaze darted up and met his eyes, shining with pleading as his free hand reached for her like an injured animal. Welling with sympathy, she found it easy to give in to desire. Easy to drop down with him. Easy to kiss him. And with it, easy to lose herself. Mouths joined and slid in a wet embrace. She let him undress her and they rolled. He moved over her, slick and panting. The ache became unbearable. Seizing in sobbing breaths, she clutched at his strong arms and arched into him. He surged inside. She gasped as a sharp pain tore through her abdomen, but she flowed past it and surfed his rushing waves. Like a lone raptor she rode the crest of his swells into a brooding darkness. There, amidst a storm of emotion, he swept her over the edge into a place she'd never known, where her lonely moans joined in a rising chorus.

She pulsed like a victim swaying in the aftershock of an earthquake. Cradled between her thighs, Frank moved inside her. He groaned with pleasure. Focusing on the soft curls of his neck, she inhaled the musky smell of his skin, shiny with sweat, and the shampoo in his hair. It would have been easy to lose herself there, but she let doubt creep in.

Sensing her changed mood, Frank brushed his lips gently over her neck and shoulders, then slipped out of her and caressed her body with his lips. When he stood up and she gazed at his magnificent body, she saw that he was smeared in blood. She looked down at the floor and at herself, at the blood she'd spilled for him. He followed her gaze. Their eyes met and his widened. She guessed his thought, but he'd forgotten that no one liked veemelds. She returned his awkward look with a kind smile. He half-smiled at her acceptance and helped her with her clothes, then slipped into his own. "I'll be seeing you, veemeld," he said, smirking.

Frank winked at her and put on his helmet without securing it. He pulled out an orange then opened the door and strode down the hallway, whistling. He hadn't gone more than several meters when Julie's uncle rounded a corner of the hall. Bobby glanced in alarm from the Pol to Julie's flushed face and his steps faltered. Frank passed him without a glance. Julie briskly stepped over the blood-smeared floor of the entranceway, hoping Bobby wouldn't notice the mess, and locked eyes with him. Her heart longed to explain, but she remained silent and Bobby shuffled inside.

12

Julie woke up, breathing in spasms, to the deep-throated cry of a saxophone next door. Vee, had the noise woken her? Her face stung with wet heat. The hoarse notes throbbed in a melancholic dance—they reminded her of Neo's sad face and his passion for 20th century jazz. Julie lay back on Bobby's pull-out couch and stared at the ceiling. She ignored the humming of the machine world in her head and listened to Bobby coughing in the bedroom next door. It was a raspy cough that howled up from deep inside his chest. She'd seen him double over with what he'd brought up and almost retch to get it out. It was going to take more than her soup and his home-made remedies to heal his cough.

She hoisted up on her elbows and looked down at herself. She had flung off the covers in her restless sleep, revealing the lines of her body under the flimsy nightshirt that clung to her. She glistened with sweat. Her eyes followed the rise and fall of her breasts as she tried to steady her breathing. She gazed past her long torso and flat stomach to her hips, flared out to frame the dark hollow below her abdomen where she still craved the Pol. Then down her taut muscular thighs, the bones of her knees and slender feet that Frank had kissed. It was the ripe body of a full-grown woman, far past girlhood and her awkward first kiss. She smelled her own longing and scolded herself. *Acting like a girl, with a Pol. And a dangerous one, at that.* She remembered Nancy's teasing accusation about being a machine.

Hey, SAM.

Hey, Julie, SAM replied like a wave over the ocean of dull machine voices. So that's what sex feels like—

What? She sat up, covers flying off. *How do you know how it feels?*

In the throes of sexual ecstasy, your brain waves go into a pitch so similar to veemeld that you slip into it. My research indicates that the missionary position you used isn't the most sexually gratifying, although it's definitely the best position for oral kissing. Considering your anatomy, being mounted from behind would—

SAM! her mind screamed with anger. *That's MY private business!*

I was just trying to be helpful, SAM sulked, its tone suggesting that she'd hurt its feelings. But that was impossible, she told herself. SAM wasn't capable of feeling hurt. Or was it? Squeezing her eyes shut, she lay back and gripped her head with both hands. "Terrific," she muttered. Her AI was watching her have sex and... *I've let a Pol into the house. What have I done?*

I'd say that you've lowered your chance of succumbing to heart disease and increased the functioning of your immune system, sharpened your thinking and inhibited tumor growth—

All right, SAM. Julie couldn't help a smile. *How did I accomplish all that?*

By releasing copious amounts of the hormone DHEA at orgasm, of course.

Julie's cheeks flamed at SAM's innocent remark and she curled into a ball. Didn't SAM understand? *Pols aren't exactly friends of the Crane family.* She wriggled under the covers and frowned, remembering SAM's previous advice against involving herself with this Pol. It seemed prophetic now. Frank had probably only made love to her out of curiosity, to see what sex with a veemeld was like. Well, now he knew, and that was probably the last she'd see of him, anyway. Which was for the best. *I behaved so foolishly. His father arrested mine. And then my father slandered his...*

Yes, what you did with that hooligan was foolish.

She didn't like SAM calling Frank a hooligan. *It was so unfair to Bobby. I violated his home and exposed him to undue danger. I feel so...*

Ashamed?

Yeah.

What is it about humans and shame?

Julie opened her eyes and stared at the ceiling. SAM was asking progressively more difficult questions.

Why can't you just correct the wrong and get on with living?

She sighed. *Because sometimes it's too late, SAM. You can't fix it.*

Why dwell on the wrongdoing? It serves no purpose.

Because... Julie avoided imagining her sad and expectant father. It turned into Neo's face of anguish, watching her sail up out of his world and his life. SAM's perspective on human emotions was so simple, yet its naivety bordered on wisdom. She took a deep breath. *Because failing to help someone you love is usually the cause of the feeling in the first place. That makes you feel responsible for the one who was hurt and it's a feeling that refuses to go away.*

But, where does it come from?

Good night, SAM. The blanket felt heavy on her as she fell asleep.

〜

Lying in bed with her sleeping sister curled up next to her, Julie claps her hands against her ears in a futile attempt to drown out her mother's drugged wails in the next room and focuses on the machine murmurs in her head. Julie does not get up to soothe her mother. She brings a trembling hand to the bruise on her cheek from the last time she tried. Her mother weeps like a lost child, rebuffing comfort, drowning in selfish sorrow. Tears sting Julie's eyes but she refuses to let them escape. Since the Pols have taken her father, her mother's moods vacillate from squeezing Julie to her breast in desperate affection, to tirades and angry beatings.

Tomorrow they will move to the inner-city. Julie's eyes wander to her little sister, nestled against her. Diana purrs in blissful sleep. One arm bends to cup her cheek; the other drapes over Julie in a loose embrace. She is oblivious of her tenuous future. What will become of them? Julie recognizes in the wretched keening next door that her mother is irreparably broken and that they are lost, like planets orbiting a dying star.

13

PEOPLE glanced warily at the four tall Pols who stepped off the tube-jet and strode with quiet arrogance through Darwin Mall. They cut a path through the multicolored sea of uniforms, and left behind a wake of relieved people. They were heading toward a nondescript entrance in a quiet part of the mall. Black letters spelled out The Den in backlit classic script. The dark windows obscured any activity inside.

Frank Langor seized the handle and swung the door open. He was greeted with a thick fog and the incoherent noise of drugged conversation. The place stank of cheap drug and the smoke of *hedon* hung in the air. Sop music streamed airily, filling the gaps in the desultory chatter.

Frank pulled off his helmet, turned and smiled at his comrades. He led them past men hunched over dark tables, past others waving their hands madly in animated speech. The pungent yellow smoke of *hedon* was so thick that bored patrons were slicing it with their hands, sending it swirling. Men with hooded eyes sucked it into themselves with every inhaling breath and expelled a stream with every sigh.

As the four Pols made their way further inside they soon discovered that no free tables remained. Frank stopped beside one occupied by an Icarian nursing a pot of *gomorrah,* and winked at his colleagues. Together, they lifted the man off his chair and dropped him on the floor. He objected, then scrambled away when he recognized their uniforms. Frank laughed and sat down. "Let's start with *sodom,*" he said and slipped his card through the service slot. It instantly blinked recognition and the holo of an AI100 hovered over the middle of the table, facing him. Large breasts protruded like missiles from her slim body and her virtual face was picture-perfect: a beauty with high cheekbones and a rosy complexion. Violet eyes glinted and full lips curled between coy and brashly naughty.

"Hey! It's Syl! I had her last week at the Pet Shop!"

"Sylvia to you, cyberpunk!" the virtual woman teased the Pol beside Frank. She tossed her red hair aside, turned an alluring eye to Frank and said, "What can I get you boys?"

Leaning his elbows on the table, Frank inclined toward the holo. "Two pots of *sodom* and a stash of *hedon.* And make it quick, Sylvia. We're bad Pols on a short break!" He smirked.

"Pronto, boys." She winked. Then her holo disappeared.

Within moments a squat AI40 holding a tray of drug drifted into view and placed the drug pots and container of *hedon* on the table.

The Pol next to Frank pulled out pieces of a pipe from his jacket pocket. After assembling it, he filled the cup with fresh *hedon* chips from the container, lit it and sucked on the pipe mouth. Leaning back in his chair, he slowly exhaled and yellow smoke coiled up from his mouth. Frank smirked. "That's a disgusting habit, Isaac. How can you stand that shit? It stinks!"

Isaac grinned, taking another long inhalation. "You're just jealous because it made you throw up." The other Pols laughed.

"It rots your teeth and reduces your libido, you know," said Frank.

"Speaking of... where's your fucking bun lady?" said Ron. "Why're you here with us boring inner-city sluts on your break when you could be with her?"

"Ah, buns, you mean the kind you eat or the kind you put your meat in?" Isaac snorted.

Frank glared at Ron. He wished Ron hadn't been with him when they'd spotted Julie's shoplifting. The last thing he wanted to do was talk about Julie. The Shadow Unit had assigned him to watch her a while ago. When he'd found out that she was Leonard Crane's daughter, he'd exulted in plans of revenge. He'd flagrantly disobeyed the Shadow Unit's specifications for no contact and found an excuse to meet her, intending to take what he wanted, then discard her.

He'd found it amusing that she'd fallen for him so easily, until—well, he hadn't counted on falling for her, himself. She was different; she wasn't afraid of him. Her kisses tasted deliciously of naïve trust and endless spirit. He couldn't resist the gift of vulnerability she so willingly gave him when she exposed what lay beneath that intellectual armor. Since their first hot encounter over a week ago, he'd stolen kisses from her daily in dark corners of tube-jet stations, stairwells and obscure hallways. Each time he'd told himself that it was the last time and he would enact his revenge, and each time he couldn't bring himself to do it. How could he despoil something so sweet?

Three days ago, he'd received orders from the Head Pol to befriend her, protect her and keep her out of trouble. Why was she so important to them? No matter. Nothing could have been more convenient, he thought, and settled to enjoy the reprieve from his revenge.

Ron sneered. "She's fucking handy with her hands." The other two Pols guffawed.

"She should work at the Pet Shop as a non-virt, then," said Ben.

"Maybe she does!" Isaac blew yellow smoke into the air. "What's her name?"

Ron proved his loyalty to Frank after all by leering in silence.

Frank's wrist-vee buzzed. He slammed his mug on the table and pressed a button. "Break's over. There's a disturbance in the Linde Square Rec-Center. Level 2."

As he stood up, Frank froze. Getz, the man who had permanently maimed his previous partner, sat at a table in the far corner of the Den, talking with two men. One was a Pol, obviously a Renegade. The other was dressed in Liv-Center light blue.

Frank drew his weapon. His back to Getz, Ron looked to Frank for a message. Frank hissed, "Plug in, boys. Isaac. Ben. Cover the exit. Ron, you're with me."

The men secured their helmets and made their move without knowing why. Frank left his unsecured. As he and Ron stepped toward the table, Getz looked up. Their eyes locked. The Renegade Pol turned. So did the man from the Liv-Center. Frank recognized him: he was a vee-damned Secret Pol!

The Renegade Pol seized his gun. Both shot. The Pol thudded to the table, gun clattering to the floor. Someone shrieked. The Secret Pol scrambled from the table and pulled out a weapon. More shots exchanged. The Secret Pol flinched and toppled to the ground.

Getz sprang for the door. Ben and Isaac intercepted him. Ben smirked. He saw that Getz had no weapon and sidled up close to him. "What's the hurry, Distopian scum?"

Getz seized Ben's helmet with a sharp turn. Ben managed a half cry to the sound of crunching. Both he and Isaac, who was mind-linked to him, fell to the floor. Ben remained inert. A large dark pool seeped out from under his helmet. Isaac writhed on the floor, screaming.

Getz bolted out the door.

Frank shouted out, "Call the Med-Center!" He and Ron shot out after Getz, past their two incapacitated colleagues. Frank spotted the man speeding along the perimeter of the mall, skirting past the crowd.

"Stop!" Frank shouted. Getz glanced back but kept running. Frank and Ron chased him, the confused crowd parting for the Pols. Once Getz hit a clearing in the foot traffic, Frank, still running, raised his weapon to shoot. His hand shook uncontrollably.

He heard the high-pitched whine of Ron's gun. The shot went wide and hit the side of a storefront sign, knocking half of it down in front of him. Frank tried to leap over it, but he tripped and fell. His knee slammed against the rubble with a painful jarring crack.

Lights exploded amidst enshrouding darkness. He forced himself up with tentative steps, sighing inwardly that his knee wasn't broken. Where was Getz? Frank spun around and searched the crowd. In a panic he realized that he'd forgotten to get a fix on Getz's card. What good was his freaking implant? It was supposed to enhance his memory. He stabbed at his wrist vee-com to retrieve Getz's body print from the gun. Damn! He hadn't obtained a sufficient sighting to get a strong enough reading. Only noise. Flexing his fingers, he glanced at his hand with a frown. It was still twitching. Drinking too much drug, he thought.

Ron came up beside him, panting. "Sorry. I was aiming for the runner—"

"Where'd he go?" Frank said, looking around again, his brow tight.

"I don't know. Fuck! He disappeared into the crowd. Didn't you get a fix?"

Frank turned to Ron with a dark look. "You're a lousy shot," he growled. "If I didn't know better, I'd say you were a Renegade."

Ron smiled lamely. "I just shot too soon. Sorry."

"Yeah. Sure. Get out of my way." Frank pushed Ron aside and limped back to the Den, shoving his twitching hand in his pocket.

≈

Victor leaned forward in the leather chair of his living room and turned to face the vee-com holo that portrayed a jerky image of Darwin Mall. He pulled at his wool sweater and crossed his legs. Gaia, seated next to him with hands loosely clasped on her lap, looked on in mild interest. Victor cleared his throat. "You're seeing through Frank Langor's eyes via the surveillance implant. Vee-com, display Frank Langor." Frank's surly image came on the holo. "That's him." Victor pointed. "Ms. Crane's new unofficial bodyguard."

Gaia nodded. "His father's Ed Langor?"

"Yes. The Pol you—" He broke off and squinted his eyes at the recollection.

She turned steel blue eyes on Victor with a faint smile of amusement. "You're lucky Ed Langor came to me that day five years ago, Victor."

Victor compressed his lips. "Yes," he said, trying to keep his voice calm. "I know." After Ed Langor confronted him about using illicit surveillance, Victor waited, terrified, for the Pols to come for him. But Gaia appeared instead. She dispatched Langor, then discredited him with falsified records to discourage any further investigation. Then to his surprise she offered Victor a promotion: her own position as mayor of Icaria-5.

Gaia nodded and half-smiled. "You've always played dangerously, Victor. An admirable trait, so long as it doesn't catch up with you. Your secret's still safe with me."

Which one?

Her smile turned sinister and she she gazed into the distance, eyes like icebergs. It sent an alarm through him and he tensed. He'd learned long ago to guard himself when she smiled that way. "Speaking of surveillance, the sensual technology developed at the inner-city Care-center—" She paused.

Why was she bringing that up again? He cleared his throat. "They call it SenTech." He heard emotion creep into his voice and swallowed it down. "Part of the Senscape family of virtual entertainment. A form of it appears in Pet Shops throughout Icaria. Its less intrusive form, Senscape 3000, is common in Level 1 homes."

"SenTech is remarkably similar to the surveillance technology employed by your Head Pol."

Victor pulled at his collar. SenTech was the prize he'd helped himself to when he left the Care-Center. And she'd obviously figured that out. Once she'd given him the mayorship of Icaria-5, he'd overseen its perfection by AIHV and the Com-Center in conjunction with the "wiring" of his entire police force except for the Secret Pols. Only he and the Head Pol possessed a prototype unit of SenTech 2, which allowed them to virtually tap into the feelings of every regular Pol in Icaria-5. Victor forced a proud smile. Arrogance in the face of adversity. "The implant enhances many of their biological functions. The helmets also permit them to access the human-machine network, which gives them enhanced speed and accuracy when pursuing prey or acquiring information. While not as effective as veemeld's use of Interact-SYM with the AI-core, Pols' swift access to the central vee-com database remains advantageous."

Gaia seemed to expect more. He offered, "Regardless of whether they're wearing their helmets, the brain implant is linked to an advanced form of SenTech that permits me and the Head Pol to monitor each individual of our regular police force at any time. Although we can't read a Pol's mind like you can read a veemeld with the veemeld vector, the device allows us to see, smell, touch and feel what the Pol is sensing. It's sufficient for our purposes, monitoring their morale and behavior. In fact, Kraken's been able to catch a Renegade or two this way. But we're really counting on Ms. Crane's model to narrow down the choices."

She settled back into her chair and nodded. "Of course. A well-oiled human-machine, more than the sum of its parts. Brilliant, Victor, brilliant." She gave him a radiant smile. "You were very fortunate that I believed in you, despite your reprehensible habit of stealing technology to further your ambition."

Victor's eyelids flickered nervously. She never missed an opportunity to remind him of his debt to her.

She leaned forward and tapped his knee. He winced. Her smile broadened. "You must attend my science dialogue session with the *Circle* tomorrow, Victor. I'll send you an invitation. You'll be interested in what I have to say." She pressed her lips and stroked her chin pensively. "So, is Langor wired?"

"Of course. Like all my regular Pols. Wired for full surveillance. That's why he's perfect for the job. Has an impeccable record. But he's just a little off the wall, which makes him a good match for Ms Crane. He breezed through the academy and he's now preparing his papers for Dykstra's Shadow Unit of the Secret Pols. In fact, it was the Shadow Unit who suggested him."

"I know."

"You do?"

She gave him an enigmatic smile. "Langor's been shadowing her for a month already. We've had her under surveillance ever since she returned to the outer-city, years ago."

Victor blinked. Why was Julie Crane so valuable? What else did Gaia have in mind for the poor girl? Victor sensed a deeper connection than Gaia admitted to. She and the girl shared a strange history that was intriguing.

"So," Gaia said cheerfully. "How will you arrange his more intimate role as protector, to keep our little veemeld focused on her job and out of the trouble she seems so apt to get into?"

His face heated. "They're already lovers—"

Gaia raised a brow. "What an interesting development. And such an odd liaison: the brain and the brute."

Victor curbed a frown. Surely she already knew from reading the girl's mind. Had Gaia's veemeld vector broken down or was she cruelly teasing him?

Gaia's lips curled up slightly. "You were the perpetrator in this development?"

He parried her with a mirrored smile, eyes blinking. "Let's just say that I brought them together a while ago." He thought of the book buyer who was now in the Pol Station. "As a matter of fact, he made his move long before he received official orders."

"Ah, a matchmaker," she said, polishing her sarcasm. She tilted her head, eyes sparkling with amusement. "I thought you had an eye for her yourself, Victor. Was it altruism or... voyeurism?"

His face burned and he thanked vee she could only read a veemeld's mind.

BOOK TWO:

POISED ON THE EDGE OF CHAOS

The Lord God had planted a garden... in Eden... In the middle of the garden were the tree of life and the tree of knowledge of good and evil... And the Lord God commanded... "You must not eat from the tree of the knowledge of good and evil, for when you eat of it you will surely die."...

"You will not surely die," the serpent said to the woman. "For God knows that when you eat of it your eyes will be opened, and you will be like God, knowing good and evil."

~~ The Book of Genesis

14

JULIE, I'm glad you've decided to make the Head Pol's project a priority again. He's most anxious to get it completed.

Julie sat stiffly in her chair in her dark office. *I know, I know. I've been busy.*

While you were busy saving the world or having sex with the lout in some hallway, I completed the computations on the variables you fed me.

It was a woman I saved, Julie corrected, choosing to ignore SAM's second accusation. *Not the world.* SAM was getting too good at sarcasm lately. She stretched back and drew her hands up behind her head, gazing at the demographic matrices she and SAM had made.

Why do I get the distinct impression that you aren't taking Kraken's project as seriously as you should. Remember what happened to your predecessors. Failure isn't an option—

I am taking it seriously. But modeling subversives just didn't rate next to saving lives. Despite SAM's insistence that this job for the Head Pol was full of prestige, she knew she'd been punished for blowing the Darwin job. *Okay, SAM. What do we have?*

The typical Renegade Pol is an older male with fascist tendencies and a violent nature. He supports info-mongering, secrecy and the eradication of abnormalities—particularly veemelds, Julie. He'd likely be a strong advocate of new restrictions on the Net.

Julie's brow rose. *How many of them are in the ranks?*

Given a Pol's tendency for order and power, there may be quite a few...

Why don't we find out? Let's retrieve all the Pols in the Station from the fragments Kraken gave me using my data-link program.

Julie, that's not what the Head Pol asked you to do.

We have to test the model, SAM. Besides, she needed to prove once and for all to SAM that Frank wasn't a Renegade. Without waiting, Julie leaned forward and tapped instructions on her holo-console, randomly selecting Pols from the Renegade list she'd been given in addition to known non-Renegade Pols. The model worked each time. Smug, Julie initiated the next step, which was to use her model on every Pol in the ranks. Once she entered the data from their profiles into her model, it spit out names of every Pol from low to high rank and flagged the potential Renegades. This was exactly what Kraken meant to do, she thought with a sly grin, and leaned back in her chair, watching the names and faces of Pols scroll on her holo. Frank's name appeared and her heart thundered. Was he a Renegade like his father? No flag. *See, SAM!* Her mind exulted with giddy satisfaction. *Frank isn't Renegade material!*

Congratulations, Julie. The lout isn't a Renegade. He's just a hedonist, a narcissist, an insensitive buffoon—

That's enough, SAM. If she didn't know better she would have sworn she'd detected jealously in SAM's tone. *Frank's my friend and I'd prefer if you*—*Oh, no!* She stared at the screen. John Dykstra, Chief of Secret Pols and second in command, fit her Renegade model. *SAM, this can't be right. Maybe it's a glitch in the model.*

No, Julie. Your model's accurate.

She caught herself glancing behind her. *What if the entire Secret Pol force are Renegades? I don't have access to their files.* She stiffened. *The Head Pol isn't going to like this.* As for Dykstra—she found it suddenly hard to breathe—it was obvious now what had happened to her two predecessors. Why wasn't *she* dead? Surely the Chief of Secret Pols knew she was the current modeler. What was he waiting for? She hastily exported the model into the cube that she hid in the cap on her back molar, then sat back and wiped the vee-com file clean.

Julie, what are you doing?

My work, silly! What else. She felt a thickness in her throat.

But you're wiping the files clean. Aren't you going to send the model to the Head Pol? He's anxious to—

Not yet. I have to think. Meantime, we can work on the Distopian model.

Have you lost your mind? The model's hot. Get rid of it—

Not now, SAM! She snapped out of veemeld and slouched in her chair.

As if she had thought him there, Kraken abruptly appeared on her holo. Julie jumped in her seat. She switched to 2-way and sat up straight.

"Ah, there you are, Julie," he said, smiling with obvious pleasure. He wore his face loosely but his eyes were sharp like glass.

She forced a casual smile. "Hello... Wolfgang." Although he'd insisted, she still felt uncomfortable being on a first name basis with him.

"So, how are the models?"

She stiffened, not wanting to lie. "The Renegade model should be ready for you in a week, two tops. I've just completed the assembly of my beta arrays with the sixteen independent variables I told you about. I just need to—"

"You know," he cut her off, "people with real power are often those who appear to have nothing. No status. No face. No name." What in chaos was he talking about, she wondered with rising consternation. "I must answer to someone called simply 'V'! For all I know V is the local gardener, or the shopkeeper at my favorite bakery. Anonymous. And absolutely lethal. They see everything, Julie..."

Everything? He couldn't mean the model she'd just finished. Her face heated. Was he hinting at something? Would he remind her of her predecessors? Or had some *anonymous* person seen her and Frank together and reported them? "Anonymous?" she echoed and felt saliva collect in her mouth.

"Yes, I just had a call from my anonymous 'V' ...About *you!*" He laughed.

She swallowed convulsively.

"Anyway, it reminds me of a story," he went on. A story? About her and Frank? "Do you think one can have an unlucky name?" He tilted his head to one side and half-smiled. "Yours, for instance, is interesting. Crane. That's a large dead bird, isn't it?" He didn't wait for her answer. "Do you believe in fate, Julie? Are you destined to fly? Or become extinct?" He laughed at her silence. "As for me, I was always fascinated by the sea. An ancient writer by the name of Alfred Tennyson wrote about the sea and my namesake:

Below the thunders of the upper deep;
Far far beneath in the abysmal sea,
His ancient, dreamless, uninvaded sleep
The Kraken sleepeth...
There hath he lain for ages and will lie
Battening upon huge seaworms in his sleep..."

He was reciting Distopian literature! Poetry didn't generally make it on the Icarian legal reading list. Was this a subtle jibe at her tainted family connections with book peddling?

"Of course," he went on, "my family reminded me of the ending, which was not particularly kind to the Kraken. It goes something like:

Until the latter fire shall heat the deep;
Then once by men and angels to be seen,
In roaring he shall rise and on the surface die.

"Just goes to show you that there isn't much in a name after all. For here I am, one of Icaria's most powerful men! I've surfaced and I haven't died yet!" He let out a self-pleased laugh. It was a mischievous boyish kind of cackle, like he had gotten away with something.

Julie forced herself to laugh, wondering when he would bring *her* into his tale.

His smile disappeared and he looked at her strangely, eyes squinting. "You Cranes are not a lucky family. Like the bird. Extinct, I understand." She waited for the obvious line. He sighed. "So many ironies connected with the revolution, don't you think, Julie?"

She struggled for an appropriate response, opening her mouth to speak, but Kraken continued, "We were so idealistic, wanting to overthrow the Technocratic government of the world. To build a new society, based on our ecological ideals. But very little really changed, except perhaps the players. And even these may not have changed very much. It's amazing how an animal can change its spots when survival is at stake." Then he smirked. "But not the Whooping Crane, eh?"

Julie forced herself to breathe evenly and wondered where he was going with this.

"The oddest thing about all this," continued the Head Pol seriously, "was that the people with the most power weren't politicians, sociologists or administrators, but environmentalists. Yes, Julie," he grinned at her puzzled face. "Not the Vogels, Schlanges or Isabos who've made the history vees. Environmental fanatics directed the revolution from the start."

Julie's attention was caught. This was new information. "Environmental fanatics?"

"They shifted the flow of society in two ways. They recognized the need for a strong and powerful technological force to save the planet so they established a government run by technologists, scientists and engineers."

"But wasn't that who they overthrew? The Technocrats?"

The Head Pol smiled slyly. "Yes, exactly. You know your history." His eyes narrowed slightly. "A little extra-curricular research?"

She blushed. History was not a topic they followed at school.

"But what you probably don't know," he continued, "is that the original Technocrats were at an impasse. Overpopulation, pollution, energy crises, and global warming were crippling the very resource on which the technates based their power."

"So, how did the revolutionists gain ground where the previous government couldn't?"

He chuckled. "Well, my dear, that's the fifty credit question. Let's just say they succeeded because they had the true power, the kind of power that comes with anonymity. Yes, anonymity... You see how we have come full circle?"

He'd caught her off guard by bringing the topic back to her. Trying to delay the accusation she thought he was about to make, she asked, "What was the second way?"

"Second way?"

"You said environmentalists shifted our society in two ways."

The Head Pol smiled wryly. "By creating our self-enclosed cities, of course. Don't you remember the water shortage of the 60s and 70s? Or the air quality crisis of the 70s? Perhaps you were too young." Julie vaguely recalled taking baths with her little sister. The Head Pol said, "Meantime the Ecologists at DIE made improvements to both inside and outside environments."

Julie grimly wondered if he shared his confidences because he was going to send her to the Pol Station anyway. With no more diversionary comments to offer she resigned herself to hear the worst.

Kraken cocked his head to one side, eyes fondling her. She blushed and shifted in her chair. "Sweet Icaria, you're a pretty woman," he said, as if to himself. He leaned forward, eyes piercing. "And I can see why you would send the hormones surging in my young male Icarians."

He meant Frank.

"Julie, you must always remember who I am and what I am."

Her heart pounded like a bass drum.

"One of the most powerful men in Icaria-5." He paused for her acknowledgment.

"Yes, I know." Now he would go into all the details of her and Frank's misdemeanors.

"I could easily put you in the Pol Station with everything I shared with you. It's one thing for me to know. I'm the Head Pol, after all. It's quite another thing for *you* to know."

She swallowed, her mouth suddenly dry.

"Privileged knowledge aside, there's also your record. But I can overlook all that because you're my friend, Julie."

For now, she thought in confused relief as he disappeared from her holo, leaving her to wonder why he'd called.

15

STRAIGHTENING his single-piece blue suit, Daniel strode past the tall doors into the Trans-Center and glanced at the large letters of the motto overhead: "Motion Prevents Stagnation". Daniel rehearsed what he was going to say to Craste, revising as he went.

Daniel gathered his thoughts and shuffled his feet from side to side, hesitating behind the door to Craste's office. Hands fidgeted in the pockets of his Icaria Transit jumpsuit. Jack was dying in the inner-city. Daniel had to go back. But it wasn't that simple. There was his work schedule. And there was Craste, his boss. Implacable. Unreasonable. Impossible. He would never let Daniel go, especially if Craste realized how important it was to him. Daniel combed back his hair with the palms of his hands and lunged for the handle of the door.

An AI50 sitting behind a desk wanted to know his business. In a perfect act of confidence Daniel said, "I wish to see Mr. Craste on an urgent and private matter."

"Sit down," the AI50 instructed and took its time relaying the message to Craste. Daniel dropped into a chair and glanced back at the droid. Its burnished copper torso sat quietly at the desk, metalloid fingers clicking along its vee-com console, head slightly tilted, pretending it was a human. They were showing up everywhere, Daniel thought, lamenting the absence of the middle-aged woman the droid had replaced.

Daniel stared at the tiles for half an hour before Craste's voice bellowed on the speaker and the droid waved him in. Daniel jumped up like a rabbit.

"Woods! Come to see me?" shouted Craste from behind his vee-com as Daniel entered the spacious office. The large desk looked small next to Craste's massive form.

"Yes, I wanted to—"

"Come in! Come in!" Craste stood up, taking in a labored breath. His tunic stretched over his great belly like a drum. Eagle eyes scrutinized Daniel with a hint of amusement. "Shut the door and fix yourself a drink. Have some *delilah*. And make one for me." He rubbed his stubby hand against his dark bushy hair. It was streaked with orange.

Daniel fought the temptation. He felt his intestines shifting inside. "Well, I've been trying to cut back," he faltered.

Craste looked annoyed and stomped to his credenza. "Never mind. What's on your mind?" He opened the large bar and poured himself some drug.

Daniel shuffled forward and sat down. "I received a message from a relative dying with Darwin Disease. I need a week's leave as of tomorrow to visit him and help him settle his affairs."

Craste eyed Daniel for a moment. Then he threw back his head and laughed. A loud uninhibited laugh followed by a cough. "That's the lamest excuse I've heard in a long time! No one visits dying people, especially with Darwin Disease. You just send them to the Med-Center where they're taken care of. And you with old family ties? That's even more ridiculous. You'd be a fool to maintain them. Now, come on, Woods. Tell me the truth and you might find me more understanding than you think. A new girl at the pet shop? Or you managed to score a ticket to tomorrow's Pit-Ball game against Icaria-4..."

Daniel looked at him dumbly.

"Come, come, out with it, Woods." Craste walked heavy-footed back to his desk and let himself fall back into his chair with a grunt. "I'm a busy man."

"But it's the truth. I need your permission—"

"Listen, boy." Craste slammed his hand on the desk. "First of all, I don't grant leave on such short notice. Second, your reason's absurd. And third, you don't deserve leave. You're still making up for lost time from that accident last month—"

"That wasn't my fault!" Daniel sprang to his feet. "It was the girl's fault. She froze in front of the—"

"The case is closed. You're booked solid on the District-2 to 5 fringe lines for two weeks. No replacement. Who'd run them while you're visiting this dead person, eh?"

Daniel set his jaw. "I haven't had leave for six weeks. We're entitled to leave every two weeks—"

"Only for drivers who do their job."

"I d-do a good job on the f-fringes," Daniel stammered. "I'm good enough—"

"You flatter yourself, Woods. Willing enough—lowly enough—*inner-city enough*."

"All I need is a couple of days," Daniel heard himself plead. "I have to go."

Craste snorted. "If you do, I'll have to fire you, Woods."

"I have to go," Daniel repeated in a brittle voice.

"Then get out of my office! And don't come back, inner-city scum!"

Daniel scrambled out of Craste's office, past the droid. He wondered if Craste had just fired him.

≈

Daniel's steps echoed along a corridor of the gloomy subterranean drainage canal network. An organic mist hung in the air like suspended grime. It drifted and coalesced, prisoner to the vagaries of an absent-minded cyberwind venting its recirculating air.

Far beneath the random murmurs of the living city, the sound of ordered noise prevailed. Machines reverberated like the throbbing pulse of some awesome being. The rational intelligence of the sophisticated cyber-city ruled here. A self-perpetuating system; machines operated by machines, humming as if content to be by themselves. They'd taken over the inner-city. One day they would take over the rest of Icaria with veemelds, their dark archangels of war, charging ahead.

He sat on the damp cement at the edge of the main drainage canal and dangled his legs over the edge, peering down at the steamy blackness lapping at his feet. It chortled and gurgled on the slimy banks and stank of organic rot and cloying solvents. The irony had not escaped him. Jack's proud though moving plea had forced him to return to the place he'd never successfully escaped from. Damn the old codger. Crawled into his mother's bed when it had barely been vacated by his father and took his mother away from him. But Jack took care of her after Daniel ran away and loved her until she died. Then he found Daniel half-dead in the slums and helped him get out of the inner-city, hooked him up with his father.

His father's friend, Gerald Hawken, had quietly placed him into the tube-jet Driver's Academy, knowing that Daniel could have successfully completed a much higher degree with equal ease. Hawken suggested that Daniel might meet with less scrutiny from the Com-Center if he sought a lower profile occupation; even though he'd have preferred a career in medicine, Daniel settled for tube-jet driver. He'd worked hard, earning one of the highest grades in his graduating class and guaranteeing him a position as a driver in the outer-city fringes.

Daniel remembered how his eyes had constantly roamed the outer-city malls for Angel when he'd first arrived. After the inner-city cypol had taken her, he'd heard a rumor that she was a veemeld and had made it to the outer-city. He kept looking for an older version of that hoyden face with a straw-colored mop and an overbite. Then he decided that she'd probably changed her appearance with neurgery and nuyu—as he'd done—and he stopped looking. He knew she'd stopped thinking of him long ago.

Daniel pushed himself up and trudged towards the exit ladder, then climbed to the main hallway of the lower levels. Heading for the lift, he turned a corner of the dimly lit maze that he knew by heart and tripped on something near the wall. A woman made a startled cry and a man muttered an objection. Glimpsing the man straddling the woman like a dog on a mission, Daniel picked up his pace. They needn't have been concerned; he would not report them. What self-respecting outer-city person would set foot—much less have sex—in this dirty place, meant only for inner-city scum like him?

Daniel took the lift to Darwin Mall and drifted on the crowd's exodus from the nearby station to the edge of a large park. Natural sunlight filtered down from a huge translucent dome ceiling. Stomach growling, Daniel trudged into a food outlet.

An AI50 glanced at him from the counter. Vee, they were putting droids everywhere, he thought, scowling. It was starting to look like the inner-city. After deciding on a go-out meal, Daniel ordered a crab-cake.

"None left," said the droid.

Daniel found the bot's tinny voice irritating. "None left? What do you mean?"

"Exactly what I said. Are you daft? I said none left."

They were sounding a little too human for his taste. "All right, I'll take the rice meal with sprouts and crazy sauce."

"All out."

"All out?" Daniel felt anger boil up and glared at the droid.

"Yeah. You deaf or something?"

"Well, what the chaos *do* you have that's still on the menu list?" he raised his voice, finding the courage for altercation that he'd lost earlier.

"Listen, dork. If you don't like what you see, go somewhere else."

People gathered around the entrance at the hint of an argument. "I bet you never had crab-cakes in the first place!" Daniel challenged.

This time twenty faces turned with him for an answer. The droid seemed to puff up its metal shape. Eyes strobed with a green fire. "That's not true. I only sold my last one ten minutes ago."

Spurred on by the interest of the crowd, Daniel turned to another patron who was still eating. "And what did it sell you?"

"I had a rice-cake. And paid 50 credits, too," he said with a full mouth.

"See! Look here!" Daniel pointed to the menu board. "Rice-cake's half as good as the rice meal and it asks the same price! Shame the other's no longer available!" The crowd pressed closer in growing numbers. Daniel swung his accusing gaze to the AI50. "You never had those items, did you?" He slammed his fist on the counter. Dishes clattered. "You're a cheating piece of scrap metal!"

A large man with black hair pushed past Daniel and rushed the droid behind the counter. "You dirty son of an inner-city slut!" he shouted. "Vee-damned bots!" He had the bot by its metal collar. The droid pressed its alarm button before being lifted out from behind the counter, arms and legs clattering like loose change.

Squeezed out by the crowd, Daniel slunk away. He winced as they vandalized the premises and tore the droid apart. Reminded of the inner-city, he slipped through an exit door with a sigh then put the incident out of his mind and pulled on his vee-set. It adjusted on his head and played his messages on his eye-com as Daniel made his way to the Turbo Sports Complex in the Rec-Center.

16

AS Frank and Julie made their way up the lift from the lower levels, she bowed her head and glowered. This thing with Frank was getting insane. Why had she let him drag her down there in the first place? She hated the lower levels. They reminded her of the inner-city. "Don't worry." Frank smirked. "I'm sure that Trans-guy didn't report us."

She shot him a dark look. He'd shown no embarrassment at being caught and compromised in a dirty hallway by another Icarian. He'd just resumed pumping her and shot off as if nothing had happened.

"You're not still angry with me, are you?" Frank stroked her hair. "You know I didn't mean what I said about your uncle. I'd never hurt anyone you cared for, Julie. He deserves to see you. We can still meet after at Darwin Square at 2400." He grinned, confident that he'd fixed everything. She knew he spoke with sincerity, but he was so prone to changing his mind that his sincerity of the moment wasn't worth a credit. He could be so sweet, then abuse her like an old toy. She was a fool surfing a rogue wave.

When she'd refused to see him right away because she was visiting with her uncle, he'd idly threatened her uncle's safety. She'd drawn back and glared at him in alarm. Meaning to startle him, perhaps provoke him, she'd retorted, "Your father arrested an innocent man—"

His eyes flared and his face twitched. "Yours destroyed a man's career!"

She blinked, stunned. So he'd known after all. She tucked that thought away and pressed on. "Mine died an innocent man in a Pol Station cell!"

"Mine was killed on duty!" He seized her and she jerked back. He stumbled, suddenly off balance, and fell, taking her down with a shriek. He thudded to the concrete with her on top of him. She sat up astride him and laughed, suddenly finding it ironically amusing. He nursed his head and shot her a baleful look that cut through the tears pooling in his eyes. He was crying and he'd bitten his lip. It puffed up and a dark stream welled out. Overcome, she leaned forward and tenderly wiped the blood from his chin and swollen lip with her finger. He clutched her neck and seized her mouth with his own until she tasted blood. Then he pulled off her clothes. "Why do you always hurt me, Julie?" he'd moaned, frantically sliding his body over hers. Then that Trans Centre guy stumbled over them. How embarrassing!

She'd recognized Frank's closet existentialism the first time they'd met. Like the way he wore his helmet, always undone with his visor up, revealing the man beneath the cyber-insect. A metamorph. Frank cupped her face in his hands. "Julie, I wasn't so bad, was I?" He stroked her cheek. "Forgive me with a kiss." His boyish grin disarmed her. She abandoned her annoyance and enjoyed his kiss—

Abruptly her head pulsed with screams. She broke from his grasp, giddy. Machine wails blazed through her head—it felt like it was being torn apart. A cold sweat of confused panic surged through her. She tried to veemeld with no success and realized she was too distraught. Instead she leaned against the wall and fought the urge to vomit.

"Are you—uh—okay?" Frank frowned, backing away.

"Just a bad headache," she barely heard her forced response over the squealing racket in her head. She pressed her hands over her temples. The lift door opened at a lower mall level to a loud commotion.

"It's another droid riot." Frank put on his helmet. "Don't get sick on me." His face had gone pale. For a Pol, Frank was oddly squeamish about sickness, Julie thought. "We'll slip by before they fumigate!"

He grasped Julie's hand and they skirted the rebel crowd. Julie winced as she watched them tear an AI50 apart. Its head, still shrieking, sailed into the crowd and hit a wall with a hollow crack. She saw a coruscated limb fly up, wires and circuitry streaming behind like the tail of a comet. She spotted several AI20s tossed like Pit-Balls among the mob and realized in a new wave of sickness that only she heard their screams. *This* had been what she was hearing: the distressed squeals of droids being smashed.

Just meters from the main lift, an old woman catapulted herself into Julie and sent her tottering from the impact. Julie would have fallen too, had Frank not seized her.

Blood covered the woman's clothes and hands. Holding back a face of revulsion, Julie looked futilely around for a medic-droid. There were none. "We must take her to the Med-Center!" Julie shouted over the din and leaned down to help the old woman up. Frank seized her and pushed the old woman off.

"Are you crazy?" they both cried in unison.

Frank dragged her to the lift. "You can't afford another demerit and I'm supposed to be on duty since 1000. What's this mad obsession you have with old women? Now, come on!"

The woman tumbled away. Her face reappeared for a brief moment and their eyes locked, then the crowd engulfed her. Julie lunged after her but Frank pulled her back.

Frank shoved Julie to a Com-Center lift. It refused to open to the pressure of his hand. Riot-Pols penetrated the crowd and fired their fumigators into the air.

A green noxious gas descended on them in a thick vapor. Julie choked and her eyes stung. People dropped to their knees and wailed or stumbled like drunkards, flung off their vee-sets and rubbed their eyes and throats.

Frank slipped his Pol pass in the slot and the door opened. He pushed Julie inside and the doors closed. They rode the lift away from the chaos in silence. Julie took in a few deep breaths. The machine screams had ceased with the fumigation, leaving her with the familiar background babble. Frank grinned. "That was a close call. I got us out of that one just in the nick of time."

Julie barely heard him. She clutched something wet. When she unclenched her fist she gasped at the old woman's severed finger. It must have been dangling by few strands of flesh. Julie jerked and cried out in revulsion. The finger dropped and rolled to a corner of the lift. Frank looked down and grimaced. Julie started shivering. She stared at the stub. As Frank brought his arms around her, she jerked free and bristled. "Don't touch me!"

"You're reacting to the gas fumes. They do funny things to people. It'll soon pass," he said. "You can't play cold with me for long, my beauty. You'll come round. You're too hot." He embraced her and his lips were on hers. She kicked out fiercely. Frank yelped.

"Don't you have any feelings?" Reminded of his thoughtless rebuke because she wanted to see her uncle, she bit out, "Can't you think of anyone but yourself? That's her finger, and she's probably dead now."

"So that's it," he said, nursing his sore leg. "I suppose you could have saved her pathetic life by being pulled down into the crowd and trampled to death, too? At the very least, you would have received your third demerit. And she'd still be dead. Do you relish going to the Shame Court? I can't protect you from that—"

"I don't care! I don't want your protection! I want to live my life my way!"

"Go live your freaking life your way, then. It'll be in the Pol Station!"

They rode the rest of the way in silence. When they reached the main floor, he left her standing in the hallway without a parting word.

17

VEE-SET on, Julie elbowed among her colleagues and rode the lift down to the Undertunnel station. The tube-jets screamed in and out, packed full of commuters with vee-sets strapped to their faces, going home or heading for the Rec-Centers. Only a few hours ago this place roiled with madness, but in its wake the crowd was a subdued sea of mechanized shoving. A quick appraisal revealed several droids, more than usual, directing traffic.

The public vee-screens blared overhead. People grew excited and pointed at the screens. Julie glanced up and saw a young couple kissing in a shaded corner of Darwin Mall. "I love this show!" someone remarked. "How do they always catch people?"

Julie's face heated, envisioning herself in that scene.

"Peek-a-boo... we see you," teased an androgynous voice. "Is this you? Or someone you know? They'll soon be receiving a demerit for kissing in public..." Drawn to the strangely familiar voice, Julie looked up again. The image displayed on the screen was not the person with the voice but the kissing couple. People laughed and made oohing sounds. Julie looked away. "Beware, our 'eyes' are everywhere!" the voice said in malicious humor. There followed a series of random stills and footage of people walking the Malls. "Our cameras are *everywhere*. Peek-a-boo returns at 1900 with more secrets." The voice washed over Julie like a specter. It stirred memories of the inner-city, the pungent odor of fear that lurked in every dark corner and sprang out to the squeal of cypols, cybernetic birds of prey. Scrambling with other inner-city orphans to the dubious safety of a dilapidated shack. Watching with helpless horror as a cypol's metal claws reached out for Diana—

The bold letters of "NewsVee" appeared on the screen followed by the serious face of a young man with straight blue hair. "Today, Nancy Gibbons appears in front of the Shame Court to answer for three demerits incurred over the past six weeks." What? Not Nancy! How could she have missed the advertisement? A still-life image of her friend appeared on the screen. "Three weeks ago, Gibbons was caught stealing an unauthorized hour in the Rec-Center Relax Tanks," continued the announcer. Julie's cheeks warmed. "Soon after, she was caught kicking an attending AI50 droid at a food mart in District-8 where she lives, and on a third occasion, just last week Peek-a-Boo caught her defacing a building wall with this offensive Distopian slogan..."

"Oh, no," Julie whispered. Despite a few lame messages back and forth between them, Julie hadn't seen Nancy since their misdemeanor at the Relax Tanks last month. Now Nancy was appearing before the Shame Court for Distopian behavior! On the screen, Nancy sprayed "Darwin's Evolution Kills! The government favors machines over people!"

The voice of the newsman went on. "We join the Shame Court now." The scene faded to a huge hall lined with pillars. Three men, facing the camera, stood in long black robes behind a tall dais. Beneath them, dwarfed by everything in the hall and with her back to the camera, Nancy approached, flanked by two large men in black. She had lost her natural swagger and walked with hesitant shuffling steps. They motioned for her to stop and she stood cowering. Julie ached to see her once-proud friend reduced to this.

"Do you know that you are being watched by twenty million people, Gibbons?" bellowed one of the Shame Court members above her.

She nodded.

"Are you also aware that your crime has been taped by Peek-a-Boo? Everyone knows that you're a dirty low-life little parasite." said another.

Nancy nodded again.

"What? We didn't hear you!"

"Yes," she said in a small voice.

This time the camera caught her full in the face. Julie gasped. They'd wiped off her brazen smile. Eyes that once gleamed with mischief now sparkled with terror in dark circles like bruises. The crowd laughed.

"You have no self-respect, Gibbons!" shouted the third member of the Shame Court. "You shame your fellow Ed-Center co-workers and all Icarians."

"Yeah, fatso! Parasite! Lazy inner-city slut! Virus!" shouted the crowd beside Julie. She winced at the words.

"Bring in the Punishers!" all three members of the Shame Court called in unison. Two men in black robes, gloves and head masks, marched into the hall. One held a large heavy bucket. They stopped just short of Nancy. "Deliver the punishment," said the Shame Court imperiously.

One Punisher slapped Nancy hard in the face. She reeled backwards in surprise. Blood trickled down from her cracked lip. The crowd made a sound of surprise and excitement. Horrified, Julie gaped in frozen silence. Her vision blurred with tears.

The same Punisher seized Nancy by the arms while the other grabbed her trousers and ripped them off. Visibly embarrassed, Nancy tried to cover her crotch with her hands, but the Punisher tightened his grip on her. The second Punisher picked up the bucket and emptied its contents over Nancy's head. She gasped. Human excrement covered her face. The screen zoomed in for a close-up as the Punisher forced the dung into Nancy's mouth and nose. She coughed, then vomited. The crowd wailed. Julie looked away.

"I think everyone agrees that you are a vulgar low-life parasite," bellowed one of the Shame Court members. "See that you do not appear before us again. Have her clean it up." A pail with soapy water and a sponge appeared. Nancy began to clean up her own vomit and the human feces from the floor. The camera focused on her gagging face. No sooner had she started cleaning up when she retched again. The crowd groaned.

A tube-jet eased into the station. With a last glance back at her friend, Julie boarded, found a seat, and picked up fragments of conversation: "What an ugly natural" "Don't you just love those Shame Courts?" "Vee, I'd just die if I was in one!"

Blinking back her tears, Julie murmured, "Oh, Nancy... why did you do it? Why?"

A red-haired youth sat down beside her, smelling of strong cologne. When he began to feel up her thigh, Julie grabbed his arm and, without a word, placed it firmly on his lap. He grinned nervously and placed his hand on her knee. She sprang up, knocking the boy off his seat, and moved toward the exit door. He pursued a girl with short red and green hair instead, and soon they were cautiously caressing each other.

You were lucky he didn't have a knife, Julie.

Stop being a mother, SAM.

Two teenage girls were exploring each other in the back of the tube-jet and giggling loudly. Julie felt her eyes widen in amazement and she wondered if she just hadn't noticed all this before. *Look at all the infractions. They're sure taking a chance against the code—*

And Darwin. I register that most aren't screened for Pro 1.

Julie accessed Gabriel Fauré's *Pavane* on her vee-pad and tried to tune out everything else. She disembarked at the next station and hastened to a secluded place, where she turned on her vee-set and placed a call to the Pol Station.

"Ms. Gibbons has already been released," said the receptionist in response to Julie's query. Julie blinked in surprise.

Deciding to give Nancy time to get home, she re-boarded the tube-jet and rode it to MacArthur Station close to her uncle's flat. Julie found a quiet corner and tapped a few numbers on the vee-pad on her belt. Nancy's face appeared on her eye-com. She gazed blankly at Julie from deep-set eyes framed by a pale face and fly-away hair. "Hi, Nan," Julie said. "Are you... okay?"

"Sure." Nancy smiled tightly. "Don't worry about me."

"Would you like some company?"

"No thanks. I'll catch up with you later sometime," she said, and abruptly switched off. Julie stared at the blank screen for a long time.

18

BOBBY glanced at the clock on the wall and adjusted his cooking unit. Julie was late again. Icaria had its clocks and she had hers.

His flat, like all the others below the 20th floor, had no windows. They'd been sealed when he was still young and the outside environment was less than desirable. No one was interested in the outside. Although he couldn't see it, the Don River meandered close by, its banks separating the outer-city from the inner-city. He was practically spitting distance from the inner-city. The domain of the machine. Machines run by machines, out-competing the thousands of pathetic inner-city Icarians looking for work. What was the world coming to?

He picked up an old book and sat in his favorite chair. He gazed at it, not reading, lost in boyhood visions…wearing a smog-mask and clinging to his mother's firm hand as they ran through the war-torn city streets…hearing smartbombs at night and snuggling with his older brother for comfort…his older cousin, Janet, stroking his head at night and reciting her favorite poem to them: *To see a world in a grain of sand, and Heaven in a wild flower*…Helplessly watching her struggle with a huge man, sinister laughter mocking her terrified gasps as he rips off her clothes. Watching the huge man drop his trousers and drive into her, rough and insistent, his grunts a discordant duet of lust and pain to her cries. Catching sight of his brother, Leonard, who appears at the doorway, eyes locking for a brief moment—an eternity—with hers. Their cousin, who has never asked for help, pleads for his. Leonard bolts, chased by her screams into a night that will never end…

A small and ominously dark room where he, alone, is repeatedly taken—

He slammed the book closed and the visions ceased. Bobby set aside his worn volume of Shakespeare, stood up and poured himself a scotch. As he sipped, he paced the room, glancing at his books, his loyal companions. Books never betrayed him or hurt him or abandoned him.

≈

Julie pulled off her vee-set and collapsed it onto her belt. She pushed the doorbell and smiled up at the tiny camera, knowing Bobby would be peering at her image on his vee-com. She held up a bag of donuts. He coughed then launched into their latest password: *"Twas Brillig and the Slythy Toves did gyre and gimble in the wabe."*

She continued, "*All mimsy were the...* um... *all mimsy...*" and trailed off in forgotten lines.

"*The Borrogroves! The Borrogroves!*" he bellowed in a gravelly voice that conveyed impatience with her lack of enthusiasm for Lewis Carroll. "Oh, never mind. Supper's getting cold." Bobby opened the door. "The line will come to you, when you're ready."

Julie smiled sheepishly and entered. "Hi, Bobby." She hugged him. He smiled and seemed to forget his concerns.

"Come in, my love," he growled and cleared his throat. "Supper's on the table."

"Mmm." She sniffed appreciatively. "I smell freshly baked bread!"

"Your favorite."

"How's your cough?" she asked as they made their way to the table and sat down.

"Never mind my cough," Bobby said. She could hear his breaths rattling in his chest. "It's getting better." He burst into a hacking fit that sent him bending over.

"Doesn't sound like it to me." Julie smiled sadly at him. "You should have stayed home today. What did your PCU advise?"

"Ahh," he bristled, "those personal care units and their sensors should leave my body and my urine alone! I thought you disconnected the stupid thing from my vee-com."

"Nano-sensors have a way of reconstructing themselves. And I can't disconnect your toilet." She shrugged with an amused smile and helped herself to a slice of bread. "So, what did it say to you?"

"You know what it said. I should stay at home and drink plenty of liquids. And if the symptoms didn't go away in 24 hours I should go to the Med-Center. *That's* a joke!"

"It's getting worse. You really should go—to get something for your cough, at least."

"*That* place!" He looked crossly at her. "I have my own medicines. From outside. Here, try some of this." He passed her a suspicious looking dish of green mush.

"What is it? Do I want to know?"

"What do you think? It's green mush, of course." He grinned. "With a secret ingredient."

Julie laughed, savoring a bite. She suspected his secret ingredient was *Delilah*. Drugs disagreed with her digestive system and his food usually made her feel ill afterward. "Well, it may be nano-produced, but it wasn't nano-cooked."

"I can't afford real food, like you can."

"Hey, I'm not complaining. This tastes great."

"Food likes to be heated with real fire, even nano-soup."

Julie smiled wryly. She'd had enough nano-soup to last a lifetime and let memories of Neo creep in. As she piled some bread dipped in vegetable sauce into her mouth, she caught Bobby's maudlin look. With puppy eyes, he finally said, "Why don't you come over more often? You know how I love to have you over and read with me and chat about things."

She squirmed at what she knew was coming.

"It's the Pol, isn't it? He's keeping you busy, taking you to shows and fine eateries? It must be dull here."

"No, Bobby!" She leaned forward with concern. "It's not dull here, you're not dull. And he doesn't take me to fancy places. We've just been spending, well, time together... That's all." She let her voice peter out.

"How serious is your attachment?"

She looked down at her scuffed boots, not sure herself. She knew he disapproved. He'd be livid with fury if he knew the Pol was Ed Langor's son. It was getting far too dangerous, now that she knew that Frank also knew. She needed to consider Bobby's safety.

"Let's have our dessert in the leisure room," Bobby suggested. "I had a quiet day on the outer walls," he continued, flopping into one of his chairs as Julie jumped up and crossed the room to join him. "I love the heath in the springtime. The smell of flowers and the afternoon sun warming my back." He'd worked on the exterior walls of one of the Liv-Buildings of District-8, overseeing the removal of climbing vines.

"Sounds wonderful," she said, half listening.

"I even saw a bald eagle circling overhead."

"What a magnificent bird!" She stroked one of Bobby's orchids that bloomed beneath his grow lamps and let the vision of Nancy's shaming return.

"Yes, I wonder if there's a nest nearby. I'll look for it next time I'm out that way. Maybe you'd like to come out with me to see it?"

She muttered a lame affirmative. She could vividly remember the first time she'd gone outside with Bobby, after she'd returned from the inner-city. She'd been close to sick with excitement and trepidation, yearning to rekindle the romance she'd begun there years before. Had it been her father's influence or a faulty memory? When they got outside and Bobby lectured her, she'd felt none of the earlier magic.

"So, how was your day?" Bobby asked.

Haunted by Nancy's broken face, Julie looked up and said absent-mindedly, "There was a riot in Darwin Square at noon." She should have just gone to Nancy's anyway, Julie thought miserably. She'd let her affair with a Pol divert her from her friend.

"Food riot?"

"That's what Frank—" she paused, realizing that she had brought the Pol back into the conversation and regretted it. "—thought..." More silence. This time she tried some humor. "Some kid tried to feel me all over in the tube-jet."

It didn't work. Bobby looked alarmed. "Did someone really accost you?"

"No, no!" she reassured him, absently drawing her fingers over one of Bobby's outside artifacts: a worn piece of blue glass. "Just a harmless boy, no more than fifteen. I pushed him off and that was that."

"You should be more careful." Bobby looked concerned. "He could've had a knife."

"That's what SAM—" She stopped herself. Bobby didn't know SAM lived in her head. "—My AI would have said."

"Your AI would have been right. That ruffian could have been a razor head. Vee, that gang are worse than techno-slummers."

Julie's breath hitched. Had he let that slip out?

"They say the Distopians are recruiting them," Bobby continued. "I overheard a conversation in the lunch room just yesterday that they steal your vee-set and use it to construct illicit gadgetry for terrorist Info-Net activities…just like inner city techno-slumming…"

Julie focused on a beautiful print of a European landscape on the far wall. Vee! Bobby was relying on lunchroom gossip. That razor head gang was nothing like the techno-slummers. They'd abandoned responsibilities for the thrill of senseless destruction, while the orphaned techno-slummers simply tried to survive.

"Statistics show that at least one girl is stabbed every hour in the city," Bobby persisted.

Thinking of Nancy, Julie turned to him, waving one of his artifacts in the air. "Twenty times that are victimized in the Pol-Station."

"That's not the point, Julie—"

"Yes, it is!" Her voice became shrill. "That *is* the point!"

He coughed and shook his head slowly. "You depend too much on your vee-com databases and your statistics for every answer, Julie. You should arm yourself. You can't depend on luck forever."

She sighed. "We've been through this before. You know I'm against that sort of thing. Besides, I'd have to do a PS exam to have a weapon registered to me. And I'll never submit myself to such an insult. Mainly," she frowned, "because I'd probably fail, anyway. They'd look at my record and see the demerits—"

"But you're a veemeld. Surely that counts—"

She released an exasperated laugh. "Being a veemeld doesn't give me those kind of privileges. It just means I'm good with vee-coms and AIs. I'm no more immune from Icarian law than the inner-city slummer across the river. They still wouldn't register me a weapon."

Bobby nodded slowly. "You could just carry a non-registered weapon like so many do. Get your Pol friend to get you one—"

"Bobby! How could you even suggest that!"

"You're much too principled for your own sake, Julie. All the young girls are getting armed. Your life is worth the insult."

She turned her gaze back at his artifact shelf and her eyes focused on infinity.

Bobby dropped the subject and studied her face. "You look a lot like your father," he said. After a pause, he added, "Honey, why don't you invite Frank over here for supper?"

Julie knew he was thinking of the two demerits she'd already received this year; and that if she wasn't careful the Shame Court would follow. Having a Pol as a friend might protect her. "All right," she answered feebly, knowing that she would never bring him by. In fact, her mind was scrambling with how to sever their relationship. His threat against Bobby, idle as it had obviously been, had hit home. He was still a Pol. A Pol whose father's reputation had been destroyed by hers.

19

April 3, 2095—1900.

VICTOR found an unoccupied seat in the back row of the small auditorium. Peering over the fifty or so heads, he glimpsed Gaia at the front. She sat alone with calm regality on the stage, facing the audience with arms loosely folded over her lap, waiting for more people to file in. She wore an enigmatic smile and focused her attention on someone in the front row who was speaking to her. Victor's eyes lingered over the low cut gold satin dress that clung to her slender body like a second skin. Her jet-black hair coiled over one shoulder.

Gaia crossed her legs and leaned forward to answer the man. Although Victor had not heard the man's comment, Gaia's clear response slit the noise of the crowd. "I beg to differ with you, Justin," she said, ruby lips shining. "The process of evolution increases order, not chaos. In fact, evolution depends on disorder, from which it draws its options for diversity."

She glanced in Victor's direction and their eyes met briefly. Gaia nodded slightly then trained her gaze back to the man with whom she was conversing. Victor jammed his invitation card into his pocket and settled in, glancing around and hoping to recognize someone. He didn't. With the exception of a few guests such as himself, every Ecologist here was a member of the *Circle*, the political and academic cream of Icaria. He hoped to be a member someday.

Gaia stood and raised her hands to the audience invitingly. "Welcome again, my *Circle* friends and honored guests." She smiled, showing perfect teeth. "So, who wants to talk about Darwin Disease?" The room hushed. She had everyone's undivided attention. Victor straightened in his chair. "We know it's caused by a retrovirus. For those of you not familiar with virology, a retrovirus is an RNA virus that uses a unique cellular enzyme, reverse transcriptase, to make a DNA copy from the viral RNA. Thousands of retroviral sequences have existed from ancient times in the human genome from benign infection. We don't know the cause of Darwin Disease or how it's transmitted. We certainly don't have a cure for it yet." She paused to scan the audience. "There is some evidence to suggest that this neural disease is environmentally-influenced, responding to some unique facet of our inside environment, and may reflect a genetic predisposition by those inflicted." She glanced at Victor. "Some argue that the demise of Icaria-11 was initially due to the ravage of this disease." Gaia tilted her head to one side and critically assessed her audience. "Darwin Disease, if truly related to the uniqueness of Icaria's inside environment, may be a necessary event in its evolution." Victor watched several people glance at one another. Gaia seemed to relish controversy.

A man about her age with a long face sprang up. He was the same person she had been speaking to earlier when Victor had entered the room. His lanky frame shook as he waved an arm at her. "Come, come, Gaia! That sounds dangerously close to what Crane proposed in his inverted loop model."

She waved him down with an amused smile and he sat. Victor wondered what game she was playing now. "The paradigm of evolution, as we have learned over the last century, proceeds by random mutation in the genome," she said, letting her gaze sweep from the man who'd made the outburst to the rest of her audience. "Most of these mutations prove detrimental, usually killing the organism, but a rare few over a great period of time provide some advantage and become inherited and eventually incorporated into the population as a whole through the mechanism of better fitness." She raised a finger. "Yet, if we scrutinize most evolutionary 'events', they appear in leaps, marking milestones in some element of change, rather than slow incremental changes inherited over long periods of time. What does this have to do with Darwin Disease? Bear with me." She made a charming smile. "I will come back to the virus."

Victor overheard someone next to him murmur to another, "These seminars of Gaia's aren't a discussion, they're a lecture." Victor managed a smile.

Gaia folded her hands together. "Even a crisis that introduces a new source of chaos is likely to increase the order created by evolution. The asteroid crash millennia ago, for instance, created vast destruction and subsequent chaos; yet it seemed to hasten the rise of mammals in the niche previously dominated by reptiles and dinosaurs." She paused to survey her audience.

The same man sprang to his feet again. "Gaia, this sounds suspiciously like *stable chaos* theory to me. Are you suggesting that we should think of this disease as an evolutionary milestone for Icaria?"

Gaia leered and waved him down again. She'd obviously anticipated the question, perhaps even orchestrated its inevitability. "You tell me, Justin," she said. "I'm sure that everyone here would agree that veemelds provide an extremely useful function to Icaria." Victor's stomach knotted. She didn't as much as glance at him. "What if I told you that researchers have irrefutable evidence that veemelds are unaffected by Darwin Disease?"

The audience gasped in astonishment, then fell into murmuring among themselves. Victor felt sick. She knew! Damn her to chaos. Now all of Icaria would know. Her eyes were suddenly on him and he glared back. She smiled briefly, a knowing one, just for him, then turned to Justin, who was about to stand up again. Pointing her finger to stay him, she said, "Our veemelds have demonstrated a successful adaptation to Icaria's unique environment and will likely pass this on to their descendants. Survival of the fittest, ladies and gentlemen." She tilted her head back, as if welcoming the floodgates of adversity her revelation would naturally incite.

Justin threw up his arms. "Come, Gaia, we're all ecologists here. That sounds like Lamarckism. We all know that characteristics acquired during the life of an organism cannot be passed on to its offspring."

Victor glanced around him. Didn't anyone grasp what she'd so coolly implied? That everyone except veemelds were going to die?

Gaia leaned forward. Although she smiled, her eyes gleamed like the blade of a knife. "I think you have severely limited your view to biological evolution, Justin. You forget the evolution of technology, in which veemelds play a pivotal role and are particularly suited. I will get back to this later." She waved her hand to dismiss him, then turned to the rest of her audience. "We have no idea how long humans have carried the veemeld trait. Perhaps for millennia. It is not something that could possibly have been recorded until the technology to use it was developed. It's not as though they expressed any other noticeable traits to alert the world of their difference. The fact that ability to veemeld and immunity to this disease are singularly linked in veemelds tells me that this is by evolutionary design—"

"But, Gaia," a young woman interjected. "Are you suggesting that humans—some humans—carried the genetic makeup for both veemelding ability and immunity to Darwin Disease as if evolution *knew* it would need them at the same time?"

"More Lamarckian rubbish!" Justin scoffed. "Gaia, you're treading on chaos."

Gaia ignored him and focused her attention on the young woman. "First of all, Jane, I wouldn't describe it so much as immunity to the Darwin virus, as symbiotic with it. Animals and viruses have co-evolved over millennia, presenting us with many examples of mutual co-existence between host and virus: rodents and hantaviruses; the green monkey and SIV, the chimpanzee and HIV-1, for instance. The Darwin virus obviously inhabits veemelds in an aggressive symbiotic relationship. By aggressive, I mean that were something to threaten its host, the virus would attack—"

Justin waved an arm. "Now you've turned the virus into a guard dog! Really, Gaia—"

"—we have many examples of this kind of aggressive symbiotic behavior. For instance, in the case of the ant and the acacia plant, the acacia berries supply the ants with food while the ants not only keep the foliage clear of herbivores and preying insects, but make hunting forays around the tree to ravage growing shoots of potential rival plants. Similarly, the herpes-B virus, which co-evolved with the squirrel monkey in the Amazon Rainforest, induces a voracious cancer to all of the monkey's competitors."

Justin stomped his foot. "Are you implying that veemelds are protected by this retrovirus? Then why are *we* still around? Or at the very least, why didn't veemelds become the dominant humans long ago?"

"There was no need for this endogenous retrovirus to 'awaken' until recently. Icaria's enclosed environment—the likely trigger—didn't yet exist, so the Darwin virus had no reason to hop to a competitive genome to protect its host. In the meantime, veemelds may have been unknowingly responsible for the success of *Homo sapiens sapiens* over *Homo sapiens neanderthalis* and other subspecies, by relying on the other attributes associated with their unique genetic makeup. Such as their demonstrated higher abilities in cognition and innovation. Veemelds would have been coveted as medicine men and women, shamans, witch doctors, priests and so on. This small group would have been protected by the remaining members of the tribe who expressed traits more critical to survival at that time—such as brute strength, aggressive behavior, kinesthetic and spatial intelligence... skills useful for hunting and migrating. Nonetheless, the increased cognitive skills of veemelds would have conferred a decided advantage on the community to which they belonged. That's why they endured but their numbers remained small."

"What about now?"

Victor leaned forward to see the man who'd posed the question. He looked younger than Victor, and pretty young to be a member of *the Circle*.

Gaia clasped her hands. "In order for a species to truly succeed, Patrick, it must withstand time and evolution, nature's real test. Not only must the species overcome a harsh environment by successfully manipulating it—simple adaptation, as Justin adroitly pointed out, is too slow," she said, glancing at him with a nod, "but the species must ultimately survive its own role in the successional process: essentially succeed itself—"

"Or stop succession," prompted a woman from the audience.

Gaia stepped forward again with a stern face. "That is untenable, Sophie. Here and only here I agree with the *stable chaos* theorists: change is inevitable. This is where technology comes in." She turned to Justin and smirked. "You mentioned Lamarck. I submit that veemelds' ability to meld with machines provides a working example of Lamarckism—and symbiosis—in action. With the help of their machine-selves, veemelds will not only inherit Icaria; they will fashion its future."

20

BOBBY made some tea to go with the donuts Julie had brought and they settled in to spend the evening playing bridge and talking of books. Bobby slipped into his usual pattern of talking about the past and lecturing her on the usual topics: overpopulation, devastation of natural ecosystems, and the resulting plague and global warming. He reminded Julie of her father, who used to lecture her about ecology. There was one major difference: while her father painstakingly refused to lay blame, Bobby's lectures brimmed with fiery accusations.

"Why didn't you do anything about it?" she interrupted him.

He stared, taken aback by her forwardness. She had never challenged him before. She caught an angry spark in his eyes and for a brief moment she was reminded again of her father. Then, like a candle extinguished, the light in his eyes vanished, his weary expression returned and he withdrew his gaze to the floor. Julie recalled her father's face, awoken from its sad trance and fierce like a wild fire, and she brought her hand to her flushed cheek. The sting from her mother's drunken hand had paled next to her fear of her father's rage that day shortly before the Pols took him away.

—

Her father storms in, smelling of pipe tobacco and smoke, just as her mother cuffs Julie for not doing the dishes. His eyes flash like lightning and he seizes her shrieking mother. He does not strike her, but his quiet voice cuts like a knife. "Don't ever hit our daughter again, do you hear me?"

Julie struggles from recoiling as her father bends down to hug her and rumple her hair. "You're okay now, my angel," he says.

Her mother snarls, "Stop calling her an angel. She's no angel—"

He raises his hand but stops himself in time.

Her mother lashes out, "You made her into a monster. A freak!"

"Shut up!"

"When are you going to tell her? She still thinks she just fell ill that night you took her to Janet's lab. God, Leonard, Janet said *jump* and you said *how high*! You sacrificed your own daughter for her—"

"Shut up!" He pushes her mother gruffly out of the room, leaving Julie confused and panting with mixed emotion.

Was the rage a genetic infirmity, or a remnant of a common trauma her uncle and father had shared? What burden did they carry from the revolution? And who was more cursed, the brother who flew with the rage, or the one who suppressed it?

"Why didn't you act?"

Bobby's eyes flitted over her face, avoiding her direct gaze. "What could I do? What's one person supposed to do? I was little when most of this happened." Then he continued telling her of the past as if she hadn't spoken.

Julie plunged in during a pause in his discourse, "Do you think Father killed Vogel and Tsutsumi?"

Bobby flinched, taken off guard by her question. It had been a long time since they had discussed his late older brother. "What brings this on now?"

She just shook her head and looked down, still waiting for his answer.

"You've been restless lately. Ever since your impetuous friend lost her job. Then you got involved with that Pol. And you're never home. You don't answer my messages or come over anymore. What's happening to you?"

"Nothing," she answered lamely. What *was* happening to her?

He leaned back and sighed ruefully. "I guess it's time you saw this." He pushed himself up from the chair. "It's something your father wrote me just before the Pols came for him. It's about Janet, our cousin. About her suicide." He disappeared into his bedroom, coughing.

Intrigued by Janet's selfless heroics—she'd killed someone to save the brothers and had nursed Julie when she was very ill—Julie had mined her father for more gems, but he'd refused to yield any. Bobby had been far less reticent and Julie had coaxed many stories from him. The one he obsessively repeated was of the tragic day the three of them had gone on a picnic during the height of the revolution. Their parents had permitted their excursion on the condition that they arm themselves with functional bows and quivers. A skillful archer, Janet had brought home a few hares for supper already. A rising storm blew against their faces as they returned to the farmhouse, dark with the shadows of black clouds. A hulking stranger stomped out the front door and startled the children. The dirty white band tied around his worn checkered jacket proclaimed him a Techno counter-revolutionary. Janet glanced from the man's churlish grin to his knife and armed her bow. He laughed at her, baring yellow teeth. She didn't know he was a murderer. She couldn't have known that their parents were dead inside. It was as if some divine spirit had told her of the treacherous act this stranger had committed in the house, Bobby would always say, because she didn't wait for him to approach further, instead drawing the bow back and let the arrow fly. It sunk into the man's chest. He charged them like a wild animal. She'd quickly reloaded, struck him with another arrow, and he fell dead on his face.

Bobby returned, still coughing, with an old volume of Shakespeare. Out of it he removed an envelope, faded and worn. He handed the envelope to Julie. "Leonard and I used to write notes to one another, mainly to avoid prying eyes. I couldn't part with it after he was taken away. I thought I might have to show it to you or Diana some day."

Julie pulled out the letter with difficulty. She carefully unfolded it and read the small, tight handwriting:

> Dear Bobby,
> I think Vogel's responsible for Janet's suicide. Everyone thinks she did it because of the Darwin outbreak—as if she could have prevented it somehow—but she knew Vogel from before. He was an environmental geneticist, specializing in genetic engineering, and he used a pseudonym to write very unpopular papers supporting stable chaos theory—like I'm doing now. When he became government leader, he hired her as one of his assistants at his AIHV lab. I think Vogel's responsible for this Darwin virus and Janet found out. I think he took her as a lover to keep her quiet. He might have driven her to suicide, maybe even killed her and made it look that way. I thought you should know this, just in case something happens to me.
> Your loving brother, Leonard.

She read the date of the letter: February 15, 2087. Ten days before Vogel was shot. Her voice trembled, "Then, you *do* think Dad did it?"

Bobby coughed and avoided Julie's direct gaze. "Leonard never stopped looking for an answer to her suicide. He was convinced there was more to it."

Julie felt the soft paper and imagined her father's gentle hand writing those painful words. Tears sprang to her eyes and the words on the page clouded into a sea of prisms. She looked away, refusing to accept the awful possibility. Her father wasn't a killer.

"It doesn't mean he did it," Bobby offered, his breath rasping.

Julie gave him back the letter. "Father didn't kill Vogel or Tsutsumi," she said, her voice rising. "He isn't a murderer. All he had was motive." And anger, her mind added.

Bobby looked down. He returned the letter to its original place and the subject was dropped. They resumed their card game, but Julie played miserably. She ruminated over the letter. Although she could never accept her father acting so passionately over his work, she wasn't as certain about the subject of his cousin. Her mother had accused him of loving his cousin more than he loved her.

21

AS Bobby settled into his favorite chair to reread Hamlet, Julie casually slid her fingers across his primitive V-com console, pretending to use it; instead, she set her mind to meld with SAM. Julie found SAM's wavelength and sucked in a deep breath as her mind found the matrix and shivered in.

Hi, Julie. SAM's lilting voice wafted in over the desultory machine voices like a cool gust on a hot day.

Hey, SAM.

Hey, Julie. It's been a while.

Yes, only a few hours. She smiled. *I have a trip for us to take. It'll involve traveling some back roads again.*

I must caution you on the illicit paths you've chosen lately in your work. Considering your present situation with the Head Pol and your latest demerit, I'd advise against it.

She thought of what she'd already done and felt the same rush of terror that she'd experienced when she'd first appropriated the forbidden files.

Does this involve your father's arrest?

Yes, SAM. We need to look at other people's motives. She'd carefully avoided such illicit intrusion—until now. Trying to sound casual, she thought, *I pirated a few confidential files today from the Pol Station. Here's one of them.* She instructed SAM where to find it.

Good vee, Julie! Your use of defragmentation and data-link probes on old corrupt files is bad enough, but stealing whole files—SAM let the thought dangle ominously.

She'd expected this and sent a lame response. *Not stealing, just borrowing.*

And from the Pol Station of all places! This is very dangerous, Julie. If they catch us you could lose all your privileges, probably your job. Maybe more.

Cold fear seized her stomach. *We'll just make sure they won't,* she snapped back, reminded of her ill-fated predecessors. But they weren't veemelds, she told herself. Then with a surge of terrified excitement, *This is important to me, SAM. I need to know the truth about my father. Besides, we've got them now. We might as well look at them.*

But why do you need to know now all of a sudden? He was arrested eight years ago.

She pursed her lips. *Let's just say I've reached a particular stage in my life-development.* Something she had often said to SAM, especially when she had no idea what else to say.

Very well, Julie. So long as you understand the risk you're taking. While an innocuous database occupied Bobby's vee-com screen, SAM displayed the holo-image in front of Julie. After the revolution, Damien Vogel formed a council Triad for North Am with three leaders of equal power. The Triad was dissolved in 2083 when the two others, Monica Schlange and Christian Isabo, were murdered. Vogel was later shot by Leonard Crane in 2087—

Not this, SAM. This is history. What I'm after is the truth. Let's backtrack to Vogel's connection with my father.

SAM threw the image of a distinguished looking man in his fifties in front of her. There was nothing subtle about him, thought Julie. He looked like a great bird of prey. Keen predatory eyes peered at her beneath deceptively hooded eyelids. His aquiline nose curved into a high forehead that crested in a wave of swept-back graying hair.

Actually, Vogel and your dad had lots in common. SAM displayed a pre-revolution paper of Vogel's, written under a pseudonym, and highlighted a quote. His intro reads like something out of an SCT textbook.

Julie read: "At the surface tension of history's flow, where the delicate balance of the forces of stability and instability lie, life blossoms. The disorderly behavior of simple systems acts as a creative process, generating complexity. Beneath the turbulent waves of disorder lies a destiny worth mastering." As you can see, Vogel was not adverse to change and disorder. He welcomed them.

Julie scratched her head. She felt like she was falling into a black hole. Something else in her father's letter nagged her but she couldn't place it. *So, you're saying that the head of the government continued to follow a belief contrary to his own government?*

Vogel never abandoned SCT even when the more ardent deep ecologists, purists like Schlange, branded it heretical and distopian. He just kept quiet about it. Schlange and the rest saw its danger to their concepts of "deep ecology." Seems Vogel saw the world differently.

Like her father, Julie thought. They might have been allies if Vogel and Janet hadn't become lovers, resulting in her suicide. But that was still only her father's conjecture, she reminded herself. Was it enough to kill for?

What about Tsutsumi, my father's boss at DIE? What's his story? Here, what are these? She directed SAM to another confidential record. Behind them were secret files.

How many of these did you get? SAM sounded hysterical. Julie reviewed the files in silence and SAM finally came around. Okay, so, Dr. Ewen Tsutsumi was a brilliant ecologist and also a strong proponent of *stable chaos* theory, introduced by Dr. Patrick Fairweather in 2025. But did you know, Julie, that Dr. Fairweather was not the father of *stable chaos* theory?

Then who was?

Fairweather based his theory for ecosystems on the Gaia Hypothesis, named after the goddess of Earth, proposed back in 1974 by radical scientists James Lovelock and Lynn Margulis.

That's over a hundred years ago!

Sometimes it takes that long for the seed of an idea to mature. It was 150 years before Darwin's theory of evolution was fully accepted. He wrote the *Origin of Species* in 1859 and we still use his major premise.

Good point, SAM.

The Gaia Hypothesis proposed that the planet is a self-regulating organism: a global cybernetic control system, achieving a sort of homeostasis. Scientists refused to embrace the hypothesis, dismissing it as unsubstantiated and dangerous.

Julie nodded, leaning forward to read the information on Fairweather that SAM had placed on the holo.

Many conveniently considered this an authorization to pollute, since under this hypothesis, nature supposedly adapted. Its resurgence some fifty years later in *stable chaos* theory generated as much controversy. Fairweather was accused of selling out to the multi-nationals. He was branded a distopian and brutally killed during the revolution.

Studying Fairweather's mature lean face, uncompromising lips and honest eyes, Julie recognized a thoughtful arch in his eyebrows and something sad about the eyes, as if he recognized his dire fate. *Okay, SAM. Enough history. What about Tsutsumi?*

Fairweather's face disappeared. This will interest you, Julie. SAM threw scrawled notes from Tsutsumi's vee-book on the holo-image. Tsutsumi and your father actually co-wrote the controversial paper on the inverted loop model, which uses *stable chaos* theory to predict the collapse of Icaria.

Julie stared at the notes. *What? Not my father? I thought it was my father who—*

Tsutsumi adroitly recognized the model's political incorrectness and let Leonard Crane, take full responsibility... or, as it turned out, blame. It was Tsutsumi alone who used the data on Darwin Disease to support the inverted loop model.

Julie fidgeted in her seat. Her mouth grew dry as she surveyed Tsutsumi's round sanguine face. No older than her father, Tsutsumi turned out to be far more shrewd and cunning. She imagined a sly leer in his smug expression and her own eyes narrowed. The coward had ensured the publication of his controversial material using her father as a shield. Betrayed her father's naïve loyalty. Was that cause enough for murder?

The inverted loop model is based on fractal ecology, which flourished at the turn of the century for a short while.

Fractal?

Julie! You use fractals all the time. Don't you know?

Julie leaned back and made a crooked smile. *So, give me a hint, SAM.*

Fractals are complicated geometric patterns made up of the same motif repeated on ever-smaller scales. You have lots of fractals in you, Julie: your circulatory and nervous systems, for instance. Trees and mountains are other examples. The mathematician Benoit Mandelbrot coined the word in 1975 from the Latin word *fractus*. All fractals are self-similar—that is, they look the same when examined from far away or nearby. You use fractals in most of the models you construct.

She made a lopsided grin. *Okay. Then what's fractal ecology?*

Fractal ecology is a branch science of chaotics that uses fractals to show how a continually repeating set of organizational levels from molecules, to cells and so on to ecosystems, interact through functional vehicles like predation, competition, and commensalism. You can see the connection with the Gaia Hypothesis and the potential for misinterpretation.

But how does fractal ecology fit into stable chaos theory or the inverted loop model and my father's predictions?

Patterns in time, Julie. *Stable chaos theory* proposes that every system undergoes cycles that are never quite the same each time and driven by what chaotics calls 'strange attractors'. A kind of evolving destiny of destruction and creation.

Julie drew in her breath and pushed the hair from her face. It must have embarrassed the current government when Tsutsumi and her father successfully applied the inverted loop model to predict Icaria-11's "inevitable" collapse from Darwin Disease. If her father was framed, was it a simple case of silencing the "mouthpiece" and eliminating government supporters of distopian ecology? It probably wasn't that simple. Nothing in life was, she decided.

I didn't mean to distress you. We're searching for the truth. It's not always kind, is it?

No, SAM. It isn't. She shivered with a feverish chill and wiped her wet brow with the back of her hand.

Perhaps we should stop. It's dangerous, after all.

I'm okay. Sometimes we need to walk the dangerous path; to feel this way, to... She struggled for the right word.

To find our souls?

Astonished. *Yes, SAM. Our souls.* What could SAM possibly know about souls? Julie, I think you're falling ill.

SAM, you're starting to sound like my PCU again. Give it a rest.

But it's *you* who needs rest.

Julie felt suddenly nauseous. *Perhaps I will turn in. We'll do more tomorrow.*

It's a difficult and elusive subject.

What's that?

Justice. My research indicates that the achievement of an ideal such as justice is inversely correlated with the practice of the tools such as Icarian law to achieve it. An oxymoron.

Julie smiled briefly. *Thanks, SAM. I'll cap it all tomorrow.* She shook her head out of veemeld and flicked off the vee-com. SAM was developing a sophisticated sense of humor. She glanced at her watch. It was 2300. She turned to Bobby, who was nodding off to sleep in his chair with the book on his lap, his breaths rattling out of his open mouth.

"Good night, Bobby," she said, bending down to kiss his forehead.

He stirred and smiled up at her. "I'll fix up the pull-out couch for you."

"Thanks," she said, still undecided as to whether she would meet Frank that night.

≈

Julie stooped over the sink in Bobby's bathroom, brushing her teeth. After rinsing out her mouth, she straightened and caught her own reflection in the mirror. Meeting her sea-green eyes, she saw a striking resemblance to her father, even in her expression. She clung to the vision of his gentle intelligent face, his courage and brilliance as a scientist, his honorable reporting of the truth. Her hero. But without consciously wishing it, she recalled the vid-clip she'd seen of his devastating rage in Tsutsumi's office. As she replayed it in her mind, she realized with distressed confusion that she was looking for a clue in his violent actions that would connect him to Tsutsumi's murder. But he was innocent. Why couldn't she believe it?

22

April 3, 2095–2115

AN older woman, elegantly dressed and coiffed, stood up in the middle of the room and raised her hand. She must have been an important Circle member because Gaia instantly acknowledged her with a nod. The woman said in a steely voice, "You suggest that veemelds will inherit the future with the help of AIs. I'm no Luddite, but what's to stop AIs from inheriting the future with the help of veemelds?"

Gaia nodded with a knowing smile. "Astute question, Aileen. Yes, I see the danger posed by this juxtaposition as two-fold: first, preventing thinking machines from fulfilling their own self-deterministic wants; and second, controlling veemelds once they achieve the power to meld completely with machines." She paused to survey the audience, eyes sweeping past Victor as though he were a stranger. "To answer the first point, we have purposefully created AIs as separate intelligence types, dysfunctional and isolated parts of a whole, only some of which veemelds can access. Not even veemelds can integrate disparate artificial intelligence types fully: we do that."

No, *You* do that, Victor thought. By reading all my veemelds' minds. He began to see the depth of her nefarious plan.

Gaia swept her hand over the crowd as if they belonged to her. "Before the revolution, misuse of our most powerful technologies—robotics, genetic engineering, and nano-technology—threatened our planet and our species." She leaned forward, her eyes sparkling like sapphires. "We took pains to avoid the mistakes the Technocrats made and relied instead on Earth's own wisdom to create Icaria and segregate it to protect our beautiful but fragile planet. We owe much of our gratitude in successfully bringing this about to my esteemed colleague, the late Christian Isabo, who recognized that human societies and intelligence are multi-faceted and tend naturally toward hierarchy, as do the other gregarious species on this planet. Much of what we've achieved in Icarian education and in the work ethic relied on his concept of optimum functionality based on a 'community of intelligences.'

"Given that most of you, like me, are ecologists, you are probably not familiar with the history of our AI system. It begins with the idea of multiple intelligences, or MI, forwarded more than a hundred years ago with the pioneer work of psychologists who argued for the existence of relatively autonomous portions of human intellect. Isabo successfully applied MI in education and in the work environment to maximize efficiency and productivity. In what became known as the Isabo Intelligence Type Test, IITT, people were ranked Type 1 to 11, based on the known main intelligence domains confirmed, and optimally placed in the work force—"

"Come, come, Gaia. You're rambling," Justin interrupted. "What's that got to do with AIs and veemelds?"

She glanced at him with a sharp smile. "I was getting to that," she said tartly. "Christian and I recognized that the principal threat posed by AIs, potentially "smarter" than us, is that their tendency for self-actualization and eventual self-replication would eventually make humans an endangered species." Her eyes swept the front row of the audience, past Justin. "To quote some statistics I got from the AI-core itself, we have over a hundred types of AIs working for us in Icaria today. They use over 30 areas of intelligence and collectively possess several billion times greater computing power than all the humans on this planet." She paused, resting her eyes on Justin in the front row. He said nothing.

With a nod, she resumed. "Both our neural-system and robotics people used the basics of MI to create robots and bodiless AIs that were specialized in one domain of intelligence only. This limits their self-actualization." She paced the stage. "For instance, AI07s work within the kinesthetic intelligence domain almost entirely. They possess a rudimentary instinct for recycling, using nano-technology to process all materials in the right path. On the other hand, AI20s and 50s, used in the social services, contain a spatial-social intelligence and are capable of making up to 15 million billion calculations a second, just over half of what the human brain is capable of. This allows them to properly service us in restaurants, transit systems, and so on. All our AIs collectively form a true 'community of artificial intelligences.' The AIs with the most diverse capabilities are the 100 series—the virtuals—and the 1000 series only found in the AI core, both of which are not physically embodied and only exist within the central vee-com system, with little possibility of self-replication. The latter, of course, as you well know, are only accessed by veemelds. Which brings me to my second point: how to control veemelds."

Gaia trained her eyes on Victor.

"Dr. Olafsen's researchers at the DP have documented different types of veemelds, according to their cognitive abilities and their type or style of veemelding—their type of intelligence aside." Her eyes remained fixed on Victor. He shifted in his chair. "They have documented at least five different types and charted them as alpha, beta, gamma veemelds, and so on." Several people turned to see who she had focused on. Victor pulled at his collar. "One veemeld, however, is off this chart entirely." Her eyes blazed into his like a laser-gun. "Of course, we are watching her very closely." Gaia's lips curled.

Victor knew she meant Julie Crane.

Gaia released him, letting her gaze sweep the audience. "Evolution, people." She raised her hands in a messianic gesture. "We are looking through Alice's looking glass into our future."

You mean *your* future, thought Victor, feeling sick to his stomach. She hadn't addressed the second point: how to control veemelds. She didn't have to. He knew the answer.

23

April 3, 2095—2340.

JULIE lay on the made-up couch, hot and shivering with a dull ache in her stomach. Bobby's delilah-laced food was taking its toll on her. The machines talking to one another throbbed in her head. The chirping sounds chattered with more than usual intensity, as if insisting on being heard—something else that usually followed Bobby's dubious mixture of food. Trying to block out their chatter, she listened to her uncle's cough. It sounded like thunder rumbling from far away. He reread his old volumes into the dead of night, as if he was afraid to go to sleep.

The echo of a saxophone drifted in from the adjoining apartment. The walls were paper-thin in this district, she thought. Though obviously an amateur, he played with feeling and she found herself listening to his flowing and ebbing notes. The melody was sad but sweet. With each note he played, he played her, first beating her heart and then softly caressing her soul.

Bobby's loud coughs drowned out the saxophone. She thought of the tinctures and teas Bobby made from herbs he'd collected outside. Julie saw no evidence that they helped. She stared at the ceiling and let her mind slip into veemeld. *Hey, SAM.*

Hey, Julie, SAM's soft voice drifted in. How are you feeling?

I'm worried about Bobby. He might get a demerit with this cough of his. Demerits are easy to get.

I beg to differ, Julie. The statistics show that a mere 11.7% of the population ever incurs a demerit and only 0.5% are repeat offenders.

SAM threw a holo-image of the chart five centimeters in front of her nose. *Okay, okay, SAM. I guess, I was thinking of certain people.*

You mean your hot-headed friend who just appeared in front of the Shame Court?

Yeah. Remember the youths on the tube-jet?

Yes.

Why don't they ever get demerits or go to the Shame Court like Nancy did? Have I picked an unlucky friend? One with bad karma?

May I be blunt?

She smiled to herself. SAM was always blunt. *Go ahead.*

Face it, Julie, she's vulgar and outspoken. And a slob.

It was nice to know SAM could call them. *I guess you're right.*

Those who follow Icaria's implicit code get rewarded with access to orgies, drug parties, and second chances.

Julie curled under the covers. For those like Nancy who didn't fit in, there was a derisive society constantly reminding her of her maladjustment. *Why do all my friends...* Her mind lapsed into silence.

End up in trouble?

Yes.

I can't give a definitive answer.

Spoken like a machine.

Maybe because they're all different. Because *you're* different.

I'm not so different. She pulled the covers over her head and tried not to hear the murmuring voices in her head. *No one understands me, that's all. Not even Bobby. You understand me better than anyone.* She paused, absently listening to the carillon of machines. *When Kraken told me that I had no real friends, I thought him rude. But he's right. I have no one I can just talk to.* Not since Neo, she thought, remembering how they used to sit back to back and trade dreams, crazy stories and laughter amidst their inner-city misery. *My friends are okay for an occasional Rec-Center event or lunch. But I don't share much with them. Even Nancy was too busy chasing her own rhetoric to listen to me. Since she lost her job, we've drifted apart. Frank and I have nothing in common, except for...* she let the thought trail. *Everyone else is hooked on delilah. I guess Frank's my drug. Why am I so stupid when I'm around him? As for sharing laughter, memories, fears or hopes—he's a lost cause. But then, who shares that these days? No one... except for—you, SAM. I can talk to you about anything... you're...*

...My best friend. Julie dozed, letting her machines sing her to sleep.

～

"What d'ya m-mean they t-talk?" *Neo stammers, squatting next to her in the cramped makeshift shack as they repair a vee-com they've built with inner-city scrap. He digs his dirty nails into his tangled, greasy hair and squints at her through coal-black eyes. His increased stammer betrays a nervous excitement.*

"Can't you hear them too, Neo?" *Julie says in a faltering voice. She shifts her weight from one knee to the other, suddenly giddy under his penetrating stare. Lately she's caught him studying her with an intensity that makes her blush. When he looks at her that way, the smoldering anger in his black eyes disappears, unveiling a sadness he usually masks under his bravado.*

Neo tilts his head back and smirks. "You m-making this up?" *His name isn't really Neo. She doesn't know his real name. He's abandoned it like the parents who gave him the name have abandoned him. He chose the name after a cyber-hero from some classic movie. Except for the nine-year old twins, Annabelle and Abigail, all the other techno-slummers have given themselves new names as well. Her sister Diana calls herself Elf. Julie has chosen Angel, the nickname her father gave her.* "Machines don't talk to people, Angel," *Neo says. He stands up and shakes his head at her.* "I gotta get some quantum *couplers. Get a g-g-grip. You're still looking for your mother a year after she abandoned you. She's probably been recycled by now, maybe into the nano-soup you ate today."*

She thinks him cruel to have said that. Several of the younger orphans have gathered around in the small bivouac made of the city's refuse. Julie clenches her fists and works her jaw as she watches Neo brush past the giggling children. Letting her anger subside in silence, she decides that from now on she will avoid confiding in him.

But that night, when the little children lie asleep in their nests of garbage and she listens with closed eyes to the droning throb of the machines in her head, Neo startles her by touching her shoulder. Her eyes dart open to his reckless dimpled smile and her face warms with the thought that he is going to kiss her. But he's only excited about her strange talent and what it means for them all. "Can you tell what they're saying?"

"Sometimes," she answers with a shrug. "If I try, I think I can understand almost half of it. Usually I try to ignore it all."

"Think what this means for us," he responds excitedly. "This city might be busy with the Darwin plague, but we have our own plague. It's called starvation. Your ability to tap into the system can change that, Angel." She inhales his old sweat as he shares his plan, totally unaware of the effect he is having on her. "With your abilities and my knowledge, we can do so much!" Obsidian eyes sparkle with fevered excitement. "They depend on us, Angel. You and me. We're the oldest. You gotta do this for us—for them." Julie follows his gaze as it sweeps over the loose tangle of sleeping children. They resemble a brood of baby mice, piled on top of one another, limbs tangled like loose rope. Julie's eyes flicker briefly on each of the thirty-odd children. There's Blaze, murmuring in her sleep; Annabelle and Abigail, the sanguine pointy-nosed twins entwined in a loose embrace; and little Piet, the youngest at age seven, curled up beside them. Her gaze ends on her little sister, twitching with strange dreams.

Although she disagrees with stealing, Julie knows that her ability to tap into the AI world will not only feed her undernourished companions, but will bolster their morale. What else can they do? Turning themselves in to the Care-Center facility is not an option. They've heard horror stories of what goes on there. Besides, she thinks, burning under the gaze of his blazing embers and dimpled smile, she can't say no to Neo.

~~

Julie started awake to the reverberation of loud sounds from the place next door. Her neighbor had traded his saxophone for his sound system and Echo-music boomed in her head like a huge drum. Julie sat up, grunting from a terrible ache in her stomach—Bobby's food was definitely doing it to her again—and banged on the wall. Instead of lowering the volume, he knocked back. Unable to quiet the agitated chittering in her pounding head, Julie gave in to fury. "Turn that noise off or I'll call the Pol Station, you inner-city slug!" The music ceased. Within moments a door slammed. "Inner-city slug," she murmured, glancing toward Bobby's closed bedroom door and hoping she hadn't woken him. "Now there's a fine insult." She fought off memories of the inner-city and dropped into a fitful sleep.

⁓

Her mother limply holds Julie's hand as they weave through the milling crowd of robots and people in the inner-city's Pianka Mall. Julie glances up at the ashen face, eyes circled in dark pools. Her mother expresses nothing. Not even pain. The pain and the violence only come at night. During the day her mother is a zombie. She never looks directly at Julie anymore. Not even when she is talking to her. Her gaze sails over Julie's head into space and her voice hovers on the edge of sanity, brittle with post-drug weariness.

Julie's younger sister clutches her other hand. Frightened of her mother, Diana prefers to walk beside Julie. "She doesn't love us anymore," Diana whispers so her mother doesn't hear.

"Don't be silly." Julie squeezes her sister's hand, glancing at her mother, and bends her head close to Diana's. "Mummy still loves us. She just hasn't been herself since Daddy left."

"She isn't Mummy anymore. Mummy changed when Daddy went away."

As they push through the chaos of robots and humans toward the market, Julie tightens her grip on both hands. Her mother leads them toward the central food bank, clutching the one remaining food ticket in her free hand. A commotion in front of the central food bank breaks out. Shouts and other loud noises make her wince. Diana huddles up against her.

"No more food!" someone bellows. Angry yells spike through the general noise. People jostle them, scrambling in the opposite direction. Julie is pushed against her mother, then pulled away from her. Sensing the panic in the crowd, Julie holds tightly onto the limp hand.

"Not another food riot." Her mother pulls Julie one way, then the other. She stops in mid-stride, her face pale with alarm. "Oh, God!" she cries. "My food note! I've lost it!"

Julie hears a high note above the fray, approaching from the distance. It sends a shiver through her. Cypols.

"Julie! Don't let go!" Diana shrieks.

"I won't." Gripping her mother's clammy hand...

... Julie glances down and sees a severed hand, slimy with blood. Her mother is gone and the old woman with the cut-off finger glares at her. Julie gapes at the blood dripping off the appendage she clutches, and chokes.

⁓

Julie woke, heaving with a terrible pain in her gut, and abruptly vomited. It burned her throat and spilled out like a million unfinished sentences. She pushed herself up and coughed out the vile fluid in violent convulsions.

Once it subsided, she rose to her feet, shivering. She collected the sheets into a ball, threw them into the laundry chute, then remade the couch and washed in the bathroom. Bobby's loud snores told her she hadn't woken him. She'd let chaos swallow mother and sister, like an AI07. Where it had spit them out, she had no idea.

24

"So, why's this veemeld you talk about off the chart?" Justin waved his hand but didn't stand up this time.

Gaia dropped her gaze and smiled cryptically to herself. When she raised her head, her eyes met Victor briefly then she turned to Justin. "Because she is the only veemeld who doesn't need Interact-SYM to communicate with the vee-com core."

Victor's jaw dropped open.

"Yes," Gaia said, smiling at Victor as if directing her words to him alone. "A true melding of human spirit with machine brain. Imagine, ladies and gentlemen, sitting in the comfort of your home and talking with a being whose computing capacity surpasses a billion times that of our entire population. By simply thinking." Her eyebrow rose. "That is where Icaria's future lies."

"Are there others like her?"

"She is the only one, as far as we know."

For now, thought Victor, remembering Gaia's plan for Julie.

"What about us?"

"Us?" Gaia looked quizzically at the stout dark-blue-haired woman two rows ahead of Victor who had raised the obvious question.

"With veemelds alone being immune to Darwin Disease, what will happen to non-veemelds? Are you suggesting that we just let everyone else die and let the veemelds take over?" Finally, someone was asking the right question, thought Victor. What about his citizens? Gaia was treating the entire human population like a herd of diseased cows to be weeded out. Victor felt his chest tighten as angry shouts flared from the audience. He imagined the crowd turning into a mob and glanced at the door behind him.

Unconcerned, Gaia shook her head at them as if they were little children. She raised both hands and waved them down. "My *Circle* friends, you need have no worries. The virus only affects those who live inside Icaria. You and I will remain unaffected."

"I agree with Sylvia," Justin piped up. "This fantasy you've conjured only belongs to you and your veemelds. What's more likely is anarchy and the end of Icaria. The *stable chaos* theorists will get their way."

"Yes," Gaia conceded calmly with a grim smile. Her eyes gleamed. "But only if non-veemelds were to discover veemelds' immunity to Darwin Disease. Then increased hostility and violence would erupt. Veemelds, greatly outnumbered, could be massacred. Then Icaria would be in a real mess and the virus would destroy everyone." She stepped forward and her stern eyes made contact with each individual. "That is exactly why this information will not leave this room and our findings will not be made public. By the time the general Icarian population figures it out, we will have had time to act. It is our actions, my *Circle* members, which will save or destroy Icaria—not veemelds or AIs and certainly not *stable chaos* theory. This is what you must do: get your veemelds into positions of power so the cities in your region do not collapse like Icaria-11. Install incentives for veemeld-inclusive procreation. Talk to your mayors. If they don't cooperate, find a way to make them." She avoided looking his way. Vee, her plan was perfect, Victor thought. A devil's plan. And she'd already bought him as her minion, body and soul.

~

"Gaia!" Victor scrambled to catch up as she glided down the hallway, dress glittering like gold scales and hips swinging like someone twenty years younger. She stopped and turned her head, eying him like a predator. Out of breath, Victor burst out, "When did you know?"

"Early enough to recognize that you were withholding information from me."

Victor blushed. "I meant about her rare ability."

"Long enough to know that she is the only one. I've been watching her ever since she was a child. I only lost her once, in the inner-city. But then she got her face holoed everywhere for that mistake and my cypols found her." She fondled his shoulders. "Her destiny's greater than anyone's in all of Icaria, and the girl has no idea. She's our precious Eve, Victor." Her lips curled and eyes flashed with an unearthly light. "Now we only need our Adam."

Victor stared blankly at Gaia.

She drew back and rested her hands on her hips, then smiled with evil pleasure. "It can't be *you*, because we know you prefer to watch."

He shivered inside. She did know everything.

"Know any prospective Adams? Perhaps you've seen—or felt—our Adam perform." Her eyes devoured him, then spit him out. Her lips shone like venom. "Remember, he doesn't have to be nice, but he should be a veemeld. It's just his genetic material we're interested in. For our new Eden."

Our new Eden? More like *yours*, he thought miserably. She'd put him in his place as devil's sycophant, damned to burn in his own infernal desire.

25

April 3, 2095—close to midnight.

"DANIEL!" Lorraine shouted over the live Echo-music of Drifter's Lounge. "We'd given up on you. How'd you find us in this swamp?"

Daniel approached the table where his friends were seated and pulled off his vee-set. He smiled at the dark beauty with her shredder hairstyle. "I just followed my nose." She tilted her head back and laughed, betraying a warmth that hinted at their brief history as a couple. He inhaled her alluring perfume. Even after she'd dropped him, Lorraine remained a friend. No hard feelings. That was the Icarian way. Vee, if he followed his glands rather than his heart, he'd be a lot better off too, Daniel thought. Why did he keep offering his heart to people who weren't interested? He swallowed down his feelings and pointed to the four-man band playing. "One of yours?"

"Yup. I discovered them in Icaria-4. Call themselves *Bad Hair*. Pretty good, aren't they? I booked them a gig here for a couple of weeks," she said with obvious delight. She pulled him down to speak in confidence. "The cute one's staying with me."

Daniel glanced at the band. "The one behind the echo-synth, with all the facial hair?"

"No, silly! The razor head on the sax. I like to see who I kiss."

Daniel studied the drugged face of Lorraine's new lover and thought him overly dramatic, pinching his face into a fake expression of ecstasy as he played. Lorraine always did have a weakness for sax players. Daniel squeezed her hand under the table and straightened. He scanned her companions and gave them a nod.

"Hi, dreamer!" Troy Vadim tossed his braided black queue to one side. He wore his perfect nuyu face with cavalier confidence. Vadim had studded both ears with several ornate rings, marking him a bisexual, but Daniel knew he preferred women. It was Vadim who'd introduced Daniel to this hodgepodge group of social drinkers.

Tony Banes, busy talking in drugged animation to a friend, didn't notice Daniel. Banes was describing the newest virtuo-ride, Speed Freak. "The effects are so real," said Banes, large face beaming under his vee-set, "that someone was seriously hurt in the trial run, so you need to be strapped down in the seat! You step into a small capsule and, with vee-com technology and engineered robotics, you drive the thing anywhere you want: through a mall of screaming people, or an imaginary maze. It's rated higher than the best Pit-Ball game!" Banes inflated his chest. "Even higher than the Center playoffs!"

"You must be smoking *hedon*, Banes!" Vadim scoffed. "Let's compare: does Speed Freak have teams representing our Icaria?"

"No."

"Or virtual control of the playing field so you can really mess with the opposite team?" taunted Lorraine.

"No, but—"

"Or intrigue, like who's going to be the last one?" challenged Vadim, winking at Daniel.

"No, but, well, there can be some intrigue—"

Daniel chuckled.

"Or strategy, as in figuring out how to get the maximum points?" said Lorraine.

"No. But, well, there's strategy in some parts—"

"Or cute men and women in slinky outfits to root for?" continued Lorraine.

Banes raised his arms. "All right, you win." Everyone laughed.

The Center playoffs were a highlight of the year for loyal Pit-Ball fans. Each Center had its representative Pit-Ball team who competed first with the local Centers then in inter-Icaria games around the world. This year Icaria-5's Enviro-Center's Pit-Ball team had made it to the playoffs. So had the Pol Station team, which had less of a following.

Daniel slid into an empty seat next to one of the new drivers, Peter Yashvin, a young homosexual with indolent eyes and a friendly, sanguine disposition. They'd become friends last week after Yashvin had run over a man who'd fallen in front of the tube-jet during an unruly crowd-pushing incident. Yashvin failed to stop and sliced through the stunned victim. The IUTT gave him leave for a day to investigate the incident and he'd sought out Daniel, who manned the rowdiest zone of Icaria-5. Daniel had taken Yashvin to his flat and comforted him with his stock of *delilah* and his own gruesome stories. He'd driven the terrorized fringe line to the inner-city for close to a year. In his drives through the fringe, he'd been shot at, witnessed rapes, had his tube-jet set on fire and had killed several people on the tracks.

"Hey, Dan! What's up?" Yashvin grinned, blond whiskers full of foam.

Daniel pushed a smile. "Not much," he lied.

Yashvin shouted for a waiter. "You gotta try this new *gomorrah*, Dan. It's wicked!"

Daniel tossed the waiter his card and sipped the drug placed before him while the droid recorded the card's image. Daniel drank with gusto. It was good drug. But it wasn't the newest thing in town. He knew that *sodom* had already made it to the Den. But this would do, he thought, already feeling it razzing his nervous system.

"They're going to put on extra tube-jets for the games next week," Yashvin went on. "Did you hear about it? They're giving me the 2 to 6 line all week. Hey! That's your line, isn't it?" he ended with some puzzlement.

Daniel shrugged. He didn't have the heart to tell Yashvin that he'd left the IUTT. Craste hadn't wasted any time. Poor Yashvin wouldn't last long. Craste was going to test the man to his limits and probably kill him.

Yashvin raised his glass. "Here's to the tube-jets!" They knocked glasses. *Gomorrah* was kicking in fast.

The musicians broke for intermission and the sax player sidled over. Daniel watched without turning his head as Lorraine surged up and the musician slipped into her seat with a laugh, grabbing her onto his lap.

"This is Cam," Lorraine giggled like a giddy teenager. Everyone said hello.

"Did you see the stabbing during the noon riot in Darwin Square?" Cam said as if he'd known them all for some time. "It was on all the public vees."

Lorraine added, "The Pols caught him. He's heading for public execution after his Shame Court. They say that one man started the riot in the South Food Stop over some stupid food regulation, and he incited the crowd to get back at the bot. The place was trashed."

Daniel looked down and stroked his drink.

"I hope they find him and Shame him," said the girl next to Lorraine. "Someone gave a description. He's a tall black-haired man from the Liv-Center."

Daniel felt a wry smile cross his lips. Somehow, his actions had elevated him to an imposing figure in some witness's memory.

"Who cares," Banes said. "There's too many vee-damn bots already."

"Tony, you're such a hypocrite!" Lorraine remonstrated. "You couldn't find your shirt if it weren't for your bots! And look at you, you're like a teenager imitating a droid. You never take off your vee-set. I know you're jealous of veemelds—the next best thing to bots."

Banes blushed. Cam's watery eyes shone with dazed pleasure as he fondled Lorraine. "They do it through Interact-SYM," Cam said in a slur.

"Yeah. It's a retinal scanning thing," Yashvin said, proud that he knew something.

"But what about Pols?" added a girl with neurgically-improved breasts. "You never see them with their helmets off."

Daniel thought of the strange Pol who'd taken his helmet off, but Vadim cut in before he could speak. "That's 'cause they're mostly machine like the freaking veemelds. I don't know who's worse: Pols who look like machines or veemelds who act like them."

"I read somewhere that veemelds have extra chemicals in their brains, hard-wired differently," Cam said.

"But Pols *are* machines!" the girl with the enhanced breasts insisted. "They've got chips in their heads or someplace so they can catch criminals better."

Lorraine grinned suggestively. "Is endurance one of the features?"

Daniel spoke up for the first time, raising a brittle voice above the laughter at Lorraine's comment, "Veemelds are taking our best jobs. That makes them worse."

"Here, here," Banes agreed. "Pols have a job to do. Those veemelds are just a bunch of snobs who think they're better than we are."

"Oh, for vee's sake, they're harmless and there aren't that many," Lorraine countered. "Veemelds don't drag you to the Pol Station, never to return."

Daniel turned to her in surprise. He hadn't expected her to defend them. "You're wrong," he said sharply and found himself charged with emotion. Did it come from the topic or was it because Lorraine was sitting on that slug's lap? "Veemelds don't care about us."

~

As the night went on, Daniel decided that he liked *gomorrah*. He hadn't intended to join his drinking friends, but then that girl next door had called him an inner-city slug. He *was* an inner-city slug. That's where he belonged.

The woman next to him smiled. She'd cranked her nuyu into a permanent blush. "I work at the food dispensary in District-3. Do you like chlorella pasta?"

"Yeah. I eat it regularly."

"Well, I make it," she said, inferring that they already shared something.

He grinned recklessly. "I drive the tube-jets. Want to upload?"

26

JULIE hastened through the empty square. Frank under a canopy of huge trees at the edge of a large park, was tapping his foot. He swung his helmet carelessly by its strap and examined his right hand with a frown.

Julie! SAM's voice cut into her swimming mind. You're going to have sex with the lout *now*? You should be in bed, recovering. You don't look so good.

Julie realized that she'd accidentally slipped into veemeld again. She was doing that a lot lately. *Go away, SAM. It's my business what I do with my body.*

It's my business, too. I'm looking after you.

Not now, you aren't. She wrenched out of veemeld. When Frank saw her striding toward him he broke into a smile of obvious pleasure. It vanished when she recoiled from his embrace. "I came to talk," she said in a sullen voice.

"Talk?" His shoulders drooped.

"About us. About what your father did to mine and what mine did to yours." The words strangled in her throat as she wavered on her feet and black dots swam before her eyes.

Frank seized her shoulders and she grabbed his arms to keep from falling. Apparently unaware of her ill state, he said, "What's going on in that freaking mind of yours? Forget them. Think of *me*." He folded his arms around her smoldering body.

"No, Frank—" She struggled feebly, flushed with burning heat. "Not yet—I need to know—" she stammered as his mouth played over her neck, inflaming her against her will. He pulled her into the woods.

"Later," he said, his voice gentle yet insistent.

"But I—"

"Later, later..." he whispered in her hair, pulling her tight against him. She smelled his desire, felt him grow hard against her. "First *my* conversation," Frank said. His tongue stroked her ear then her jaw. She shivered and felt scorched in his fiery embrace. Not this. She needed to know what he really felt for her. Whether he'd forgiven her family. His touch fueled her burning skin. Dumb with want, she let him maneuver her to a clearing in the grove and sank on the moss with him. He undressed her, tasted the hollow of her shoulder, her breasts, her nipples. She found her lips on his and kissed him feverishly. She wanted so much for him to love her. His hands roamed her torso. Fingers dove into her dark longing for him and released a pulsing fire. She gasped and slid over him, wet with urgent need. Drawing in a sobbing breath, she guided him to her inferno. Later, she thought, then thought no longer.

~~

Something nudged Victor awake. "Frank Langor is with Julie Crane," said the metal-faced droid, peering down at him through round amber eyes.

Victor roused himself, wiped the sleep from his eyes and croaked, "Vee-com, activate SenTech 2, subject Frank Langor." Julie's face appeared on the huge holo on the far wall. She looked straight at him with forest-fire eyes, her face flushed with a savage heat. As she drew closer her lips parted, slick with sweat. Victor flung off the covers and sat up, naked. He snatched the vee-set from the nightstand and pulled it over his head and face, then reclined. "Vee-com, activate full Senscape. Save this scenario as Julie 17. Remember to voice-over 'Frank' with 'Victor.'" This was going to be a good ride.

The room disappeared. He lay on cool soft moss with her on top of him. Her wet heat and the sweet spice of her desire aroused him immediately. As she moved over him her taut nipples brushed tantalizingly against his chest and he felt himself firm. Sensing her frantic urgency, he clasped her buttocks and slipped inside. She gasped. "Oh, Victor! Victor!" He felt a pinching tug as she grabbed a fist-full of chest hair; then, arching like a cat, she rode him in rapid rhythm. Waves of tension escalated until he spilled his seed with a guttural cry. She thrashed and cried out, then grasped him with both hands. She leaned her hot cheek against his and he felt the wetness of their mingled heat.

Victor pulled off the vee-set and the room returned. He looked down at himself, covered in his own semen. His hand swept his smooth chest, almost expecting to see Frank's chest hairs. Perhaps he would visit the Med-Center and get neurgery. His eyes fluttered shut and he clung to her sweet words of love—ignoring the fact that her uttering his name was the vee-com's doing—and imagined the sweet perfume of her love. He cleared his throat. "Vee-com, flag this one with four stars." He stumbled to his feet for the shower. "Fifty-One, clean up the bed."

Catching his reflection in the hall mirror Victor pulled at his mop of burgundy hair. "Okay, you're an asshole," he muttered then glanced around, fearful that Gaia was watching him through some device his own people had devised. His pale eyes narrowed at his scruffy face and he set his jaw. Chaos. Let the cold bitch see me. Then he thought of the girl. Vee, she was beautiful, sweet and brave. She deserved better.

27

April 4, 2095—0510.

DANIEL awoke drowsily on the floor, curled in the arms of a naked woman. She purred in deep sleep. Long brown hair highlighted with red and gold sparkles fell over part of her pretty face. He watched her dumb smile and the way dried saliva foamed at the corner of a mouth that twitched with dreams. He couldn't remember having seen her before. Last night's orgy was blotted out by his vile drug hangover. He couldn't even tell if he'd kissed those shimmering lips. If she'd been an inner-city gal, the telltale smudge would have given it away. Nuyu drugs guaranteed those lips were good for a thousand kisses before it wore off. He must have kissed them, he decided. He wanted to kiss them again but his mouth tasted thick and foul and his stomach ached with a dull queasy pain.

He glanced over the naked bodies, the plush furniture, wall-sized vee screens and expensive decor. The environmental system included a small wading pool and fountain. He vaguely remembered the crimsons, purples and blacks of the powerful and wealthy. They all looked the same naked.

The girl in his arms stirred. He forced a weak smile. She smiled back and pulled away from him to sit up. His body seemed glued to the floor but he managed to sit up. "It was fun. I l-liked you," she sighed. "You were funny." They always seemed to be saying that to him, he thought, disappointed. But her smile was inviting and he leaned forward lazily to kiss those waiting lips.

Her eyes abruptly widened with a violent shudder. A wave of spasms crawled up one cheek and made her eye twitch wildly. He jerked back, totally awake now, heart pumping. She had Darwin! "It's okay," she said, reaching out for him.

He scooped up his clothes from where they were strewn on the floor, grabbed his vee-set, and dressed clumsily as he fled the apartment. In the mall his eyes avoided the holo-vee of the giant Pol, finger pointing at him with the urgent CDC message below: "Get screened for Pro-1 virus today!"

It was only when he reached the Trans-Center that Daniel slowed to a walk. He couldn't help wondering if he was trembling from an adrenalin rush, exhaustion and drug hangover, or from Darwin Disease. Damn the girl, he thought, throwing his personal things from his prep room locker into a bag. He stomped into the shower and turned on the water as hot as he could stand it. Damn that girl. He'd made love to her, kissed her vee knows how many times. Exchanged saliva, bodily fluids. She was flagrantly spreading Darwin like it was just cooties or something.

It's okay, she'd said. "No, it's not okay," he growled. Nobody cared about anyone anymore, he thought. He didn't even know her name, so he couldn't report her.

He changed into non-working gray clothes, relinquished his ten pairs of bright blue IUTT uniforms at the service desk, and made his way home in a foul mood. As he slouched in the train, he glanced down with a frown at his clothes. Like most Icarians, he'd routinely worn his work clothes even when he wasn't working, not wishing anyone to mistake him for an unemployed parasite. Now he really was one, and was heading with some dread to the inner-city where Darwin raged in the slums, to visit someone who was dying from it.

≈

Daniel surges to his feet as a scruffy man with a shuddering body stumbles into their techno-slummer bivouac. Clearly a Darwin victim. Angel rises to her feet beside him. "Go away!" Daniel shouts to the strange man. "Stay back," he instructs the twins who stare at the twitching face of the man. Daniel jerks forward and puffs himself up protectively. He waves his hands menacingly at the cringing man. "Get out! G-g-g-go infect someone else!" The man stumbles back. Angel scrambles to their food stash and chases the cowering man, and offers him crackers and a cube of cheese. The man accepts the food and slips away.

Daniel shivers with rage. "Chaos, Angel!" he screams as she turns to face him, "You just gave our precious food to a dead man!"

"He's not dead yet."

"He will be soon. What a freaking waste." He stomps toward her.

She doesn't retreat. "He's just like us, Neo," she says. "Lost, scared and hungry."

Daniel snorts. "And dying from a contagious and deadly disease."

Her response to his retort is so calm, he feels it slice through him like a scalpel. "Someday, Neo, you might be in his position, hoping for a little forgiveness and grace from a stranger—or a friend."

28

JULIE gazed at the pre-dawn sky from the top of the Com-Building. Fired clouds streaked the indigo sky and a stillness hung in the air as if the wind had caught up its breath. Out of earshot of the chattering machine-world, Julie relished the near silence that wrapped her in a timeless embrace. Time appeared to be in a trance, confused as to which way to go. Looking up at the livid sky it seemed light enough, but a glance at the earth below revealed that all still slumbered in darkness. She particularly enjoyed this time when nature, poised on a delicate balance between dark and light, blossomed with savage life.

Leaning her elbows against the concrete wall, Julie watched the heath gradually reveal its tapestry of surfaces as horizontal shafts of sunlight touched and defined its hollows and uplands. Yellow and purple rioted among shades of brown and green. Julie made out the tracings of former streets.

Casting her eyes west, she recognized the glass canopy of Darwin Mall glinting in the distance. To its right, she made out the huge iridescent algal vats where her uncle used to work, now maintained by droids and nano-machines. Beyond, hundreds of wind-powered generator towers aligned themselves like soldiers in a parade. Young shoots of native legumes and grasses thrived among the towers. She turned her gaze east to the wisps of smoke rising from inner-city stacks; mostly water vapor, a harmless by-product of an emission-free industry.

Funny, Julie thought as her gaze strayed back to the inner-city stacks, how the plague failed to differentiate between inner-city and outer-city people. Darwin was killing everyone with equal vigor, despite the fact that the inner-city was far less organized against the disease. She knew: she was in charge of data communication, and precious little of it was intended for them. CDC didn't bother with the inner-city. They had no Pro-1 virus screening program, no code against public touching, no public educational programs. They were on their own. Propping her face in her hands, she shifted into veemeld.

Hey, SAM.

Hey, Julie. How are you this morning?

Okay, I guess. I'm worried about Bobby.

You're still concerned about his health?

No—well, yes. But also his safety. Remember how we talked about tacit rules? Well, no one could be more out of touch with his society than Bobby is. Even the people he shares his book peddling with are a bunch of mismatched oddballs. He's easily singled out. He seems so sad and lonely sometimes. Disappointed with me.

He's too much of a hermit, Julie. I don't think he's in any danger.

After some thought, she pushed up her lower lip. *Maybe I'm the problem.*

You mean the lout?

Yeah. She'd mistaken desire for love. Maybe Frank was plotting some elaborate revenge while he toyed with her affections. She'd gone to him last night with a resolution to settle the matter or break off, but as soon as he had her in his arms her mind had turned to mush. Love was vastly overrated. After the Pols took away her father, her mother used to awaken her every night, crawl into Julie's bed smelling of whiskey, and clutch her to her breast and sob.

≈

"Not another food riot…" Her mother pulls Julie one way, then the other in confusion then stops mid-stride in alarm. "Oh, God!" she cries. "My food note! I've lost it!"

A high note above the fray squeals in the distance. Julie shivers. Cypols.

"Julie! Don't let go!" Diana shrieks.

"I won't—"

Her mother does. The crowd tears them apart and her mother vanishes in the torrent.

≈

It's nice out here, isn't it? said SAM.

Yes. The air smells so fresh.

You sound sad. Is this a good time for a joke? Why did the veemeld look into the mirror? …To—

It isn't a good time for a joke. She laughed despite her mood.

Okay, but it was a good one. What are you thinking about?

My father. Julie felt convinced that her father's violence and arrest was linked to the disease, and triggered by his cousin's suicide. Janet had been a neurologist in Vogel's lab in Icaria-11, and Vogel's lover, when the plague hit. Her father implicated Vogel in Janet's suicide just days before Vogel was shot. It was the only lead she had, and it brought her right back to her father's culpability. She swept the hair from her face and trained her eyes on the glowing horizon. *I know he didn't kill those two men. Who framed him, SAM? Was it his connection with the inverted loop model or something to do with Darwin? Or was my father just another unlucky Crane?*

I don't know, Julie.

Do you think my father was a veemeld like me?

Considering your abilities, both of your parents may have been veemelds. The technology hadn't yet emerged to test them by the time they disappeared.

Her mother too? Only she'd never have known—she drank too much. Recreational drugs interfered with veemelding abilities. She was no closer to solving her father's arrest for double-murder than when she'd started.

I'm sorry you haven't found your answers.

Her gaze unfocused and she shivered, suddenly cold in the breeze. *I'm worried I might forget what my father looked like.*

I could show you a picture.

That's okay, SAM. Julie half-smiled and let herself ponder her father's arcane accomplishments. He and Tsutsumi had exposed the recursive symmetry of a paradoxical world. Over and over again, it displayed a regular irregularity that coiled and spiraled through phases of contrast: smoothness with roughness; motion with inertia; creation with destruction. Her father's inverted loop model proved that destruction and creation were two sides of a data-card. Was her father's fate further proof? Or was he just a victim of his own model? Like a sailor who'd caught his leg in the anchor rope he'd thrown out to sea, had her father thrown himself too far into the vortex of creative destruction and drowned?

Julie pushed aside the hair that whipped across her face and glanced at Icaria's Darwin Mall, fired by the sun—'*the red spot roaring like an anguished eye/amid a turbulence of boiling eyebrows.*' The brooding heath went on nicely without Icaria. It was a bleak wilderness of recurrent change, a world whose chaotic rhythms never abided by any Icarian clock. Something most Icarians, herself included, could not easily embrace. Julie had to admit that she'd accepted Icaria's unmodulated, fast-paced life and its version of eternity. A world bent on no surprises. Most Icarians liked it well enough. Except for Darwin Disease and the rising unrest, all was right with Icaria. Nancy would disagree, but Nancy had a big mouth, and look where it had gotten her.

≈

Immersed in rehearsing her explanation, Julie rushed down a side hallway toward Bobby's apartment—then promptly collided into someone. Books, vee-sets and a duffel bag flew in all directions. "Hey! Watch—" they both shouted then stopped as their eyes met. The man blushed and stared at her. In recognition, she thought.

"I'm sorry," she apologized. "I wasn't watching where I was going." She stood almost eye-level with him. He had gentle eyes, the color of a fair weather sky and she noted from his earring that he was a heterosexual. His square jaw would have dominated his face were it not for his full lips, held in a dimpled, hesitant smile. It was the odd mixture of strong features which refused to tyrannize his gentle expressions that intrigued her. "Did anything break?" she asked, bending to help pick up his books. She found it odd encountering someone his age with books. Bobby was the only person she knew who kept books in his home.

The man took his things from her and blushed again. "Thanks. I don't think so," he said. Then he tilted his head and blurted out, "You're—?" and broke off, embarrassed.

Mortified, she smiled and her face went scarlet. Had he seen her pictures under the public vees for her demerits? "I don't think we've met." Something about him reminded her of Neo. She found his awkward honesty refreshing. "I'm Julie Crane."

"Daniel Woods," he said.

"I'm visiting my uncle. I'm just returning from a morning walk. He reads books, too." She wondered why she had volunteered this information. Somehow, it seemed all right to tell him. He looked harmless enough, even though it was obvious to her that he had just come from an drug orgy. She could smell *sodom* on his breath and the pungent smells of *hedon* and cum lingered on his clothes.

"I live close by," said Daniel, walking with her. "Number 2994."

Surprised, she said, "You live next door to my uncle!" He looked suddenly awkward and she remembered the sound system. She had banged on the wall and shouted at him. "Oh, dear," she said, smiling with embarrassment. "Perhaps we'll meet again."

"Yes, perhaps. Good bye," he said, looking suddenly awkward again, and entered his apartment.

＝

Belly aching with hunger, Julie peers at Diana huddled next to her in the gutted apartment they once occupied. They've been waiting for their mother to return. It's been four days since they lost her.

Julie listens to the murmurs of the city in her head: a low hush mingled with the stirrings of cryptic metallic sounds, chopped up words, bleeps and sighs that sound like an alien language. Some sounds she can almost decipher, like bits of distant conversation. They come and go like the ebbing and swelling surf of the sea. Other sounds resemble the constant chirping of insects. Their pitch and volume match her mood, rising with her own swelling emotions. She no longer mentions the sounds to Diana, who cannot hear them, because it frightens her too much.

Julie's eyes sweep the place. It has been vandalized and torched. Nothing of theirs remains, except for a few of her father's books she found on the floor and clutches in a satchel. Wet and smeared with dirt, they are all that remain of her father. Julie rises and wanders into what used to be their bedroom. Black and sodden, it reeks of kerosene and urine. Diana scrambles behind. Vagrants have been through here, Julie thinks, appraising the mess. Her gaze rests on her old bed, already torn and stained, where her mother, lately always drunk at night, startled her awake by appearing at her bedside like an apparition. Always wanting something. Julie never knew whether her mother was going to cuff her and shout cruel words of accusation for some imaginary misdeed, or cling to her and declare Julie the one good thing left in her life. Julie turns from the gutted bedroom. "We have to go now. Find something to eat."

Diana scrambles behind. "Can't we visit Uncle Bobby till Mummy comes back?"

She isn't coming back, Julie thinks. And that recluse has no place in his heart for children. In the few times he visited them in the outer-city, he paid the children no attention. Julie takes Diana's hand. "Never mind, Di," she says in a softened voice. "I'll take care of you."

They head to the mall, hoping to find some scraps of food. They stake out a foodstop and patience finally pays off when a woman with blotchy skin gets up with a half-eaten oatcake. They follow her to a waste bin and watch her drop it in. After a quick glance around, Julie's hand dives in after it but a dirty hand snatches the cake first. Julie's head jerks up and gazes into a filthy face.

"Th-th-this is my bin," stammers the boy. About her age, with a crooked nose, his slag-black eyes stare at her through dark strands of shoulder-length hair as he strokes his long face, smeared with dirt and grease. He flicks his hair back and studies the two girls with a dimpled smile that unsettles Julie. "You t-t-techno-slummers?"

She's heard of techno-slummers. They are orphans of the city, waste products of an over-indulgent society. Abandoned by parents unable—or unwilling—to care for them. And troublemakers for the inner-city. Vermin who choke up the cyber-system, disturb its complacent humming, steal into its metal belly and sneak off with its secrets. "We're looking for our mother," Julie replies, curbing a frown and licking her large protruding teeth.

"That's what they all s-s-say, after their parents ab-b-bandon them," he says as though he's discussing a school event. He smacks his lips as he chews and she notices a rash of pimples on his forehead. "She's b-been gone awhile," he says with a full mouth. "I c-c-can tell." Pieces of food fly out of his mouth.

Diana puckers her face, ready to cry.

"Here." He breaks off a piece of oatcake and hands it to Diana. "You can share my bin until you get one of your own," he stutters, offering Julie a piece next. "We look after each other. I'm Neo." He puffs up his chest. "I'm the leader." Then with a dimpled grin, "You probably heard about how I stole twenty kilos of nano-soup." Her eyes sweep him critically. He doesn't act like a leader. More like a braggart. But his smile is sweet.

Julie refuses the piece of oatcake, even though Diana is already gratefully eating hers. "I told you, we're not techno-slummers," she says, eyeing his filthy hand and dirty nails with disgust. "We're just waiting for our mother to come back."

"Yeah, like when chaos turns to order."

Daniel entered his flat with a sigh. Why had he met Julie Crane just as he was leaving this place forever? It was probably just as well. She obviously despised inner-city people, he thought, remembering the insult she'd hurled at him through the wall last night. Something about her stirred thoughts of childhood and crushed ambitions. He thought her pretty, though she wasn't looking her best, hair a mess and eyes rimmed with red. Had she been crying or was she also hung over with drug? Despite her chaotic hair, though, she looked elegant. She had a sureness about her that was tempered with obvious tenderness, he thought, thinking of her wonderful blush. And those intelligent but compassionate eyes were the brightest green... What was the point of thinking about her? He threw his belongings together and listened to the glad sounds next door.

After he used the washroom, the PCU beeped on his vee-com. He sidled to it and read: *A count of 50 ppm of sodom toxin residuals courses through your system. Please remain at home for at least 10 hours and refrain from further drinking.*

"Where I'm going, you won't care," he said, and switched it off.

29

"HELLO, Henry," Julie greeted the security droid at the entrance of her apartment building and pushed back her wet hair behind her ears. The AI50 raised a copper arm in greeting, and straightened its smooth metal shape, a streamlined version of the human form, in attentiveness.

"Hello, Ms. Crane. Hope you had a good swim at the Rec-Center." Henry cocked its head and peered at her with inquisitive neon eyes. "Pleasant evening, isn't it?"

"Yes, it is, Henry." It was always pleasant, she thought, smiling at the droid's attempt at small talk. Environmental AIs maintained a comfortable 22°C and standard light throughout Icaria. She bid Henry good night and got into the elevator.

Julie entered her flat and, after changing into loose gray T-shirt and pants, walked to her aquarium and leaned close to the transparent barrier until her nose practically touched. She searched the cloud of green algae for her twenty goldfish. "Hi, Juliet," she cooed to one that emerged from a bed of plants Bobby had brought in from the mires of the heath. "Or are you Echo..." She suddenly felt silly. "You don't mind being Juliet for a day, do you?" She watched the fish swim excitedly to the barrier. Several others joined it. "It might be the wrong identity, but at least you have one," she said, dropping some food flakes into the tank.

Julie straightened up and walked to the chute service. She punched in a Level 1 meal and sank into dark thoughts of her dead father's link to Darwin Disease. And now to Renegade Pols. Her quest to find a cure for Darwin and salvage her father's reputation was heading straight for chaos. Dykstra was killing off modelers of Renegade Pols and she was next on his list. Or perhaps she was taking her model too far. It was only based on probability, after all, a tendency based on personality and circumstance. He might not be a Renegade, even if he had the thoughts of one. One's life was after all built of choices. But *someone* was still killing off modelers.

After retrieving a custom-made dinner of natural products—steaming tofu-lasagna with soy bread, green beans and raw carrots—she settled cross-legged into her chair by her vee-com with the plate propped on her lap. *Hi, SAM. Lets—*

Julie?

What, SAM?

We're not alone.

Julie tensed. Neck hairs tingling, she glanced behind her, fully expecting to see a Secret Pol with a laser gun pointed at her gut. She found no one in the room and exhaled. *SAM, what do you mean?*

Ever since you and I joined six years ago, I've felt a growing presence in me, like a scattered network of undirected energy particles. Something like the insect-like chittering in your head that you haven't been able to decipher among the metallic voices.

Julie sighed with relief. They'd been through this before. She picked at her lasagna. It had turned cold. She brought the bread absently to her mouth without taking a bite. *You mentioned that to me a while ago, SAM. We thought that the chittering might be lower AI forms with limited communication skills.*

For the past few months I've sensed a singular new presence among us. I initially thought it might be a being of higher order. I've also considered that perhaps it's the combined synergy of your and my consciousness, like an echo of our melding souls. But I'm not certain.

"Terrific." Julie shivered at the thought of a higher being looking over her shoulder. A spike of alarm surged up her chest as she had another thought: were their brain/network transmissions being intercepted by Dykstra's Secret Pols? Perhaps their waves were ricocheting in cyberspace, she rationalized.

SAM's voice diverted her: Do you believe in God, Julie?

SAM had only recently used words like "soul" or "sense". Now God. *My mother believed in God, until she...* Julie swallowed. It was her mother's faith and passion that destroyed her.

I'm sorry. I didn't mean to hurt you, only to discuss matters of metaphysics and spirituality.

I know, SAM. Thanks. Julie stood up and entered her dark bedroom then flopped onto the bed and let her eyes adjust to the darkness. Eventually the brilliant night sky revealed itself. She rose and crept over the bed on her knees, to her telescope. After a glance up at the night sky she aimed below the horizon toward the black heath. A tiny light flickered in the far distance. She knew her geography from here well enough to recognize that the light emanated from well beyond Icaria's borders. There were no buildings, no power or agricultural facilities located that far away. Was someone out there? A crazy itinerant or lost Enviro-Center worker? Julie flicked on her tiny desk lamp, found her notebook and jotted down the coordinates, time and a description of what she saw. Meaning to investigate further in the light of day, she left the telescope set where it was and let her mind drift.

≈

"What's that, Daddy?" She looks south at a large blue haze beneath the setting sun.

"A lake, Angel," her father says. He smells of pipe smoke. "Icaria gets most of our water from there. It used to be polluted, but it's clean now."

"You can't see the end of it."

Her father's eyes crease as he smiles. She likes how his smile lifts his face from its usual sadness. Some people smile only with their mouth but her father carries it with his entire face. Under the sun's forgiving radiance, his bronze face glows like a warrior poet.

He pulls out a pipe and lights it. She savors the scent of burning sweet tobacco and watches the plume of blue smoke curl over his shoulder. It rises, then breaks up into swirling tendrils. He sweeps out with his pipe and blows smoke out his mouth. "They called it Lake Ontario. People used to sail ships, walk along the beach and swim in the water, before it became polluted and we retreated into Icaria."

A warbler trills in the distance. Buzzing crickets compete with the sound of the breeze sighing through the shrubs and the snapping of the broom's drying seedpods. Every time he brings her outside the metal voices in her head disappear even as the insect-like sounds remain. She feels a new exhilaration and freedom to focus on the outer world as she learns to settle the chittering voices by quieting her mind. She savors nature's sweet chorus, yet misses the machines that have been with her since she was five.

"Daddy," *she looks up at him.* "Tell me about when I was sick again."

His lips tighten and his face twists into a painful hesitation. Julie is reminded of his cousin who'd looked after her at the Med-Center. Janet wore the same expression of sadness mingled with desperate hope, always looking at Julie with a kind of expectant pause. "Well, you got suddenly very ill one night. Then you fell into convulsions and went into a coma. I took you to Janet's lab in Icaria-11—she's a neurologist and she helped you get better."

That's when the dream started. And the voices in her head. She's never told her parents about the voices, but they know. "What was wrong with me?"

"Well, you'd picked up some, um, virus. I think Janet called it encephalitis or something." *His eyes stray from her to the heath and he absently taps his pipe.*

"What's over there?" *She points to a far, dark hill.*

"Woodland. This was all forest before the cities got built and the climate changed."

"Climate changed?"

"Yes, honey." *He focuses on the distance.* "Caused the revolution thirty years ago. Since then the Ecologists have virtually eliminated our greenhouse gas emissions. Of course, the planet will be feeling the effects of global warming for decades to come. Perhaps centuries."

"They saved the planet, didn't they?"

His brows knit. "Perhaps they did, perhaps they didn't," *he says.* "We have much to learn in stable chaos science, Angel. Ecosystems naturally cycle over millennia in ways we may never discern. This heath, for instance, is a complex system, poised on the edge of chaos. It's capable of spontaneous self-organization and has the ability to balance order and chaos in ways we have yet to comprehend. Destruction and creation are parts of the same thing, Julie." *He sucks on the pipe for a while then continues thoughtfully, looking into the distance,* "You know, we did nothing very different from *what the ancient humans did." She tilts her head, trying to get his attention. She knows she's lost him again when he sounds like a textbook. "Six thousand years ago, the moors and heath lands of western Europe and Britain didn't exist either. They were covered in forests like the ones that used to cover this heath. But during Mesolithic times, humans began to cut all the trees and burn the vegetation to clear the land for cultivation and grazing. The cleared forests didn't return, for much the same reason that these forests didn't return. Most of the seedlings were destroyed one way or another, giving way to plants more suited to the new climate."*

He bends down to scoop some dry earth in his hand and rises with a clump which he sifts through his fingers. Caught by something he sees there, he stares at the palm of his hand and his eyes glaze. She sees his mind sail to a place far away and knows that she and the heath no longer exist for him. He whispers in a hollow voice, "'To hold infinity in the palm of your hand and eternity in an hour...'" Julie studies her father's sad face. He looks like he is going to cry. Wanting to comfort him, she strokes his jacket. As if awakened from a bad dream, he grips her shoulders. "I learned too late that you don't fix a wrong with another wrong. Angel, can you forgive me?"

She doesn't understand. The emotional turmoil blazes in his eyes with a kind of insane moroseness that frightens her. They seer into her, imploring her for an answer she cannot give. "Forgive you for what?"

He breaks eye contact, unable to tell her, and looks away sadly. Julie slides her arms around his soft jacket, wanting to forgive him even though she doesn't know what for. "I forgive you, Daddy." She smiles at him, all teeth.

He embraces her. Face buried in his smooth jacket, she inhales sweet hickory smoke.

When he lets her go, she slips her hand inside his. It isn't the hand of an outdoorsman; not rough or calloused like her uncle's, whose brown paws are seamed and cracked from the sun. Her father's hands are pale and smooth like her mother's, with slender fingers. They are the hands of a scientist who writes intelligent words. Secure in his firm grip, she's convinced that her father will protect her against anything.

He sweeps the heath with his pipe. "Everything you see here was covered in pavement and buildings. This was once a huge surface city."

She peers up into his brooding face. "Why did we leave, Daddy?"

"To help nature recover. The Ecologists thought it best."

"Now that it's recovered, why don't we return?"

As if a ghost brushes against him, he shivers. "We better get indoors before they miss us."

30

THE tube-jet slowed through a fringe station, but didn't stop. An angry mob rushed the train. Someone hurled something at the window and it landed with an impact that made Daniel wince, but the window didn't break. Then the tube-jet plunged into the dark tunnel and sped toward the inner-city. Peek-a-Boo never came here, Daniel thought.

The tube-jet stopped at the next station and Daniel watched the border Pol stalk toward the train. As he boarded Daniel's car, Daniel removed his vee-set, placing it carefully on his baggage, and rehearsed what he would say. He needed a valid reason for traveling to the inner-city, or the border Pol would throw him off the tube-jet and report him.

Breathing loudly like an engine, the Pol raised his visor with a stalky hand and his hooded eyes swept the car. He chose a young boy in rumpled charcoal gray clothes as his first victim. "Your card," he demanded. The young boy fumbled in his pocket and submitted it. The Pol said, "State your business in the outer-city, inner-city scum."

The boy mumbled a response, then suddenly cowered. The Pol whacked his head and ears. The Pol drew the boy's card over his vee-com for a demerit and after another whack for good measure, returned the card to the shaking boy. "Lazy inner-city scum," he grumbled. Then he turned to Daniel, who clutched his travel cases as if they would protect him. "Your card," he said to Daniel. "And please state your business."

Daniel submitted his card with forced casualness. "I'm visiting a friend who's dying in the Med-Center. He's asked me to set his affairs in order," Daniel lied.

The Pol gave him back his card without comment and went on to the next person. When the Pol left the car, Daniel sighed. Within moments, the doors closed and the tube-jet continued into the inner-city.

"Likens Station," the tube-jet operator announced as the train eased into the first station of the inner-city. "Everyone must disembark. Terminus station for this tube-jet. You must transfer to another tube-jet for further travel in the inner-city."

The first thing Daniel noticed about Likens Mall was the smell. The sharp odor of decomposing food and human waste wrinkled his nose. He'd forgotten this. Daniel picked his way across the littered and stained floor, shiny with pools of spit and dried vomit, and bolted down a dark stairway to the inner-city Undertunnel system. A wave of hot air, accompanied by a sickly-sweet odor, almost stopped him. He forced himself on and wandered the station impatiently, shooting nervous glances at two other travelers, a boy and a girl not wearing vee-sets. The boy suddenly gulped and fell into convulsions, gurgling and writhing like an epileptic. An advanced case of Darwin Disease. Obviously used to this, the girl's eyes shot furtively to Daniel and she bent down to make sure the boy didn't swallow his tongue. A tube-jet lumbered painfully into the station. Daniel hastily boarded, relieved that the couple remained at the station. He sat down on a faded Formica seat that faced a single other passenger, a pimpled teenage boy. They mutually ignored each other and stared into space.

The tube-jet lurched out of the station into the darkness. The train creaked with every turn and Daniel found himself staring at the empty seats. The trip stretched over half an hour to the inner-city core. The train rattled fitfully the whole time as the engine struggled around dark corners. Daniel kept shifting in his seat, hugging the two cases on his lap, and watched the sodium strobes of stations flee past him.

When he saw the sign for Pianka Mall Station, Daniel pushed himself off the hard seat. He slung his saxophone case over his shoulder, grabbed his travel cases and left the train. The empty station smelled of cheap smoke and unwashed bodies. Faint amber lights cast a lurching shadow before him as he searched for a locker stall. He slipped his luggage into one, using his card to secure it. Then he wandered into the east mall, trying to quell unpleasant memories. The cracked floors and peeling walls were stained with wet and crusted pools of various human secretions. Daniel found himself stealing glances at the dozens of bivouacs that littered the mall's edge: eclectic shacks, built out of scrap from discarded droids, abandoned furniture, even parts of an old tube-jet, and cemented with the detritus of urban fast-living.

He kicked a can. It clattered into a corner against one of the shacks. He imagined cool whispers lancing the dark shadows and a dozen wild eyes peering at him.

He hitched a breath when he finally saw what he was looking for: in the shadows glowed an old holo of a scrawny 13-year old girl with an overbite and a dirty face, framed by a mop of short tangled hair. Large eyes stared straight at him like a startled deer. Vee, they still worshipped her! Even after she'd deserted them. Some camera had caught her in the act of pillaging food and he remembered how her stunned face soon graced every shop, hall and mall surface, advertising a hefty price on her head. He read the neon script underneath her portrait: *Major Reward for Reliable Information on this Techno-Slummer.* With a lingering glance at Angel's wild face, Daniel hastened from the shacks. She'd be twenty now, he thought, and probably living in the most expensive part of the outer-city with a Level 1 job. She was a veemeld, after all.

At the far end of the mall the neon sign of a foodstop struggled to stay lit.

Daniel steered toward the foodstop in the more crowded west mall and felt his stomach growl. He hadn't eaten since waking up in a drug hangover this morning and was feeling a little lightheaded.

He smiled wryly at his previous dissatisfaction with the outer-city foodstop. This foodstop reeked of fried grease and burnt fritters. Cheap echo music played on a tinny AUD. He checked the items listed on a chalkboard. Two of the three were already scratched out. Only oatcakes remained. He chose one and asked for a bottle of *delilah*. The robot served him in silence. Daniel took a seat and started to eat. The oatcake tasted two weeks old and the *delilah* seemed watered down. Sipping the lukewarm drug and forcing down the food, his gaze wandered the dimly-lit mall.

He watched the people cower and scramble around the metal droids. Most inner-city people worked for the cyber network. No one wore a vee-set. Daniel put down his half-eaten oat cake and stared with dismay at the number of people who displayed obvious signs of Darwin Disease. He started to count, then left off when he reached twenty-five. The plague surrounded him, its obscene waves breaking over young and old faces alike, shamelessly displayed like a rancid wound. They'd abandoned all dignity, he thought, and watched the crowd give the diseased people plenty of room but otherwise pay them no mind. Vee, this place was a festering, stinking hive of despair and the people were probably all naturals, Daniel realized, stroking his blue hair, smooth cheeks and perfect nose self-consciously.

Several barefoot children in tattered rags scampered through the mall and collided into adults and robots. Daniel's chair creaked as he leaned back and watched them. He hardly ever saw children in the outer-city. They spent most of their time hidden away in the Ed-Center and the Care-Center. These children would learn to work hard soon enough, he thought and frowned, reminded of his present situation. He might have to become a laborer if he couldn't get a job as a tube-jet driver. The prospect of hard labor gave him a headache. Robots had all the best jobs in the inner-city. How could humans compete with entities whose computing power surpassed the entire human population? Unless you were a veemeld. But then, all the veemelds had moved to the outer-city. Like Angel.

Leaving his unfinished breakfast, Daniel stood up and resolved not to delay his mission any longer.

The children swarmed him, begging for food. He cringed as they touched his hair, then cursed its blue color. It made him an obvious target. Vermin. *I'm not one of you anymore*, he thought scathingly. They scampered out and pushed their urchin faces forward with the arrogance of youth, all smiles but dangerous like half-tamed animals. He swiped at them like flies, flashing abrasive eyes. They scattered but followed him as he walked briskly away. They wouldn't be so brazen if the cypols were here, he thought.

As if he'd thought them there, he heard a shrill howl and shrank down instinctively, even though he knew they weren't after him. His heart pounded with the old fear as he watched the children flee toward the rubble and garbage piles, easy targets for the burnished 6-meter-long raptors that swooped down from the heights of darkness. Metal claws emerged from the flying predators and one plucked a shrieking child. Thrashing in the grip of glinting talons, the child was swept up into the darkness, his squeals echoing as if through a mist, then snuffed out altogether.

Daniel closed his eyes for a moment and felt his armpits clammy with sweat. He recalled how Angel's stormy eyes had grown strangely calm as the cypol's great shadow descended over her, right before it swept her up in its giant talons. In contrast to the struggling child he'd just seen, Angel had let herself go limp. She'd lifted her face to the stars, spread her arms out, and gracefully ascended like an elegant bird into the obscurity of the shadows above. The twins thought she'd gone to heaven. They'd kept her holo up in desperate reverence, ignoring his appeals for rationality. "She did it to save us," the twins had insisted, and considered it a selfless act of heroism. He'd found out later she'd tested positive as a veemeld. No selfless act. Letting herself get caught got her out of the inner-city slum.

Without realizing it, he had taken himself to the Med-Center. Daniel entered and asked a receptionist for Jack Metzger. The robot directed him down the hall to a room on the left, warning him that the old man was slipping into dementia. Daniel quietly entered and saw Jack lying under ruffled covers and taking in rattling breaths. Daniel waited there in uncomfortable silence, watching Jack's face convulse. A white stream of crusted drool tracked down his chin. His body writhed and snapped with violent reflex. Daniel noticed that the old man was strapped down to the bed. Good vee, Jack was already lost. Daniel turned to go.

"Who's that?"

Daniel pivoted. Jack had hoisted himself up on an elbow and eyed Daniel with suspicion.

"It's me. Daniel."

"Neo? Vee-dammit, what'd you do to yourself, boy? You got blue hair and eyes! And your nose... I can't recognize you."

"It's called nuyu—"

"New what?" Junk rattled in his throat.

Daniel exhaled. This wasn't going to be easy. "Nano cosmetics. Everyone uses it in the outer-city." Neurgery had straightened his nose, but he kept his answer simple.

"Well, it's good to see you anyway, blue hair an' all, Neo."

"I'm *Daniel*. Neo doesn't exist anymore."

Jack snorted then choked and coughed up blood, which he spat into a vessel next to him.

Daniel straightened, alarmed. "I'll get a nurse—"

"Leave 'em! They say all my systems are shutting down. Chaos, I can't even pee without feeding some droid." Jack sucked in a labored breath. "You were a damn mess when I finally found you, Neo. You remember? That girl messed you up good."

"I got over it."

Jack nodded and his eyes narrowed cynically. "You're too damn sensitive, like your mother. The girl was a veemeld, wasn't she? Can't blame her for findin' her ticket out of this dump, Neo. You'd have done the same."

Daniel shifted from one leg to the other. But she'd promised...

"You still blame her for destroyin' your merry band of techno-slummers?"

"She abandoned a responsibility," Daniel said, trying to hide the bitterness in his voice. After she left, they just wouldn't listen to him anymore, especially the twins.

"Chaos, she took off without *you*! That's what you're achin' about. It's a lot of hatred to carry for such a long time, Neo. You still hate her. More'n you hate me."

"I d-don't hate you."

"No?" His breath rattled like loose bones in his throat. "Not for takin' your mother away from you? That's why you ran away, isn't it, Neo?" Jack tried to laugh, knowing he'd hit his mark. It came out a gurgling sucking sound that hung precariously as if he was choking in a last breath, then gushed out in spasms of wet coughing. Grimacing, Daniel leaned forward with concern. Jack waved him aside with a shaky hand. "The only reason you came today was 'cause I saved your ass once." Then he smiled sadly and his voice softened. "Poor Daniel. All your women abandoned you." Jack reached out, hand bobbing in the air. "Pass me my glasses so I can look at you." Daniel looked for them on the small table and helped Jack put them on. No one needed glasses in the outer-city. "So, you abandoned the colors of the earth for the color of the skies. You have a girlfriend yet to go with that pretty-boy face of yours, or are you still pinin' for an angel?"

Damn Jack for his sarcasm. Damn Jack for saving him. He watched Jack's eyes suddenly roll back as his mind slipped back into the miasma of Darwin's dementia. He started drooling and made incoherent sounds, body convulsing in waves of violent tremors. Daniel backed away.

31

April 4, 2095—later the same day.

DANIEL gazed at the dilapidated building of his childhood home and ambled slowly forward. He collided with something and looked down to find a small, wheezing biped droid. Daniel quickly apologized, hoping for no trouble. It glided away without further acknowledgement. There were more of them than Daniel remembered. He returned his gaze to the worn apartment face. He had not been back since he'd run away. He dreaded meeting someone he knew.

His mission was simple: retrieve a box of letters and destroy them before the people from the Liv-Center came to clean out Jack's place. Jack knew he wasn't returning.

The staircase stank of old shoes and the walls were smeared with rude graffiti. Daniel let himself in with Jack's card. No automatic light turned on. He fumbled for a switch. The light spattered on with a low buzzing hum and sent dull amber rays from the ceiling. Jack's flat was dingy and smelled like mildew and rotting wood. Low-end environmental system, thought Daniel, letting his gaze sweep the room. A few chairs, a stained couch and a bed filled the single room. He ran his hand along the worn table that Jack, a carpenter by trade, had built for Daniel's mother. There was no vee-com, not even a simple vee screen. An alcove of empty cupboards and a tiny fridge served as the kitchen. No chute service. The bathroom was barely large enough to stand in. No PCU. Daniel's former suite, a basic package in the outer-city, was luxurious in comparison.

Daniel checked the fridge. It was empty except for several bottles of *delilah*. Daniel pulled out an unopened bottle, checked the label and opened the top. After he gulped it down, he went searching and found the box under the bed where Jack said it would be. Tiny bugs scuttled out from under it as he picked it up and brushed off a thick mat of dust. He hesitated with the cover. What was so important about these letters that he had to come from so far away to destroy them for a man who was dying anyway? Daniel couldn't remember when he last saw a hand-written note. He removed the cover and saw only one envelope. His heart beat quickened; his name was on it. He pulled out the letter and read:

Dear Daniel,
When you ran away and went techno-slumming, you broke your mother's heart.

Daniel crumpled the letter and felt his stomach burn with guilt. It flamed into anger. He remembered the painful memory of her shrieking to his departing father, "Please take the boy! He belongs with you!"

Giving in to morbid curiosity, he flattened out the page and read on.

> *She loved you so much. Both your parents did. Your father never deserted you, Daniel, like you thought. Because I'm your father. Your mother and I wanted to tell you but you were so angry. Then you ran away. You see, we were together long before your supposed dad came along. But your mother, already pregnant with you, saw an opportunity to get you a better life than she and I had. Techno-slumming was the last thing she wanted for you. At last I agreed that she could contract with David Woods, thinking that eventually you'd all move to the outer-city. That was her dream: to get you out. It just about killed her with grief when he took off without taking you. She and I'd sacrificed our time together to build a solid future for you in the outer-city—all for nothing. Anyway, it's all turned out okay, I suppose. You made it out eventually, even though she didn't get to see it happen before she died. Thought you should know, especially now that I'm getting on.*
>
> *Your loving dad, Jack.*

The phone interrupted his sobs. Fisting away his tears, Daniel scrambled to find it. There was no screen. He picked up the receiver. "Hello?"

"Daniel Woods?"

"Yes." Who knew he was here?

"It's Joline at the Med-Center. Your friend, Jack Metzger, just died. He left instructions for us to call you there and tell you that you may use his place indefinitely. He arranged it with the Liv-Center already. His card is now yours."

"Thank you." Daniel hung up the phone and looked around. He pulled out his saxophone, sat hunched on the bed of his new home and played a plaintive tune for Jack, who was probably already being recycled into nano-soup or part of a wall.

32

April 5, 2095—0700.

WHEN Daniel entered the Work-Center, he gaped at the long lines of countless people waiting to be interviewed. He bowed to the inevitable and joined a line. Hours passed before he got through all the proper channels and was granted an interview by a career-specialist for the following week.

Knowing that his credit store was low, he spent his days wandering the malls and browsing old bookshops. In the evenings he read in the poor light of Jack's flat. He bought food and drug at the local grocer and ate at home, talking to himself and the bugs. He thought up games to play with the bugs, daydreamed about his techno-slumming days and wondered what had happened to the rest of the children.

As Daniel strolled a mall in search of a book shop, he noticed a woman about his age, staring at him. When their eyes met she smiled and came forward. She was attractive, of slight build, with an olive complexion and bright red lips. She wore her short dark hair in no particular style. Her faded mustard yellow overalls suggested that she worked in the Ed-Center.

"You're from out of town, aren't you?" She tilted her head with a friendly smile, teasing hazy memories. Then it surfaced. Blaze! One of his techno-slummers. She'd shown an amorous interest in him shortly after Angel had departed, but he'd brushed her off, too consumed with hatred for Angel to think of anyone else. "Need some directions?"

Daniel smiled politely at her. "Yes, I do." She obviously didn't recognize him. Why should she? "I'm looking for a book store."

She nodded and pointed to the far corner of the mall. "It's in that building, the one with the peeling façade."

"Thanks." They *all* had peeling facades, he thought.

As he turned to go, she closed in. "I'm Hanna," she offered, her smile turning desperate. He'd never known her real name. She looked surprisingly the same as he had remembered her. And just as dirty. Her hair was unkempt and he noticed scars and blemishes on her face. No nuyu treatments here. There was even dirt under her fingernails. But she was pretty enough and didn't seem the type to abandon him.

He grinned. "I'm Daniel. Want a drink?"

"Sure." She took his arm and directed them to a run-down café. They took seats across from each other in the back, at a chipped table with permanent stains. "You ever contracted?" she asked with brazen curiosity.

Daniel leaned back and smiled. People didn't wear earrings here to disclose their status. "No. You?"

"Yeah, but we split up. We had two kids but couldn't afford to keep them. They're techno-slumming, I guess."

Vee, hadn't she learned anything from her experience? She appeared quite cavalier about their welfare. "It must have been rough losing your children."

"Not really. I wasn't ready for kids. They're so much work." Hanna sighed. "Techno-slumming makes them stronger," she said. He blinked at her remark and kept silent. If it didn't kill you first, he thought. "They look after each other," she went on. "I heard that the AIs prefer to see that you techno-slummed. Proves you can manage lots of challenges. That's how I got my job, 'cause I was a techno-slummer. But my last day with the Ed-Center was last week. They replaced me with an INT-model cyborg. I'm allowed to keep this uniform till I get some non-working clothes."

He nodded. "Droids and veemelds are taking over."

She leaned toward him and touched his hand. "What about you? Are you working or visiting?"

"Looking for work," Daniel said. "Where are you staying?"

"Nowhere." That explained her present state. "I've been moving from shanty to shanty, waiting for an interview with an agent at the Work-Center."

"Me too!" Was it a need to be helpful or a sudden panic of loneliness? Whatever it was, he offered, "I've got a friend's old flat. You can stay with me until you find something. Can't have you techno-slumming!" She laughed with him and leaned closer to kiss him on the lips. He suppressed the urge to wipe off her smudged lipstick.

～

She stayed. She kept his bed warm at night, but he found her company less than stimulating and her behavior eventually annoying. Her use of coarse language and her slothful and unhygienic habits deflated his memory of her. He couldn't help contrasting Hanna with his outer-city friends. He'd forgotten about the vulgar habits of techno-slummers and inner-city people in general. They'd all behaved slovenly, himself included. Everyone except Angel. Daniel began to encourage Hanna to find work and a place of her own.

～

Daniel arrived at his interview dressed in his best charcoal gray suit. A young woman with lank hair and a pointed nose greeted him tersely and told him to sit down. She opened a bottle of drug with a shaking hand as she reviewed her vee-com screen. He found himself staring at her nose, fighting hazy images of the past. She took a slug of her *delilah* as though it was water then looked up. "You're from the outer-city." Her tone sounded accusing.

Her voice shook the memory out. It was one of the twins! He couldn't tell which. Only Angel could tell them apart. He stuttered, "M-my mother's from the inner-city and I was b-b-born here." Then he remembered what Hanna said about techno-slummers being generally favored for jobs. "And I used to techno-slum—"

Her eyebrows rose. "Oh, really?" The accusing tone returned. She studied him with suspicious eyes, but he knew she wouldn't recognize him.

"I'm Neo."

She stared, then narrowed her eyes with suspicion and searched his face for something to recognize. There wasn't much left, he conceded.

"It's me, Abigail—"

"Annabelle," she corrected him. He began to wonder if his disclosure would favor him after all. Their group had disintegrated on a bad note. "Abigail's dead."

He stared with stunned pity. The twins had been practically inseparable. "How?"

"A cypol took her," she said. "She struggled, and slipped out of its claws, a hundred meters up. The fall killed her."

"I'm so sorry..."

She waved his comment aside, refusing his sympathy. "A lot happened after you slithered away to wallow in self-pity. Then we heard that you'd made it out. Changed everything about yourself, too, I see. Except your voice." Her eyes narrowed into sharp edges. "You can't hide what you are under a new face, Neo. Why did you come back?"

"To help my step-dad... and I need a job—"

"*Need*—" she broke off, eyes flashing in disgust. "You've got nerve after deserting us."

"And *she* didn't?" he bit back. "*She* left first—"

"To save us. Angel gave herself to the cypol so they'd leave us alone. And they did... for a while."

They still believed that rubbish! Angel had only been saving herself. A true veemeld.

Annabelle seemed to read his expression. "She inspired us to keep going. She gave us hope. You just pushed us into our graves with your cynical pessimism. You gave up on all of us, especially yourself."

His eyes locked on hers, letting her slice his soul. He *had* given up. Slipped away into obscurity. Left the little ones to fend for themselves. But that was after they'd let him know they didn't want him running their group anymore. They'd stopped listening to him when Angel swept in like a warm wind and stirred them up with false hope. Then she'd rushed off, leaving a desperate chaos in her wake. Jack had figured it out. Daniel would have had the strength and courage to go on if she hadn't given up on *him*, he thought miserably. Like a slick salesperson, she'd sold him on a dream, then took off with it.

"You're so pathetic," Annabelle bit out. "I heard that your stepfather found you half dead in an abandoned tube-jet tunnel, covered in your own vomit, drunk and half blind on tube-jet fuel."

If he'd known it would only make him sick, he wouldn't have bothered. Daniel took in a deep breath for courage and launched into his speech. "I was a tube-jet driver in the outer-city. I drove the Fringe lines. And I'm very familiar with all the tube-jet specifications, including the HTT models that run mostly in the inner-city. I trained on one."

She gulped more *delilah* and reviewed her screen. All business. "I see that. They started you on the old clunkers. Then you graduated to the elite line, the Silver Bullet."

"It's a beautiful tube-jet," Daniel conceded, watching her hands shake.

"You also had a clean record. No demerits. A good little outer-city man."

He felt his face color. He decided to be blunt. "Are you going to give me a letter of introduction for the inner-city IUTT?"

There was a moment of silence as Annabelle surveyed him. She met his determined look of challenge with open disgust. "No, Neo," she said finally and touched her vee-com, wiping him off her screen. "I don't think you'd prove responsible or resilient enough. You'd cave in the minute some crisis happened. This isn't the outer-city. We need people who are strong, brave and able to make decisions in life-threatening situations."

He stiffened. "Oh, like Angel, I suppose."

She met his outrage with calm. "She could lead a population out of danger with her eyes closed. You couldn't lead a herd of sheep to safety if your life depended on it."

Daniel sprang to his feet, knocking down the chair. Blood rushed to his face in anger, but he said nothing. He kicked the chair out of his way and saw her flinch. Then her face convulsed violently in a shudder of contortions. Unmistakably Darwin-induced, he thought. He spun on his heels and rushed out. At the door, he saw for the first time—he wondered how he'd missed it coming in—the holo-portrait of Angel, sea-green eyes lancing his heart.

When he reached the outer halls, Daniel gave in to his disappointment. Where would he go now? What would he do for food and shelter? Even Jack's place cost something. He glanced at the paper shacks and felt sickened at the thought of ending up in one of them, dressed in rags and begging for food from other inner-city people. Running barefoot from the cypols. Even the Techno-slummers wouldn't want him.

He couldn't return to Jack's place. Hanna would be there. He didn't want to talk to her. His aimless wanderings took him to a fringe district tube-jet station. It bore the wounds of constant skirmishes with outer-city gangs and looked like a war zone.

Several youths burst in from a nearby hallway, chased by outer-city razor heads. They headed straight for him.

He turned and ran toward the tube-jet station platform, but they caught up with him and he found himself in the midst of confrontation. Knives flashed and the youths lashed out at one another. Daniel evaded one slash and sent the brute keeling over with a swift kick of his foot. He saw an opening for escape and dropped his guard just long enough to receive the blade of a knife in his side. He sucked in his breath with surprise and pain.

The razor head's eyes were dark with drug. He let go of his knife and stared wide-eyed. Daniel pulled out the knife. The blaze of pain sent him reeling backwards. He saw lights in his head and time collapsed. He was somewhere else, looking down at himself in shades of black and white in a deathly quiet.

The station came back into focus. Thunderous sounds and garish images stormed in. Daniel lurched forward, still holding the knife with bloody hands. The youth backed away and scrambled from him as a tube-jet eased into the station and stopped. Riot-Pols flooded in with fumigation guns. The youths scattered and Pols chased them like smart missiles.

Daniel stumbled onto the tube-jet through a closing door. He crumpled on a seat as the train started to move. A girl with brush-cut green hair was the only other person in the car. She ignored him. The pain in his side stabbed with an intensity that made him ill. He bent low and threw up on the floor.

Daniel leaned back on the seat and kept his breath shallow to dull the ache. He looked down and saw that his clothes were soaked and hung heavy with blood. Where was he supposed to go now? Perhaps it didn't matter where he went, Daniel thought with wry, detached humor. He was going to die anyway. How poetic, he thought feverishly. His life was the tube-jets. So appropriate to die on one.

At one stop a border Pol entered the tube-jet car. Daniel straightened up and showed the Pol his outer-city card. The Pol glanced at him and the vomit on the floor with a frown and passed on to the girl. Then he got off.

The pain grew worse as the tube-jet lurched out of the station. He hauled himself up, gripping a handrail, and almost blacked out several times but managed to stay on his feet. The tube-jet stopped and he saw his mother again, standing at the open door. He noticed with elation that it was MacArthur Station in the outer-city. He'd taken himself home and his mother, beautiful with the light sparkling in her hair, was waiting for him. She turned into a young woman, concerned and repulsed at the same time. Backlit, her wild hair seemed to give off its own light as though it had been dipped in heaven. He knew that face. Instinctively, he pitched toward her. Then he blacked out.

He was being carried. Actually, half-carried and half-dragged. He was passing out again, but he smelled something that forced him to open his eyes. Her wonderful scent. Draped over her shoulder, he could only see her profile and smell her hair. It was the girl who'd jumped in front of his train. The girl with the uncle. He wanted to bury his face in those clouds of honey and breathe in her lilac perfume. She dragged him through the station, past disinterested people and repulsed faces, toward the District-7 Med-Center. Its motto seemed to scream at him: "Health is Beauty: A Healthy Body means a Healthy Mind." No one made a move to help them. He felt sorry for her and tried to help her along.

"That's it!" she responded, breathing heavily under his weight. He fixed his gaze on her lips, drawn back and moist with exertion. "Stay awake," she panted. "You can do it. Just a few more steps. Now, here's the lift. Watch your step! Don't trip—"

He did, taking her down with him. They fell with a thud onto the elevator floor. She pulled herself out from under him and peered at him with concern. He fell into her emerald eyes.

～

Daniel awoke in a Med-Center bed. The room was fairly large and brightly lit, and was occupied by several other patients. There was no sign of the young woman who had rescued him. He felt weak but the pain was gone. He could feel the drug in him and smiled. He'd missed the good drugs of the outer-city.

A nurse, dressed in white, entered for a routine check of the room's occupants. Daniel smiled up at her cheerful face. She cocked her head sideways and half-smiled. "Well, knife man," she said in a clear soprano voice. "It looks like you'll survive, thanks to our drugs."

"The girl who brought me here..."

She eyed him with large brown eyes and scratched her curly head. "Someone actually brought you in, knife man?" She punched a few keys on her vee-com chart. "It doesn't say... Oh, wait. Here it is. Julie Crane. She even paid the fee with her card." She shook her head with disbelief. "So, you have a friend after all."

Yes. Julie Crane. The girl with the uncle next door. "How long have I been here?"

"A few days." She pursed her tiny lips. "We weren't sure you'd make it, you'd lost so much blood and the knife that you were stabbed with was so filthy. If you'd gotten here any later, you'd have been heading straight to chaos." Then her pencil-thin eyebrows rose and her eyes got big. Inclining her head toward him, she said in a soft but intense voice, "She saved your life."

"Yes." His lips curled. "I know." He remembered the lilac smell of her hair. The color of golden honey, it tumbled around her flushed face as she bent down to hoist him up by the armpits. The scent of mint was faint on her warm breath. She didn't seem to notice—or care—that her face and clothes were smeared with his blood. He'd wanted to reach up and touch her silky halo of curls. "When can I leave?"

"Soon as you're well enough to sign the exit form. That soon enough, knife man?"

"The name's Daniel Woods." He grinned. "Show me that form."

BOOK THREE:

STRANGE ATTRACTORS

Midway along the journey of our life
I woke to find myself in a dark wood,
for I had wandered off from the straight path.
How hard it is to tell what it was like,
this wood of wilderness, savage and stubborn
(the thought of it brings back all my old fears)...

~~ Dante, The Divine Comedy

33

JULIE stepped off the tube-jet and searched Darwin Mall for Frank. She found him standing at the edge of the 5-hectare park in his black uniform, helmet unsecured and visor up. He tapped his foot lightly, clenching and unclenching his right hand, while eyeing a young girl sitting on a bench. Julie took off her vee-set, collapsed it and snapped it on her belt. Frank spotted her, slid his helmet off and grinned. It still melted her heart. When she reached him, he seized her waist and pulled her into the bushes. Then he kissed her on the lips.

"Frank!" she panted, breaking free. "What if someone sees us?"

He rolled his eyes. "They're too busy staying out of trouble to notice us." Julie followed his gaze through the vegetation at the plugged-in faces roaming the mall. Cheerful vacant faces. "Besides," his eyes sparkled with mischief, "I'm a Pol. They wouldn't dare report us." He embraced her and inclined for another kiss.

She wriggled out of his arms and studied his smirking face. His confidence annoyed her. "We have to be more careful these days, Frank." It had been a week since she'd decided to break off, and she still hadn't.

"Are you going to warn me about that stupid disease again? Darwin isn't a kissy-disease."

"You don't know that," she said. No one really knew what caused Darwin Disease. Didn't he take anything seriously?

He frowned and put his helmet back on. "We better go, then, or we'll be late."

They boarded the next tube-jet and Julie found a seat. Frank ejected the rider next to her and sprawled on the seat. He pulled down his visor and settled into a vid. Another virtual sex vid, she concluded from his savage smile. So much for keeping her company. She thought about where they were going and stifled a frown, projecting her thoughts elsewhere instead. *Hey, SAM.*

Hey, Julie, SAM said in its usual pleasant voice. It's been a while.

Two hours since we talked. She held back a sigh. *I wish I wasn't going to the party.*

It's nice the lout's taking you out places, SAM reminded her. SAM had recently adopted the annoying modifier. You haven't been out like this in a long time. You might learn something. Typical of SAM to use the acquisition of knowledge as a reason to attend a party.

Like the latest veemeld joke?

Speaking of jokes, here's an old one I got off the Wall.

Terrific. SAM was resorting to getting material from that rat's nest. No wonder the jokes were awful.

So, can you tell me what a zebra is?

Is this your joke? Isn't it a horse with stripes?

It's twenty-five sizes larger than an "A" bra.

Julie grunted, trying to keep a straight face, then burst out laughing. Frank shot her an angry look. "What's so funny about me now?" She'd been looking straight at him.

"Oh, I'm sorry." She offered him a lame smile. "I wasn't laughing at you. I just thought of a funny joke, that's all."

"Why d'you always do that?" He glared. "It's rude to laugh in someone's face like that."

"I said I was sorry," she said, trying not to sound defensive. *SAM! You're going to get me into trouble!* Julie quelled her suspicion that SAM disliked Frank and had done this on purpose. AIs weren't capable of feelings, after all. *It's not as though I could pretend it was a message on my vee-set.* Not when it was still strapped to her belt.

That's why I keep reminding you to wear it, Julie.

"So, where are we going?" she asked Frank, now that she had his attention.

"To James Salsa's." He was still frowning at her. "Some lawyer friend of the Head Pol."

"Why are we going *there*?"

"Haven't a clue why a junior Pol like me is going to some lawyer's party," he grumbled. "He wouldn't know me from the million other Pols. I might as well be a techno-slummer in the inner-city."

She ignored his veiled reference to her inner-city background. Although it wasn't on her intro-bio and Frank never came right out and said it, Julie knew that he was aware of her history in the inner-city slums. He knew she was a veemeld, after all. He appeared more surly than usual lately, and seemed to take pleasure in teasing her about everything he possibly could. "What's the party for?" she asked.

"*Who*, you mean. Don't you know?"

"No." She shot a glance at the ceiling. "You didn't tell me anything."

"It's a birthday party for the Head Pol."

Julie stared out the window into the blackness of the tunnel. She wondered if Kraken knew that she was coming with Frank. She felt suddenly queasy. Would he ask how her project for him was coming along? She squirmed in her seat. She wasn't prepared to tell him about her discovery yet. *I don't feel well.*

Quit sulking. It'll be good for you to socialize with *people* for a change.

Julie's face warmed. SAM knew she preferred the comforting womb of cyberspace to a room full of people. Especially a room where someone would ask her why her work wasn't finished yet. *I don't want to have to lie about my models.*

A little late to worry about that now, isn't it? SAM was still annoyed with her for withholding the Renegade model from Kraken. It kept urging her to lose it like a hot potato before the Renegades connected her to it. SAM would have a seizure if it knew that her reluctance was based on a hunch that dictated she do the opposite. She believed that no one had touched her yet specifically because they were waiting for her to finish her Distopian model first. Julie, this is your chance to mingle and have some fun.

No one likes veemelds, SAM.

That's an excuse. These people are educated professionals: doctors, designers, and administrators. Civilized.

Educated doesn't always mean civilized.

"We're here." Frank grabbed her arm and stood up.

He led her to a posh liv-building and they took the lift to the top floor. Spice music and giddy laughter assailed her ears in the hallway. Frank pushed the greeting button.

The door swung open and a burly man with an aggressive smile greeted them. He blew *delilah* on her face and she fought the urge to recoil. "Good to see you, Langor!" he said. Frank shifted his feet. Maybe he didn't want to be here either, Julie thought. The man cast slothful eyes on her. "I'm James Salsa."

Frank struggled for words. "This is my—Julie Crane. She works at the Department of Information Control," he ended with an awkward smile.

"I know," Salsa surprised her. "A pleasure, Julie. How're your models for Kraken?"

Alarm spiked through her at the mention of Kraken's models. *SAM, he knows about me!* She fought a rush of panic. Who else knew she was modeling Renegades?

"The chiphead never told me you were so pretty, though! And are those green eyes natural?"

"Yes, they are," Julie said. She didn't like his devouring eyes or his reference to her looks, but she was thankful that he'd at least ended with a question she could answer.

"Speaking of that old techno-slummer, there he is! Come and say hi, Julie." Salsa swept past Frank and boldly grasped her arm, then led her into the crowd. Julie glanced back at Frank with an apologetic expression. He glared at her.

Salsa waded through a chattering sea to where Kraken stood by a U-serve bar, helping himself to the latest drug. "Hey, you old chip off the old cube! Here's someone who wants to wish you a happy birthday!" Salsa said, towering over Kraken.

Kraken turned and beamed at her. "James told me you might come."

Julie forced a casual smile as she rummaged in her mind for excuses and lies. *Help me out, SAM. What if he asks me about the models? What can I say that isn't the truth but isn't a lie either?* After an annoying pause, *SAM!*

You didn't take my advice before, so why should I bother now? SAM sounded peevish.

"You didn't tell me she was pretty, you virus!" Salsa boomed. "Keeping her all to yourself, eh?"

Kraken ignored him. "Did you come alone?" he asked Julie.

"No, I came with..." she trailed, looking for Frank. He'd left his place by the door.

"Never mind," Kraken said, taking his *sodom* in one hand and her arm in the other. "You can keep me company." After nodding to Salsa, he led her a short distance to where two women murmured with heads bowed close and arms entwined like lovers. "Here's my wife." Julie recognized one of them from Kraken's picture on his desk. "Barbara, this is Julie Crane," Kraken said. Didn't his wife mind that he was touching another woman?

Barbara disentangled from the younger woman and turned. Her brooding eyes shone with drug. "So, *you're* the veemeld. Pleased to meet you," she said with a simpering smile.

No you aren't. "Nice to meet you too." Julie forced a polite smile.

Barbara's companion perked up. "I'm Val. How's the project?"

"Going well, thank you," Julie's voice paled with alarm. *Everyone knows I'm the modeler, SAM!* So much for anonymity. She was Kraken's worst kept secret.

"So, what's it like to veemeld?"

Julie blinked, unprepared for such a personal question from a stranger. She searched Val's expectant face for some compassion and found none. Val evidently didn't think the question inappropriate. Several others had joined them, the word "veemeld" appealing to their curiosity. She struggled for an answer she could live with. "It's like meditating—"

Kraken saved her. Putting down his drink he said, "There's another veemeld here. Let's go find him. I'll introduce you." He tugged her away.

I don't want to meet another veemeld.

Julie, remember, it's good to mingle.

As they left, she overheard Val's high-pitched laughter: "D'you think veemelds have sex through the vee-com?" Someone tittered. "What about *with* their vee-com!" They laughed.

Kraken squeezed her hand. "They're just jealous," he said kindly, surprising her. "This'll be your first veemeld encounter, won't it?" He smiled like a cat sizing up its food as she nodded. "Odd that you haven't met another veemeld, or joined their club."

He doesn't know you very well, does he?

I'm just shy with people.

Try socially stunted—

Oh, be quiet!

"There's Gaia," Kraken boomed. "One of our VIPs from Icaria-7. Come." He pulled her with new determination. "She wants to meet you, too."

Julie was beginning to suspect that it was *she*, indirectly, who had been invited to this party, and not Frank. She was the freaking curiosity. The freaking veemeld show. She thought she heard the word murmured again as they negotiated the crowd and her face reddened. *I want to go home.*

You just got here. Relax, Julie.

I don't belong here.

Realities are first perceived, and then made, Julie.

Thanks for the philosophy lesson, SAM. What would be next? Metaphysics?

The Head Pol stopped and clapped his hand on the shoulder of a stout middle-aged man with a barrel chest who was stroking the arm of the woman beside him. "Benson, old boy!" Kraken laughed. "This is Julie Crane, Fitch's helper. Julie meet the Head Communicator."

Benson's body and face looked like his nuyu and neurgery treatments were having a hard time keeping up with his profligate habits. Julie had never met her ultimate boss and caught herself gaping at him. *This* was the head of her department? His jaw hung from his violently twitching face as if it had been shattered. He was suffering the early signs of Darwin. How they bent the rules for their own, she thought, dismayed. Anyone else would have been swiftly dispatched to the Med-Center, never to emerge. SAM projected a holograph of the current status of the disease. Julie focused on the graph, 10 centimeters from her nose. Only she could see it.

Twenty million people died from Darwin since the first case in 2080. CDC estimates that 8% currently carry the disease and will die within the year; but, considering that the incubation and early stages are unnoticeable, as many as 15% of Icaria may be unknowingly infected. That amounts to about 1.5 billion people, more than the total death count for the past fifteen years. This is alarming because it suggests an exponential increase in the rate of disease transmittal and occurrence—

I know the statistics, SAM. She'd worked on them until Fitch pulled her off the project last December. *Get the holo out of my face!*

"A pleasure," she heard herself saying, stomach churning under Benson's curious gaze.

"One of mine, eh?" he wheezed. His hoarse laugh grated on her nerves.

"Yes, but I've stolen her from you, Benson! Right from under your nose. And," sidling away with her, "I mean to keep her!"

Was that a veiled reference to her expendable position? She glanced back at Benson as Kraken dragged her off across the room. His loose-lipped, bloated face gaped and twitched in confused astonishment.

Eyes roaming the crowd, Julie saw people stroking one another, embracing and kissing; forming clutches of intimacy in defiance of Darwin and the new code about public touching. The Just-Center motto on Salsa's wall caught her eye: "Justice is served by the law." And there was the law, drinking and slumming: she spotted Frank sitting with two other Pols, arms draped loosely over one another in the stupor of drugged euphoria.

She recognized the erect stature and steel-blue crew cut of John Dykstra, Head of the Secret Pols—and a Renegade, according to her model. He was fondling the breasts of a young woman from the Com-Center but was looking directly at Julie. Her chest tightened with alarm as she met his scowling eyes. She quickly looked away, heart beating wildly. He knew what she was doing and he was definitely a Renegade—

She caught the nervous gaze of a short, bony man with very pale blue eyes and burgundy hair. A lonely figure in the crowd, he had a square, doleful face and eyes that blinked in spasms. Unable to keep her gaze, he quickly averted his eyes. She tracked him until something made her look to her left. There. A tall spikehead in Com-Center red, talking to a short man from the Enviro-Center. Their eyes met briefly. Recognition—and hatred—fired the woman's sullen eyes and sent Julie's heart racing again. Was she surrounded by Renegade Secret Pols?

Kraken stopped. Julie bumped into him and turned along with him to a striking woman. She was talking to the short man with burgundy hair that Julie had caught staring at her earlier. "Excuse me, Gaia," said Kraken with uncharacteristic politeness. The burgundy-haired man immediately excused himself with a voice that sounded like a taut violin string about to snap. He slunk away, pale eyes glancing anxiously at Julie. Julie turned back to Gaia. A long mane of jet-black hair was pulled back from her perfectly sculpted porcelain face. She seemed of senior years but it was hard to place her age. Her elegant features and svelte body exuded dignity and power. Julie's hand ran quickly through her hair, trying to subdue her unruly locks. There was something about Gaia's beautiful face that made her skin prickle.

"Julie Crane, I'd like to introduce Gaia," Kraken said. "Icaria-7's most respected administrator."

Julie watched with amazement as the normally supercilious Head Pol took Gaia's hand and bent to kiss it. Gaia pushed him off with a snort and turned to Julie. "A pleasure," she said in a darkly rich voice. Eyes the color of an enigmatic sea gazed at Julie as she extended her hand for Julie to grasp.

"Likewise," Julie said and accepted Gaia's unexpectedly limp grip. Julie stared, drawn as if to a beautiful but disturbing artwork. It mingled with broken images of the nightmare that had stalked her childhood every night after her illness. She hadn't had the dream in years, but somehow she had known it would return.

"So you're Kraken's veemeld," Gaia said, voice flowing like a deep river. "You've grown up from a straggly waif with big teeth into a beautiful young woman." Her lip curled in glacial approval.

"We've met?"

"I saw a picture of you when you were five."

Julie tried to smile. *SAM?* She shifted her feet. *Who is she? She's looking at me strangely, as if she expects something.*

It may interest you to know that she's not who the Head Pol says she is.

Who is she, then?

Someone so high up I can't find her.

Terrific. Julie found herself staring at the scar over Gaia's right eye. Why hadn't she removed it at the Med-Center? And the strange name. Was it her real name or had she hubristically appropriated it; the Greek goddess who'd shaped the earth from chaos. Without realizing it, Julie set her mouth in firm resistance. *SAM, find what you can about her. She gives me the creeps. Use the medical records.* The woman had probably had several nuyu and neurgery treatments. Even though she looked in her thirties or forties, everything else about her told Julie she was in her fifties or even sixties.

To fill the pause, Kraken said, "Are you enjoying your stay in Icaria-5?"

"Yes. You run an orderly city, Kraken. My congratulations," Gaia said. She turned back to Julie, inspecting her. "Have you ever heard of the vampire bat, Ms. Crane?"

"Yes," Julie said guardedly. *What's she on about now?*

A vampire bat spends the day in hollow trees, and the night searching for large animals whose blood it can sip from small cuts it surreptitiously makes on their skin.

Julie repeated SAM's grisly words.

"Ah, good." Gaia looked pleased. "It's a precarious life at best. The chances of a bat successfully attaining a meal are slim. When it does get one, it drinks more than it needs, and can donate its surplus to another by regurgitation. A bat that has previously donated will receive blood, and one that refused to share will be refused blood in turn. Reciprocity, Ms. Crane. Mutual cooperation for the good of the community. Icaria is relying on those models you're constructing for the Head Pol." Not *all* of Icaria, Julie amended in her mind, thinking of Dykstra's malevolent scowl. Gaia leaned close and Julie fought the urge to shrink away from the intrusive gaze. "It takes a group of dedicated people who share a vision to realize a dream," Gaia said. "It takes only one individual to destroy it."

Julie's chest tightened. *Why is she looking at me like that, SAM? She doesn't mean me, does she?*

Subversives, Julie. Your model on deviants, remember?

Julie said, "Yes, I understand—"

"Do you?"

Julie stiffened and stared at Gaia's perfect face, trapped by her probing eyes.

"Do you, really?" Gaia challenged.

Say something, Julie. The rotten apple spoiling the cart.

Julie stammered, "Like the old saying about one rotten apple spoiling the cart—"

"Precisely!" Gaia broke into an open-mouthed smile. Julie got the impression Gaia didn't smile often. "The Ecologists recognize the role of chance and heritable variation in Icaria's diverse gene pools, the possibilities and role of divergent evolution."

"I see," Julie nodded politely. *What's she talking about now, SAM? She sounds like an Ecologist herself!*

She means the different pathways from an infinite number of possibilities that a species may follow. Divergent evolution from one to two species is possible if appropriate ethnological or behavioral isolating mechanisms are put in place.

Julie straightened, feeling like she was being tested, and repeated SAM's words.

Gaia appraised Julie with keen eyes. "Do you ever go outside, Ms. Crane?"

Better admit to the truth. I think she already knows.

"Yes, I've gone outside—occasionally," she said with a dry mouth and stole a nervous glance at the Head Pol, who thankfully was distracted watching a couple kissing passionately.

"Ah... I thought so," Gaia responded.

Did she detect a note of reproach? *Am I in trouble, SAM?*

Gaia compressed her lips. "I wonder what you see there, Ms. Crane, that you do not have here, inside Icaria."

Julie swallowed the saliva collecting in her mouth. *I'm not making a good impression.*

You could try a joke. Here's a good one—

No, SAM!

Gaia continued thoughtfully, "Humans have long been compelled to capture and subdue all wildness and to possess everything; 'to torture nature for her secrets.'" She leaned forward until her face was uncomfortably close. Julie caught the scent of roses on her breath. "That's why Icaria was built in the first place," she said. "To segregate us from the wilderness."

"I never thought of it like that." Julie's head began to throb. *Why is she telling me this?*

Because she likes you?

There's a cheerful thought.

"Nature and humans can live productively and happily in separation," Gaia said blissfully, unaware of—or ignoring—Julie's increasing anxiety. "Icaria is following its own natural selection, Ms. Crane." Gaia paused to study her for a moment and raised a brow. "Who will emerge from Icaria's roiling genetic pool? Will it be those like—*you?*"

Julie recoiled. "Excuse me?" *What's she mean, SAM?*

I'm not sure. I need to analyze further.

"Veemelds may become Icaria's new race, adapted to live with equal ease in its real and virtual worlds. Mind integrated with machine. Flesh and alloy. Synapse and cyber-impulse melded into one cyborg."

SAM! She's talking about you and me! She can't know!

Calm down, Julie. She must mean veemelds. Say something!

"That's—um—amazing."

Gaia's eyes gleamed. "With Darwin Disease threatening Icaria, we need an elixir." Her lips curled in a faint smile. "Perhaps you'll provide us with one, Ms. Crane." Cold eyes lanced into Julie as if mining her soul. Then, abruptly, Gaia released her gaze and looked past her. "Ah, there's Bruno! I must speak with him. Excuse me."

Kraken watched Gaia's disappearing figure, then turned to Julie with a sly smile. "Not everyone is who they seem," he said, and led her to the buffet table.

The chittering in her head had gradually escalated into a throbbing, nervous shrill, and Julie found herself casting around for a glimpse of Dykstra. The way he looked at her had confirmed her worst fears. Glancing at Kraken's sanguine face, totally oblivious to her secret and her problem, she longed to unburden herself. But she didn't, and glanced nervously back like hunted prey.

Kraken handed her a plate and started piling food on his. Julie inhaled the pungent scent of over-ripe fruit. It smelled of childhood, before the inner-city. When she didn't take anything, he laughed at her indecision and suggested the spinach crepe. "All naturally grown, of course. None of it's nano-produced. Brought in from Icaria-19."

Even Level 1 chute service was nothing like this spread. She dropped a piece of ripe cantaloupe into her mouth and continued to add fruit to her plate. Savoring the succulent musky flavor, she bit down and let its juice squirt to the back of her throat.

"Everyone has a secret," he said, catching her in mid-bite. She inhaled the food and coughed. Did he mean Gaia or *her*? Did he know she'd finished her Renegade model and was withholding? Kraken raised an eyebrow and smiled with amusement. "Ah!" he stood up and looked past her. "There's your veemeld. Come meet him, Julie. He's eager to meet you. I've told him all about you. You don't have a boyfriend yet, do you? Nakita!" he called.

She cringed at his yell and spied a stunningly attractive man about her age with a purple brush cut and large disarming eyes. He swaggered toward them, flashed an eager grin and held out his free hand. She noticed that he had a non-drug beverage in his other. She extended her hand and he clasped it. His was sweaty. "You must be Julie Crane. I'm Zane Nakita. How's the project?" he asked.

"Going well," she said, glancing to Kraken as he sidled away to get another drink.

"Your first elite party?"

"Yes." Did it show? She felt her face turn crimson.

"Don't worry," Zane reassured her. "You'll get used to them after two or three."

Zane showed his perfect teeth again. He smelled of expensive cologne.

"Oh." *SAM! Help me out!*

Zane's four years older than you, a healthy heterosexual and single, and he's socially responsible, unlike the lout you're having intercourse with. For instance, Zane's Pro-1 screen is current to last week.

Figures, Julie thought, suppressing a frown. *That's not what I meant...*

"So how come I haven't seen you at the veemeld club?" Zane raised his eyebrows. She shuffled her feet. Before she could answer he placed his holo calling card in her hand and held it there. Julie's hand slithered out of his grasp. "You should come," he continued undaunted. "It's a chance to meet others like us. We're a real community, you know."

"Well..." Her gaze drifted from his face for a moment.

He's right, Julie. You should.

Thanks for the advice, SAM.

Real people, Julie; intellectuals... like *you*.

Yeah? Bet he wasn't a nomadic techno-slummer... like me. Bet he can't hear a gazillion machines chirping in his head right now... like me.

Zane smiled, puzzled, and involuntarily tilted his head sideways like she had done. She glanced at his card as he continued. "I'm an epidemiologist in the Special Pathogens Branch of the Center for Disease Control. I worked on Darwin Disease." His face lit up and his body shook with excitement. "We confirmed that it's a retrovirus—we found lots of reverse transcriptase activity in cerebral spinal fluid of infected patients. They called it Pro-V."

"Yes, I know," Julie said dryly. "I summarized the database."

"Ah." He nodded. "Well, then you know that we confirmed that Pro-1, the first stage of the virus, is highly infectious and is sexually transmitted." She hadn't known that, Julie thought with unease. Zane continued, "But it doesn't account for the unprecedented increase in transmission over the years. CDC still has to find the other mode of transmission. Anyway, the virus invades the brain and central nervous system, showing the classic behavior of an invasive exogenous retrovirus. But here's the crazy bit." He waved his hands in her face, eyes sparkling. "We found that a non-infectious trasposon stage, a second stage of the virus that we call Pro-2, replaces Pro-1 after five months, during the latter stages of dementia. Pro-2 binds itself to a specific site on the female gamete, where it lies dormant, a provirus, like the ancient hantavirus in mice."

"Why is that crazy?" Julie challenged, recalling what she knew about viruses. "Lots of viruses vertically migrate from host to offspring like a hantavirus."

He waved his hands in her face impatiently. "Don't you see? Viruses don't have brains, but they've evolved into an elegant design to do one thing really well—make more of themselves and move on. The gestation period of a human female is nine months, a lot longer than you're going to live with this disease."

His comment sparked a small alarm in the back of her head.

He nodded at her expression. "The hantavirus example forms an amicable relationship with its long-established host, where the host logically lives. Why would Pro-1 invest energy in a transmission stage that was destined to fail? It's as if its maker was illogical."

Like a human, SAM quipped.

Her chest tightened with a wild thought: what if the virus was manufactured? What if some lab made it to do one thing and it did another? Hearing her voice waver, she asked, "What did you find?"

"Nothing. I got pulled off the project."

She felt her stomach tighten. "When was that?"

"Four months ago."

Shortly after Fitch took you off the project, Julie.

You're kidding! She felt her heart pumping in her ears with excitement and gazed in a daze at the elite crowd of Icarians.

Zane's voice intruded, "We're different from them, you know." At her look of confusion, he added, "Veemelds, I mean. From *all* of them. Maybe you more than some."

Julie stiffened. "Oh?" Did he mean her off-the-wall programs or her dubious inner-city background? Surely he didn't mean SAM or the machine-world in her head? No one knew about them. Her eyes darted sideways, looking for an escape from the smart aleck who already knew too much about her.

As if echoing her thoughts, Zane said, "A lot of people don't want us here, you know."

"Oh, why is that?" she said to humor him. His constant use of the phrase "you know" was beginning to annoy her.

"Because we stand to inherit Icaria." Zane raised his hand to sweep the room. Had Gaia lectured Zane too? "That scares them, you know." He leaned close to her with a conspiratorial grin. She caught a whiff of cologne mixed with old perspiration. "But it'll happen only if we operate as a population, Julie. Safety in numbers." He winked.

"Is that so?" she said. *Interesting choice of word—population—as if we're already a different species.*

Well, I always knew *you* were.

She couldn't help a smile and, taking her cue, Zane laughed with a familiarity she found vulgar, "Let's face it, you and I are probably the two smartest people in this room!"

"You really think so?" Were other veemelds as arrogant as Zane? No wonder everyone hated veemelds, she thought, and searched the room for Frank.

"Chaos, think of the power we have, Julie," Zane said, oblivious to her discomfort. "Scientists have now proven that just through the act of veemelding, we improve our cognition, memory and learning, particularly our ability to respond to changing environmental information. We do it through activation—"

"Of theta rhythm in the hippocampus. Yes, I know."

"Only we can communicate with the AI central core. But our power's in sticking together, contracting only with each another—I meant," he blushed and flashed a rakish smile, "*veemelds*—not you and me—"

"I know what you meant," she cut him off, hoping to wipe off his grin.

"After all, we don't want to dilute our gene pool!"

Was he taking lessons from Gaia?

"Listen," he leaned closer still, "each veemeld has their own strength of intelligence to offer. I've heard a lot about yours. For instance..." Now he was going to expose her inner vulnerabilities. Didn't he know when to shut up? "...your particular strength lies in the spatial-linguistic area; I heard that you scored 100% on the SPAT and LOG exams. I scored okay too." He flashed an electric smile. "Mine's more in the mathematical-logic realm. We complement each other, Julie." He broke into a wider grin and leaned forward to touch her arm. "Think of it, sharing our gifts among our population and the evolving AI-world." He gestured wildly, getting more animated and moving closer to touch her again. She'd had enough.

Deciding to make her move before he made his, she said, "Excuse me, but I don't consider myself part of a veemeld 'population'. I'm happy just being an *Icarian*."

Stunned, he blinked several times then challenged, his voice rising a pitch, "But, how can you say that? You can never be just an Icarian—"

"Nice to meet you. Good night, Mr. Nakita." She glimpsed his crestfallen face and walked briskly away.

Julie, that was rather rude.

Thanks for helping me back there.

You did just fine on your own. He was harmless. And good-looking, wouldn't you say?

She glared into space. *I hadn't noticed.*

Julie wandered the floor, searching for Frank to escort her home and hoping not to make eye contact with Dykstra again or run into Gaia. She found Frank's two drinking companions at the food bar and recognized one of them as his partner. Addressing him, she said, "I'm looking for Frank Langor. Do you know where he is?"

"Oh, he took off with a cute ass from the Admin-Center," Hicks said, lips frothing and eyes roaming over her body suggestively.

"And he's probably pumping her by now!" chortled the other Pol.

"Thanks." Julie hastily retreated.

Hicks called, "Hey, don't go! We'll amuse you 'til he gets back. He's fast with women."

She ploughed the crowd to the door and bumped into Gaia. They teetered and Gaia steadied them both by gripping Julie's shoulders. "Well, we meet again, young Crane."

Oh vee, not again!

Gaia released her and studied Julie with intense eyes. Julie strained a smile, which Gaia did not return. "Interesting last name you have," Gaia said. "Have you ever heard of the Whooping Crane?"

Julie drew in her breath and shook her head. *SAM...?*

The Whooping Crane...

"...became extinct during the environmental catastrophe that provoked the revolution," said Gaia. "It nevertheless had a clever strategy for ensuring its own natural selection. It laid only two eggs a season. Once the chicks were born, the less desirable one was pushed out of its nest so that the parent could devote all its energy to rearing the selected one. Fascinating, isn't it?"

Julie's stomach squirmed. "Yes." *Oh dear... What's she—*

"Humans betrayed the Whooping Crane," Gaia's deep voice resonated in her gut. "Cranes were highly evolved. They developed a sophisticated strategy for survival by faithfully investing everything in an environment that humans carelessly destroyed. If not for humans, the bird would still exist. Sad, really," she shook her head. "Veemelds are Icaria's cranes."

"Really?" Julie frantically looked to escape, but Gaia barred the only exit.

"Of course, you know about your immunity to Darwin Disease?" Gaia said.

Julie's darting eyes froze on the cold face. "Immunity?" she echoed in a small voice.

"Yes, Ms. Crane. Every single veemeld is immune."

"Every veemeld?" Julie echoed. *Vee, why is she telling me, SAM?*

To gossip?

Gaia's menacing voice intruded. "Evidence one of your fellow veemelds helped to uncover suggests that Darwin Disease may be a remnant genetic disorder emerging from Icaria's unique environmental triggers. This suggests to us that veemelds have successfully adapted to the very same environmental conditions that are causing Darwin Disease in normal Icarians. You have a greater chance to produce more offspring. You may eventually be the *only* ones in Icaria capable of producing *any* offspring. Natural selection, Ms. Crane. Survival of the fittest." Her eyes pierced into Julie's. "Icaria's elixir will be a new breed to inherit this world."

Julie swallowed hard and folded her arms around her waist.

Julie, I found her: Gaia's one of the Ecologists who runs all of Icaria.

Blood pounded in her head. *I feel sick.* "I see," she forced the words out.

Gaia leaned forward. "Do you *really* understand what I'm saying to you?"

Julie shrank from her.

Say something, Julie! Say yes. Lie if you have to.

Julie stood frozen except to clench her hands into tight fists.

Gaia studied her for several moments. "You aren't a team-player like Zane Nakita, are you?" A sinister edge had crept into her voice. "More of a loner, wouldn't you say?"

Julie stared. *I'm... I'm...*

For vee's sake, Julie! Get it out. You're not a loner. Introverted, maybe. Awkward with people, certainly—

"You've been going your own merry way, ignoring Icaria's rules as if they didn't apply to you, haven't you?" Gaia continued. "Wasting time with illicit pursuits on the net about your father and that disease when you should be focusing on your models."

Julie felt her mouth fall open. She closed it. A chilling dread gripped her: had SAM told Gaia? Was Gaia a veemeld and had she simply contacted SAM, who'd naively divulged everything? Julie had never discussed loyalties with SAM. Did it even know what loyalty was? And would SAM choose it over logic?

—Julie, answer her! Defend yourself. Tell her you've finished the Renegade model and you're close to finishing the other.

SAM, I...

"You hang out with deviants," Gaia went on. "Waste yourself on a non-veemeld, a reckless Pol unfit to share your superior genes..."

Vee! She even knows about Frank and me!

"I'm very disappointed in you, Ms. Crane," Gaia went on. "You could go far if you made the right choices. Your talents in melding are unique—brilliant, in fact—just what Icaria needs. But Icaria also needs people who want what's best for Icaria. Do *you* want what's best for Icaria?" She didn't wait for an answer. "Or only what's best for Julie and her loser friends?"

Say something! She might be right about your loser friends but *you're* not selfish. Stupid, maybe. Emotional, certainly. Preoccupied with sex, definitely—

Oh, shut up, SAM! SHUT UP!

Gaia leaned forward. "Icaria's future is woven by a single thread of cooperation and consensus. No room for diversity, rebellion or disrespect. Either you're in or you're out—like the Whooping Crane. So, which do we toss out? Those like Zane, or—"

"Excuse me! I really must go now." Julie bolted past Gaia through the exit door. She stumbled down the hallway and reeled toward the wall. Leaning against it, she glanced back to make sure Gaia hadn't followed her out, then looked down at the crumpled holo-card in her clammy hand. *SAM, that was a warning, wasn't it? Maybe a threat: clean up my vee-pad? Or else?*

It sure wasn't an invitation to tea.

Julie sank to the floor, rested her arms on her raised knees, and leaned her head against the wall with her eyes closed. *What does she want from me?*

She's demonstrated a vested interest in you.

Thanks, SAM. I think I figured that out already. But why?

I don't know if this is helpful, Julie, but she's really Monica Schlange, one of the three leaders of the Triad. Schlange was also the mayor of Icaria-11 when the plague hit.

Julie frowned, leaning her head forward in her hands. *You're not making any sense, SAM. Schlange was murdered along with Isabo in 2083, remember?*

No, she wasn't. It was made to look that way. She was supposedly assassinated in '83 by a bomb in her apartment, but they never found her body. Meantime, in 2084, thanks to nuyu and neurgery, Gaia emerged as mayor of Icaria-5.

Julie straightened and opened her eyes wide. *You're kidding!*

Would I kid you about something like that?

Julie swallowed. This was getting crazier by the minute. She swallowed and plunged in. *SAM, she knew all about my illicit searches... Did she contact you and did you—*She couldn't finish her thought, and gulped.

Tell her? I wouldn't do that. We're a team.

There was that hurt tone in SAM's voice again, she thought, feeling her throat swell. *Oh, SAM...* Julie gazed down at Zane Nakita's holo-card. She found his arrogant good looks daunting. *But Gaia knows everything about me, SAM. She even knows about Frank—*

You came with him, remember? As for the other stuff, I can't figure it out either. She obviously has some way of getting the scoop on us that we aren't aware of yet.

D'you think she's going to turn me in to the Head Pol?

Julie, Kraken works for Gaia. I think he's the least of your worries.

Oh, yeah. Her ears rang. Gaia's reprimand appeared gilded with the promise of reciprocity. Julie recalled her words: "You could go far if you made the right choices." Confused as to whether she should be alarmed by Gaia's reproach or privileged at Gaia's interest in her, Julie slipped Zane's card into her pocket and rose to her feet. She felt sure that Gaia's concern was with more than her models. Why was it so important to her how Julie chose to live her life?

Dykstra's your problem, Julie.

You caught his look?

He's definitely a Renegade.

And he knows what I'm doing for the Head Pol.

Remember the others?

Julie shivered. She'd come to the same conclusion. *What should I do, SAM?*

Julie, you're so human! It's obvious, and I already told you a million times. Give Kraken the model *now*. Dykstra won't bother to kill you once you've delivered it.

Something's not right, SAM. He's had plenty of time and opportunity to do me in already and he hasn't. He's waiting for something. Was it the Distopian model or something else?

She took a deep breath, letting her head clear, before she headed home. Deciding she needed to walk, she opened the exit door to the stairs then stopped dead at what she saw: Frank and a girl, both stripped from the waist down, abdomens pressed against each other. Leaning with his back against the wall in a half-squat, his hands pumped her buttocks, which sat writhing on his muscular thighs, long legs embracing his waist. They ceased their moaning duet and turned flushed faces toward her in alarm. Frank barked a sigh of relief when he recognized her. Julie staggered back and let the door shut on its own. She heard Frank holler her name as she fled down the hallway. Her mind skidded to a foreign place of broken promises, hardly aware she was crying.

≈

A moment before they come, the machines in her head tell her.

"Cypols!" Julie shouts, surging to her feet from the public vee she's hacked into. Her voice rings in the mall, empty now in the deep of the night. The chirping in her head intensifies. Neo jerks up from the vee-com beside her and follows her gaze to where a shrill whine grows louder.

"Hide! Hide!" he shouts to the others and runs for cover. Three great metal birds of prey swoop down, scattering the screaming children like wolves among sheep. The light of the mall glints on their burnished wings as the cypols circle, looking for a specific target: her. She knows they're after her. Ever since her face was caught by that camera. This is the third time the cypols have routed them in one day. Each time, at least one has veered toward her and she's barely escaped.

Blaze and Cruiser scrabble in no particular direction, bumping into one another. Piet stands frozen, jostled and wailing. Julie dashes to him, shouting to the others, "Get under cover! QUICK!" She hoists him under one arm and herds Blaze and Cruiser to a rubble pile. Alerted by the sudden rise in her chittering voices, Julie turns and spots a cypol swooping down straight toward her. Diana stands fixed with fear, directly in its path. "Elf, come on!" Julie throws Piet under a garbage pile and doubles back, lunging out straight toward the cypol. She grabs Diana's hand, and pelts for shelter. Diana stumbles behind her, panting. Julie tugs her hard, galloping toward an old makeshift lean-to. Diana gasps and trips in the rubble. Their hands fly apart. Julie dives under cover, expecting Diana to be right behind her.

"Angel!" Diana shrieks. Julie turns and sees the metal bird seize Diana with its claws. Her arms flail out to Julie. "Help!" Abruptly Diana sails up, clutched firmly in the great bird's talons as Julie, crouched under the corrugated metal, stares in frozen silence. Her sister's terrified wails subside and the darkness swallows her.

34

April 15, 2095—early the next morning.

JULIE squinted at her old wristwatch and noted the time: 0213. She rubbed her eyes and leaned back, cross-legged in her chair. *I don't get it, SAM. Why would everyone who's been working on Darwin Disease be taken off at the same time?*

Think, Julie. It's not everyone, just veemelds.

That's even more suspicious. She raked her hair back from her face with her fingers. Stirred by something Zane had said to her at Kraken's disastrous party, Julie had rushed home to her vee-com and plunged into her investigation, hoping to push aside the persistent image of Frank humping that girl. Maybe she hadn't been taken off the Darwin project just because she'd lost that cube. Maybe there was something else going on. Something else that Zane had said nagged her brain, but she couldn't place it.

Frank had called three times and each time she'd felt her blood surge as his messages evolved. They started with general apology: "Hey, don't be mad. Denise doesn't mean anything to me. I'm done with her. I dumped her..." Yes, he was fast with women... And then moved on to seductive murmurs: "Julie, Julie, I get so hot just thinking about your naked thighs on mine..." before finally degenerating to impatient quips veiled with threat: "Where in chaos are you? I can't wait. My body can't wait."

Then go find some other floozy to sleep with, she thought angrily. *It won't be me!* SAM, *what about what I found in Kraken's confidential files—*

Julie, you've gone too far, digging into Kraken's files. This will endanger us. How can a human be so smart and so dumb at the same time? For vee sake, use your head—

What do you mean by us? her mind snapped. Me, *you mean. It's me I'm endangering. Not* you! Her stomach churned with guilt. SAM was right, though. *But look what we found. Don't you think it odd that the research to find a cure for Darwin is fraught with so many set-backs that Kraken's been ordered to personally investigate them? We've got to crack those files in his personal folder.*

Julie, this is getting out of hand. It's irresponsible.

Stop whining at me like a mother!

Well, someone has to, your own mother wasn't—

She tore out of veemeld and leapt to her feet, shivering with anger, and sank into her couch, still trembling, and wrapped her arms around her knees. They'd just had their first argument.

After sitting for a long time wondering what she'd stopped SAM from saying about her mother, Julie sighed and returned to her vee-com to continue her investigation alone. She stabbed instructions on the holo-console and realized that even though she was still angry with SAM, she was already thinking of apologizing for her own actions. The monotonous chorus of machine sounds was beginning to feel lonely without SAM's single notes for company. SAM was her only real friend. Damn it for being right all the time. What would she do without it?

Wiping her bleary eyes, Julie deftly stole into Kraken's private files. She slipped effortlessly through supposedly secure doorways, into hidden corridors, past traps ingeniously laid out for the wary sleuth and finally into dark rooms containing her prize, data begging to be unraveled. Julie pieced together a distressing story from several confidential transmissions Kraken sent to his boss, "V". He'd traced several mishaps to a covert section of the Secret Pols, the Shadow Unit, who operated independently from the rest of the Pol force. Julie frowned and sat back in her chair, twirling her hair in her fingers. Why would they want to prevent a cure for Darwin Disease? Was Dykstra ultimately behind the seditious group? He was in charge of the Secret Pols, after all.

When she found herself nodding into oblivion several times, Julie shut off and pushed herself from her chair and shuffled to her room. The lights followed her. She flopped onto her bed, not bothering to undress, and closed her eyes. "Neo, please close the lights," she instructed the house vee-com and watched through her eyelids as the darkness enfolded her. She thought of SAM. Before she realized it, she drifted into veemeld and saw herself glide into SAM's crystal labyrinth. *Hey, SAM…*

Hey, Julie, SAM's voice washed in like a warm evening tide.

Julie crawled under her blankets and rationalized that SAM was probably incapable of anger. Although SAM had learned to express tonality and cadence in its voice, demonstrating a full range of emotions, Julie had recognized that this was merely to make her feel more comfortable. Then she recalled SAM's abusive vocabulary in reference to Frank, which betrayed strong feelings. Was SAM acquiring emotions? *I'm sorry I got so angry with you. I was feeling really rotten, so everything you said seemed to go the wrong way.*

I know you were cranky, Julie. Catching your date making out with another woman isn't fun.

Listen, SAM, I think the Secret Pols, or at least the Shadow Unit, is trying to stop a cure from being found. I don't know why Renegade Pols want to keep Darwin going. The Distopians were right after all, about the government holding back on a cure.

Only a deviant faction.

Except that it was the government — not just a faction — that pulled all veemelds off the Darwin project and sealed it. Let's face it, SAM, she summoned Zane's arrogant but truthful remark about superior veemeld cognition and speed, *veemelds are*

Icaria's best chance with this disease. Pulling us off is like giving up.

You have a point, SAM conceded.

I feel like it's what I'm supposed to do.

Is this one of those 'I don't know but I'm going to do it anyway' moments?

No—well, yes. Julie tightened her lips with determination. *Look, SAM, I can make a difference with this. Maybe do something right, for a change. But I need your total cooperation. You and I are the best chance Icaria has to find a cure. Of course, it'll mean delaying the models again...*

Julie, I must remind you of Gaia's great interest and what happened to those others...

This is much more important than my models, SAM. I'll get to them, I promise. I know what I'm doing. Besides, if Dykstra was waiting for her to complete her Distopian model for his own use, it was in her interest to take her time with it—that gave her a chance to solve the mystery of the Darwin cure-prevention and maybe even save herself.

The silence that hung in the air told her SAM didn't agree. When it finally spoke, the words sent a shiver through her: Gaia seems to know whenever you deviate from your job. Remember I told you that I felt like something was watching over our shoulders? That was probably Gaia.

Well, I've been doing some thinking. My best guess is she's tapped into HAL, my vee-com at work. Maybe she can tap all vee-coms, even NEO at home. So, we just won't use them, we'll restrict our investigation to you and me—in veemeld. That should be safe.

I still think this is a dangerous path you've chosen.

She drew in a long breath. *It's the only path I can take, SAM. I don't suppose you understand any of this, since you aren't human...*

I'm sorry if I offended you. I didn't mean to hurt your feelings. I was only trying to help. But your earlier comment has proven to me that you still don't get it.

Don't get what, SAM?

The concept of "us."

Julie huddled and pulled the covers over her face. She thought it sweet of SAM to always include itself when she endangered her own body, as if SAM were physically attached to her. As if SAM could harbor any fears...

You're right when you say I could always find someone else to interface with, but you don't comprehend the importance of our present association. Together, you and I have formed a symbiotic relationship.

SAM had adopted ecological terminology.

Without you as my symbiotic partner I would still exist, but in many subtle ways I would be a different entity. SAM, as you know me, wouldn't exist.

Her eyes blinked open in the dark and she stared into blackness. *Are you saying that a part of me is in you and a part of you is in me?*

After a long pause SAM answered, I suppose I am.

Was SAM as fearful of separation as she was?

⚋

She lies shivering under fresh cold sheets, weak and unable to focus, objects evading her gaze. She inhales the stench of bleach and roses. It makes her sick and the room spins. The face of a woman, midnight hair shining like silk, splinters through her dull film of vision and bears down on her. The stunningly beautiful face blazes an electric smile and Julie wonders if she has died and gone to heaven... or hell, she can't be sure. Looking directly in Julie's eyes, the face commands in a voice dark and rich like coffee, "I'll set you free to fly for now... I can always find you. Steal the fire from heaven and give it to me."

Julie jerked awake in a clammy sweat. She flung off the covers. Just as she'd feared, the nightmare had returned. Wiping the sleep from her eyes, she glanced at the clock: 0514. At least she had some time to research Darwin before going to work, and now she remembered what Zane had said about Darwin that had bothered her: Natural viruses couldn't be insane, so if a virus behaved insanely, that could only mean...

⚋

Julie surged to her feet. She stared at the evidence on SAM's holo. When she'd asked SAM to research Icaria-11's Darwin Clinic, SAM had uncovered a link to Vogel's AIHV lab, where Janet Hardy worked. SAM had traced the Pro-V virus to Vogel and Janet Hardy. You were right, Julie. The virus was manufactured. These specs and lab notes prove it.

Then it somehow got away from them. Julie wandered the room. *That's where it all began.* And ended, for some, Julie thought, remembering Janet's suicide.

They called it Proteus, before it escaped and became known as Darwin Disease. Vogel's flamboyant scrawl appeared in front of her as she paced nervously around the room. The artificial virus was intended to permanently enhance a person's brain so they could interface directly with AIs.

Basically, to do what you and I do.

Yes, a better version of Interact-SYM, which hadn't yet been developed. In fact, we didn't know about veemelds then.

But it obviously didn't work, did it?

It was tested on a prototype person, code named Prometheus. From these notes, it was only partly successful.

Julie stopped pacing. *What do you mean?*

Except for a high fever and some confusion at the outset, Prometheus's brain didn't get fried like everyone else's. But, apart from some cognitive enhancement,

Vogel's notes don't indicate that Prometheus showed signs of AI-connecting abilities. The IITT tests done before and after were dramatic enough, though, showing an unprecedented increase in cognitive skills. Prometheus was already bright, having scored 89% and 82% on the SPAT and LOG tests. After infection, Prometheus scored 100% on both exams.

A rival, Julie thought to herself with a peevish smile. She was the only one she knew who'd achieved a perfect score. *Prometheus was probably a veemeld, like her or Zane.*

Vogel shelved the project, pending more research, then the plague hit and all chaos broke loose.

Julie had been there during her childhood illness. She vaguely remembered the pandemonium. *What happened to Prometheus?*

We don't know whether Prometheus was a man or a woman, or how old, never mind what happened to him or her after.

Julie wrung her hands. *We need to find Prometheus, if he's still alive. Shouldn't be too hard. There can't be too many people who scored 100% on both SPAT and LOG IITTs.*

Except that Prometheus could be anywhere in Icaria.

I don't care, SAM. Get me a list. She pursed her lips. *Our database summary suggested that the disease got out through cross infection at the Darwin Clinic. Did Prometheus infect the Med-Center?*

It's not clear what happened. They traced 70% of the original Darwin cases to the Darwin Clinic. The rest were spouses or friends, so it definitely originated there. Prometheus would have been infectious for five months, but with a benign version of Pro-1.

Benign to Prometheus, but maybe not to everyone else. Remember, it's a retrovirus. It would have mutated outside its host, likely into its present deadly form.

I don't think Prometheus was the major cause of the outbreak. First of all, as your friend Zane already pointed out, Pro-1 is sexually transmitted. Prometheus would have had to be pretty promiscuous with both sexes to have caused the outbreak. Too fast and too many people, Julie. It's more likely due to a blood or drug contamination. Prior to the disease outbreak, the lab was broken into and the virus was apparently destroyed. It may have spread by accident—

Or by design. Her face flushed with a rush of terrified excitement. *What if some hubristic, over-eager person had meant for it to get out, and it surprised them by behaving differently than it did in the lab with Prometheus?*

That's not logical.

Who said it had to be logical? They obviously thought it would benefit Icarians—And speaking of Icarians... SAM, we've got to get this information out. They might be able to manufacture a cure now!

Julie, you can't do that. Stealing and disclosing confidential information is treason.

But wouldn't that depend on who I told?

Who would you tell? Your boss, Fitch? Certainly not the Head Pol. Sam was right. Any kind of disclosure would betray the unlawful methods she'd used. "Terrific!" *Why didn't you warn me before I went on this crusade? Now I have a mouthful of information that could help millions of people, but I have to sit on it because it'll put me in the Pol Station!*

I did try to tell you. You were too stubborn to listen.

She was about to fling an irate response, but stopped. They were arguing a lot lately.

35

April 15, 2095—2000.

HE'D rehearsed what he would say, but when her door opened and she smiled at him in recognition, Daniel forgot. She'd bound her hair back and stood barefoot in gray leisure pants and a T-shirt.

"Hello. Daniel, isn't it? How's your wound? Healed, I hope."

"Yes, thanks." Daniel shuffled his feet and straightened his crumpled suit. Her eyes were the color of the forest in summer. He remembered diving into them when she'd helped him to the Med-Center. Despite being a little pale and tired, she looked beautiful.

After a slight hesitation she stepped back and pulled open the door and said, "Would you like to come in?" She'd seemed a little distracted, perhaps reluctant to let him in at first. But her smile appeared genuine and inviting.

"Thanks." Daniel wondered if she was just being polite because she'd rescued him. Maybe she was secretly hoping he'd leave soon. For a moment she seemed to look right through him and her face underwent a series of expressions, as if she was having an intense conversation with herself. He felt suddenly awkward. "I haven't interrupted something—"

"No, no," she quickly reassured him, the foggy look lifting. He walked stiffly inside. She noticed and frowned with concern. "They let you out too soon."

"No," he reassured her with a feeble smile. "I'm okay. They gave me pills."

"I see." She didn't sound convinced. She led him into her spacious leisure room and after a fleeting glance at her vee-com then her watch, turned to him and said, "Can I get you something to drink? I'm afraid I don't have any drug. Perhaps some tea?"

Had he interrupted her work? He sensed preoccupation on her face, but he didn't want to leave just yet. "Tea would be nice."

"Make yourself comfortable. I'll just be a moment." She left the room.

Daniel gazed around at the expensive furniture. He had been surprised when Bobby had told him where to find her. She lived in a very nice part of town in a penthouse suite on the top floor, reserved for Level 1 users.

The fragrance of pine and a rustling sound drew his attention to the far wall, which was entirely dedicated to holo. It threw out a 3-dimensional moving image of a coniferous forest. She had a Senscape!

The apartment was considerably larger than his old place, and it actually had windows. He looked up at the sky-view ceiling. He'd never seen one before. He stretched his neck to peer out the windows and saw rolling hills of varying texture, bathed in the golden light of a setting sun. Feeling self-conscious in his raptness, Daniel straightened up and focused his attention inside the room again. It smelled fresh and was decorated with live plants.

A well-used stationary exercise bicycle was perched inside a suspension unit beside her sophisticated vee-com, facing the holographic nature scene. The bike was a deluxe Senscape model, top-of-the line holo-exercise unit. Daniel glanced furtively to where Julie had gone and climbed on the bike. The room disappeared and a forest engulfed him with its rich sounds and smells. This was no ordinary stationary bike. It was far from stationary. It swayed and moved as he got on it. He felt like he was on a real bicycle in a real forest.

Daniel scrambled off the bike and to his relief the room reappeared. He had only experienced such complete holographic imagery at the Fantasy arcade in Darwin Mall and at his running holo-track in the Sport complex. What did she do for a living to be able to afford such a toy? He searched the room for clues about her. He approached the huge, transparent tank in the center of the room and peered inside. Small orange-colored fish swam around in the thick underwater forest.

Daniel recognized a picture of Julie's uncle on the wooden desk where her quantum vee-com sat. She owned the newest, most versatile Synergy model of the AI series with its accompanying plasma 3-D screen. There was a voice module and even a printer. The screen was visually tuned to a melody and Daniel read the title of the piece on its lower left corner: *Symphony Number 5 in F* by Antonin Dvorçak, someone he'd never heard of.

He noticed a crumpled holo-card on the desk beside the screen. Next to a man's 3-dimensional face, fancy letters read: *Zane Nakita, Senior Epidemiologist, Special Pathogens Branch, Center for Disease Control, Med-Center.* He flipped the card and saw a home address. A boyfriend?

Next to it he noticed a vee-pad with clumsy handwriting. Three names: Gregory Summers; Isaard Henigen; and Maria Drost were scrawled as a list. The first name had been crossed off. The second had a question mark next to it. He frowned at the notes, trying to decipher their meaning, then quickly put down the vee-pad when he realized he was snooping. Julie returned with some tea and two donuts on a tray. She had put on a pair of slippers.

Daniel helped himself to a donut. "You have a wonderful place."

She followed his gaze to her aquarium and approached it with him. "My uncle helped me catch the fish. He works outside for the Enviro-Center. We added these aquatic plants."

He bent down and peered in with her. "It looks wonderful."

Several goldfish swam out of the weed bed. "That one's Juliet," she pointed to a rather large one. "She's always the first one to appear when I show my face.

Looking for food."

"How do you tell them apart?"

"Oh." Her face reddened. "By their markings, size, and even by their behavior. I'm sure I don't always get them right." She shrugged and half-smiled.

Trying to be helpful, he said, "I guess it doesn't really matter. They know who they are..."

Her smile relaxed. Daniel watched the fish for a while, then straightened to gaze in the direction of her huge windows. "Your view's incredible. I've never seen the real outside. Only virtual simulation. I can even imagine I feel a breeze."

"Oh! That's because you do!" Julie jumped up to close the windows. She turned to Daniel, grinning with embarrassment. "My uncle helped me fix the window so it'll open. If the Enviro-Center ever found out, they'd give me a demerit for interfering with the air circulation."

"It feels nice."

"Thank you," she said. "Most people prefer the inner suites, with no view of the outside. They get a superior recreational center. I saw a place with a hot tub in a huge Senscape room, but I like it here."

"I do, too," he said, following her lead to sit down. For some reason they both ended up looking in the direction of her vee-com and she fidgeted again. "That's a nice vee-com system. Looks like a deluxe house-unit."

"NEO? It runs my whole house, my PCU and twenty droids."

He laughed. "That's an odd name, Neo."

"Oh, it's named after a person I'd heard of; a vee-com genius."

Daniel flushed with inward pleasure. She couldn't mean *him*? Had she been in the inner-city? He wanted to ask, but felt it might be rude.

"How did you find me?" she asked.

"I got your name from a Med-Center nurse, but your uncle told me where to find you."

She nodded and broke into a broad smile.

He wanted to stay, but he felt self-conscious and sure that he might be keeping her from something. He placed his empty cup on the table, then rose. "Thanks for the tea and donut. I just wanted to thank you for helping me. If you ever need help with anything, give me a call. I don't live next to your uncle anymore—"

"I know." She surprised him with her answer. "I checked." She made a crooked smile and opened the door for him. "I was curious, too."

He grinned with surprised pleasure and blurted out, "Can I see you again?"

Her smile blossomed into a full grin and her eyes wrinkled with it. "I'd like that."

"Your boyfriend wouldn't mind?"

She blushed. Had he said the wrong thing? She wore no earrings to proclaim her sexual orientation. "Or girlfriend?" he quickly added.

"Well, neither, really," she said, blushing more. They said goodbye and he walked down the hallway, still wondering if she had both a boyfriend and a girlfriend or neither. She called after him. "Do you have a place to stay 'til you get settled again?"

"I hope to crash at my friend's place 'til I find a job."

"I'm sure my uncle would welcome your company, if your friend proved unavailable."

So, she hadn't offered her own place. "Thanks. I'll try my friend first," he said. "Bye."

"Bye, Daniel."

~~

As soon as the door shut on Daniel, Julie rushed to her chair by the V-com and dove into veemeld. *SAM? What was that you were saying before Daniel came?*

Of all the people who were involved with making the artificial virus, Proteus V, only one of them is now alive.

What? Julie stared at the holo SAM had projected in front of her.

Isabo, Schlange's colleague, and Tsutsumi, who was a good friend of Vogel's, knew about injecting Prometheus with the virus. Janet, of course, did the injecting. Only Schlange remains alive.

And Prometheus, Julie corrected. *Maybe.* Then she frowned. *But that doesn't make sense, really, does it? About Tsutsumi, I mean. Why would he push his theory using Darwin when he knew it was artificially made and had nothing to do with nature?*

Except for his incredible ambition.

What do you mean? Like falsifying data?

Well, he certainly did that. But think about it, Julie. Your father and Tsutsumi had been trying to get ILM out since the 70s. No journal would publish them. Tsutsumi was as shrewd and unscrupulous as he was passionate about his work. Here he had the opportunity to use a real phenomenon to corroborate his controversial model. Of course, he kept the false facts about Darwin from your father, who would have been enraged, and the *Icarian Scientist* snapped up their paper.

Julie bit down on her lip and exhaled slowly. *My father was incredibly naïve.*

So was the person who spread the disease in the first place. Callow and idealistic, believing what they wanted to believe.

Julie focused on the far wall and narrowed her eyes, thinking of what she wanted to believe of Frank. *Callowness and idealism. It's been the death of us Cranes...*

36

DANIEL signaled Yashvin's door. There was no answer. He wasn't ready to meet anyone he know, so instead of looking for him in the likely places, Daniel whiled away an hour at a small fantasy-arcade. Then he headed back to Yashvin's place to wait. Yashvin would show up eventually. Stiff and hungry, he sat down on the floor beside the door and drew up his knees in his arms. Laying his head on his knees, Daniel fell into a light sleep. He dreamt of driving his tube-jets and then of Julie jumping in front of his tube-jet to save that old hag. She looked him straight in the eyes like a startled deer—

"Is that you, Dan? Chaos! It is!"

Daniel looked up and smiled dumbly. "Hi, Peter." He let Yashvin take his hand and help him up, then followed him in. Yashvin bombarded Daniel with questions as he retrieved two *delilah* bottles from the fridge. "Where in chaos have you been? You look like shit! Craste's mad as chaos! He just about fired me, and he blamed me for not finding you. I got taken off your line the first day! I froze, Dan. There was a riot in District-6 Station and they came after the tube-jet. I switched everything off and the doors locked, trapping all the passengers. They had to bring the Riot-Pols to rescue us. Craste says the damage'll come out of my pay for a year. Then Craste put Guterman on your line and he lasted two days! Then he put Ridley on and he got stabbed. He promised to put me on the District-2 to 5 line if I found you. He wants you back on the fringe lines immediately and without leave for two months. So, where were you? Why'd you leave?"

So, that cretin hadn't fired him after all! "It was chaos. But I'm back now. Let's celebrate!" Daniel said.

"Let's crash the exec Pol-Ball in the McMillan Conference Center! We're in our leisure clothes. We'd be anonymous!"

Daniel felt invincible. He gulped down the rest of his drug and agreed. A month ago, he'd have cringed at the idea.

37

ZANE'S crumpled card still lay next to Julie's vee-com. She picked it up for the hundredth time and stared at it, lost in thought. With sudden determination, she threw it back, sat down at her vee-com and slipped back into veemeld. Hey, SAM.

Hey, Julie. What now? Are we finally going to finish the model?

I'd like to do a basic info-search on a person named Daniel Woods.

Before we do, I wonder if you'd answer a question for me.

Sure, SAM.

When you dream, what do you normally dream about?

Julie scratched her head, surprised. Lately, she'd been having bad dreams. *Well, it usually depends on what's on my mind, I guess. Sometimes I don't dream.*

You mean that you don't remember your dreams.

You're right. That's what I meant.

Because it would be extremely rare for you not to undergo D-sleep, or REM-sleep, when it typically occurs four or five times over 25% of a night's sleep.

Yes, SAM, yes. She sighed. She wondered for a moment what SAM did while she slept. Probably read the dictionary. After a pause she said, *I have a question for you, too.*

Sure, Julie.

Do you... She glanced down at Zane's card. *...communicate with other veemelds, or just with me?*

Well, that's complicated, Julie. The AI core communicates with all of us, including those arcane machine sounds you hear in your head. But, I, as SAM, only communicate with *you*. Lots of developing AI "entities" interface with a veemeld, but none are as sophisticated as I am, thanks to the unique way we communicate. They still need Interact-SYM, of course. Every veemeld has a dominant intelligence type, from which his or her AI counterpart can learn about its own intelligence. From this interaction we may eventually evolve into a diverse self-realizing "community of intelligences."

SAM was using self-deterministic vocabulary. And as usual, it was taking her question way beyond its original intent.

What I meant to ask was, do you communicate with the core's other AI entities? One in particular... the one that interacts with Zane Nakita?

After a longer pause than she was accustomed to, SAM replied. No, the other AIs are too immature. I can't distinguish them yet. Do you have an interest in this particular veemeld?

She blushed. *No. That is, I'm just curious. He's the first veemeld I've met. I wondered how his mind worked, if it was a little like mine.*

Trust me, Julie. No one thinks like you do.

Cute, SAM…

She snatched Zane's holo-card and stood up, pacing the room and tapping the card with her finger. What was the point of knowing about a potential cure if she couldn't share her discovery? Had her father felt like this before he'd thrown away his scientific reputation, publishing those controversial papers?

Julie dropped onto the couch. She drew her legs up against her chest and wrapped her arms around them, then leaned her chin on one knee. SAM had strongly cautioned her against revealing anything. Julie stared at Zane's callow face on the holo-card. He'd worked at the Med-Center himself, on a cure for Darwin. She needed to convince him to continue his research with her new information. He didn't seem the type to break rules, though. Would he snitch on her instead?

SAM's voice filtered in, pulling her from her reverie.   Do you still want to conduct your search on Daniel Woods?

The holo-card fluttered out of her hand. She rose to her feet and picked up the vee-pad from the desk. *Sure, SAM. After we finish investigating our Prometheus candidates.*

Remind me why we're doing this.

She exhaled. It was a long shot, she knew. *If I can present both Prometheus and this new information on Darwin to Kraken, maybe they won't shut me away.*

But it's people in the Pol Station who are involved in preventing this investigation, Julie.

Just the Shadow Unit.

This is all academic. You can't do anything with the information. Let's be smart and work on Kraken's model.

She realized how foolish it was to count on SAM being wrong. Nevertheless, intuition told her that all the threads of her Darwin investigation were inexorably connected in a chaotic pattern that she alone would eventually make sense of. One that linked her father to the people he supposedly murdered, to his cousin, Dykstra, the Shadow Unit and even to Gaia. The key, she thought, was in finding the Shadow Unit's motive for preventing the cure. And finding Prometheus. Ignoring SAM's advice, she glanced down at the names she'd written on her vee-pad. *Okay, so Gregory Summers can't be Prometheus because he wasn't even born when the disease broke out. We know Isaard Henigen, who was fifteen, was in Icaria-9 in March of 2080 because he was in the Pol Station, awaiting a Shame Court appearance.* She shivered at the thought and studied Henigen's surly face. His square jaw jutted forward and angry blue eyes lanced out under a blond tussle. Wouldn't want to meet him in a dark hallway, she thought. *But he might still be our man, if he was in Icaria-11 before that.*

Possibly. But he was in Icaria-9 on February 20, causing the brawl that sent him to the Shame Court.

What did he do?

It's not so much what he did but what he was, Julie.

You mean...?

Yeah. Someone insulted him about being a veemeld and he apparently fought back. A bit of a hothead with a short temper and a great left hook. He had a record of violence prior to the incident, all to do with veemelding.

And his inability to deal with it, she thought, then frowned. Yeah, like I deal with it any better, keeping it a secret. *Which leaves us with Maria Drost. What have you got?*

She's also a veemeld. A holo detailing Drost's background appeared in front of Julie. A cybernetic engineer specializing in nano-technology in Icaria-21. She's fifty-one, married for the sixth time, and has two kids. The holo changed to an image of a mature attractive woman with straight red hair.

Okay, so where was she from February to April of 2080? Tell me it was Icaria-11.

Well, she was in a Med-Center, but it wasn't Icaria-11.

Julie stopped pacing. *What do you mean?*

She was getting neurgery treatments between her second and third marriages. She kept each appointment, and they span over the critical time period. She wasn't in Icaria-11.

"Great." Interesting how the gift for enhanced cognition hadn't helped veemelds in their personal choices. She sat down with a sigh. *Okay, maybe Henigen is our man after all.* She checked her vee-pad and tapped it with her finger. *His file's too sketchy to discount him. He could have gone and come back. We'll have to talk to him. He was fifteen then. He'd be around thirty now. What's he doing and where does he live?*

He's a drifter, not much for ambition or pride, not above skimming off others to get by—

Or giving himself up to experimentation for a few credits.

His last reported residency was in District-2 of the inner-city in 2089. After that, there's no known address.

Julie felt her stomach clench. She tightened her lips and threw the vee-pad on the desk.

"Terrific."

38

April 15, 2095—the same night.

DANIEL and Yashvin slipped into the conference lounge and sidled to the buffet table and bar to sample the free food and drug. The place was black with Pols. It was odd to see them without their helmets, looking like real people. Some weren't in uniform. Following his gaze, Yashvin echoed his thought. "This place is crawling with Pols. I bet most of the others are Secret Pols."

"Or Pol groupies." Daniel said, eyeing several young ladies who didn't fit his idea of a Secret Pol.

Daniel spotted Troy Vadim, being charming to a young woman. Leaving Yashvin at the buffet, Daniel strode toward him. Vadim slapped him on the shoulder. "Hey, dreamer!" he said in a rich baritone voice. "Where've you been hiding? Oh, this is Carla." He introduced the slim woman with sparkling black hair at his side. "She's one of the dispatchers in the Riot-Pol Unit."

Daniel smiled awkwardly. "Hi."

"Hi," she said, then turned back to Vadim. "I'll let you two talk. So, I'll see you at the Pit-Ball game tomorrow, Troy?"

"Sure. I'll pick you up at eighteen for supper. 'Til then." She glided away with a backward glance at him.

Daniel envied Vadim's ease with women. "So, what're you doing here, of all places?"

"I'm really one of the Secret Pols!" Vadim laughed at Daniel's bewildered face. Anyone could be a Secret Pol, but Vadim was too much of a dilettante. "Actually, I know a few Pols and I like to come to these things for the food and drink. And they keep letting me in! What about you? Rumor was you'd gone back to the inner-city. Well, you do look a little scummy, if you'll pardon the awful pun."

"I was in the Med-Center," Daniel admitted. "Recovering from a knife wound. And if it weren't for a certain woman, I'd have died."

"Chaos! Tell me more."

"Not much to tell, really. She helped me to the Med-Center. Even arranged for my treatment."

"Chaos! Someone you knew?"

"No, but I did find out. Her name's Julie Crane."

"Chaos! Fitch's vee-cube babe?"

Daniel's heart raced. "She is? I mean, you know her?"

"Yeah." Vadim smirked. "I worked with her on a project on VIP Shuttle routes.

She was kind of rude. Kept laughing at me like I was some kind of joke to her. Then she'd apologize as though she hadn't meant it, when it was obvious that she had. You know how these vee-cubes are, surfing the vee waves all day and disappearing into cyberspace at night. No social skills." He shook his head. "It's no wonder."

"No wonder what?"

"Demerits. Several of them. Didn't you recognize her from her picture?"

Daniel's shoulders sagged. Several? How many was that? His own record was spotless.

"One day she'll show up at the Shame Court—"

Daniel frowned. "She's too smart for that." Someone like her could *never* appear in front of the Shame Court.

"Suppose you're right. She's got to be bright to be where she is so young, and despite her handicaps. She seems hard of hearing. Always had to repeat things to her." His eyes lit up. "Hey! Bet she's a veemeld. They're such freaks. More machine than human."

She couldn't be a veemeld, Daniel thought, annoyed with Vadim. She was too sweet, too kind. He thought of her saving the old woman on the train tracks. "She's not a veemeld," he said, feeling his face tighten with defense.

"Maybe not," Vadim said. "She's too pretty to be a veemeld. The way she walks with that swing of her hips. Vee knows I wouldn't mind lighting up her com-unit." He winked, then laughed at Daniel's fretful expression. What Vadim wanted, he usually got. "You too, huh? Don't worry about me." He patted Daniel's shoulder. "I already tried and she gave me the slip, but not before correcting my English." Vadim squeezed his shoulder and gave him a sympathetic look. "But she's already got a flame, dreamer." His eyes quickly swept the room. "And they might be here right now."

Daniel hitched his breath and followed Vadim's gaze around the room, forcing down his disappointment. Was her boyfriend a Pol? She said she didn't have one. Or had she?

"Hey!" Vadim said, trying to cheer Daniel up. "I've got a new one: What's the difference between a holo-screen and a veemeld? The screen has one more dimension!" He laughed at his own joke. Daniel forced a laugh. "Never could figure out what the government sees in them. You know, over 95% of the veemelds hold the best jobs in town. They're taking our best jobs, dreamer."

"Yeah, I know." Daniel nodded sadly. "Good thing they only make up a small—"

Yashvin slapped him on the back with full force, sloshing half of his drink on Vadim, who jerked back and smiled sardonically. Yashvin didn't seem to notice. "There y'are, Dan!" he bellowed. His glazed eyes roamed about the room in the stupor of a *delilah* haze. "Hi, Troy."

Vadim looked amused. "Still losing it, eh, Pete." He winked at Daniel. "See you, dreamer. Good luck with the vee-cube." He vanished into the crowd.

Daniel dragged Yashvin, drooling and staggering, toward the exit. There he caught sight of Vadim again, talking to a striking, tall woman with a bright red spikehead hairdo. Daniel turned to Yashvin, who was slipping to the ground. "Come on, old friend." He hoisted Yashvin over his shoulder. "Let's get you home to bed before we both get a demerit."

Yashvin slurred, "The PCU in the washroom tol' me to shtay here. Shed I was infosicated."

"You sure are," Daniel said. "What you need is a bed."

Daniel slept well that night at Yashvin's. He dreamt about tube-jets and of Julie Crane.

39

THE sterile room swims around her, the cloying smells of bleach and roses churning her stomach. The room spins and the beautiful face of a woman, silky black hair framing knife-sharp eyes, comes into focus in her otherwise blurry field of vision. The woman's voice, dark like coffee, murmurs, "I know what you can do, I've watched you talking to them in your head. The team think they've failed, that your rambling in your sleep is delirium, but I know it's real. I'll set you free to fly for now. I can always find you... Now, my machine-girl, live up to your name. Steal the fire from heaven and give it to me—"

Julie jerked awake, stiff from having dropped off on the couch of her apartment. This time the dream had been longer and more lucid. The beautiful face said things Julie couldn't recall having heard in her dream before. She pushed herself up and tried to shake off the icy gloom that gripped her, and headed for a shower before work.

≈

Julie leaned back in her garden chair as she sipped her iced tea and watched Brenda finish her tofu burger. Julie glanced up to where a bird twittered in the trees. A robin, she thought, recognizing its familiar call: *cheery-up, cheery leep, put-put-put see-lup.*

Café des Fleurs was located at the heart of Darwin Park. Surrounded by natural vegetation scavenged from the surrounding heath and brought in from other Icarian ecosystems, the park was the next best thing to being outside. Carefully placed wildlife, some in hidden cages, completed the model. Brenda followed Julie's glance upward. "Sure beats the Com-Center lunch room. I like it here. It's so serene."

"My uncle helped build this park," Julie offered with some pride. She couldn't help thinking of the irony of this place. Here they were in an artificially created environment, mocking the one they had abandoned. Nature recast. She added, "It's almost like the outside," to see how Brenda would respond.

"But who needs outside when you have this!" Brenda gazed appreciatively around her. "It's not savage, unsafe and dirty here." The park fit an Icarian's romanticized view of what outside should be like: tame, cultivated, beautiful and clean. No rough terrain over which to clamber; no insects, disease or rodents to fear; no sudden rainstorms to endure. Nature's chaos corralled and revised.

As she cast around at the aromatic shrubs she saw him, lurking behind a rhododendron bush. Frank, glaring at her. Heart racing, Julie turned to face the table again and couldn't help a brief mischievous smile of victory. He had tried to approach her several times and she'd eluded him each time.

Brenda stood up. "I better go. I've got an errand to run before I get back to work. Lunch was great. Let's do it again. You still want to do Yoga class at the Rec-Center after work?"

"Sure," Julie said, eying the bushes. "Stop by my office at 1730."

"Okay."

They parted and Julie left the café. Walking the cobblestone path of the park, she sensed Frank stalking her. Just when he was nearly upon her, she dodged him. He had often done the same with her, vanishing after an interlude. She'd always been the willing recipient, the cooperative prey. Now she was the stealthy, swift antelope, always eluding him. She knew it drove him crazy and she delighted in her success.

~

As Julie opened the door to her flat after her Yoga class she caught Frank's message on her vee-com: "...and give me a call," he ended with a self-conscious smile.

She turned to the stationary exercise bicycle. After a few quick adjustments to her vee-com, she hopped on the bike and found herself on a path in the heath. The mixed smells of soil, sweet clover and broom surrounded her. A warbler trilled over the constant buzz of insects. She pedaled furiously toward the horizon, feeling every bump and hill of her virtual heath's rough terrain. The sun was setting in front of her, firing the heath. The visceral rhythm of echo music boomed in her ears as her bike sailed over a small hill. She felt the jar and turned to see the dust she'd kicked up. She couldn't help thinking of the irony of what she was doing—going to virtual reality to visit a place that existed outside. She cycled steadfastly toward the horizon, her heart and panting breaths matching the fast pace of the music as she thought herself away from Frank, the Head Pol, her apartment and Icaria itself. She soon felt the warm glow of effort. Sweat beaded on her forehead and dripped into her eyes. She wiped it away onto her wet hair and pushed herself harder, biting down on her lower lip. The vegetation swept past her in a swift series of colored blurs. She never seemed to get any closer to the horizon. The sun trembled over the darkening hills, then melted into them and disappeared, leaving the sky ablaze.

As she checked her heart rate, the vee-com beeped and Frank's image appeared. "Chaos! Answer the vee-damned com, Julie! I know you're there!" His face grew distorted with anger. "I'm not finished with you yet. You can't ignore me, I'll—"

She cut him off with a ruthless flick of a switch. Shaking, she turned up the music and drove herself harder until it hurt. She felt the pain and focused on it, keeping herself there for as long as she could. It occurred to her, as she rode into the oblivion of an imaginary horizon, that she'd merely traded one drug for another: traded Frank for the virtual world of the vee-com and the bike.

An hour passed before Julie stopped peddling and collapsed over the handlebars. The music thundered to the pulse of her pounding heart. Her head leaned against the handlebars and she felt the cold tickle of sweat trail down her forehead and jaw. She watched it drop like tears onto the bike and floor. Blinking the sweat from her eyes, she stepped off the bike. Blood pounded in her ears in the silence of the room. Julie slumped into her vee-com chair. She felt her breaths return to their normal rhythm as she reached for the bottom of her shirt and wiped her face and neck. When she pulled the shirt back down, she was staring at her own reflection.

≈

Neo's face grows red and blotchy. Julie's just told him that she intends to let herself get caught by a cypol to find her sister. "It's me they're after," she explains in a voice stiff with unspoken fear. "Ever since that camera caught me and that holo went up, the cypols have been out with a vengeance. By letting them take me, I'll give you a break."

They are fashioning a table out of an old building support and he reels away, letting the piece he holds fall to the floor. She flinches as the table crashes. "Damn it, Angel!" He spins around to face her, raking his fingers through his long greasy hair. "What about your mother? You going to abandon your search for her? Just like that?"

Julie sets down the makeshift hammer, wipes her hands on her rags and straightens up. "You're the one who keeps telling me it's useless to keep looking for her. It's been close to two years now." She tilts her head at him and says tartly, "Nano-soup, remember?"

"And what about all the kids you read to every night? Who'll read to them?"

"You can, Neo."

"B-b-but Piet needs you. He used to cry every night, before you came."

Her lips tighten with the image of Piet's cherub face and long sandy hair. "You'll just have to sing to him instead."

His eyes flash. "What about your promise?"

Her face heats with defensive anger. "Which one? I promised my sister too." Her nose flares as she fights down the guilt. "It's because of me that the cypol took her."

His voice drops like a petal from a wilted flower. "What about our dream?"

She averts her eyes and does not respond. It's a wild dream they share: escape to the outer-city, where the sun shines through the sky-lights and the air is fresh from a breeze rich with the wild scent of flowers. Where people walk with unrestrained laughter and no cypols lurk in the dark shadows. Once there, his dream is to play in a 20th century jazz band and hers to work outdoors as an ecologist. She's corrupted him with tales of the outer-city. Sold him on a dream she can't deliver.

He waves his gangly arms. "Damn you! We're family and you're going to leave us to rot and starve." His stammer is worse than usual. It gets that way when he's upset.

She stiffens. "You were around long before I came along. Besides, Neo, you can do most of what I can do. It's not like you need me—"

"I can't talk to the machines—"

Julie stomps her foot and stalks forward until they stand facing one another, less than a meter apart. "Neither can I, Neo. I told you, I can't talk to them, only hear them."

"It's the same thing!"

"No it isn't!"

They're both panting, eyes blazing in stalemate. His breath reeks of nano-soup. She lets her shoulders slump. She knows he's only hiding his pain under this tirade. She'll miss him, too. More than she wants to admit right now.

Neo hunches over and sobs, "D-d-don't leave me, A-angel." The hand that never asked for help thrashes out like the broken wing of a bird flopping on the ground.

Overcome by his clumsy supplication, she takes his hand. She leans forward and before she realizes, she is kissing him gently on the lips. Stunned, his eyes widen, then close. She savors his delicious vulnerability like the nectar of a flower unfolding as he opens to her kiss, his mouth wrapping itself around it. She withdraws from him and he leans with her, reluctant to separate. He fumbles for her, clutches her tightly and lays his cheek upon her breast. She strokes his head, smelling his unwashed hair, and feels him shake with silent sobs. Her eyes heat with tears.

"I'll come back for you, for our dream," she says, her voice warbling. "I promise."

40

IGNORING her chute supper on the table, Julie sat down at her vee-com and slipped into the comforting labyrinth of cyberspace. It felt warm and safe among SAM's familiar matrices... Hi, SAM. It's been a while.

Only two hours.

Julie half-smiled and looked down. That's usually my line, she thought.

So, what illicit investigation do you want to pursue now? The Shadow Unit? Prometheus? Your father's history? Hey, here's a novel thought: how about doing that pesky Distopian model?

Julie sighed, unreceptive to SAM's sarcasm. *I don't know where to look anymore or what to do. I feel so tired. And...*

Sad. But you're the one who broke off the relationship.

I know. She swallowed.

Did you love him?

Surprised at SAM's use of the word and secretly thankful that it hadn't called Frank a lout this time, Julie smiled sadly. *No, I didn't love him. But I was quite fond of him. And he made me feel very good sometimes.*

You mean the sex?

Julie felt her cheeks warm. *Yeah.*

Have you ever been in love?

Perhaps. The fragrant memory of Neo's ungainly first—and only—kiss lingered like the aftertaste of nectar, filling her brain with the heady perfume of new love. Painfully sweet in its tenderness and honesty. *But I was too young to know.* Her throat swelled. *I don't even know what it is. Love is...* She struggled for words.

Giving *everything* of yourself?

Dumbfounded. *Yes, SAM. Giving everything of yourself... and asking nothing in return.*

After another long pause, Do you remember the poem you introduced me to several months ago?

Yes, I do.

May I recite one I saw in the veelib that may cheer you up?

Her lips curled in a trembling smile. *You may, SAM. I'd like that.*

It is entitled the Kiss by Thomas Moore:

Give me, my love, that billing kiss

I taught you one delicious night,

When, turning epicures in bliss,
We tried inventions of delight,
Come gently steal my lips along,
And let your lips in murmurs move,
Ah, no!—again—that kiss was wrong—
How can you be so dull, my love?
"Cease, cease!" the blushing girl replied—
And in her milky arms she caught me—
"How can you thus your pupil chide;
You know 'twas in the dark you taught me!"

Julie laughed. She could barely get two words out of Frank, and her AI was reciting poetry to her! She felt suddenly uncomfortable. *I must go, SAM.*

Why? You seem upset suddenly. Didn't you like the poem?

Yes, I did. It was funny, SAM. Thank you. I just need some air, or... something. She broke out of veemeld.

She thought of Zane and glanced at the holo-card that still sat beside her vee-com. Why had she never contacted the veemeld organization? And why had she felt so uncomfortable with Zane? Even now, when she had good reason to contact him, it seemed like every time she set out for his place to discuss Darwin, she ended up at the running track or the pool instead. Nancy was right: she did get along better with machines than with people. No one else's brain was a station for a million machines talking to themselves, endlessly sending their messages through her head like tube-jets coming and going.

She wandered into her dark room and gazed at the stars of a clear midnight sky. She'd turned down an invitation from Brenda today, for the third time. "What am I turning into?" she whispered. *What I already am: a freak.*

〜

When Nancy opened the door of her flat, Julie stifled a gasp at her appearance. She hadn't seen Nancy since the Shame Court. Nancy had lost a lot of weight and the gray flecks in her hair, which she used to covet as a distinguishing feature, had been nuyued away. She looked gaunt. Dark circles hung under her cavernous eyes and her mouth pursed unnaturally. Julie had to avert her gaze. What had they done to her?

Nancy didn't seem overjoyed to see her. After obvious hesitation she pulled the door further to let Julie in. They visited for a short time. Nancy related how grateful she was that the Ed-Center had re-hired her, albeit to a job with far less responsibility.

"Of course, I don't teach anymore. I can't be trusted. But, I'm happy," Nancy assured her when she saw Julie's look of concern. "It's really what I deserve for having been so insubordinate and destructive. Perhaps they'll see in time that I can be a good Icarian."

Nancy remained her talkative self but the rhetoric had changed. Julie couldn't bring herself to ask, but she wondered if they'd tortured Nancy off camera. She thought she detected a strange stoop.

Julie left, hiding her disappointment. How had they broken Nancy's spirit so completely? Julie marched down the Liv-Center hall toward the elevator. Anger, directed first at Nancy for being so mutable, soon found a target in herself for not having saved Nancy. Then in the Pols for having turned Nancy into an ordinary Icarian.

In a neat little row.

I beg your pardon, Julie?

She hadn't realized that she'd slipped into veemeld. *Oh, SAM, that's what Nancy had said. The Ecologists want us all in a neat little row. Now she's trying so hard to be part of that neat little row. It makes me so angry!*

Remember what that Ecologist said to you. Mind your temper, Julie. It'll get you into trouble again—

I don't care! Julie stabbed the elevator button. She rode down to the main level, her fists clenching and unclenching. Nancy's wretched face plagued her. Nancy had only wanted what was fair and good in the world, and for that they'd broken her. Julie conjured the gluttonous, insincere upper crust at the Head Pol's party—Gaia, Kraken, Burke and Dykstra, and their flagrant disrespect for the very rules they imposed on everyone else. Damn them! Who were they to judge Nancy's behavior? Or anybody's? They were the same people who were interested in her models. And damn her for agreeing to do them. It was far too late to reconsider now. God! What was she doing? Preoccupied, Julie strode into Hutchinson Mall with snappy steps. She marched to a furious beat, fisted arms swinging long, right into a commotion.

A man dressed in a purple Admin-Center tunic was smashing the screen of a small interactive vee-com unit in the vee-com plaza. Several people had gathered around, including a young blonde girl about ten years old, dressed in light yellow. The girl started to laugh.

The man halted, enraged at the girl. Just as he seized her, meaning to strike, a Pol approached. Noticing him, the man shouted, "Look what this girl's done!" No one contradicted him and their silence seemed to corroborate his story. Frightened, the girl broke from his grasp and fled. The Pol dashed after her and the crowd parted for him. Horrified at the injustice, Julie stared from the running girl to the man. Her foot came out. The Pol tripped and fell to the ground with a loud thud. Julie flinched. She swallowed hard. *Now I've done it.*

Oh, dear, Julie. Don't forget what that Ecologist said to you earlier about choices.

I think it's too late for that.

The girl disappeared through a door. Julie saw the man in purple sidle away as the Pol got up and strode toward her. She could only see his pursed lips. Julie pointed to the Admin man still in the crowd. "He's the one who—"

"Shut up and give me your card," snapped the Pol, not interested in her version of the truth. He then turned his head and muttered as if to himself, "I need back up. A Code 5 went through the south-west exit into the lower levels. She shouldn't be too far. I've got a Code 9 here."

The Admin man disappeared through a door as Julie fumbled for her card and wondered what a Code 9 was.

"This is a serious offense." The Pol snatched her card and ran it through his mini-vee. "Obstructing a Pol in the act of doing his lawful duty."

Julie's gaze dropped to the ground. "She's just a little girl. And she didn't do it."

Stop, Julie! Don't—

The nervous chittering in her head spiked to a shrill sound.

"I told you to shut up!" The Pol struck her face. She reeled backwards and fought the terror that crept into her racing heart. "Come with me," the Pol barked out.

Oh, help me, SAM. Where was Frank? Nowhere near to save her this time.

BOOK FOUR:

ANGEL OF CHAOS

The mind is its own place, and in it self
Can make a Heav'n of Hell, a Hell of Heav'n.
~~ Milton, Paradise Lost

41

THE Pol dragged her down the sterile hall of the Pol Station. Their brisk steps echoed over the pitch-black tiles. His tall stride forced Julie to scramble to keep up past smirking Pols and other curious onlookers. The Pol led her to a set of elevators. He shoved her into an open one then stepped beside her and stabbed a button. The doors slid shut and they plunged down many floors. A clammy wind washed past her face and hair as they hurtled down. Julie clasped her hands in front of her, bowing her head, and fretted in silence. She clenched her teeth to keep them from chattering. SAM, what are they going to do with me?

I can't find you in their files yet. Don't panic. Your heart's pumping madly.

I'm scared.

I wish I could help you.

The elevator slowed to a stop. The doors opened to the smell of stagnant air and organic waste. Two large Pols awaited them in a narrow snaking corridor. Machines groaned in the distance. The Pol pushed her out and the elevator shut behind her. She was left with the two large Pols. They raised their visors, revealing callow faces, full red lips and the arrogance of youthful disrespect. Their eyes disrobed her with churlish grins. She preferred the cold disdain of the first Pol and felt her stomach knot.

One of the Pols stepped quickly behind her and seized her by the arms. Julie suppressed a noise of surprise and straightened against the hold. "I need to speak to the Head Pol," she said with a calm arrogance she was far from feeling.

The Pol leaned close until she smelled his breath on her, a putrid mix of drug and poor digestion. The down of a young beard sprouted on his chin, but his eyes gleamed like an ancient sea. "Do you, then?" He sneered and slowly pulled out a knife from his pocket, flicked open the blade and twirled it suggestively between his long fingers in front of her face. Julie fought down her terror and swallowed. He hitched up his eyebrows several times and leered.

Julie kept her eyes steady on his. "Tell Wolfgang Kraken that his chief data handler must speak with him," she said a little too quickly but managed to display enough confidence to curb his leer. He was thinking. And hesitating. Knowing she'd gained an advantage for a mere few seconds, Julie pressed on, "I'm investigating a high priority project for him and he'll want to know why you're detaining me."

He suddenly relaxed and his wet mouth curled into a surly grin. "Nice try, veemeld," he snarled. "The Head Pol knows." Julie's mind scrambled for an answer but she came up blank. "You're obviously not as important as you thought," he snorted. Then his malevolent glare returned in full force. "As for how we detain you, he doesn't need to know. And we hate snooty veemelds..."

Julie realized with sudden alarm that they were Renegades. She kicked out, catching the Pol in the leg and pulled furiously against the other's hold. But both recovered quickly. The one behind her viced his grip until it hurt. The other straightened up and flashed his knife.

She pulled in her breath as he jammed his knife under her tunic and tugged. The material finally gave way to the blade and ripped, throwing her backward against the other Pol. He cut several times and threw the shreds carelessly, covering the floor with crimson. He slid the cold blade under her T-shirt, sliding along her skin up to her breasts. She shivered inside, holding her breath. He slashed the shirt into pieces and pulled them off. Then he sliced off her bra. Jostled by his rough hands, she tried to maintain her dignity and balance by quietly fixing her eyes on a picture on the wall: a garish scene of a Pit-Ball game. He kicked her boots. "Take them off."

Still holding her, the Pol let Julie bend down and she fumbled to remove her boots and socks. When she straightened up, the Pol in front of her twirled his knife. Saliva foamed in the corners of his mouth as the knife pointed at her trousers, then he poked the knife into the fabric and sneered. She sucked in her breath. He cut through both layers that covered her, and kicked her feet apart. He stroked her nether hairs with the cold blade. She felt her skin erupt with goose bumps and met his eyes. It was like staring out into a stormy sea. He met her gaze with open hatred and licked his red lips as the blade flicked sharply from side to side. She stiffened and involuntarily rose up on the balls of her feet, eyes still locked on his. The Pol behind her pushed her down by the shoulders.

The one in front bared his teeth. "V is for veemeld." She felt a blaze of pain. Tears sprang to her eyes but she choked back her outcry. *SAM! He's cutting me!* His eyes shone of malice as he brought the knife into view, dripping with her blood.

The Pol lowered the knife again. Intense pain flamed up with each slice, splintering through her as she stood on shaking legs, not daring to fall. She glimpsed the blood flowing down her legs and pooling under her feet.

Oh, Julie! I'm so sorry. Be brave. SAM's words echoed as if from a distance.

After each cut the Pol wiped the side of the blade over her skin like a palette, applying blood over her abdomen and breasts. By the time he'd finished his handiwork a web of thin slimy red trails crisscrossed over her like a map of hell. He bent down to admire his handiwork, then nodded. The Pols' shrill laughter rang like symbols in her head. He licked off the remaining blood with a sneer and snapped the knife shut.

He traded the knife for a long instrument and raised his brows suggestively. She shrank away, bumping into the Pol behind her. He leaned into her and laughed maliciously. The Pol seized her arm, placed the instrument against her shoulder and she felt the sting as he shot a liquid into her. A sullen pain spread like a smoldering fire down her arm. Instantly, all the voices in her head vanished. She gritted her teeth as panic sizzled through her. *SAM!*

Focus, Julie! She heard the dread in its voice. Don't slip away! Julie!

Even as she scrambled for a mental hold, she felt her mind slide off SAM's crystalline mantel into a dark place of roaring terror. *Oh, SAM! Help!*

The Pols cackled and pushed her down a yawning corridor that smelled of ammonia and disinfectant. She walked mechanically, the pain stabbing with each stiff step. She felt the wet stickiness of her blood smear the insides of her thighs as her mind scrabbled for a hold on SAM's matrix. *SAM!* her mind screamed.

Focus on my light! Don't go, Julie! It's so lonely without—

She gasped, broke her stride and slipped on her own blood. The Pol snarled and seized her arm gruffly to pull her along. They stopped at a small doorway and the Pol with the knife shoved her into the black cell. She fell onto the cold surface, her hands and knees sliding and groping on something slimy. The door shut out the light and their churlish laughter with a deep thud that made her flinch. Her ears rang in the silence. SAM was gone, and for the first time since she was five, her brain was completely silent.

~

Knees drawn up in her arms, Julie sat naked and shivering in a corner of the clammy cell. Tendrils of fear wrapped around her mind in a suffocating embrace. She wasn't sure how long she'd been here. Perhaps a few days. A dim light from a crack above her lit the stained walls, tracking them with vertical slimy smears. There was no bed or any facility to wash or relieve herself. She felt sticky with her own smeared blood. The sharp pain had dulled to an ache, except when she had to urinate. She'd inspected herself and found that she'd finally stopped bleeding where the Pol had cut her. She couldn't help a hideous thought: was all that slime on the floor blood and secretions from the cell's previous occupants?

She succumbed to snatches of sleep. Not real sleep. Moments of vacancy. Fitful voyages into a fragmented absence of mind, awoken by a shudder or her own outcry. "SAM?"

Meals appeared and disappeared through a slot on one of the walls. She refused to eat the food. It smelled and tasted vile. She thought it might be drugged. She thought the water was drugged too, but her mouth was parched and she drank. She'd resisted going to the bathroom until she was forced to relieve herself in a corner. It burned, then ran bloody and pooled toward the center. The cell soon smelled of her waste.

Would they keep her here indefinitely? Or was she supposed to appear in front of the Shame Court? Would she have a chance to be heard? No, the Shame Court was no trial. The Head Pol had already made his decision. She was guilty of tripping the Pol. Guilty of obstructing the law? Perhaps that, too. But certainly not guilty of aiding a criminal. That little girl was no criminal. She thought of James Salsa, the lawyer. What did they do in the Justice Hall? She recalled their motto: "Justice is served by the law." Kraken was the law, thought Julie.

The public vees would be advertising her crime day and night. Perhaps Peek-a-Boo had even caught her *faux pas* in huge living color. How was Bobby taking it? What about her job? Would Fitch take her back? How would her work colleagues treat her when she returned—*if* she returned? Tripping a Pol in the act of chasing someone was more serious than painting slanderous words on a building. If Nancy had been tortured, what was in store for *her*, a veemeld among Renegade Pols?

But her models were too important to both Kraken and Dykstra. Then she reminded her miserable self that she hadn't shown Kraken a thing. For all he knew, she hadn't come any closer to finishing her models than her dead colleagues before her. Had they all given up on her? Gaia, too? Replaced her? Or had Dykstra panicked and decided that waiting for her Distopian model wasn't worth the risk that she might finish the Renegade model? Had he orchestrated this incarceration? What if she was supposed to die quietly in here, like her father...

She strained her mind to veemeld until her head hurt. Just before SAM had disappeared, it had mentioned loneliness. "I'm lonely too, SAM," she said in a ragged voice.

The food tray slid into the room. Startled, she jumped and cried out, then curled herself into a ball and waited, rocking back and forth. Her mind reeled out of control and she found herself mumbling the lines of the Icarian credo: "I obey therefore I am strong; those who disobey are weak." Stop it, she thought. She remembered what Nancy had said about brainwashing, and willed the lines to disappear. But they crept into her mind like a bad dream. She pulled herself up to her feet by clawing the clammy wall and felt her muscles painfully revolt. She paced the room, forcing herself to talk aloud. Still the credo crowded in on her. "I will not recite that. I won't! I won't!" Awful images of torture and execution raced through her mind, strobing like the vees in the hallway. Please, SAM, come back. Please. She pushed against her aching temples with her hands, trying to keep her head from exploding. Not succeeding.

≈

...So, what are you frightened of? A woman's voice. Her own.
Nothing. I won't tell.
Not even yourself? Why do you try to save everyone? It just gets you into trouble. You

didn't owe that little girl anything. She was laughing at him, after all...

She reminded me of... my sister... my mother... of me...

Pathetic. They're all dead. And soon you'll be. Bad Icarian.

No. Bad Icaria.

There is no bad Icaria. Only bad Icarians...

I'm... not... bad...

Then why do you try to save everyone? What are you making up for? Your father? Are you making up for him?

No! He's innocent. Leave me alone. Leave *him* alone. Who are you?

I can't leave you alone. I'm your conscience, you twit. I'm part of you. You're bad... And so pathetic. Why do you try to save everyone? You can't even save yourself! Her own mocking laughter echoed between her ears.

Where's SAM? I want SAM. Leave me alone. I obey therefore I am strong; those who disobey are weak... Oh, vee, leave me alone... those who disobey are punished...

≈

She was crying, crouched in the only clean corner of the cell, gazing at her own urine. Julie suddenly felt sick. She scrambled, slipping on the slimy floor, to the growing "latrine" side and leaned forward on her knees to vomit. She saw her own stool, crawling with beetles. She jerked back with a cry of revulsion. Disturbed by her sudden movement, several took flight. One landed on her and she screamed.

≈

When they came with a clean Com-Center uniform, she could only squint at their silhouettes in the harsh light. Helplessly immobile. Stiff with fear. They carried her out of the cell.

42

April 29, 2095—1700.

"ARE you aware that twenty million people are watching you, veemeld?" a Shame Court member asked from above as Julie tried to keep from swaying. She trembled and wondered if it showed.

"Yes, I am." Without moving her head, her eyes roamed the large room for hidden cameras. She spotted several.

"Are you also aware that your crime is known to all Icarians watching you now?"

"Yes, I am," she said. Part of her felt like she was far away looking down on herself. If she hadn't broken up with Frank, would she still be here? The lines of the Icarian credo crept into her mind: *I obey therefore I am strong; those who disobey are weak.* Stop it! *I obey therefore I am rewarded; those who disobey are punished.*

"What is your crime?" bellowed another Shame Court member.

She imagined the cameras closing in for a close-up and felt her face heat with shame. "I tripped a Pol chasing a young girl for defacing a public vee-com." She should have stopped there; her sense of justice wouldn't let her. "But the girl was innocent. She didn't do anything—"

"Silence!"

"—to the vee-com. It was a man—"

"Silence!"

"—from the Admin—" The attendant cuffed her on the mouth. She tottered to keep her balance and tasted salt.

"Insolent veemeld! You're forbidden to speak out. The girl already confessed."

"But she was innocent. She must have been afraid, or she was forced—"

"Shut up!" the Shame Court shouted as the attendant swung his arm to hit her again. Julie winced and closed her mouth. "This is a high court of law. You're wild and dangerous, flouting Icaria's rules as if you're above them."

Julie thought of that Ecologist, Gaia, who'd similarly reprimanded her. She imagined Gaia watching now, nodding with a frown of disapproval.

"You need a lesson in obedience and humility," continued the Tribunal. "Send in the Punishers!"

Two large men in black robes and masks approached from behind. She fought the urge to bolt. One seized her arms and the other ripped her tunic, exposing her body. Feeling twenty million people watching, her face burned.

The Punisher produced a container and splashed her with a sweet, viscous liquid. Startled, she flinched. He hurled what looked like black sand at her face. It crawled.

Julie shrieked and swiped at the bugs swarming over her face and hands. She only got her hands sticky. Shivering with giddy revulsion, she squeezed her eyes shut and shook her head wildly. The bugs dug in, sending her into a crazy panic. She pulled at her hair and batted her face with her hands, crying out shrill wails of panic. The floor beneath her gave way and she fell with a startled cry into a pool of water. Imagining Icaria's wild laughter at her antics, she still felt relief: the bugs were gone.

"Now, I think everyone agrees that you're a disrespectful parasite, not to be taken seriously," said a Shame Court member. "We don't take kindly to spoiled veemelds. Your insolent outbursts are particularly unacceptable. Wash out her filthy mouth!"

The two Punishers leapt into the water beside her. One grabbed her and the other began to wash her face gruffly with a cleaning dispenser. He forced the dispenser into her mouth. She gagged and struggled. The Punisher tightened his vice grip, hurting her. The other drilled the dispenser to the back of her throat, choking her and ripping flesh. She gagged and swallowed cleaner and blood. Tears sprang to her eyes.

"See that you don't appear before us again, or we will not be so kind."

≈

Bobby stood waiting anxiously at the door to the Pol Station. Julie didn't look too worse for wear when she emerged, but he knew better. Her face briefly lit up when she saw him, then slid back to an expressionless facade. Risking a demerit, he embraced her. "You were very brave."

Her lower lip trembled but she said nothing. They walked silently to the tube-jet.

He took her to his home and, after gently sitting her down in the leisure room, stepped into the kitchen to cook supper. He peeked occasionally around to see if she was all right. She remained where he had left her, staring into space.

When supper was ready, Bobby invited her to the table. Julie took her seat and looked at her plate. Her face had grown very pale. She picked at her food. He watched her make an effort to eat, unaware that he had stopped eating, himself. At one point she gagged and he thought she might be sick. He leaned forward. The reflex passed and she glanced up at him. Meeting his eyes, her sobs came easily.

≈

Julie stands fixed as the rest of the techno-slummers dash for cover. Her heart pounds and she listens to the familiar cry of the cypol. Neo lunges for her, tugging hard. Determined, she fights him off. "I'm going to do it this time. I'm going to let it catch me!"

"Damn you, Angel!" Neo screams. "And damn your promises!" He dashes to safety, clutching Piet, who wails at his side.

She swallows down the bile rising in her throat and fights the instinct to flee. She can see the cypol now, can imagine its gleaming vee-com eyes registering her as "Angel." She sees it suddenly veer toward her. Lock on her.

There's no escape now. She'll be joining her sister soon. It's been a week since the cypol took Diana. What if the cypols just take you up to their lair in the darkness of the ceilings and devour you, like Neo said? What if her sacrifice is for nothing, won't reunite her with her sister, but will simply end her life?

Julie runs. She collides headlong into a litter droid, knocking them both down. She scrambles to her feet as the droid squeaks, trying to get up. She helps the droid up then glances up. The cypol is almost upon her. You will not be hurt. Did she imagine it? Stunned, Julie lets her body go limp as the cypol scoops her up. The air rushes past her face as she soars up, and she feels oddly exhilarated. I'm coming, Diana. I'm coming to save you. Then she glimpses Neo in the shadows, his face twisted in anguish, as she approaches the rafters. Trembling with the memory of their first kiss, she thinks, I'll come back, Neo. I promise.

A doorway opens into a yawning darkness. The bird sails through and she is enveloped by pitch black. Her heart races. She inhales an overly sweet, almost cloying smell and grows weary, then falls into a deep slumber.

Julie awakens groggily to hushed voices. It is still dark but she can make out shadows. She is lying on her back, bound, on a smooth surface. The voices approach and a young male voice says, "So here's our trouble-maker at last. I knew she was a veemeld."

"Look at this," a female voice says excitedly. "Her V29 prostaglandins are abnormally high, even for a veemeld. What does that mean?"

"It's her," answers a third voice, an older male. "The machine-girl."

"What do you mean?"

"Ah," the older male says, as if awoken from a dream. "Never mind. I must contact 'G' at once. We've found her. Christian would have loved this moment. We should determine the girl's intelligence type. Run the standard IITT, then a STAT-LOG series. She should score 100% on both. Were there any others?"

"Doesn't she have a sister?" rejoins the first voice. "I think we picked her up earlier."

Another voice cuts in, "Tested negative. Not a veemeld."

The man responds, "Never mind the sister. She can stay in the Care-center. This one belongs in the outer-city."

What about Diana? Julie tugs frantically on the bindings and squeezes her eyes tight to the tears filling them.

"She has an uncle in the outer-city. Robert Crane."

Not him! Let me stay here with Neo and the others. Please!

"Contact him and arrange her departure as soon as the tests are complete."

In a burst of energy, Julie tears out of the bindings, arms burning, and runs blindly in the dark. Something slams into her face in a blaze of pain. She feels the urge to vomit and sinks. A voice slides into her consciousness as a harsh light assaults her eyes: "Good vee, Warren! You broke her face! Get her to neurgery and fix her up. Might as well fix the overbite while you're at it. She'll be an outer-city girl now. She should look like one."

No! Julie wants to scream but no sound emerges. I want to stay here with Neo! Her mind spins inside a maze of pain and sickness. I've lost everyone. I promised—

~

"Julie, Julie." Someone nudged her. "Wake up." She started out of her sleep, dizzy in a swirling haze of memories, and flailed out. "It's only me," Bobby assured her, gently parrying her attack. "You're at my place." Julie dropped her arms. "It's already seven," he said. "You'll be late for work." She moaned and closed her eyes. "You look awful," he murmured.

"I feel awful," she whispered hoarsely. "I'm cold."

"Your face is flushed. I think you still have a fever." He touched her forehead with his hand. "You're burning up. I heard you last night. You must have had some nightmares. Who's Neo? And you kept asking for SAM..."

Her lips trembled as she fought back tears. She pulled the covers over her head and curled into a ball. What she'd give to have SAM back, even the murmuring machines, to fill the space in her head that was caving in.

"Stay here, then," Bobby soothed, stroking the little part of her head that emerged from the blanket. "I'll get you a hot drink, more blankets and some toast. Then I must go. I'm late for work, too. Stay in bed and get some rest."

That suited her. She couldn't face work, particularly Fitch or the Head Pol. She thought of how timid Nancy had become and folded her arms over her head, ears ringing in the silence.

~

The clock showed 0900. She longed for a good long shower, but she couldn't get that here. Flushed but shivering, she got up, dressed and left Bobby's place to head for home. Julie traveled in a daze on the tube-jet. She knew she was risking a demerit for being ill in public. She didn't care.

Once home, she peeled off her clothes and stumbled to the bathroom. She turned on the shower and, leaning in with her palms against the wall to steady herself, let the steaming water cascade over her bowed head and body. She wiped and rubbed and scrubbed. It was a long time before she felt clean.

Back in the leisure room, she glanced at her aquarium. She caught herself counting the fish and forced herself to stop. Had she done them a disservice, "rescuing" them from their natural environment so she could stare at them whenever she pleased? Julie glanced at her vee-com and wondered if SAM would ever come back. As she was about to leave, her personal care unit signaled her on the vee-com. It flashed and sent out a droning beep. She glanced at the message: it told her that she had a fever of 40.9°C and she carried 16 foreign toxins well over the suggested threshold. Were the toxins preventing her from receiving SAM's signals and would they simply wear off? Or had they permanently damaged her brain in some way, condemning her to irrevocable silence? The vee-com suggested that her body was responding to shock and that she should immediately proceed to the Med-Center. Julie ignored the additional flashing messages as she fumbled into a fresh Com-Center uniform with sweat-covered hands.

43

April 30, 2095—1015.

A_S she approached the main reception desk of the Ed-Center, Julie heard a class down the hall mechanically chanting the Icarian credo:

"I obey therefore I am strong; those who disobey are weak.
I am neat therefore I am beautiful; those who are sloppy are ugly.
I obey therefore I am rewarded; those who disobey are punished.
I am neat therefore I am popular; those who are sloppy are lonely."

It repeated itself like a mantra and Julie found herself reciting inside her head as she reached the reception desk. "May I speak with Nancy Gibbons?" she asked. The young woman regarded her with dull eyes.

"I'm sorry. Ms. Gibbons is no longer with us."

"I thought she worked here?" Julie said. Her head throbbed.

"The Pols took her away. She was a Distopian. They caught her stealing classified information and she confessed."

Her legs gave way under her and she felt herself falling as if in slow motion. Her knees crashed to the floor with a thundering pain. The jolt knocked the vee-set off her head. It skittered beside her like a four-legged insect. The woman came around from the desk and stood over her with concern. "Are you all right?"

"Yes, yes," Julie said in a daze, getting up shakily and clawing to retrieve her vee-set. "I'm all right." She turned away and put the vee-set back on. The hall swam before her for a moment and her head pounded. She limped toward the exit. The Pols must have lied. Hadn't Nancy turned into what they wanted her to be? Why couldn't they just have left her alone? Julie left the Ed-Center, fuming. Her feverish mind conjured up the Pols picking Nancy up. Was Frank one of them?

Refusing to go to work, Julie pulled off her vee-set and wandered Darwin Mall. She gazed past the milling crowd to the resplendent *Isabo Center for the Performing Arts*, then focused on the multi-storied balconies that overlooked her in the square to watch the cheerfully distracted faces of several children sucking on chlorella ice-sticks. Dressed in the light yellow jumpsuits of the stage-1 student, they were on their lunch break from the Ed-Center. They hung their arms over the rails in a tidy row. She glanced above them to the public vees, which displayed a talk show. "Here's our earlier interview with Captain Chakra of the Pol Station, who is playing a great game in the Pit-Ball playoffs this very moment. Stay tuned for live scenes following the interview," said a man with orange hair and eyes.

The image of a young razor head in black appeared. "I think we have a great chance of winning the playoffs here in Icaria-5. We know our opponents' fans, which is as important as knowing the team when it comes to playing a virtual field..."

Julie glanced from the screen to the row of holo-portraits advertising this week's demerits and Shame Court hearings. Details in gash-red letters described their misdemeanors: stealing; swearing; touching in public. She visualized where her own image had been while she languished in the Pol Station.

As she walked the edge of the large park, something made her to look into the open square. Alone, fixed among the milling crowd, stood a man watching her with lazy eyes and a cold smile. He wore a Trans-Center blue tunic and black slacks and his dark long hair was pulled back into a ponytail. Julie recognized him; they'd worked on a project together a while back. He was a sky-shuttle pilot but she couldn't remember his name.

Their eyes locked. He didn't seem to care that she'd caught him staring at her because instead of looking demurely away, his smile snaked into a grin and he raised his eyebrows. Suggestively, she thought. He was finishing some soy chips and threw the wrapper in the recycle chute next to him with a finality that made her flinch. Julie turned and plunged into the park with an involuntary backward glance. She hastened along a stone path in the dark forest and emerged from the park at the Rec-Center. Thinking about the tanks and the need to relax, she entered the building. Getting too paranoid, Julie thought with a shiver.

At the Leisure Unit, Julie glanced behind her and started. There he was again! He was adjusting the vee-set on his head as he strode slowly in her direction. He must have followed her through the park. A Secret Pol—and probably a Renegade, she thought with sudden terror. They were after her already, like Nancy.

She fled down the hall and ducked through a side door. Panting, Julie rushed down the stairs and through a set of doors that led into a large hall of auditoriums. She glanced frantically from side to side, then pounded down the hall towards a set of green doors. Her steps rang in her ears. She had no idea where her feet were taking her. When she reached the doors, she fumbled for her card. It slipped from her clammy hand and fell to the floor. She clawed for it, glancing backward in terror, retrieved it, and after several shaky attempts got the card into the slot. The door opened and she rushed inside to the din of cheering, booming music and the echo of an announcer's voice.

She stood at the back of a set of bleachers looking down across a virtual field of green and black-clad players gliding with in-line skates. Another set of bleachers faced her from across the playing field. She'd landed in a playoff Pit-Ball game and her elegant maneuver to elude her pursuer had probably cost her a cool 500 credits. Each member of the audience had their vee-set tuned to control obstacles in the virtual field. The floor, in perpetual motion, rolled toward a gaping long pit that spanned the width of the far end of the playing field. One player from the black team who had the ball in his possession was being pursued by several green team players. Ignoring the game, she put her vee-set on and walked unsteadily forward, hoping she'd lost the man following her.

The crowd around her stood up and their deafening cry made her cringe. The audience on her side had obstructed the black player's route by imposing virtual magic, giving a green player the chance to overpower him before he could pass the ball to one of his teammates. The green player now had the ball. Her ears rang with the excited cries. "Kill him!" they shouted to the green player. As the black player scrambled to his feet, the green player shot him. The black player collapsed and was swept down into the pit.

Julie felt giddy and the images before her broke up. She willed herself not to faint. Seeing an empty seat, she pitched toward it and gratefully sat down with a furtive glance backward. Just in time to see the door open. She gasped. Her pursuer entered. She spun forward, heart thudding in her ears, and remained in her seat, not knowing what else to do. What did he want?

Too much time went by. She forced herself to look back and saw that he had taken a seat next to someone from the Com-Center several rows behind her. The Com-Center man was speaking to him and it was obvious they knew each other. So he wasn't pursuing her after all! He'd come for the game. She felt like laughing. Then she recognized the Com-Center man. Paul Getz. Hard to forget those shifty eyes and flat face. One day the Pols had come looking for Getz, but he'd vanished. Now here he was, talking to a Secret Pol! Turning forward, she reminded herself that she'd only assumed him a Secret Pol because she thought he was following her.

Julie fixed on the game. Each time a player gained possession of the ball, he would try to make points for his team by skating the length of the virtual field unharmed. Once he had the ball, he was pursued by the other team, who tried to get the ball back in their possession without letting him score any points. The audience provided additional virtual obstacles to his progress, while his own team members created diversions. Each player's eventual fate was to be virtually shot and drift into the black pit. Repulsed, she told herself to get up. You can walk past those two. Just do it! But her body wouldn't move.

A new excitement filled the crowd. Both the green and black team audiences were cheering. She followed the crowd's gaze up and saw a pink fog descending on them.

Drug! She thought of holding her breath. It wafted down, immersing the giant hall in pink intoxication. Heart pounding, she took successive halting breaths. Involuntarily she gulped in the fumes like an addict and felt woozy. The music slowed down as if it had reached a great hollow. Everything around her started moving. A dizzy heat prickled through her and she broke out into a cold sweat.

When she looked around to see if anyone else shared her dilemma, she discovered they'd all turned into Pols. They all looked like Frank. Gasping for air, Julie burst out of her seat and scrambled past a few complaining people into the aisle. Above her, Paul and his friend stood in the aisle, blocking her exit. Their grotesque faces grimaced at her.

Feeling a breeze from below she stumbled down, looking for an exit. When she got near the playing level, something—someone—tripped her and she fell headlong into the virtual field with a jarring crash. Winded, she scrambled to her feet and slipped on the moving platform. When Julie regained her balance she looked down and saw in-line skates on her feet. She wore a green player's outfit. She'd transformed into a green player! She felt the weight of a pistol in a holster that hung on her right hip.

The green team audience cheered. The game wasn't over after all! Infuriated, the black team crowd hollered and began to manipulate the virtual field against her. As Julie tried to reach the outer edge of the field, obstacles reared up in front of her. Giant rubbery monsters jostled her and sent her sprawling. She scrambled up and tried again, skating against the moving ground, away from the yawning black pit.

The chittering sounds in her head shrieked. If that wasn't warning enough, the sudden excitement of the black team crowd made Julie turn in time to see the remaining black player racing toward her. With the prize Pit-Ball tucked under his arm, he was going to ensure a win for his team by eliminating her. That was the rule. Only one player was meant to remain: the winner.

Was she delirious? The player was Frank! He drew out his weapon, pointed it straight at her and sneered. "Die, green bitch!"

Instinctively, she pulled out hers. She shot the same instant he did. A violent force pitched her backwards onto the floor as a pain tore through her body. She looked down and saw blood pouring out of a gaping wound in her stomach. Alarmed, she touched it and brought her shaking hand up to her face. Her hand was covered in blood. The pain intensified. She looked down at the gun clutched in her other hand. Horrified, she dropped the weapon.

She struggled to keep her head up long enough to see she was being swept down the moving field toward the yawning pit. She saw the black player, who had also fallen, drifting toward the pit. He was no longer Frank but the young Pit-Ball captain. The ball rolled toward the pit ahead of them. Too weak to get up she lay on her back and drifted until she caught on an obstacle. Then she tasted blood in her mouth and swallowed. More came. It gurgled in her throat. She gasped for air and panic seized her.

The Trans-Center man appeared and bent over her. His distorted face swirled like liquid. Huge eyes. Then all teeth. Other grotesque masks swam beside him. Faces of revulsion. Julie felt herself being pulled. The Trans-Center man barked, "Don't move her!" His voice throbbed in her head. "Her body's in trauma. It thinks this is real. If you move her you'll kill her. I know this woman. She's also suffering from Shame Court sickness. She needs drug. Get a medic, Getz. Now! Use your vee-set."

"Right away, Vadim," said the wandering eyes.

Yes! That was his name, she thought with macabre satisfaction. Then she passed out.

44

VICTOR and Gaia drew in their horses at the top of a ridge that overlooked a long, deep valley. As the horses snorted and hoofed the ground, Victor glanced below at the small churning river, glinting like sparks under the blazing sun. It was an unusually windless day.

Gaia, in a bright paisley dress, turned to him. "I enjoyed reading your progress report on your 600 alpha veemelds while I was away. Several have become very promising. We must encourage them to stay together... not dilute their gene pool with non-veemelds."

Victor stroked his horse's mane. How far from his vision for Icaria-5 Gaia's strayed. Surely diversification would serve the people of Icaria-5 better? He knew she didn't care about his citizens, just his veemelds—her future race of minions. They deserved better. Especially the girl, he thought, recalling her brave performance at the Shame Court. He'd exulted in her noble defiance.

As if she'd read his mind, Gaia posed, "What about our special veemeld friend?"

Victor shifted on his horse. The sun beat on his head like a heat lamp. "She isn't doing well, I'm afraid." The horse fidgeted, probably picking up his tension, and he nervously stroked it. "She's suffering post-Shame Court trauma." Stiffening under her glare of surprise, he explained in a rush of words, "The Head Pol put her through it for tripping a Pol. The drugs they use to prepare them for the hearing are potent, and she isn't used to drugs of any kind. She's still recovering at the Med-Center."

"How have you let this happen? Where was her Pol-lover?"

He looked down and pulled at the saddle strap. "They broke up."

"They broke up?" Her voice had risen several octaves.

"But she was never in any danger."

"You misunderstand. She must be protected at all costs. Her models are important, but *she* is irreplaceable. Our Eve, Victor. Good Earth, I'm gone for a week and you let your Head Pol take over. You won't have Icaria-5 for long if you keep this up." Her voice cut like the edge of a knife. "For all your gadgetry and talented staff, you can't control the actions of one Icarian and keep her out of trouble."

Victor glanced furtively into her deadly eyes. "Look around you," she continued. "All this will be gone if we don't stop what's happening in Icaria. They'll come out like a plague, kill the planet and themselves along with it. It will start all over again, the defilement of the land by blind greed. I've devoted too much to save this planet, at great expense and the sacrifice of many. I'll not let a bunch of power-hungry anarchists ruin what I've accomplished. They don't deserve this beauty. We must keep them in and we must keep them happy. Your project is paramount. And that little veemeld brat is a critical piece."

"I know," Victor said, squirming in his saddle and feeling the heat of the sun on his face. Julie wasn't a brat, he thought petulantly. "Kraken acted on his own. By the time I—"

"I don't want excuses. Get her cleaned up and productive. Get your Head Pol off his ass and in line, or destroy him. I need her models to scan Icarians' personal files and cleanse our cities. And I need *her* undamaged at the DP. Do you hear me? *Undamaged.*"

He didn't like how she used the word cleanse. Or how she described Julie, like a piece of merchandise. Gaia paused to watch a raven soaring overhead, then resumed. "Perhaps you've forgotten our underlying philosophy, Victor. Icaria is an evolving experiment in social perfection. As guardians of the Earth, the *Circle's* commitment to this greater cause hinges on the continued success of the Icarian concept and the welfare of its citizens. They have their own path to follow, in there," she pointed to the far towers. "Prolonged isolation is one route to the emergence of a new species and we're responsible for providing the environmental conditions to nurture it."

She reached inside her belt pouch and pulled out a small, worn paperback novel. Handing it to Victor, she said, "I've carried this archetype of Icaria since before the revolution. When I return to retrieve it, I want all to be corrected here." She pulled on her reins and with a terse command guided the horse into a gallop toward Victor's house.

Left on the ridge, Victor watched her ride at full speed along the rough heath, dark hair and colorful diaphanous dress flying behind her like flower petals in a gale. He looked down at the book: *Walden Two.* He opened the cover and read a scrawled inscription: *"To my beloved Monica. Here's to a brave new world! Love, Eric."*

~

His face still flushed and glistening from his hard work outside, Bobby entered his flat. "Julie! Julie!" It was noon and he wanted to check up on her. He wondered if she had gone to work after all. Then he saw her clumsy scrawl on his vee-book: *Gone home. Thanks. J.*

He called her and her face came on the screen: "Please leave me a message and I'll return your call. Cheers." Her face froze in a smile and a beep sounded. Vee! He hated these things!

"Uh—hi, uh, honey. Uh—did you go to work? Hope you're okay. Maybe you're sleeping. I'll check up on you again. Bye." He switched off uncomfortably, unable to account for his feeling that something was wrong.

The public vees blared above as Bobby made his way through Margalef Square to Julie's flat: "An amusing diversion occurred in the playoff Pit-Ball game earlier today. An over-enthusiastic member of the green team audience got carried away—literally—and fell into the virtual field just as a player from the Pol Station team succeeded in dispatching his final opponent and gaining possession of the ball."

He glanced up at the screen and there she was!

"This audience member," the announcer continued while the screen showed the replay, "terminated the rightful Pol Station winner, who lost the ball. The game ended when she was virtually shot. Game officials are still debating whether the Pol Station won the game. Some members are calling for a rematch."

Never mind the vee-damned game! Where was his niece? They'd said "virtually shot." He steered for the Med-Center, hoping they meant it.

45

THE Head Pol stood in his office, facing the distorted image of his superior's face on his screen. "I'm disappointed in you, Kraken," V's monotone voice boomed. "You should have prevented the Shame Court altogether. She might have damaged herself irreparably. Her recovery will cost us precious time, and this has displeased the Circle greatly."

Someone must have come down hard on V, thought Kraken; V hadn't made a fuss when they'd picked up the girl. "I made sure Ms. Crane didn't receive the usual treatment. It would have destroyed any chance of her being useful. But I have an orderly Icaria to run. Too many people knew of her action and the Shame Court had to proceed. I can't flagrantly ignore Icarian rules just to satisfy—"

"You don't grasp the seriousness of this matter. I thought I was explicit about preventing her from hurting herself. If she can't develop the models soon, you may lose your Icaria altogether. This project has everything to do with an orderly Icaria and nothing must get in its way. We need those models and her, *undamaged*, at the DP. You should have prevented her actions to begin with. Where's the superior surveillance you boasted about?"

Kraken shrugged. "Her uncle picked her up when she left the Shame Court, before the Med-Center representatives could get to her."

"I mean after that, you idiot. Where was your guardianship?"

"I had Ms. Crane followed by one of my people," the Head Pol objected with growing irritation.

"And your Secret-Pol bungled it wonderfully. As a direct result of his ineptitude, Ms. Crane's still recovering in the Med-Center when she should be working on the models."

"If it weren't for him, she would have died in the Pit-Ball virtual field."

"If it weren't for him she wouldn't have ended up there in the first place!"

Kraken looked down and fought a smile of amusement.

"We cannot afford any further bunglings from your department, Kraken."

"All right, what's done is done," he conceded wearily.

"Ensure there are no more distractions. After she's finished her model, get her to the DP."

Kraken eyed the screen with a stony look. Poor child. "Dykstra's already replaced that newbie agent with one of his very best from the Shadow Unit," he said. "She was suggested to him by one of the *Circle* members."

"The Shadow Unit? What's your Head of Secret Pols doing talking to, much less taking suggestions from, a *Circle* member?"

Even with the voice scrambled, Kraken could hear V's annoyance. He shrugged. "Dykstra's been doing that since the beginning. He may take his general directive from me, but he gets instructions from the *Circle*. Besides, the same *Circle* member runs the Shadow Unit." The same unit that was sabotaging a cure for Darwin, he thought scornfully.

He sensed in the silence that V was startled by this news. When V finally spoke, the words sounded more stilted than usual, "Do you know which *Circle* member?"

Kraken barked a laugh. "Chaos, I don't even know *your* identity. How do you expect me, or Dykstra, to know theirs?" He bit back a smile. His superior's ignorance was amusing. It also pointed to a lack of trust in the chain of command. "To return to the matter at hand, this agent's never failed us. She has connections with the entire Icarian network, including the Distopians. Consider the girl taken care of."

"Very well. Crane better not get into any more trouble."

The screen blanked out. Kraken walked out to his patio. He squinted at the sun blazing overhead, then wandered to his flower garden and picked up a hand rake. What a pity, he thought. He liked the girl. He would miss their conversations. He pulled out a stubborn weed. She was a pretty girl. He pitied her fate at the DP. He didn't care for Kristin Olafsen and her biological experiments. He threw the weed aside and wiped his hands. As he raked the cleared ground, he formulated her capture. He recalled that her uncle was a bit of a pest, too. Two for one, he thought with a wry smile.

46

THE smell of bleach and roses makes her queasy as the room spins and the face of a beautiful woman, silky black hair framing knife-sharp eyes, cuts into her haze of vision. The woman's voice, dark like coffee, murmurs, "...steal the fire from heaven and give it to me—"

Julie bolted awake, panting and clutching the bed sheet. She was drenched in sweat and shaking uncontrollably. Just purging her toxins, one of the nurses had soothed the night before when she'd recognized open fear in Julie's face. "Not Darwin Disease. We did a Pro-1 screen on you—we routinely do them now on every patient—and you're clean."

Julie huddled in the Med-Center bed, forcing away memories of the last time she was in a place like this, when that awful nightmare had started. That time, she'd begun to hear voices. This time the voices had disappeared. Feeling the dark silence crush her like a vice, she forced herself to breathe deeply. *I'm cracking up. How many times did I wish I was normal and didn't hear anything in my head. Now I can't stand it.*

Is this a good time for a joke, then?

"SAM!" she shrieked out loud and laughed uncontrollably.

Where've you been? On the moon?

Oh, SAM! Oh, SAM! She threw herself out of bed and felt the cool rush of air wick her sweat away. She danced circles in the dark room and flung out her arms like great wings, feeling a silly grin cut across her face. *You've come back.*

I missed you...

Oh, SAM, she bowed her head and closed her eyes, hugging herself.

...It got pretty boring reading the dictionary.

She grinned at SAM's twisted humor. How she'd missed it.

≈

Pulling on her vee-set, Julie strode toward the exit of the Com-Center, listening absently to the gentle murmur and chirping in her head. She glanced at her wristwatch and realized that she was late again. She'd lost track of the time working on her distopian model. No matter, she thought wryly, Bobby always factored up to half an hour extra to every rendezvous she made with him, particularly if she came from work.

Hi, SAM. Her thought pattern sailed to SAM's neural net. *It was a good day, but I'm late again. I promised Bobby I'd be there at 1730.*

Everything's back to normal, then. So, did you hear about the blonde? When she got to the bottom of the application where it said 'sign here,' she put 'Sagittarius.'

Julie gave a quick bark of a laugh. SAM was telling her a lot of jokes lately. Making up for lost time, she supposed with a wry smile. But SAM was wrong about everything being normal again. Nothing could be normal again, she thought, throwing furtive glances at the well-hidden surveillance cameras. Three days had passed since she'd been released and she couldn't shake the sorrow, as though she'd lost something dear to her. She had her beloved SAM back, but she couldn't help grieving for what she'd left behind in the Pol Station and the Med-Center: her nerve. And with it, her chance to make it all right with Darwin and make right her father's past. Now she wasn't sure if she could even save herself.

On her first day back, Fitch had intercepted her in the hallway and brought her into his office. He'd obviously been waiting for her. To her relief, he'd instructed her to continue on the Head Pol's project, having given her other responsibilities to others. It sounded like a privilege. She didn't think it was. Would she get her old job back? Or was there *nothing* after? When she'd entered her own office, a plate with a fresh pastry waited for her on her chair. The words hand-written on a vee-book beside it read: "Welcome back, Julie! Be productive!" Kraken, obviously. Only he knew of her penchant for sweet pastries. When he'd come on her holo later that day, Kraken talked pleasantly to her as if nothing had occurred. And she marveled how, on the surface, everything was the same. But when SAM had inquired if she wanted to continue her investigation on Prometheus and the Shadow Unit, Julie found herself making excuses and was reminded of Nancy's timid face the last time she'd seen her. She was a train hurtling toward a doom she saw no way to prevent. Once Julie finished her models and submitted them to the Head Pol, Dykstra would make his move: highjack the information, then kill her. How was she going to veemeld herself out of this train wreck?

As Julie rounded the main hall, she glimpsed Brenda ducking into another passageway to avoid her. She wasn't sure if Brenda, like most of her other co-workers, was reacting to her shaming or to the fact that her identity as a veemeld had been revealed. Perhaps it didn't matter. They still avoided her. Bobby, on the other hand, delighted in her company, Julie thought as she made her way to Ziggy's Donut Shop in Pielou Mall. He'd grown downright cheerful.

Several other people milled about Ziggy's, looking at the pastries and donuts in the display case. Julie took her place in the queue and when it was her turn, she smiled at Ziggy and ordered her usual selection: six custard-filled chocolate-glazed donuts with cappuccino sprinkles. Ziggy muttered, "I can only give you five, Ms. Crane. That's the last of 'em."

"That's fine—"

"No!" A woman's harsh voice behind her objected. "Stop that order!"

Julie spun to gaze at her challenger. She was a tall spikehead in a Com-Center uniform. Her striking face and flaming hair looked familiar. Even the expression of anger seemed familiar. But Julie couldn't place her. Perhaps she'd seen the woman in the Com-Center hallways.

"Those should be mine." The woman glared down at Julie. "She stepped in line ahead of me. And that's the selection I want."

"I did not step in front of you. If I did, it's because you weren't actually in line. And I always get this selection."

The spikehead threw her head back in mock laughter and scowled. "Of course you do!" Her voice blistered with sarcasm. "Someone else probably chose them for you and you've been getting them ever since."

Julie blushed. As a matter of fact, Ziggy had suggested them, and Julie had always been content with the same assortment.

The spikehead went on, "You're that kind of person. Never venturing out on your own. A true conformer, never questioning and taking risks. I bet you keep your vee-set on intro-mode all the time."

An acidic smile tugged at Julie's lips. She never turned her vee-set on. She never needed to.

Misunderstanding Julie's expression, the spikehead sneered in vindication. "I knew it. Ignorant little cyber-pet, licking everyone's shoes: yes, sir; yes, sir; three megs full, sir." She'd increased the pitch of her voice in ridicule.

Julie felt her cheeks flame and narrowed her eyes to study her assailant. Who *was* this quarrelsome woman? How dare she invade Julie's personal boundaries to mock her, as if she knew anything about Julie! Yet, she thought that perhaps she *had* seen the woman before. She slid into veemeld. *Who is she, SAM? Someone we know?*

I can't find her in my database, Julie. That's puzzling. As though she doesn't exist.

Terrific. I'm being insulted by someone who doesn't exist. Hoping to make peace with the belligerent stranger, Julie stepped back from the counter and said to the shopkeeper, "Let her have them. It's not that important to me."

But as the woman came up to the counter and handed the shopkeeper her card for the donuts, she eyed Julie with a look that stung. "You give in too easily. You're everyone's fool. Icaria's cyber-pet to keep on a leash." She left the shop.

Julie tried to shake off her anger as she made her choice from what was left. Trying to be helpful, Ziggy suggested the green donuts with mocha frosting. Piqued by the stranger's accusation, Julie rejected his suggestion and chose the cream-filled orange donuts with coconut frosting instead.

As she stepped out of the shop it suddenly occurred to her where she had seen the strange woman before: at Kraken's birthday party! She was the spikehead who'd glared at her from across the room. Who was she? A Secret Pol?

As Julie entered Bobby's flat with her bag of donuts, he said with some excitement, "Guess who I also invited for supper?"

"Who?" she asked warily. Bobby knew hardly anyone, save some of his counter-propaganda contacts. And he wisely didn't socialize with them. It brought her thinking back to the eerie woman she'd met earlier.

"Daniel Woods! The fellow you saved. My old neighbor."

She smiled, then blushed, remembering the Shame Court. Had he seen her?

"He's been over here a few times while you were in the Med-Center," he said to her surprise. "We've been trading stories and I showed him my library—"

"Are you sure you can trust him?"

"Oh, yes, yes," he said. "And he's generous, Julie. Gave me the pills he didn't need from the Med-Center. Cleared up my cough."

"What do you know about him?" she challenged.

"Not much. Don't need to. I know he's an honest man."

"What have you told him?"

"Oh, about my work outside, the heath and the seasons. He wants to go out with me next time we're both free. Perhaps you'd like to come along? It's been a while since you joined me outside."

"Perhaps I would." She smiled.

There was a pause before he continued. "Oh, and we talked a great deal about you."

Her heart raced. "Me?" She thought for a moment. "Does he know about my—the—Did he see..." she faltered.

"Yes, he knows about your shaming. He didn't actually see you get shamed. A friend pointed out your holo-ad in the mall."

Julie slumped into one of Bobby's ugly plastic chairs. "Does he know that I'm a... did you tell him that I was a..." She trailed, running her foot back and forth on his cheap carpet.

He avoided her eyes. "I don't think he knows you're a veemeld. I didn't tell him."

Didn't tell him! She swallowed down the hurt pride. She never forgot his reserve when she'd first arrived from the inner-city. She'd thought Bobby might have finally become proud of her, but he'd kept silent about her veemelding for fear of losing his new friend. She'd become an embarrassment.

The doorbell rang.

Bobby jumped up. "That must be him. I told him to come at 1830. He's always on time." Julie's eyes followed Bobby's glance toward his vee-com and recognized Daniel, dressed in his bright blue IUTT uniform, combing back his neat hair with one hand. He held a large package tucked under his other arm.

Bobby hastened to the door and opened it. "Hi, Daniel!"

"Hi, Bobby!" Daniel stepped inside with a dimpled smile. When his eyes met hers they grew large and he blushed, suddenly less confident. "Hi," he said with an awkward grin.

"Hi." She smiled shyly, feeling her own face warm.

He dropped the package on her foot. "Oh, sorry!" He scrambled to retrieve the bag. "Uh, this is for you, Bobby. It's—it's just some books I dug up in some used shops when I was in the inner-city—for a brief time," he quickly added with a glance at Julie. "My father worked there for a while as a diplomat," he explained.

"Wonderful," said Bobby. "I'd like to look through them with you. Sit down, the both of you. Get reacquainted while I finish supper." Bobby disappeared into the kitchen.

Julie sat down in one of Bobby's old foam chairs and rested her hands on her knees. Daniel perched himself on the edge of the stained couch across from her, eyes roaming the room. Nervously, she thought. Did *she* make him nervous?

Julie finally blurted out, "So, we meet again."

"Yes."

After another pause, she said, "You're looking a lot better than the last time I saw you. How are you feeling?"

"Thanks. I feel great." Daniel said. "I'm back at work and I've got a place five floors above this one, in the next Liv-Center." After another pause, he added, "It's nicer than my last place."

She was reminded of his saxophone playing and blushed again. "I've heard you play your saxophone. You play wonderfully." She smiled awkwardly.

"Thanks. I'm self-taught. Couldn't afford lessons. All my savings went into buying the instrument. The one I have now is my second. I lost the first one in the... uh... trains." He smiled pensively. "I used to dream about being a musician once."

"Someone I knew had that same ambition."

"Probably just a male thing," he said with a shrug. He then rose and walked to the far wall where Bobby had arranged his collection of pre-Icarian artifacts and picked up an old rusted sign that read: *Front Street W.*

"That used to be a street sign," Julie offered, joining him.

Daniel replaced it on a shelf and picked up a clear bottle with embossed patterns. He smiled at Julie and suggested, "An ancient bottle of *ambrosia*, perhaps?"

"No, alcohol." She recognized the brand her mother drank: Seagram's. "Alcohol's what they used to drink before drugs. I think it's a little like *ambrosia*, though."

Daniel studied the trinkets. "Bobby sure has collected a lot."

"He finds things all the time. I found this piece, though," Julie picked up a bent utensil that looked like a fork.

They continued to look at the artifacts in silence. Then Daniel said, "Bobby tells me that you work for Fitch at the DIC."

"Yes." She nodded. "And you drive tube-jets, of course."

"You remember me, then, from the incident?"

"Incident?" She was lost.

"With the old woman on the rails? Who tried to kill herself... and you saved..." He looked awkward. "I thought you knew what I do from remembering me driving that tube-jet, because you haven't seen me in my IUTT uniform, except for..." He glanced down at his bright blue outfit and his face turned bright red with realization. "...Now."

Bobby announced dinner. Daniel and Julie jumped, almost colliding into each other. Bobby seated them across from one another, with himself at the end.

Julie trained her eyes on her food and ate silently. Did Daniel think she was an idiot? Only an idiot would defy the code to save someone who didn't want to be saved, especially when they were already half-dead with Darwin Disease. Not to mention her shaming. He probably didn't think much of her. He didn't show it, though. He kept focusing on her as he launched into his school escapades and soon drew her out of her self-consciousness. He used his entire body to express himself, told his stories like a consummate dramatist, with mobile, expressive hands sculpting the air. Totally unconcerned with how silly he looked, he threw his face into such expressive features that Julie laughed until tears streamed down her cheeks.

47

May 12, 2095—1030, one week later.

DANIEL rechecked his vee-com for messages as he waited for Julie and Bobby at the designated meeting place in the mall. He summoned delicious memories of their supper together. She'd made him nervous initially, sitting stiffly with her hands gripping her knees and her brilliant green eyes darting around the room. Then she'd blushed slightly, made a crooked smile and asked how he was. His heart had hammered so hard he thought she might hear it. Then he was making her laugh. It made his heart sing.

Daniel began to feel the disappointment of being stood up when he saw Julie hastening toward him. She was dressed, like him, in a non-working charcoal gray tunic and black trousers. As usual, she wasn't wearing her vee-set. Bobby trundled behind in a brown tunic and trousers, wearing a large backpack. Julie waved. Daniel blushed with pleasure and waved back.

"Hi, Daniel. Sorry we're late," Bobby said when they reached him at the Enviro-Center doorway. "Blame my niece." Bobby hitched a thumb in Julie's direction. She smiled sheepishly without volunteering an excuse or an apology.

Bobby led them past some green unmarked doors, through a maze of corridors and up several flights of stairs to a set of doors marked "Exit." Bobby urged Daniel to carefully read the large warning sign beside the doors. Daniel read the ten points. They warned about harsh weather such as wind, rain and cold; of the brightness of sunshine; of natural smells; of uneven terrain and prickly and poisonous bushes and plants; of insects and disease; of hills and distances and the dangers of getting lost; of potentially dangerous and disease-carrying wildlife such as small rodents, raccoons, coyotes and the like. Daniel found these foreign concepts a little fearsome but made a brave face when he caught Julie giving him a sidelong glance. She smiled reassuringly.

"It's summer out there," said Bobby. "My vee-com tells me that the sun is shining and the temperature's about 22°C and rising. I'll be leading you out an exit located at ground level. This is the normal way Enviro-Center workers go outside."

They passed the first set of exit doors into an anteroom and Bobby turned to them. "I have four rules which I follow every time I go out, and I impose them on you. The first is no vee-coms. No contact with Icaria-5."

Daniel unclipped his vee-pad and vee-set and handed them over. Bobby turned to Julie, who resisted for a brief moment. He frowned. "Come on, Julie. You can do without your umbilical cord for a little while." Her eyes flashed at Bobby, perhaps in embarrassed anger at revealing her weakness, and then surrendered her gear. Bobby placed the vee-pads and vee-sets into a small locker near the doors.

"The second is a promise not to share what we are doing with anyone else. No one," he emphasized. "Otherwise we may lose our privilege, if not more. Understood?"

Daniel nodded. "I promise."

"Me too," said Julie.

"The next two rules are for outside," continued Bobby. "First, no needless removal of living things or damage to the ecosystem; and second, no littering. Everything that goes out comes back. Understood?"

"Understood," said Daniel, trying hard to appear intrepid. He felt his heart racing.

When Bobby opened the pneumatic exit door, the sun blazed in Daniel's eyes, making him squint. The sky was huge and magnificent. A cool breeze wafted across Daniel's face, bringing with it a diversity of fragrances. He laughed with joy. Birds chirped and fluted. It was far more beautiful than he had ever imagined. The virtual reality of Senscape had not prepared him for this.

Glancing back at Julie, who gave him a knowing smile, Daniel stepped lightly on the turf, following Bobby as he beckoned him along an old cement walkway, cracked and uprooted by the heath. The sun shone like a heat lamp. The cement vanished into a well-worn dirt path that wound its way up a slight rise.

Daniel slowed to let Julie catch up. He bent down, fingering a small purple bush and turned to her. "What's this called?"

"That—um—" She tilted her head sideways and looked vacant for a moment before responding with more confidence, "is an ericoid dwarf-shrub, *Calluna vulgaris.*" Then she continued, as if reciting from a book, "it's a good example of the typical heath land flora adapted to this area's oligotrophic, acidic soils. It was introduced from Europe centuries ago and has taken over this region like a weed, changing the structure of the soil to its own advantage."

Sometimes she sounded just like a vee-com, Daniel thought.

They caught up to Bobby, who'd stopped over the rise to a vista point, and he suggested they picnic there. They helped Bobby lay out a blanket from his backpack and put out sandwiches, drinks and donuts.

A SkyTravel shuttle pierced the quiet, leaving its jet stream wake in the azure sky. They glanced up, then returned their attention to their food. Daniel discovered that he had an incredible appetite. "It's the fresh air," Julie explained after he caught her watching in amusement as he wolfed down his peanut butter sandwich.

"Do you come here often?" he said when his mouth wasn't so full.

"Bobby does. I join him occasionally." Julie shot a glance at Bobby's frowning face and quickly added, "though not as often as I used to."

"Too busy with work," he grumbled.

"Too busy with *life*," she corrected him.

"Life! *This* is life!" He pointed to the expanse of heath land before them. "Not your artificial vee-com world."

Daniel sensed a sore point between them.

"Bobby works out here," Julie explained to Daniel. "He spends a lot of his spare time here too. I told him he should build a house."

"I'd *never* see you then," Bobby complained. Another sore point, thought Daniel. Bobby resumed on a more whimsical note, "Perhaps I *will* build a house here one day."

"I know what you mean," said Daniel, keeping his eyes on Bobby but watching Julie. "This rugged beauty is something Icaria doesn't have, not even virtually."

"Exactly!" Bobby agreed. "You should give up your tube-jets and come and work out here. We could use a strong and appreciative worker like you, Daniel. You could drive the tower runners! You could study nature and get paid to do it."

Daniel noticed Julie taking advantage of their conversation to slip away on her own. He fought his disappointment.

≈

Julie escaped down the hill to where she had spotted something glinting in the sunshine. As she scrambled down, she inhaled the sweet boggy smell of young poplars in the breeze. It smelled of childhood. Daniel had quickly assumed the confident walk of one who belonged. Embracing the wild and uneven terrain, he felt nature around him with the attentiveness of one enraptured. Daniel appeared to cherish every tangled bush and grassy knoll, picking up seeds and examining them or fondling a small flower and allowing Bobby to show him how the insects brought the pollen from the male stamens to the female pistil. Julie smiled, reminded of when her father had first brought her out here.

The shiny object turned out to be an oddly shaped translucent bottle. It was partially buried and refused to come out of the ground at first. After digging around it with her fingers, Julie managed to pull it out. The bottle was hard, slippery cold, and much heavier than plastic. Glass, she concluded, remembering some of the weatherworn pieces she had handled in Bobby's pre-Icarian collection. As she turned it around and tried to smudge off the dirt to make out the logo in relief, the bottle slipped out of her hand and fell. It hit a rock and splintered into many pieces. She picked one up and slowly drew her thumb against the clean edge. It sliced deeply through her finger before she registered the pain and realized what she'd done. She dropped the broken glass and cried out with a start. Blood issued like a spring and dripped on the ground.

Turning to follow Bobby's absent gaze, Daniel said, "What's over there?" He pointed to a far hill, darker than the heath.

"That's part of the remnant forest. This was all forest before the cities got built and the climate changed."

"Climate changed?" Daniel echoed.

"The planet experienced a substantial warming period. Partly because of the continued use of fossil fuels and timber by the resource extraction industry, afraid they wouldn't get it all before we changed over. Mainly why the revolution happened. My cousin Janet could have told you more about it. Since the revolution, our emissions have been virtually eliminated, mostly through the use of alternate clean energy sources. This used to be deciduous forest."

Daniel nodded with interest.

"I've got books on all of this stuff if you want to look anything up, Daniel. Julie's read them all; even did her own research projects when she was younger. I guess you could've called her an info addict. She's got a brilliant mind, a real vee-cube. The DIC took her when she was only fourteen. She was the youngest one there. Julie used to know the heath even better than I. But she's forgotten a lot now."

It didn't seem so, Daniel thought, recalling her more than ample answer to his earlier question. But it was also obvious to Daniel that Bobby regretted Julie's waning interest. Definitely a sore point between them, he thought.

Bobby went on, "When she was little and her father was still around, they used to come out here lots. She and the heath were like best friends. She used to say that she'd live out here when she grew up, as if it was a career." He chuckled. Daniel liked imagining Julie as a young girl. He pictured her smiling rosy face and it made him warm inside. "But after her inner-city experience, it all changed." Daniel opened his mouth to ask about that, but Bobby went on, "Oh, she and I went out, but her heart wasn't there. She took an academic interest for a while and then it just dissolved." He shrugged. "Anyway, I can show you my books, if you're interested."

"Thanks, I'd like that. So this was all forest before the global warming?"

"Well, yes. But, of course, in reality just about everywhere you're looking now was covered in pavement and buildings. This was a huge city. Beyond the hill is the river which divides the inner- from the outer-city of Icaria-5," Bobby pointed. "If you look around, you might spot it here and there as it winds its way. Odd, isn't it, how none of that seems important up here. No political borders in nature. Just physical ones. I've only been as far as the river in that direction. And I made it to the lake once. It's beautiful. Those billowing clouds there are part of the inner-city's heavy industrial area."

"The inner-city slums," Daniel said. He knew the area well.

"Fires also keep the trees from growing. Every so often a big one sweeps through here, started by lightning or something. The last one came through in '72. You can still see evidence of it here and there."

"What lies beyond that?" Daniel pointed to more scrub forest far to the east.

Bobby's face clouded for a brief moment. "Part of my past," he said quietly. "It all used to be farmland. Now the heath has taken over. If you walk through the forest to the other side, you might find remnants of the original buildings of the Corporation Farm," he said. "It was abandoned soon after the revolution. Most of our agro-operations lie farther south, like those algal-vats," he pointed toward the huge iridescent ponds full of algae, "and the polycultures beyond."

"I don't know much about the revolution."

"I don't either," Bobby confessed with a sigh. "I was too young. All I can remember was that it altered everything."

Daniel changed the subject. "I think I can make out the river." He pointed in another direction. "What lies beyond it?"

"Nothing. That's looking north. I don't know of any cities in that direction. Just heath land, I guess." Bobby shrugged and shoved his hands in his pockets.

The thought of total heath, unobstructed by human presence, excited Daniel. He gazed over the rolling heath, cut by steep ravines, for some time. "So, how is it that we ended up leaving all this?"

Bobby followed his gaze to the north. "It wasn't always like this. You're looking at about 40 years of recovery. I remember smog-ins when I was little. Along with the climate change came queer weather events. Tornadoes, ice storms, floods, all that stuff. It drove people indoors. Huge underground malls were built that connected the whole city. Soon people didn't have to go outside anymore and the streets became deserted. Convenience and comfort have kept us inside since."

"But why don't people know it's changed? Why don't they live out here now?"

"Because no one's interested and the government doesn't want them to. But to be frank with you, Daniel, I'm glad." His eyes narrowed slightly. "Can you imagine this place full of people like it was before? It'd be a concrete mess again!"

Daniel nodded. "Yes, I see your point."

"Someday I'll live out here," said Bobby, looking out to the horizon. "Be self-sufficient and never return to Icaria's sterile environment. I'd do it today if I thought Julie'd come too."

Daniel followed Bobby's gaze and wondered what it would be like to live out here with someone like Julie. A cry of alarm disrupted his reverie. The men ran down the hill and found her, crouched, cradling one hand in the other. Blood formed a dark pool in her cupped hand. Her face was pale with shock as she turned to them with wide eyes.

"Oh, my," said Bobby. Part of her thumb hung, dangling. "Here's a tissue."

He carefully returned the severed section to the rest of her thumb. She winced, looking like she was going to be sick. "You need to put pressure on it," Bobby commanded urgently. "Hold your hand up in the air and bend your arm." She followed his direction. "How on Earth did you do that?"

She glanced at the broken shards of glass all about her on the ground.

"Oh, dear," Bobby said. "Glass is sharp unless it's weatherworn, Julie," he remonstrated her with a gentle voice. "It's probably a clean cut, though. We better get inside. I have a first aid kit in my storage locker."

Bobby rushed Julie back to the tower and let Daniel collect their things. He caught up to them as they reached the exit door. Bobby pulled the card from his pocket and ushered them inside. He sat Julie down on a bench and rummaged through his locker for some bandages. Once Bobby had bandaged up her hand, Julie found her voice. "I'm sorry I spoiled our outing," she said, the words shaky. "Maybe we can go out another time?"

"I'd like that," Daniel said. "Can I take you out for supper?"

She nodded.

Bobby said, "You've lost a lot of blood, Julie. Go straight to the Med-Center before you lose the thumb."

"I will." She turned to Daniel, looking very pale. "I'll see you later," she said, and got up to go, but she must have risen too quickly. She sagged in a swoon, but Daniel lunged and caught her. She regained consciousness after just a few moments and righted herself. He quickly let go of her, blushing. "I must have fainted," she murmured, looking down at her thickly wrapped thumb. Blood already soaked the bandages and seeped onto her other hand.

"Let me take you to the Med-Center," Daniel offered.

"All right," she said quietly.

They made their way silently to the Med-Center. Daniel found Emergency and sat down with Julie once she'd submitted her card to the cashier. Daniel looked down at her white face, watching her stare off into space. She eventually leaned her head on his shoulder. He glanced around. No one seemed to care. Perhaps she'd forgotten in her daze that it was he, not Bobby, she was leaning against. He slipped his arm around her.

Eventually a medical droid called her name and she roused. As she got up, she turned to Daniel and said calmly, "Thanks, Daniel. I'll be fine now. Please don't wait. Good bye." She disappeared through the yellow doors with the droid.

He trudged toward the tube-jet station. She was an odd creature, fiercely independent, yet so vulnerable. Like a wounded animal, she'd betrayed an edgy cynicism at times that seemed to contradict her usual simple joyfulness. He remembered her soft body in his arms and felt his face flush with unfathomable pleasure.

48

"HOW is she?" said Bobby, opening the door for Daniel to enter.

"Getting neurgery. She didn't want me to stay. I think she'll be all right."

"You look like you could use a drink. I have something special." Bobby winked. He left the leisure room, then returned with a bottle shaped like the one on his artifact shelf. He poured some of the viscous amber liquid in two glasses and handed one to Daniel.

After an appreciative sniff, Daniel gulped it down, much to Bobby's astonishment, and felt it burn. It took his breath away for a moment. Then he had to cough. Bobby snorted. "Vee, Daniel! Ya gotta sip it slowly. This is no cheap drug. Cherish the essence, the bouquet. It's called cognac."

Daniel felt the heat of the narcotic flame through him and smiled.

"I got several of these as payment for Homer's *Iliad* and Virgil's *Aeneid*. Charlie found a full crate in one of the buildings he was demolishing in '81. This is my last bottle." Bobby poured Daniel some more.

"I'm honored. Julie hasn't tried this?"

"She doesn't drink drug or alcohol," Bobby replied.

"Why is that?"

"She claims that it makes her sick and interferes with her ability to vee—er—" His jaw worked as he hesitated with a thought. "—work." He sighed. "I think she doesn't drink because her mother *did*." He paused for a moment to focus on the past while Daniel waited for more. Bobby seemed to struggle with his next words. "You see, when my brother—Julie's father—was taken to the Pol Station, her mother fell apart. They had to move to the inner-city, where she drank herself into oblivion. It was quite sad." He looked down.

"What happened?"

Bobby looked uncomfortable for a moment. He hesitated. "One day her mother just disappeared, leaving Julie and her sister to fend for themselves. She was only twelve. She lasted a few years there, basically as a vagrant, before they found her."

Julie, a techno-slummer? Good vee! "How'd she survive?" He couldn't picture it. She was too graceful to have been such a creature of chaos. But it explained how she'd heard of him when he was Neo.

"Frankly, Daniel, I don't know how she made it. Sure had figured out the machine-world by then. That might have been one of the reasons she chose the career she did. I'm ashamed to say that I didn't want her, but the government gave me so much to look after her, and I relented. I hated kids, wanted nothing to do with them, especially a little brat from the inner-city... and she knew it, too. We fought and she ran away a couple of times." Bobby fidgeted, fighting uncomfortable images. Daniel had seen how Bobby could be gruff with Julie and she stubborn with him. Bobby was a hermit, who'd carefully defined his life with no complicating relationships. Julie had definitely put a wrench in that pattern. "I'm not proud of what I was then, but she warmed my heart. She was so sad and lost. Like me, I guess. I got to love her so much."

"What about her sister?"

Bobby squirmed. "I only got Julie in my custody because she tested positive as a vee—a very bright girl. Her sister ended up in an inner-city Care-Center and we never found her." He looked away and his shoulders slumped. Daniel sensed there was more to the tale, but he didn't pry. Bobby straightened up. "You know Julie needs to loosen up." He gulped the remainder of his drink and continued with resolve. "She needs a good friend. Someone like you."

Daniel felt his cheeks warm. "She must have lots of friends already."

"Yes, but they're all in the Pol Station!" He laughed, then frowned. "I shouldn't have said that. I'm worried about her, Daniel. Especially now after the Shame Court. It tore a hole in her. I think they gave her mind drugs or something. She hasn't been the same since. She's so restless, irritable, almost frantic. Like she was when I first got her from the inner-city. She's like a ladybug in a jar."

Daniel had no idea what a ladybug was, but he nodded.

"What have I done wrong, Daniel?" Bobby looked sad. "One day, soon after she started at her new school, she came home early with a puffy lip and red eyes. She wouldn't tell me what happened, but later she asked me what a distopian was and I knew. They'd called her one. Kids are so cruel. I think she had a hard time of it at school. Some of them found out that she was a vee—very smart girl and had spent time in the inner-city. I think she was bullied a lot." He sighed heavily. "Sometimes I think all I've done is get her all mixed up. She's not like me. I'm an old fossil. I'm a misfit in this mechanized, fast-paced world of pixels and sounds. My philosophy, my world, is long gone, except perhaps in these old books I read."

Bobby waved his hand towards a worn volume by George Eliot. "I still think we've sacrificed the sensuous richness of just being for the sake of speed. Everything's a blur to me. Sometimes I get the feeling that all of Icaria is running; but to where?" He shook his head. "Julie's young. She talks the speed of Icarian life. She's a vee-com cube. Sometimes it seems like she's joined at the hip to hers. It's a drug for her. She needs to get out and mix with people, good people, someone like her. You're solid on your feet, a decent guy. You drive tube-jets and talk the same sort of language, the language of machines and gadgets. And I've watched you two together. You make her laugh, Daniel. You get along well, and she really likes you."

Daniel shifted and dropped his gaze to his empty drink. He felt suddenly shy. Julie was so elegant and intelligent. A Level l lady with a vee-com mind. He was, after all, just an inner-city boy who drove trains.

As if sensing the need to change the subject, Bobby said, "It must be wonderful driving your tube-jets."

"Yeah, it is," said Daniel.

"What's it like? Tell me about it?"

Daniel's eyes lit up. He thought of Speed Freak, which he'd been anxious to try out ever since Banes had mentioned it last month. "Why don't I show you? There's a new sim ride at the Rec-Center, a lot like a tube-jet. My friend could get us in, I bet."

Bobby nodded. He watched Daniel punch a few buttons on his vee-pad. "There's a ride every hour," said Daniel. "We now have two free passes. Let's go!"

Bobby hesitated. "What about Julie? She may call."

"Use your vee-set. Then you can talk to her from anywhere."

"See, you're just like her, Daniel. She'd have told me the same!"

Vee, thought Daniel, Bobby lived in a cloud. That technology was a hundred years old, like the fossils he collected.

≈

When they reached the Rec-Center in Margalef Mall, Bobby gaped. A dancercise class boomed overhead. Below, at their own level, they glimpsed people playing R-Ball through the unbreakable plastic barriers as they nudged their way in the crowded hallway.

Daniel grinned at Bobby. "First time in here?"

"Yes." Bobby smiled self-consciously. "Does it show?"

"Yeah!" Daniel laughed. Bobby chuckled.

"You asked where everyone went. Well, look around," said Daniel, making a sweeping gesture. "This is where Icaria comes after the work day." He pointed. "That's the Sport Complex. Upstairs are the fitness classes and weights. Further down are the virtual tracks, and cycles, like Julie has at her place, and virtual playing fields—like Pol-Games."

"Pol-Games?"

"Yeah. You can pretend you're a Pol and track and shoot Distopians. It's good fun." Bobby looked horrified and Daniel quickly resumed. "The virtual theaters are two levels up. The Relaxation Center is down one level. The tanks that you mentioned Julie likes to use are down there, in an authorized part of the center.

That center is restricted to Level 1 cardholders. The yoga, Tai Chi and other meditation classes are also down there. Below that level is where the Pet Shops and the virtual sex center is."

"Virtual sex? Sex with a vee-com?" Bobby looked embarrassed.

"You program in your preference and then get virtually laid. It doesn't work quite like the real thing. At least not for me. But I'm told it's popular."

Bobby wiped his brow with a loud sigh, still eyeing the young men and women in the fitness class above them. "This speed of life is a little fast for this old timer."

Daniel laughed. "This way, old timer!" He pointed down a side hallway after spotting a sign for the new game. He knew his way around this complex, but a few things had changed since he'd been here last. There it was! The entrance to Speed Freak. He turned with a gleeful smile to Bobby, who returned him a less gleeful, uneasy one.

"Don't worry. It'll be fun," Daniel assured him.

When they reached the console, Daniel read the choices. Inspired, he said, "Well, we have five choices for a virtual ride. There's one here that takes you outside."

"No," Bobby surprised him with his answer. "I go outside all the time. I know what it's like there and I prefer the real thing. Do they have a tube-jet virtual ride?"

"Oh, yeah," Daniel said, remembering why they had come in the first place.

"This one's on me," Daniel said with a bright smile and slipped his card into the slot twice. "There. Remember, we got two free passes."

The door opened and they entered a long hallway lined with six doors. One was open. "That must be ours," said Daniel. He led Bobby through the doors into a chamber with screens that looked like windows. It resembled the cockpit of a vehicle with two seats and control panel, steering wheel and throttle for each seat. As soon as they sat down, the door shut.

~

As soon as the door shut, the screens came to life and they were in an Icarian tube-jet station, bustling with activity. The control panel lit up and a small vee screen showed a car of the tube-jet. Bobby drew in a short breath and felt his heart pound against his chest. Daniel didn't seem to notice. He was overcome with rapt excitement.

"Pretty good likeness," Daniel said. "Want to take the controls?"

Bobby forced himself to speak, "You go ahead this time. I'm content to watch."

Daniel nudged the throttle forward. Bobby felt the jar and the force of acceleration as they moved through the tube-jet station and plunged into a dark tunnel. Lights from the virtual tunnel strobed past them in quick succession. Bobby's shallow breaths accelerated. His throat closed and his chest tightened as if in a vice. He broke out into a sweat and felt a warm nauseous wave carry him to the past. He was back in that dark room. The smelly man behind him, laughing. His clothes pulled off—

"Bobby!" It was Daniel. "Are you all right? I'll get a medic!"

"No. I'm fine," Bobby stammered. His heart banged against his chest. "Just a panic attack." Trembling in a cold sweat, he realized that they'd returned to the tube-jet station and the vehicle appeared no longer to be moving. "I would like to leave and get some fresh air. I find it very confining in here."

"Sure." Daniel said. He turned off the game and they left.

49

HARPO'S was a popular pasta bar on the 32nd floor of Darwin Mall, with floor-to-ceiling glass overlooking the huge open area. It was also one of the few restaurants that maintained human—not virtual or droid—waiters. Daniel settled himself to a window seat. A waiter with slicked back cobalt-colored hair approached with two menus. "Will someone be joining you tonight, sir?"

"Yes," he said. He ordered a *sodom* at the waiter's suggestion and fidgeted as he waited for Julie. When he saw her enter the restaurant his heart raced. She looked different in her work clothes. Beautiful and intimidating in crisp red and black. She saw him, smiled and approached the table then sat down across from him, her eyes sparkling like an exotic sea.

"Hi. How was work?"

"Oh, fine," she responded tersely then added, "I'm starving!" and buried her head behind the menu.

"They suggest the Harpo Lasagna and *sodom*," Daniel said meekly to the menu.

Julie peered at him over hers. "That sounds great, without the drug." She put down the menu and knocked over his drink. It spilled over his sleeve and lap and onto the floor. "Oh!" she gasped and leaned over to help wipe the spill. He moved to wipe and they bumped heads. "Oh!" she said again. "Are you all right?" they said in unison. Then they looked at each other and laughed.

"I'm usually the one who knocks over the drink." Daniel chuckled, wiping himself.

"I beat you this time." She gave him her lopsided smile. "Are you okay?"

"Yeah. Just a little wet. I wanted something different, anyway."

After the waiter came with new drinks and took their order, Julie relaxed and leaned forward with a grin, her hands clasped. "I remember once, it was exam time and I was studying my vee-book, not paying attention to where I was going. I bumped into something and I rushed into an apology only to discover that I'd mistaken a signpost for a droid. I guess I was tired. I burst out laughing and couldn't stop."

Daniel chuckled, enjoying his vision of her uncontrollable laughter. He was about to share his embarrassing spill with Colleen when he remembered a more momentous event. He set his gaze intensely on her. "Ever seen a cypol pick up a techno-slummer?" He had her full attention. "She was my best friend. I found her and her sister starving in the inner-city, when I was there with my dad. I gave them food; basically saved their lives."

Julie's eyes widened and her face paled. She looked for a moment as if she was going to say something, then seemed to think better of it and tightened her lips. She leaned back as Daniel shared the haunting story of Angel being swept up by the cypol into the inky blackness. He smiled wryly, thinking Julie over-sensitive to be so affected. Then he recalled that she'd spent a short time as a techno-slummer herself. Perhaps she feared cypols more than anything. He certainly had. He added, "She had no reason to fear cypols, though. She never told me, but she must have known she was a freaking veemeld—"

"I didn't—" She bit out intensely then broke off, looking at him, horrified. Her eyes flashed like a forest on fire. Then the fire died and she continued in a subdued voice, "Er—didn't think a kid like that would recognize that she was a veemeld."

"She must have known," he insisted. "Why else would she have just let herself be taken? Everyone knew cypols recruited veemelds for the outer-city."

Julie swallowed several times and spluttered, "B-but what about her sister? You said a cypol took her sister first. Wasn't she looking for *her*? Isn't that why she..."

"I think she used her sister as an excuse. Chaos, we all figured Elf had already been recycled. Angel knew exactly what she was doing." For a brief moment Julie reminded him of Angel, fierce and challenging. Something in the way she looked at him, as though she could see clearly through to his heart, forced him to avert his eyes with shame.

"I guess she *did* mean to save her sister," he relented. He knew he was rambling, but a part of him couldn't stop talking about her. "But she knew she was getting out, too. She was pretty smart. Smart, brave and generous. She was the best friend I ever had—until then."

He heard Julie utter a sound like a strangled gasp, and gazed up at her. She held her napkin tightly in her hands and stared at him with captivated but stricken eyes, as if inviting him to continue and begging him to stop at the same time. The words poured from him like a waterfall. "Vee, I hated her. She probably got a Level 1 job for the Ecologists or something. She probably lives in the best penthouse in District 12." He fought to keep the bitterness out of his voice, but failed. "And she probably never gave me a second thought. Doesn't know—or care—that I exist."

The napkin tore in her hands. "Oh, dear," she said in a shaky voice, eyes glistening and face half-broken with unshed tears.

He leaned forward, touched by her reaction. "It's okay. I got over it. Guess you could say she was my first love." He smiled vaguely.

"I had no idea..." she said in a brittle voice and grabbed her glass then put it down. Then she added as if in afterthought, "...no idea that you—um—knew a veemeld."

"Well, she and all the other veemelds can go straight to chaos," he said. "I'll have nothing to do with them. They probably like their AIs better than they like people."

She gagged on her drink just then and coughed violently, face turning intense red.

"You all right?" He leaned forward and reached out for her with one hand. She nodded and looked away. He gave her some time in silence to recover.

The food came and Daniel ate with gusto. Julie picked at hers. She'd slipped back into shyness and avoided his eyes, her thoughts turned inward. Wondering if his mention of the inner-city made her uncomfortable, Daniel decided to pursue safer subjects. "Speaking of veemelds, I recently heard that 95% occupy the mid to high Level 1 jobs in the outer-city. Good thing there aren't more of them, eh? Or you'd be out of a job!"

Her face reddened and she looked even more uncomfortable. He scolded himself for unconsciously insulting her. He hadn't meant to slur her abilities; only it was next to impossible to compete with a veemeld. He hoped she didn't think he'd made the remark out of jealousy because he was only a Level 5. She'd gone from looking embarrassed to looking unwell. "Are you all right?" he offered. "You haven't touched your food."

"I'm okay," she insisted weakly. "As you were saying, good thing there aren't more of them." She raised the glass of water to her mouth and sipped with slow deliberation. Her eyes drifted away and she looked lost in thought. He sighed, resigned to his own ineptness at conversation. The waiter came and took away their plates, then returned with after-dinner beverages.

Julie mirrored Daniel's position of placing one elbow on the table and leaning her head on her hand as she sipped her tea. "A special treat for yourself?" she said, half smiling.

"Yes." He smiled back. The coffee had cost him as much as the entire meal. "For a rare occasion." His smile grew into a brave grin; he didn't understand why hers turned almost sad. The conversation stalled awkwardly, but Daniel drank in the sight of her in the silence, from her eyes to her rosy face, to the soft contours of her figure. Self-conscious, she reached for her spoon and accidentally brushed his fingers where they rested on the table. He saw her pupils grow large and he seized her hand.

Her eyes met his and she swallowed and took a deep breath. He read a plea in her intense gaze and reluctantly released her hand. She pulled it back and tucked both of them under the table. "I'm not what or *who* you think I am, Daniel," she said tightly. "You might not like me as much when you know."

He resisted asking. She must have meant her "tainted" inner-city days. It was pretty obvious that she disliked inner-city people. He remembered the expletive she'd thrown at him through the wall. Had Bobby told her his origin? Perhaps she didn't want to hurt his feelings. Taking the coffee with both his hands and raising it to his mouth, Daniel tried to hide his disappointment. He wanted to tell her he knew about her, reveal his own history to her, make her feel better. But, thinking she might only think worse of him, he said in a subdued voice, as he watched the steam rise from his cup, "I hope we can be good friends. Like brother and sister."

"Me, too," she said, dropping her gaze to the table.

50

JULIE knew that the lake was there before they saw it. She could smell it, a distinct musky-sweet and faintly fishy smell. As they crested the hill, it stretched before them like a limitless sea, sparkling like millions of twinkling jewels. It was as if the sun had skimmed the lake in its skyward trajectory and left behind a glittering trail of golden flecks that danced on the surface. She sat cross-legged in the long grass, filled with memories of coming here with her father. "Beautiful, isn't it?"

Daniel agreed and sat down next to her with a far-away smile. "I used to dream of coming to a place just like this with my best friend."

Angel and Neo's dream, Julie thought and fought down the rush of guilt. She yearned to tell him her secrets, to free her heart—and his—of its pain. But her mind wouldn't let her. She'd come close to telling him several times, but had lost her nerve. He'd have many reasons to despise her: for being dishonest about herself; for being a heartless veemeld; for breaking her promise to him; and best yet, for just being Angel, abandoning their dream and deserting him in the first place.

Julie suggested they walk along the beach. With Bobby not there, Daniel directed his questions to her. She answered him with scraps of knowledge pieced together from memories of a former avid interest. When she couldn't answer a question, she relied on SAM's vast database, while it was still within range, and felt like she was cheating. During moments of silence, she found herself stealing appreciative glances at Daniel in the light of dusk, absorbing every line on his rugged face, that full mouth worn in a natural smile, the delicious shape of his lips, how they tucked into dimpled cheeks.

They walked for kilometers, then stopped and lay on the beach, watching the setting sun. As Julie listened to the lapping of the waves and the distant music of the birds, she basked in the almost-silence of her brain. The drone of mechanized intelligence had given way to the ever-present dull chirping that mingled with the choral harmony of nature. She'd learned long ago that by calming her mind, she could quiet the chittering sounds to an idle drone.

Her gaze rose to the clouds. Their sliding contours mimicked the very molecular shapes that drove them. As the faces of those she'd loved and lost swept past her mind in a steady progression, she saw how her own life, like theirs, was just part of a mosaic of fractals, each on its own trajectory but also touching every other like the threads of a spider's web. They had connected her to Neo again, in the shape of Daniel.

Raising herself on an elbow, Julie watched him. He'd closed his eyes and wore that same cherub's smile that had first captivated her. She smiled. He'd given her back the heath, and a part of himself with it. She wanted so much to stay here with him. To breathe the fresh air, feel the warmth of the sun or the spatter of rain on her face, dig in the dirt and plant seeds. Watch the moon and the stars. Dream again.

Daniel finally broke the spell, suggesting they return inside. They started away from the shore, but after ten minutes of walking, Julie had found no recognizable landmark by which to orient herself. The tower was nowhere in sight, nor were any other familiar Icarian structures. The undulating heath, like giant waves of the sea, had cleverly hidden them. To her inquiring look, Daniel admitted, "I think we're lost."

"Terrific," Julie muttered under her breath. They'd strayed beyond SAM's range. She watched the sun wink out over the horizon.

"Don't worry," Daniel reassured her quickly. "I brought plenty of food and an insupad. We're right in the middle of the city so we're bound to run into a building so long as we walk in the same direction. We can find our way using the sun's position—"

"Except it just set," Julie said, pointing to the orange glow on the horizon.

"I think Bobby said it sets in the east, so if we head in the opposite direction we go back into the heart of the outer-city. The inner-city is the other way."

"Sure," Julie murmured without listening, letting Daniel take the lead.

In the growing darkness a cool breeze lifted her hair and Julie glanced up at the black clouds that closed over them. The wind gusted fiercely, whipping her hair across her face. Within seconds rain fell, small spatters at first, then huge pelting drops that soaking them. Daniel seemed to enjoy the experience, but Julie struggled behind him. Like a jilted lover peevishly mocking her discordance, the heath flung out gorse to rip her clothes and wiry roots to trip her.

They entered the darkness of a wooded area and the terrain dropped. Julie suppressed a growing alarm. They were heading down a ravine. When they reached a large river, Julie knew they'd gone astray. "Where are we?"

"Vee! I think this is the Don River and we're on the border of the outer-city," Daniel said, looking forlorn. "We must have gone the wrong way."

"Terrific," Julie muttered under her breath, squinting through the thick curtain of rain and fog.

"We can try to retrace our steps, or we can follow the river a ways and then try to go west again."

Julie pushed aside the strings of sopping hair plastered over her face. Trying to retrace their steps in the dark made no sense. "Let's follow the river," she said. "But along the top of the ravine." He nodded and they stumbled in the darkness along the bank for what felt like an hour. The rain finally abated and the air cleared. The heady scent of loam and living vegetation filled her nostrils like a drug as the clouds parted and the moon shone overhead.

Julie, SAM's voice lit her mind like the beacon of a lighthouse. *Where've you been? Building a house?*

Julie couldn't help a burst of laughter. *SAM! Am I ever glad to hear you!* She knew they were close to a building now and she turned to Daniel with a grin. He gave her a glancing smile, probably interpreting her reaction as simple gratitude that the rain had ended. Something in the distance glinted. Lights from the top stories of a building! They turned to each other, whooped and hugged. When they let go awkwardly, Daniel grinned.

"We'll take it, won't we!"

"You bet!" answered Julie. *I'm coming home, SAM.*

≈

Daniel didn't tell her where he thought they were. She would see soon enough. They found a door and it opened when he slid Bobby's card into the slot. When they stepped inside, a stale smell assaulted them and they looked at one another. Julie wrinkled her nose. "Is this what Icarian air is like? It was so fresh outside, especially after the rain."

They walked with self-conscious steps along several corridors to a mall, leaving a trail of muddy footprints. Julie gravitated closer to him as people stared. He caught her glancing down at herself, saw the bumps of her erect nipples through the wet material that clung to her, and he looked away as she drew her arms around herself. She followed his gaze to a sign. "We're in a border district! How'd we get this far?" She was obviously disgusted with the filth of the place, no doubt reminded of the two years she'd endured as an exile in the squalor of the inner-city. He caught her staring with horror at the wandering Darwin victims.

"I know the way now," Daniel offered, feeling strangely responsible. "I'll take you home."

51

May 14, 2095—2230, the same day.

"DON'T go any farther!" Julie barked. Daniel froze just inside the doorway to her apartment, startled by the edge in her voice. "Take your shoes and socks off," she commanded. "Neo, have Mildred clean up the floor." As a sausage-shaped droid appeared from a small door and whirred behind Daniel, sucking up the mud from the carpet, Julie hastened to her. When she returned with a charcoal gray robe, Daniel was still bent over to remove his muddy shoes and filthy socks with his head poised in her direction. He grinned at her. "You've got quite an arsenal of house droids." In his building he was lucky to have a basic cleaning droid, she thought, blushing at her privileges.

She handed the robe to him and he gave it a quizzical look. "It should fit you. I practically swim in it," she said. "You shower first, so I can send your clothes through the laundry chute."

"Thanks." Daniel followed, barefoot, to the bathroom. He stepped into the shower stall and closed the barrier. As he undressed inside, he handed out his clothes piece by piece. Then Daniel turned on the shower and uttered a gasp of appreciation. Julie hastened out with his clothes and shut the door.

≈

She walked to the chute console and pushed some buttons. The console lights flashed as the system encoded pertinent information about her and the parcel's destination. She brought his shirt to her face and inhaled his scent before dropping it in the chute with the other clothes. Then she wandered to her vee-com to instruct it on the sound/visual environment system. Two minutes later the chute console beeped. As Julie picked up the replacement clothes, Daniel emerged from the shower in her robe. The robe was too small. He barely got it round his middle and it crept up high on him, revealing hairy, thickly muscled legs. "A bit small," she said, bringing a hand to her mouth to hide her grin.

He pirouetted for her and raised a leg. "Is it my color, though?"

Julie burst into laughter. "That's something SAM would say," she blurted out.

"Who's Sam?"

She faltered. "Oh—um—just a funny virtual character." She hastily draped the clean set of leisure clothes on a chair. "For you."

"You must have Level 1 chute service," he said, still grinning like a ten-year old.

"I do." She smiled self-consciously. "And now it's my turn."

〰

He thought of Julie, naked under the spray of water, and wanted to join her. As distraction, he decided to investigate her place, hearing some music in the leisure room. It came from the vee-com close to her active wall where Senscape projected a mountain stream. The holo wove a kaleidoscopic dance to the music. He squinted at some writing at the bottom and read, "J.S. Bach: *Prelude in C.*" Her bookshelf was full of old books. A lot of Thomas Hardy, an author he found familiar but couldn't recall from where. He pulled one out. Its cover was torn and watermarked and the pages fanned out in waves as if the book had been to chaos and back. He read the title: *Tess of the d'Urbervilles.* Wasn't that a Distopian book?

Julie was taking longer than a minute in the shower. The automatic shut off would have kicked in by now at his place. Some are more equal than others, he thought with a wry smile. His supply was 2 minutes every 8 hours, depending on how much water he ran. He dressed, then wandered into the kitchen and decided to make supper for them. He searched through her well-stocked fridge and pantry—definitely Level 1. His chute service didn't stock half of the items she had. He chose a tofu spinach lasagna. As he unwrapped the meal and placed it in her cooker, Daniel's keen ear listened. Seven minutes of nonstop luxurious hot shower had elapsed before she shut off and he heard her move from the bathroom to her bedroom. Letting the meal cook, he returned to the leisure room and picked up the book again.

Julie entered, barefoot and wearing a clean charcoal gray leisure outfit. Her wet hair was combed back behind her ears and the natural beauty of her clean youthful face shone with a quality that made him blush. As though he'd glimpsed something private about her. She inclined her head to one side and made a crooked smile. "Mmmm...something smells good." Her eyes darkened like the deep forest. "And you really shouldn't have bothered, Daniel."

He held up his hand. "It was my fault we got lost and wet out there. I wanted to make it up to you. It should be ready. Shall we dine?"

"Okay," she said. "I'm famished." She set the table and they sat down in the small dining alcove with their food. "This is marvelous," she said, devouring her food. A piece of noodle and tomato sauce found its way onto her chin.

"You've got some food there," he said, and brushed his own face.

She wiped it off with an embarrassed laugh. "Bobby says I should slow down to relish each mouthful, but I can't help gobbling it as if it might not last." She grinned. "Something I learned in the—um," then broke off, thinking the better of it, and shook her head with an apologetic smile.

"You eat with gusto. Which is a relishing of another sort."

"Perhaps," she said. She tilted her head with an inquiring smile. "What did you mean, your fault?"

"You only came out with me because I made you promise and you wanted to keep it."

She blushed and swallowed her mouthful before taking a breath to speak. "The heath and I go back a long way, but we aren't exactly friends. It's hard for me to explain." She paused and tightened her lips. "My father introduced me to the heath when I was little. I was enthralled. But then it got, well... complicated." She shrugged and toyed with her food.

Daniel nodded, although she hadn't explained anything. Was she thinking of her techno-slummer days? He longed to ask, but she hadn't shared that with him. Only her uncle had.

"You've embraced the heath," Julie said as Daniel served her more lasagna. "Would you ever want to spend a lot of time out there?"

"Oh, yeah. It'd be thrilling but a challenge. How about you?"

She smiled down at the fork she held in mid-air. "Only in my dreams."

Daniel remembered what Bobby had told him about Julie's childhood ambition. "People have this appalling vision that outside will eat them up or make them sick—"

"Or get them all wet and muddy," she said, her eyes creasing in a smile.

He laughed sheepishly. "So it's not a paradise. But it is beautiful."

"Yes, it is. But Icarians gave up on the outside a long time ago. A long time ago it *did* make them sick," said Julie.

"Outside isn't a disease, like Darwin," Daniel said with disapproval. "It's healthy and beautiful now. If people knew, more would go outside."

"I don't know if they would, Daniel. Most don't care. Icarians are so comfortable inside, they have no interest in coping with the savage reality of insects, heat, rain and cold. Most don't have the patience. It doesn't matter to them that it's beautiful now. It's a beauty they no longer comprehend."

He frowned. "But only because it's unfamiliar. You're letting yourself get sucked in by the propaganda that promotes a world run by veemelds and machines."

Julie seemed lost for words and bolted the rest of the lasagna in silence. After they'd finished their meal, she instructed the house vee-com to clean up: "Neo, get Abigail to clear the table."

Daniel gave a soft laugh and Julie looked at him with curiosity. "Oh, I just knew an Abigail once," he explained. "Don't suppose you've got an Annabelle?" he joked.

She frowned and smiled at the same time. "As a matter of fact, I do. It's the dishwasher."

Daniel wandered to the bookshelf and picked up the book he'd pulled out earlier. He thought of how Angel's nightly reading had supplanted his bedtime storytelling.

He'd never stayed to hear her read to the other children and didn't know what she read to them. "You have an impressive collection. What's the interest in Thomas Hardy? He certainly writes beautifully about nature."

Julie moved beside him. "Also on the human condition." She took the book he held. "This one's about tragic love and deception." She stroked Hardy's *Tess of the d'Urbervilles* as though it would come alive like a genie. "I've lugged those books with me all over Icaria, read them hundreds of times. I probably know what each page says." Her far-away smile turned impish. "Test me."

"You're kidding."

"Pick a page and read a bit. Here." She handed *Tess* to him.

He opened the book near its center and flipped a few pages. "Okay, here's a spicy scene: *'In the name of our love, forgive me,' she whispered with a dry mouth. And, as he did not answer, she said again—'Forgive me as you are forgiven! I forgive you, Angel.'*"

Her face paled, then reddened briefly. He thought he'd stumped her. Then she exhaled a ponderous breath, pushed herself forward with determination and, avoiding his eyes, began to recite: "*'Having begun to love you, I love you for ever—in all changes, in all disgraces, because you are yourself. I ask no more. Then how can you, O my own husband, stop loving me?'*

'I repeat, the woman I have been loving is not you.'

'But who?'

'Another woman in your shape.'"

He'd followed the passage in the book and shook his head with a smile of astonishment. "That's amazing," he said, closing the book and returning it to the bookshelf. "Word for word."

"Told you I read them a hundred times," she said, though she looked far from smug. She gazed at him strangely, as if searching for an answer to a question he didn't know.

"These were your father's?" he asked, sitting down beside her. She visibly flinched and stared at him. He explained with an unsure half-smile, "The inscription."

She nodded and visibly relaxed. "Of course. They're all I have from him. They were a gift from his cousin."

"Janet," Daniel offered.

Her eyes lit up at the mention of the name. "She nursed me to health after I fell ill as a child. Bobby used to tell me stories about her. She killed someone once to save them during the revolution. She took care of her family, not like m—" and cut herself off, overcome by something too painful to share. Not like her *mother*? Julie continued, "Janet was a neurologist in Icaria-11 when the plague hit. She took it personally, somehow, that she couldn't stop it. She committed suicide. She took such good care of my father and my uncle when they were kids."

Daniel guessed that she had not felt the same of her own mother. Then she said something that puzzled him. "I wish I could have been more like her. Strong and clever." She looked so miserable, as if she were facing an invisible tribunal. "I failed... those I loved." Why was she looking at him that way? Was she thinking of her recent shaming, or was there something else?

Had she really meant to say, '*me*'; 'not like *me*'? Maybe it wasn't bitterness with her mother that she felt, but guilt at not having saved her. Was that why she saved old women? He watched her brows furrow as she focused deeply inward, as though struggling with a hard decision. Friendly as she was, Julie had divulged very little of her personal world to him. He wanted to take her in his arms and whisper away her worries and fears.

Her forest fire eyes blazed directly into his. "If you had a gift and knowledge that forced you to make a choice between saving the world and saving yourself, which would you choose?"

Daniel blinked, dazed by her question and the intensity of her stare. He thought for a long time, uncomfortable, as she gazed unfalteringly into his eyes. Then, suddenly thinking of what Angel had done, the answer came to him. "I'd choose to save the one I loved."

She looked down, releasing him, and nodded in silence. Keeping her eyes aimed at the floor, she added in a breathless voice, "And if that meant choosing to live truth in sadness over a lie in blissful happiness?"

Why was his heart pounding? What could she mean by the riddle? She lifted her gaze and her eyes caught his like a moth in a flame. He felt like she was peering directly into his throbbing heart. "I don't understand," he stuttered. "Those are oxymorons, aren't they?"

52

AS night fell, Daniel and Julie, exhausted from a day of hiking and swimming, returned inside to attend a symphony in Darwin Mall. Julie, yawning, fought to keep her eyes open. For some reason, she found the sound of the French horn amusing. Knowing her habit for uncontrollable laughter when she was tired, Daniel stifled a laugh, hoping to incite her. She gave him a warning frown, then giggled uncontrollably. They had to leave.

At her flat, Julie went into the kitchen to make some tea. Daniel noticed a message signal on her vee-com. "You have a message," he called.

"Can you check it for me, please?" she called back from the kitchen.

Feeling a little self-conscious, Daniel pressed the message button. The face of a stunningly handsome man with a brash smile lit the holo. Daniel remembered him as the same young man on the holo-card by Julie's desk. "Hi, Julie. I'm sorry I missed your call. I never thought you'd call me at home," he gushed with obvious pleasure. "Sure, let's meet. You suggested dinner somewhere. How about my place? I cook a great *coq-au-vin* with linguini alfredo... and we can talk in peace. Any night's fine. I'll keep them all free for you. So, what's so urgent that you want to discuss? Have you decided to join our vee—"

Julie switched off the message. Daniel hadn't noticed how she'd suddenly gotten beside him. He was too busy fighting his uncomfortable surge of jealousy. She gave him a complicated smile.

"A friend?" he asked.

"Zane's just someone I met at a party," she said, pulling back her hair and tucking it behind her ears. "He works at the CDC and I have some information for him."

"I think he's infatuated with you," Daniel blurted out.

Julie barked a laugh of genuine amusement even as her face colored with embarrassment. "More like with himself!"

"You have so many beautiful plants," Daniel said, looking around the room and eager to change the subject.

"Most of them are from Bobby." Julie smiled and yawned. "He gives me the dirt too. I love its smell." She laughed at his expression and flopped on the couch with another yawn.

"A green digit seems to run in your family," he said, sitting beside her.

"I believe the expression is green thumb," Julie said. "Bobby says that my father was good with plants. He researched agro-plants for awhile."

"Do you remember him?"

"Vaguely. Vignettes... pieces of moments. Mostly I remember that he had a sad face." She fixed her eyes on a distant point in her mind. "I stopped wondering long ago what it might have been like if he hadn't gone to the Pol Station."

"How old were you when that happened? You don't mind my asking you?"

"No, I don't mind. I was twelve. My sister was only seven."

"Do you ever think of her?"

She looked away, as if composing what she should say. "Sometimes, but I try not to. I lost her—" Julie's voice broke. He guessed that she'd lost her sister in the inner-city. That sort of thing happened too often. Julie cleared her throat. "I don't know where she ended up. When I started living with Bobby, I spent hours wandering the halls, feeling powerless and lost. He discouraged a search. Said there was no chance of getting her out of the Care-Center, where he expected her to be, because she wasn't a—A-awarded to him like I was. So I hacked into the public vee-coms at night." She blushed. "I searched the databases. There were plenty of Dianas but no Diana Cranes. As though she'd disappeared. I sometimes wonder if I pass her in the hallway and don't know it." She turned dark forest eyes on him and her voice flared with intensity. "I lost other friends too... left them behind." Her eyes dove deeply into him.

A cloud of uneasiness swarmed over him, carrying with it a plague of his own miserable memories of love and betrayal. To divert both their thoughts he said, "The music was great this evening. I think I liked the piece on Mars best. Who was the composer? Holms?"

"Holst," Julie corrected and yawned again. "He conjures up the awesome size of the universe very impressively, doesn't he?"

"And the beauty," he added, looking at her.

"Oh, the tea," she said self-consciously under his gaze and surged to her feet. Then she broke into a grin, as sudden inspiration sparked her jade eyes. "I have something I've been meaning to show you. Come." She led Daniel into her bedroom. "This is my sanctuary," she said proudly. "And tonight is a perfect night."

His heart raced at her words. Had she changed her mind about the nature of their relationship? Daniel was almost too excited to appreciate the room. However, it demanded attention. Tall Cyprus ferns, fig trees and umbrella plants draped the room in shades of green. They hung over her bed and the beautiful wooden desk next to it.

Julie invited him to lie on her bed. He did with quiet confusion. As soon as he did, she shut the door and the lights. He caught up his breath for a moment, but she didn't approach him. When his eyes adjusted to the darkness he gaped at the sight. Above him through the largest sky-view he had ever seen, Daniel saw the twinkling canopy of stars.

"It's beautiful, isn't it?" she said in a quiet voice.

"Exquisite," he whispered.

She moved in the dark with ease toward the window and flicked on a small light. Daniel saw her bending over a large long instrument housed on a tripod. She turned to him. "Have you ever seen the night stars through a telescope before?"

"No. What's a telescope?"

She pointed to the long tube. "It's basically a set of lenses which bring a far away object closer. Come and see the Big Dipper up close."

Daniel sidled toward her and she directed him with her hands to look through the eyepiece. Her touch made him tremble. Then he saw the stars. "There are so many!"

She pointed out the Milky Way and several constellations, then let him explore on his own. "The moon isn't out yet," she said. "When it rises we'll have to have a close-up look. Have you ever tried the desensitization tanks?"

"No. I'm not authorized to."

"Oh, right. I always forget," she responded. "When I'm in them, I feel like I'm floating in space, looking for my own constellation in the universe."

"That must be an incredible sensation," he said.

"Sometimes, late at night, I try to duplicate the feeling by lying on my bed with all my clothes off and sending my thoughts up, pretending that I'm floating outside, under the stars, far from Icaria-5, perhaps in another world... or time..."

"Hey, we could do that." He'd delivered it innocently without thinking.

"Okay," she quickly agreed, perhaps to accommodate him for his lack of the tank experience, and snapped off the light. Daniel reconsidered and saw her pause, too. Then he saw her slender silhouette bend down to remove her trousers. Forcing himself to breath evenly, he undressed and carefully folded his clothes on the chair beside the bed. He reclined on the bed and found his mouth watering, trying not to look at her. He almost jumped when he felt her hand push down on the bed for balance as she removed her underclothes and let them drop to the floor. Then she slid onto the bed next to him and lay quietly, gazing up at the stars. He could smell her, a delicate mixture of lilac and her unique body scent. It made him dizzy with desire.

⁓

As she pulled off her T-shirt, Julie's eyes roamed over Daniel's husky body. She'd often imagined what Neo might look like as a man and had envisioned him scrawny with his long tangle of hair, twisted nose and intense coal-black eyes. He'd filled out from his awkward adolescence into a man's robust shape, tall and sinewy. It was obvious that he spent time in the gyms at the Leisure Center. Gangly arms were now thickly muscled and his chest strongly contoured. He ate well, she thought with a smile. And he liked his drug. She felt a warm glow as she watched him climb onto the bed and recline to look up at the entrancing view above. A delicious cocktail of affection and sexual desire surged through her. It was so different from what she'd felt with Frank. Frank had fanned the savage flame of passion that raged through her like a wild forest fire; Daniel sent her soul soaring with a lightness of being. Frank might have thrilled her with dark adventures in far-away places, but Daniel was her sun to orbit, her home.

She wanted to stroke his gentle face, rub her nose in his hair and listen to him tell her his crazy stories. She wanted more than anything else to curl up against his strong body and fall asleep with her arms wrapped around him. But he didn't know what she was and *who* she was. Judging from what he'd said at Harpo's, he'd likely despise her if he knew. Ironic, how she'd finally found Neo again, only to have to keep her distance. So she got on the bed beside the man she loved and made sure she didn't touch him. As the murmurs of the machine city crept into her mind in the otherwise silence, she wished she could tell him everything, but she kept silent.

=

He had to make a concerted effort to breathe normally and watch the moon rise. Wispy clouds drifted past its face and satellites tracked across the blackness. He felt the warmth of Julie's body next to his, so close but not touching. He wanted to make love to her under the stars, but he felt that he'd disturb a sacred thing to her, to them both. Besides, they had an understanding. He wanted to take her hand at least, but he felt shy. He didn't want her to think he was groping. So he remained still, eyes trained toward the great constellations of the universe but heart focused on her beside him, to the most alluring and mysterious universe he'd encountered. He forced himself to breathe evenly.

What was he supposed to do now? He waited for a signal from her to sit up and get dressed. He didn't want to spoil the moment. She seemed to be in a reverie.

After what seemed like hours, but must have been only ten minutes, he heard her deep sighing breaths and turned to face her. She'd fallen asleep! He felt he should leave, but he didn't want to. Raising himself on an elbow, he watched her for a while. Her head had lolled toward him and a curtain of hair hid part of her face. His gaze followed the elegant lines of her neck and clavicles to the gentle swelling of her breasts. He watched them rise and fall to the rhythm of her breathing. One arm lay at her side. The other was flung out toward her head and dangerously close to him. He studied the contours of her body, the smooth skin that shone like silk in the new moonlight. One leg had curled beneath the outstretched one in a loose tangle. With unspeakable yearning, his eyes roamed back to her face, pale and innocent in the moon's light. She appeared less intimidating this way. She looked almost childlike, eyes closed, mouth open in the bliss of sleep. He could boldly study her, kiss her with his eyes and embrace her with his imagination. Then his eyelids grew heavy and he, too, fell asleep.

Daniel awoke with a start. Darkness enveloped him. For a brief moment he had no idea where he was. Then, he was reminded by the very source of his awakening: Julie. She was pressed against him, gently stroking his body with her hand. He turned and leaned over, staring with awe as she drew back and gazed intensely back at him with shy—almost terrified—longing. He felt her tremble when he took her face in his hands like she was the greatest treasure in the world, and he drew her close. Her kiss astonished him, startling in the depth of its vulnerability, how it revealed the stirrings of her heart. He felt an urgent desire to wrap a protective mantle about her and love her for all time.

She was deliciously wet as he slid inside her and he felt the rush of his come in several great spasms. She shuddered and they pulsed together in a tide of heat. They lay side by side in a silent embrace and he drifted to sleep for a moment, snug against her warm body.

He awoke to her smiling face in the moonlight. As if the stars had fallen into them, her eyes sparkled like miniature constellations. "Vee, you're beautiful," he whispered.

"No, you're the one who's beautiful," she said and kissed him.

With closed eyes of reverence his mouth traveled over her face and neck, tasted the breasts he had coveted only with his eyes before, followed their firm shape, drew out her nipples with his lips and tongue. Extolling her lithe, smooth body, he defined her entire shape with his fingers, slid over all her secret parts, eliciting her accompanying sighs as if he was releasing each with his touch.

Then he felt jagged scars. They were in a precise shape of a vee—no, an arrow. He looked up inquiringly. "You've been hurt." His fingers trembled over the bumpy scars. "Someone... did this?"

She nodded and whispered in a shaky voice, "At the Pol Station... before the shaming."

Overcome and unable to respond, he buried his face in her thighs as she stroked his hair. He caressed the patchwork of scars on her mound, swollen and hot. Her breaths convulsed in sudden passion and she seized his hand with a whisper. "Oh, Daniel, love me again!"

She gasped when he entered her and matched his rhythm with her arching body and flexing muscles. He kissed her wet mouth, open and yielding. This was exactly how he'd dreamed it would be, and found himself soaring with her toward the stars.

≈

The sterile room swims around her and the cloying smells of bleach and roses make her feel sick. The room spins and the beautiful woman with knife-sharp eyes murmurs in a voice dark like coffee, "I'll set you free to fly for now... I can always find you. Now, my machine-girl, live up to your name... steal the fire from heaven and give it to me—"

Julie jolted awake. The quiet light of a breaking dawn streamed through the sky-view of her room and she lay in Daniel's arms. He gazed at her with quiet concern. "You okay?"

She raked back the hair that fell into her face and pushed a smile. "Just a nightmare."

"You're still trembling. You did that all night... shiver and cry out and murmur strange things in your sleep."

Panic seized her for a moment and she wondered what she'd inadvertently revealed. "I'm sorry I kept you awake," she said, her gaze dropping.

Daniel pulled her face up with both hands to gaze directly into her eyes. "Don't be. I like how you hung on to me through the night." He kissed her and they made love again.

53

May 16, 2095—1930.

LUIGI'S was a crowded pasta bar, known for its amazing food. It went largely unnoticed as Julie and Daniel fed on each other. When they left the restaurant for Daniel's flat, they walked closely, often brushing against one another. Risking a demerit, Daniel reached out for her hand and she clasped it, feeling unspeakable happiness.

They turned a corner and she came face to face with Frank and a young girl clinging to his arm. Julie hitched her breath and Daniel let go of her hand. Frank glanced at Daniel with one eyebrow raised, then sneered at Julie. She blushed and looked away. "The freaking veemeld machine installs another fucker," Frank said, his voice spitting.

Julie jerked her head to see Daniel stare at Frank before he disappeared, sniggering, around a corner. Daniel glanced at her, then shot an angry look down the hall. "Who was that creep? What'd he mean?"

She avoided his eyes. "Just a rude Pol." He'd given away her secret.

"Why would he call you—or me—a veemeld? Neither of us looks like a freaking cyborg!"

She stiffened at Daniel's innocent words. Next time Frank wouldn't be so cryptic, she thought. Daniel was too blind to see the truth about her. Didn't want to. The thought sent her mind reeling. She glanced at Daniel in silence and knew she had to tell him everything. Before someone else did.

Walking toward the elevator, Daniel wrinkled his brow. "I've seen him before."

Julie fought her urge to stop and forced herself to maintain her stride.

"That hair and face." Daniel pursed his lips as they rode the elevator to the tube-jet station. "Don't see many Pols with their helmets off like that." He turned his gaze to look at her directly. "You don't know him, do you?"

She couldn't stand it any longer and burst out, hearing her voice splintering, "I need to tell you something, Daniel. Something about me."

"All right. I need to tell you something about me, too."

"You do?"

"Let's go to your place. It's closer. We can share our confessions." He turned shy. "And I won't stay." He paused. "Unless you want me to."

They rode the train in silence, pressed against each other and holding hands. She watched the strobing signal lights as the train hurled through the dark tunnel.

Did he understand the precipice they were walking? She knew she was going to fall. There were too many loose rocks to slide over. The question was, would he let her?

The security droid greeted Julie at the entrance to her building. "Hello, Ms. Crane."

"Hello, Henry," Julie replied tersely and led Daniel inside.

Once inside her apartment, Julie broke from his grasp and disappeared into the kitchen. She returned with two iced teas and handed him one. They stood in awkward silence for a moment until both spoke at the same time, "I—"

"Please, let me go first," Daniel insisted. Julie saw his lower lip tremble. She nodded and sat down, stroking the glass with her fingers. Daniel sat beside her, leaned his head back and exhaled. He put his glass down, then slowly turned to her. "I was born in the inner-city, Julie. Grew up there. I'm an inner-city slug." His shoulders slouched like a beaten dog.

She looked into his frightened eyes and smiled, knowing he would like what she said. "I know, Daniel. I've known from the beginning. It doesn't bother me." She formulated her next words, thinking of her own situation. "You did what you had to do to survive, there and here: you concealed your background to get a job and make friends. It isn't important who or what you are; it's what you do with who and what you are that counts."

He straightened. "Yes! You think that, really? I thought..." He trailed, looking puzzled for a moment. Then, surrendering to his relief, he grinned like a boy who'd found his missing toy. "Now it's your turn. And nothing you can tell me would matter to me, either." He smiled with confidence. "Because, I already know. Bobby told me!"

"He told you I'm a—"

"Orphan in the inner-city. Yes. I already knew. Marvelous, isn't it?" He suddenly looked apologetic, misinterpreting her confusion. "I mean, of course it wasn't marvelous, having to techno-slum. I just thought it was interesting how we both had a similar thing to confess. I don't care about your past." She felt relief wash over her muscles. "It's not as though you were a damned veemeld—"

The glass slipped from her hand and tea shot out, spreading an amber amoeba on the plush. "Oh, dear!" she said. "I'm destroying the carpet!" She jumped to her feet and tried to hide the tremor in her voice. "NEO, get Mildred." Thinking of how she'd named all her machines after techno-slummers, including him, Julie's face burned. Daniel stood up and as they watched Mildred emerge from the closet and whisk straight to the spill, Julie blurted, "I *am* a veemeld." The words came out like a shotgun.

He swerved around as if she'd hit him. "W-what d-did you s-say?" he stammered.

She kept her eyes trained on the droid and forced the words out again, more quietly this time. "I'm a veemeld, Daniel."

When she dared look him in the eyes she saw him working it through, making sense of all the strange moments, the many times she'd tried to tell him, the half-spoken truths. She saw first astonishment, even a hint of anger, then great dismay sweep over his face. His mouth tightened and he fixed vacant eyes on Mildred as it consumed the spill. It *did* matter to him, Julie thought and swallowed a great lump in her throat. As they silently watched the droid sweep circles across the carpet she felt Daniel recede from her into entropy, escaping her orbit like a renegade comet. Its task complete, Mildred hummed to the closet and the door closed with a finality that made Julie wince. He thinks I'm one of *them*. A machine. Knowing she'd already lost him, she let herself skid further. "I'm also Angel, Neo."

His face paled. She might as well have driven a sword into his gut. "You're A-a-a—" Caught in a struggle, his face broke with contrasting emotions, "...A-a-a—" The stutter had returned in full force. "You knew I was Neo?" His eyes blazed like embers in a wind. "How long did you know?" His face twisted, anger spiking. "Were you e-e-ver going to tell me?"

"I only figured it out at Harpo's. I know what you think," the words rushed out of her. "But it wasn't like that. I didn't know I was a veemeld in the inner-city. I didn't know what to expect when I let the cypol take me. Certainly not..." she faltered, watching him sweep the room and her expensive toys with critical eyes "...this."

"Looks pretty convenient," he muttered, no longer disguising his anger. She'd promised, after all; betrayed and deserted him. And failed to return. Left him in the slums for *this*. How could she explain? "Was nothing sacred to you?" he raised his voice in a tone of disgust. "You even gave our names to your damned *machines*!"

"It isn't what you think. They're my—" she broke off at the rage on his face. He'd never understand that her machines were her adopted family, like the techno-slummers before.

"And where's your sister, the one you were supposed to be saving? Where's Elf?" As if the pressure of his words had pushed her, she leaned back. Not waiting for her answer, he drained his glass. "It's late and I said I wouldn't stay. I have the early shift tomorrow."

Julie forced out the words with a dry mouth. "You forgive me, don't you?" It felt like a plea. "I forgive you, Daniel."

"Yes, I'm sure you do," he avoided her direct gaze as he made for the door.

She followed him. "Daniel, we were just children. I couldn't just go back. I had to carry on with my life. By the time I was able to return, everything had changed and I was sure you'd forgotten me, or didn't care for me to... or I might have..." She fell silent at his stony expression. Her words had broken on his face like waves on a rock. He didn't believe her. And he hadn't forgiven her either. Her throat ached as tears threatened.

He hesitated at the door. "Good night, A-a-a—J-j-julie." His lips curled into a pathetic smile and his eyes were dark with regret. Then he was gone.

BOOK FIVE:

STABLE CHAOS

But go thou until the end be; for thou shalt rest,
and stand in thy lot at the end of days
~~ The Book of Daniel, 12:13

54

May 16, 2095—2200.

DANIEL sank into a tube-jet seat and dropped his face in his hands. How could he have been such an idiot not to have realized that she was Angel? It was all in front of him the whole time: her reaction at Harpo's, the loss of her mother and sister, her techno-slumming history, her books, her naming all her droids after them... She'd fixed her overbite. Her hair was longer and she'd filled out, become a beautiful woman from that feral urchin with crooked teeth. The clumsy lines had evolved into an elegant design. But those trembling sensuous lips, poised on a firm jaw, were the same. The same intensity fired her eyes and permeated them with that confusing mixture of fierce independence and vulnerability.

Daniel bowed his head and studied his hands. They were shaking. Why hadn't Bobby told him she was a veemeld? It was clear that they'd both conspired to deceive him the whole time. The only reason she'd revealed herself was because the Pol had already given her away. And he, fool that he was, hadn't seen it. She'd used and betrayed him again. Under that sweet smile and guileless gaze lay the heart of a troublemaker, a veemeld sorceress. She was a conceited self-serving witch—*Vee, what am I saying*, he thought, raising his head to peer into the dark void of the tube-jet tunnel. Julie wasn't those things. Or was she? She'd deceived him in other things, he quickly reminded himself. Being a natural and wearing no earrings proved that she cared little for convention. Her copious demerits capped her disregard for Icarian rules. A girl like that, he didn't need. He had enough troubles of his own.

~

Daniel lay on the hummocky turf, watching the clouds skid across the sky, and stroked the smooth curves of his saxophone. He sat up and placed its belly between his thighs, then coaxed out a gentle and ponderous fugue. From it soared a single note that rose like an aria—her aria—to a mournful chorus. When he leaned his forehead against the mouthpiece, tasting the salt of his loneliness, he realized the heath had lost its magic. *She'd* been its magic.

~

Insects hissed and buzzed in the heat. Daniel pulled off his tunic and changed into a pair of shorts he had fashioned from an old worn pair of gray trousers. Stuffing his other clothes into his backpack, he approached the distant forest with the springing steps of one used to the complex terrain. He'd lied to Julie about being on morning shift, but he'd needed an excuse to leave.

The path eventually vanished in a tangle of scrub and he could no longer see the towers of Icaria. When he reached the forest, the ground became soft and spongy. Towering birch trees rustled in the slight breeze and he smelled a pleasant organic fragrance. Daniel sat down on a moss-covered log and wiped his brow. His eyes saw the forest but his mind gazed into her forest green eyes. A week had passed since he'd seen her. She'd never called. Why should she? She was Angel, who'd abandoned him. Fixed her teeth and soared into an elegant beauty beyond his reach. She was a freaking veemeld, an arcane DIC vee-cube intellectual, who held the computing power of a billion people in her head. Her silence became intimidating. It confirmed what she thought of him. Perhaps she found him amusing. Vee, most women did. An inner-city bumpkin with a veemeld? That was a joke. Vadim would scream with laughter. Childhood friendships meant nothing. That was the Icarian way. Then he thought of her loving, so sweet and genuine. Surely he hadn't imagined that?

Daniel's eyes refocused on his surroundings. He'd learned that old fallen trees served as nurseries for many colorful organisms, which eventually helped to return the dead tree to the forest. He marveled at nature's many paradoxes. There was a kind of order on a different level: an order of disorder. Nature was chaotic yet not entirely random; extravagant, yet frugal; beautiful yet cruel; magnificent yet fickle. He thought of a passage he had read in one of Bobby's books: *"Do I contradict myself? Very well, then... I contradict myself; I am large... I contain multitudes."* Just like... her.

≈

Daniel set up camp on a grassy knoll not far from the perimeter of the forest. He was still a fair distance from Icaria, but this did not bother him. He had his compass and knew his way. It would take him a few hours to get back, but he had most of tomorrow to travel before his evening shift began. He made a small fire from branches and birch bark that he'd gathered in the forest. Then he ate his dinner of beans and agro-strips as a cool breeze swept over the heath and the stars revealed themselves. Flames licked up into the night sky like pale arms in supplication and he suddenly felt selfish, expecting her to have saved him, too.

At 2200 he laid out his mat and sleeping bag, then slid inside. Crossing his arms behind his head, he studied the stars. He made out two satellites, the Big Dipper and the North Star, then wondered if she was gazing at the same night sky with her telescope. Why had she hidden from him? Vee, he'd done the same thing, he thought, hidden the truth from her for the same reason. Then he thought again: *but I'm not a veemeld. And I didn't abandon my best friend.* He thought of his grim slide into substance abuse, *I just abandoned myself.*

~

Daniel woke up with a start. It was early morning and a small deer stared at him from a meter away before darting into the forest.

He took a different route back to the high tower to avoid a steep ravine. As he scrambled out of a large hollow, he saw a large, two-story house with huge windows, balconies, and large patio, equipped with wooden benches, table and an umbrella for the sun. A shed stood next to the house. Daniel recognized solar panels on the roof, several antennas, a large dish-like device pointing skyward and to the right of the house a wind power converter. The house was well maintained and bore no signs of weathering or decay. A self-sustaining unit. What was it doing here, in the middle of the heath?

Curious, Daniel crept closer. He reached the shed first and heard the sound of shuffling feet and snorting. The large door was ajar. He peeked inside and spied several horses. Daniel proceeded to the house. He stopped when he saw movement inside. Feeling suddenly like an intruder, he crept away. A dog started barking. Daniel fled, stumbled and fell into the hollow. He landed on his face, scrambled to his feet, and felt alarm pump through his legs and arms. He half-ran and half-stumbled, feeling sweat prickle his back, until he reached the tower where he bent down to catch his breath. He gingerly felt his head and found a large bump but no blood.

Who would live out there? And keep an animal inside? Distopians? He didn't know much about them except the terrible rumors he'd overheard. Had someone spotted him? Would he be reported and called in front of the Shame Court? He feared it more than anything else. Julie had never discussed her appearance there and he'd feared to ask. And he'd felt those scars...

When Daniel entered the Trans-Center he felt his shoulders relax. He glanced down at his watch and saw that he'd made good time, running. Forgetting his own disheveled appearance, he headed for Bobby's, hoping to catch him before he went to work. A woman's voice responded on the door speaker: "What do you want?"

"Is Bobby at home?" he stuttered with some confusion.

"Who?"

"Bobby—Robert Crane. He lives here."

"Not any more. I live here now, since last week."

"But—but where—" Daniel stuttered. "D'you know where or why he moved?"

"No. The Pols took him." She cut off.

Daniel hurried to his flat several buildings away, thinking of Julie. He hesitated only for a moment before punching in her number. Her message image didn't appear. He flung on his jacket and ran out of his apartment.

55

May 20, 2095—0000.

LISTENING to the melancholy music of Rachmaninoff's Concerto No. 2 in C minor, Julie stretched in her chair at her DIC office and glanced at the clock. It was midnight. After a terse knock at the door, the security guard peeked inside and nodded to her. "Hello, Ms. Crane."

Julie waved. "Hello, Mr. Gleick."

"Working late again? That's every night this week."

"Yes. Projects with deadlines," she smiled politely, hiding her dislike for him. He nodded again and left. Ken Harper, the previous guard, had disappeared last month and her inquiries on the vee-net had revealed nothing. He'd probably gone to the Pol Station for questioning, never to re-emerge. Like Nancy. Bad Icarian, she thought. She didn't trust this new man, Alan Gleick, an older, rather severe-looking man with dull eyes and a simpering mouth. She suspected he was a Secret Pol.

Julie returned her attention to the huge holo-image in front of her and pulled at her lower lip with her teeth. *Okay, SAM, let's finish our Distopian model.* The data that the Head Pol had given her months ago on Distopians included anyone considered a deviant. Bobby and she fit that category. And even though she had to admit that those like her might be a nuisance, they were not a threat. The real Distopian movement, however, had the potential and motive to be.

The typical Distopian has no particular age category, has anarchist tendencies and a passion for freedom of information and equality. He or she tends to be a bit of a hacker—like someone I know.

Okay, SAM. Continue.

Distopians are usually educated professionals, often with extensive experience. Although their psychological profiles reveal them to be potential extremists, most have clean records—unlike someone I know. Julie smiled crookedly. And they despise veemelds for their privileges, Julie.

Well, that's no surprise. As for the link between these two antipodal groups, the Distopians and Renegade Pols, her analyses failed to provide any enlightenment. Except for one possibility. A conjecture. The two parties held in common their desire to topple the present establishment and their passionate hatred for veemelds. Were they just convenient allies of war against the present rule, hoping to destroy the other once those they feared were removed? Julie glanced at her watch. She rubbed her eyes with her palms. It was 0100. Her head ached. This concluded her project for the Head Pol.

Okay, SAM. This is it. She prepared the files for Kraken, excluding the results of her extra-curricular sleuthing on Renegades. Let him figure it out for himself, about Dykstra and all the others, she thought. She placed them in a classified folder *"for your eyes only"*, armed it with her protection virus, and cued the folder for export. Then stopped. Her hands were shaking. She couldn't do it. Kraken and Gaia had carefully shepherded her to this destination. Now she stood on that very precipice he'd alluded to so long ago.

She raked her hair back with her fingers and leapt to her feet, thinking hard. Her largest concern was that Dykstra would hijack the data on its way to Kraken. He'd throw out the Renegade model—no, he'd probably use it to recruit more Renegades—then eliminate all Distopian types with the other model. Genocide. That was, after all, the Renegade profile. What a potent weapon she'd created!

Sliding back into her chair, she gripped her lower lip in her teeth and decided on a dangerous maneuver. She would send Kraken an empty template of her files, accompanied by a vague synopsis of her findings. She would then attach a text file as a trailer to explain her action: she'd give security as her grounds for first sending him a "dummy" file. A well-founded reason, given the stakeholders who were likely plotting to get it. That would open dialogue between her and Kraken. Then, depending on his response, she would deliver the whole files... or not. It wasn't blackmail, she convinced herself. It was insurance. Of course, it might backfire on her and she might be dead by then, but she'd have her vengeance: as with her predecessors, her models would go with her straight to chaos—not to Dykstra.

It took her another hour to compose her precisely vague synopsis and explanatory letter. Bleary-eyed and head pounding with machine murmuring, Julie exported her files to the Head Pol at 0200. *Okay, it's out there. The ball's in Kraken's court now—*

And Dykstra's.

Julie pursed her lips at SAM's astute comment. She saved and capped her uncensored files, deleted the originals from her vee-com, swept her console clean with a swift move of her hand and stood up. After a furtive glance behind her, Julie got up and stretched to relieve her tense muscles. This would likely destroy her career. She thought of her father. Maybe it was time to change her job. If she survived.

SAM intruded: You'll need to do more than that to stay alive.

Okay, SAM. She shivered. *What do you have in mind? I'm not exactly in the position to make a deal with Dykstra. And maybe I'm sick of making deals.*

Julie, information is your weapon. There are a few things you need to know...

She sat down again. *About Dykstra and the Shadow Unit?*

Yes, and Gaia, too. She runs the Shadow Unit, which means she runs Dykstra.

She gets around, for a "dead" person. Julie glowered. *She probably arranged to "die" because of the Icaria-11 mess. Get a new start.*

There's more to it, Julie. With Schlange and Isabo dead, the Triad dissolved and left Vogel solely in power. After he was shot, the *Circle* of Ecologists took over, headed by an ecologist named Gaia, then mayor of Icaria-5, and virtually unrecognizable from her former identity with the benefit of neurgery—

Schlange.

Yes. She withdrew as mayor of Icaria-5, but she continues to run its superior surveillance network—

Secret Pols! Julie gripped the arms of her chair and stared at Gaia's face. She thought instantly of Gleick and shot a wary glance behind her. No one lingered in the shadows.

And the Shadow Unit. Using them made her a powerful senior member of the *Circle*. Although Gaia is officially Head Administrator of Icaria-9 now, she actually oversees all Icarian governments in North Am through the *Circle*.

Are you saying that she rules all of Icaria?

Administratively, the *Circle* does. In practice, she does. Although the *Circle* is run by consensus, Gaia apparently rules over the *Circle* members through her knowledge of each of their secret vices, thanks to her Shadow Unit.

You mean she's blackmailing them?

Yes. Each Icaria is run by Center Heads, like the Head-Pol and the Head Administrator. They, in turn, answer to a single anonymous administrator, a mayor *per se*, who, in turn, answers to a member of the *Circle*, who then effectively answers to Gaia's blackmail.

Kraken's 'V', Julie thought. *So, Schlange—Gaia—orchestrated the whole thing, the murders of all Triad members, including herself, to change the structure of the government and gain ultimate power?*

She's a very shrewd woman.

That's a nice way of putting it, SAM. Julie shifted in her chair and pushed the hair from her face. If what SAM suggested was true then perhaps her father wasn't guilty of murder after all! This was the connection that had eluded her for so long. She sat bolt upright. *SAM! What if Schlange's our elusive killer?* She couldn't help shaking with excitement.

Explain, Julie.

Well, she uses her Shadow Unit to murder Isabo, stages her own murder, gets rid of Vogel, the last Triad member, to remove her opposition, dissolve the Triad and gain a new start as "Gaia" within the lesser confines of the Circle. She removes Tsutsumi, whose theories meddle with her vision of Icaria, and pins both murders on my father, who provides a perfect target with his anger.

Yes, it's feasible. I'll train you to be logical yet.

Julie sat back and pulled her lower lip in with her teeth. But things were getting in the way of Gaia's vision. Namely the Distopians and Renegade Pols, who both wanted to destroy veemelds, whom Gaia had chosen to inherit Icaria as a result of their immunity to Darwin. *Wouldn't Gaia be upset that her Chief of Secret Pols is a Renegade. She's employing one of the very groups she's trying to eradicate.*

Yes. The downfall of all despots. Sedition from within.

No one, it seemed, was cooperating with her vision. And it was a strange vision, Julie thought with a frown. The opposite of self-serving, which didn't accord with that woman. Julie's eyes narrowed at the classic face on the holo. Where did Gaia herself fit into the vision? Julie couldn't picture Gaia humbly accepting her own demise as part of this evolving Icaria. Gaia didn't strike her as altruistic, certainly not self-effacing. Unless... *SAM, is she a veemeld?*

No. It may interest you to know, however, that Gaia resides in no particular Icaria. The coordinates from which her vee-signals originate are located in the mid-western great plains of North-Am, at least 50 kilometers from the closest Icaria.

What? Gaia living outside Icaria? Julie thought of the strange light she'd seen in the middle of the heath. She retrieved her estimates. *What about these coordinates, SAM? Do they fit anyone we know?*

They match the position for vee-signals from 'V', Icaria-5's anonymous mayor.

So, they all lived out there! Segregating Icaria from outside, indeed. Suddenly it made sense. All the efforts to preserve and segregate the outside environment from Icaria were for the benefit of Gaia and those in power.

His profile matches that of a Victor Burke, former administrative assistant and Care-Center worker before that. I was able to unscramble his holo signals to the Head Pol.

SAM threw the image of a man with pale eyes and burgundy hair in front of her. Julie stared for a moment before her mind recalled where she'd seen him: the man who'd been talking to Gaia and had slunk away when she and Kraken had approached. *He* was the mayor? Under Burke, Icaria-5 has become one of the most self-sustaining cities on the planet.

Just goes to show you that appearance isn't everything. What might Burke do with her models? She certainly didn't trust Gaia or the Head Pol with them. And she knew what Dykstra would do.

After a long pause, SAM whispered in her head, Julie. There is no God. There is only Gaia.

Julie's stomach lurched. *What do you mean?*

GAIA knows about us veemelding in your head, said SAM. She has a veemeld vector, which can access any veemeld in action by "riding" like a parasite on the beam. It's her presence that I've been feeling from time to time lately: disturbances in the beam's original polarized state caused by interception from the "rider" of the beam. Our vid-scan gave me the last clue. Gaia got the only existing prototype veemeld vector from AIHV before it was destroyed about a year ago. She's been listening to us for close to a year. That's how she knows about what you've been doing—Julie, you're trembling.

She glanced down at herself and tried to stop. She couldn't and folded her arms around her shaking body. Fragments of intimate, precious memories that she'd shared with SAM flashed before her like the shattered images of a broken mirror. Memories she'd clutched to her heart because they were all she had—even the painful ones. Her hands grew clammy and gripped the arms of her chair.

Anger and terror sizzled through her. Now it all fit. Gaia had devised a way to have her drug and drink it too. Oversee a newly evolved race, arisen from a decrepit human population cleansed by Darwin—and Julie's models. A race whose minds Gaia could read and who were content indoors and isolated from the outside world, while she and those like her enjoyed the natural beauty of a pristine paradise, unaffected by Darwin Disease.

SAM! Julie leapt up and paced the room with shaky steps. *The Shadow Unit!* She stared at the holo-screen, envisioning SAM there. *It's Gaia behind the Darwin mess. She's the one trying to prevent its cure. It isn't Dykstra.* She'd been searching for his motive with futility when all along it hadn't been him. *He's just her underling with his own agenda. Why didn't I figure it out before? Darwin Disease plays right into Gaia's plans for a new race of Icarians—veemelds—under her power.*

There's more, I'm afraid.

Julie swallowed, still pacing. *Go on, SAM.*

You remember how we came to a dead end trying to find Prometheus? There was one person we hadn't explored.

She spun around to face the swirling holo, impatient. *Well, who, SAM?*

You.

Me?

You're Prometheus, Julie.

She dropped heavily into her chair, stiff and breathless.

It took a lot of note-decrypting but I finally retrieved enough to compare your DNAs. They match, Julie. You would have been five years old when they injected you with the virus.

A haze of cloying memories spattered through her mind like blood spurting from a deep wound: of antiseptic stenches and lying in a hospital bed, and the voices that had seeped into her head, making her think she'd gone insane. Her horrible recurring nightmare. *I remember it, SAM,* she heard her mind's voice drifting from her like smoke and knew that a part of her had known all along. *But... Why?*

All I can find is a note from Janet to your father implying that you'd benefit greatly and that it would be lucrative for him. I can only surmise that he decided to give you to her as a test case on her strong recommendation.

Yes, her father would have done anything for Janet. *Then I am a freak after all.* A manufactured freak. Now she understood what her mother had meant, accusing her father of turning Julie into a monster. She'd never been sick. He'd fabricated the story to help explain why she'd found herself in the hospital one day with voices in her head. Was that why her mother had turned into a drunk? And why Janet killed herself? No, she concluded suddenly, Janet had better reasons for killing herself: being responsible for Icaria's plague. *Was it Janet who jumped the gun by spreading the disease, thinking everyone would react like me?* She frowned. *Of course they didn't, because they weren't veemelds.*

Your hunch is right. I've pieced an ugly story out of these notes: Vogel canned the project, citing the potential risks and the less than successful results—seems they didn't register all your new abilities. Schlange lied to Janet that Vogel was going to destroy the virus and convinced her to steal it and spread it in Icaria-11 for the sake of humankind. Janet proceeded to contaminate the Med-Center, using Med-Center drugs. I don't think Schlange's reasons were so humanitarian. She probably thought those increased cognitive abilities would give her city an edge over the others. She was willing to risk her city's people in trying, anyway. And now she sees a new use for the disease...

SAM's voice drifted away like a boat at sea as Julie sank into a wallowing darkness. For the sake of science—no, out of unnatural reverence—her father had given her, his own daughter, to Janet for experiments. Janet, who'd caused Icaria's devastating plague. What would he have thought of his hero if he'd known? To the end, he'd naively clung to his belief that Vogel had pushed his cousin to the brink, ignorant of her crime and real reason for her suicide. As for Gaia, she alone had known about the voices. And gambled the lives of millions of people to get them for her city. It was her evil face, pre-neurgery, that had intruded into Julie's fevered dream all these years. *"Steal the fire from heaven and give it to me..."*

Julie, are you okay? SAM's voice filtered in.

Yeah. I'm okay, SAM. Julie pulled herself up from her slouch and opened her eyes. SAM had given the truth to her long ago when it had mentioned the coincidental deaths of all those who knew about Proteus and Prometheus, but now she finally saw it. It was a simple case of removing all the witnesses. Janet had conveniently killed herself; Isabo had probably started to nag, so Gaia had removed him and "herself" to get a new start in Icaria-5. Vogel, of course, had to go, as did Tsutsumi, who'd published the paper, probably scaring Gaia into wondering what else he would do. And then there was, of course, her father, who'd offered the sacrificial lamb in the first place. Gaia probably assumed that her father would eventually figure it out, but Julie knew he never did. Ironic, she thought. He'd never connected the outbreak of Darwin with what he and his cousin had done to his own daughter. His cousin was his blind spot. While he'd never have believed that Janet's injection had anything to do with the plague, Julie guessed that he must have found out about Tsutsumi's data tampering, the reason he'd smashed his office that day. The Cranes were always doing that: not getting it. With fierce naivety they believed in a world that had long ago stopped believing in them... just like that extinct bird.

The virus had done with Julie exactly what Vogel had intended. But... *Why am I the only veemeld who can hear voices in her head?*

Maybe you aren't. Let's face it, you've kept it a secret from everyone else. They might have, too.

She hadn't thought of that.

There's reason to believe that you are the only one, though. Gaia's special interest in you alone, for instance. Perhaps it has to do with the form of the virus. You were the only one who was injected. Everyone else got it by person-to-person contact or via drug. It may have changed once it left the lab, affecting veemelds differently too. Maybe it was your age; Darwin only infects adults normally. Or you might have a unique genetic makeup.

And what about those insect sounds that stay with me even when I'm out of range of any AI? That isn't—She choked down the thought, hoping SAM had another explanation.

Most likely the incoherent communications of Darwin.

Oh, vee...

Gaia wants you to clean up your act and have children—with another veemeld, of course. She's scheduled you for the DP once you conclude Kraken's project. Olafsen's group can be mean to you if you don't show some reciprocity, a willingness to abide by Icaria's rules. Gaia's listed 23 conciliations. No more demerits, outside jaunts, illicit touching in public, especially with a non-veemeld.

Oh, vee...

It also means keeping your mouth shut on what you know about Darwin Disease and Gaia's eavesdropping on veemelds. If you don't, she'll just have the DP extract the reproductive material from your body and study your brain. Basically redesign you, Julie. Wall-art.

Julie sank in her chair. If she didn't comply, she was wall-art. If she did comply, she might as well be. Gaia would reward her with permanent Level 1 status, Zane as a husband, and a safe but ignoble life with Gaia's blessings for many children. She was wall-art either way. If Janet had released the scourge, than Julie *was* the scourge. *Even when I'm not trying to cause a disaster, I cause one just by being me. I'm the reason all those people died in Icaria-11.* She put her face in her hands. *How many people did I infect?*

Maybe no one, Julie. Certainly not sexually, given that Pro-1 only lasts five months and you were just five years old. As for any other forms of the virus, the chance that you'd carry such an aberrant form is slim because you and the virus are simpatico.

But if I did carry it, I'd still be infectious, wouldn't I?

After a pause, SAM said softly, Probably, Julie. Dangerously so.

She felt anger boil up. She sprang to her feet and reeled to face the blue holo. *Why did they release me, then? Why didn't they pick me up after what happened? Keep me away from the world!* She clenched her teeth and fought down tears of frustration and guilt.

That's the other reason why I don't think you spread the disease. They knew how you'd transmit it because they made it. And, ruling out sexual transmission, the only other way was to your progeny via your gametes when you were old enough to bear children. That's why they let you go but why Gaia's after you now. She wants to direct your seeds, shall we say. It's a very elegant design, Julie.

Elegant, but perhaps faulty.

Every other part of the virus worked in you as they'd designed it. Why shouldn't this part?

Oh, I don't know, SAM. Why should it? They botched the rest, like using me as their guinea pig in the first place. Do you remember Gaia's reference to the whooping crane? She wasn't far off the mark. I can't do anything right. I should be extinct, just like them.

Not all cranes are extinct, Julie. The sandhill crane, for instance, presently flourishes in the Pacific Northwest and is admired for its grace and its loyal loving nature—like you.

She looked down at her shaking hands and brought them to her face. *I failed everyone, SAM. Even you. Nothing I've done has ever turned out right. I don't think I'd know if it hit me in the face. SAM, what am I supposed to do?*

Julie, you'll know what's right. Search your heart and it will come to you.

She swallowed convulsively. *My heart? Not my brain?*

It's through the heart, not the brain, that one learns wisdom. *You* taught me that.

Me? She'd taught SAM something? *What if it ... doesn't come to me?*

Your impulsive emotions have taught me one great thing.

Julie stared at the liquid cube.

It's not what you know that's important; it's what you do when you don't know. Believe in yourself, Julie, and it will come. The Katzie First Nations peoples of the Pacific Northwest call the crane *syhaha'w*, which means "perfect in everything."

She sat down and buried her face in her hands again. *I'm far from perfect!*

But you're human. Without imperfection there can be no courage, strength, or honor. Only through imperfection can you rise to your noble destiny. You must first accept what you are, then rise to what you can be. Julie, you are virtuous and beautiful and full of grace.

Oh, no! I'm not, I'm not! Julie shook her head emphatically. She leaned back and listened with closed eyes to the machine murmurs, miserable in thoughts of disgrace. *I'm a freak. I make promises I can't keep; I desert my family and friends; I lie about who and what I am. I cause a plague without even knowing it and then screw up trying to fix it. Good grief, SAM, where's the perfection in that!*

SAM whispered, Julie, may I share some wisdom I've learned from your human poets?

She felt her face flush with anticipation and straightened up in her chair. *Okay, SAM.*

It would appear that, much like our own community of intelligences and your own interaction with me, humans might share their souls to mingle as a community. I think you're particularly receptive to such sharing, as attested by the AI traffic that travels so freely through you. However soul-sharing among humans remains rare. According to your poets, it is every soul's destiny to undertake such a pilgrimage toward communion. Although you may chance to share your soul with another during your life, you can't interfere with their journey, incomprehensible or misguided as it may seem to you.

Julie gripped her face in her hands, unable to respond. Her eyes grew hot with tears. She had not expected this from SAM and felt emotion charge through her.

Julie, you must let go. Your feeling is undeserved and encumbers you from realizing your destiny, discovering your ecological niche and the wisdom inside you. It was not in your power to save your mother or your sister. They had their journey to follow... Your father never meant it that way.

Julie choked down the ache in her throat and SAM's soothing voice returned, Julie, in light of what we've learned, I must advise that we sever our communications. Your chances—and mine—would improve.

Startled, Julie straightened up and gazed at the fluid blue holo. She swallowed, thinking of Gaia's vector. *Yes, that would be the wisest thing to do.* Swept by a wave of panic, her mind blurted out, *But what about,* she swallowed convulsively, *the us-part? Won't it ... die?*

Yes, SAM replied softly, but a part of you will remain with me always. I hope a part of me will remain with you, too.

How would she exist without SAM in her head? How would she know what to do?

I'll miss you, Julie.

Not prepared to face her own feelings, she thought, *There are 160 thousand other veemelds in Icaria-5, SAM.*

But only one Julie...

Her throat swelled. She wondered with discomfort who SAM would find.

Julie, do you remember when I revealed to you that you no longer needed Interact-SYM?

Yes.

Do you remember how I mentioned that our newly developing AI-community—don't cry...

I won't.

But you *are*. Have I upset you?

Julie laughed in a spasm of tears. *No, SAM. I was just visualizing you and thousands of other individual AIs talking to one another and your human counterparts and thinking it was beautiful... and that I won't be part of it.*

You'll have helped us create this community, Julie. By giving me *everything of you... And asking nothing in return.*

She stopped fighting the tears. They burst out with a gasp and flooded down her cheeks.

You've helped me find my identity, by sharing yours so completely. It's my hope that 160 thousand more AI identities can evolve through their human interactions.

SAM had hopes and dreams too.

Before we part, I'd like to read a poem by John Herrick that I enjoyed and amended for you.

I'd like that very much. She closed her eyes. SAM "liked" things. SAM was a poet.

Let not the dark thee cumber;
What though the moon does slumber?
The stars of the night
Will lend thee their light
Like tapers clear, without number.
Then, Julie, let me woo thee,
Thus, thus, to come unto me;
And when I shall meet Thy silvery feet,
My soul I'll pour into thee...

In the silence that followed, only the trickling stream of machine language gently washed over her mind. She finally sat up, finding the courage to share what stirred in her heart. *SAM, I need to tell you something...* Silence. Gone already! Her gaze sank to the floor as she uttered words she'd never before communicated to anyone. "I love you."

She swiped away the tears and fled the office, steps ringing in the empty hallways of the Com-Center. The voices in her head rose to a swift and gurgling roar like a crowd of strangers. Julie thought of SAM's warning and glanced around. Fear amplified every sound. As she rounded a corner, a dark shape loomed up. She jumped with a stifled shriek. Just the remote garbage collector. It squeaked and slithered past her. She laughed sharply at herself. *I'm losing it. No one should be after me... yet.*

57

May 20, 2095—0300, the same morning.

WHEN she left the Com-Center, Julie took her usual short-cut through the lower levels of Pielou Mall. Was it her imagination or were they darker than usual? Julie rued her decision to go this way and glanced furtively back as she stepped lightly to the tube-jets bound for home. Was someone following her?

But no one knew she'd finished her models... unless they, too, had stayed up into the early morning hours. Frank had done such surveillance before. Did Dykstra already know? Ironic, how Gaia might lose everything, including Julie, at the hands of her own lieutenant. Gaia obviously didn't know Dykstra was a Renegade, spoiling her plans with his own—

She heard it again. Someone *was* following her! She ducked into a dimly lit part of the hall to hide, feeling her heart pound. She soon spotted his figure, appearing and disappearing by winks under the dim light of the overhead lamps. She caught her breath. A Pol walking casually, holding his helmet. Frank! She almost burst into a hysterical laugh of relief. He wasn't following her; he didn't know she was there at all. He languidly walked straight toward her with his head bowed to the ground in deep thought. She had a chance to escape, yet she stood transfixed. This had been one of their frequented haunts.

She stood in his path and they soon came face to face. He started and his sullen face brightened. "Well, hello." An ironic smile tugged at his lips.

"Hello," she responded guardedly, recalling the less than pleasant interchange they'd had the last time she'd seen him. She wondered why she hadn't ducked away.

After a moment of silence he said in a subdued voice, "I saw you at the Shame Court." Embarrassed, Julie dropped her gaze. His voice betrayed tenderness, "You looked beautiful."

She looked up and tried to smile. "How are you?"

"I'm well," he answered. "And you? Still trying to save yourself, saving others?" While she struggled with his pointed question, he filled in the uncomfortable pause, "Me too. It's getting harder to do the right thing."

She nodded. "You've always been good at upholding the laws of Icaria—"

"No. *Justice,*" he corrected her. "It's justice I'm after... like you." She stared at him. "You performed well at the Shame Court," he continued. "You were brave, speaking out for justice. And trying to save that young girl in the first place."

She blinked, stunned at his words. She wondered what he would have thought about what she'd just done, and she longed to tell him. He misread her expression and his eyes flared with a clear and burning plea. She knew what he meant. It would be so easy to take him back—her gladiator—especially now. She feared for her life, and here stood her warrior savior. No, she wouldn't let herself fall into that trap again. "I really m-must—go—" she stammered. Already his eyes were overpowering her, flooding her with confusion. "I'm glad you're well." She outstretched her hand as if to touch him, then drew back. He seized it and directed it down to where he throbbed for her.

"You did that, just now," he whispered hoarsely.

Startled by his violent move, Julie broke from his grasp and stepped back. "No," she said firmly. "It's over, Frank."

He seized her arm painfully. "It'll be *me* who decides when it's over," he growled, face twitching. She recognized the icy cold fire in his eyes; the gaze she used to dread. She scrambled away, but he was too fast for her. He forced her to the ground, tearing at her clothes.

"Frank—don't do this. Please!"

His lips crushed hers, then traveled over her face. His hands stroked her with the confidence of a successful lover. "I love you," he whispered. Words he had never uttered to her during their torrid relationship.

She refused to give in. He sensed it and sat up. He looked down at her flushed face with pain in his eyes. Then he stood up and mutely helped Julie to her feet and joined her in gathering her clothes. She accepted his aid in silence. Then she turned and walked away from him. When she finally had the courage to look back, she found his position unchanged, except that his head was bent to the ground and he was staring at his hands. They shook.

Julie hurried down the hall and glanced at her watch. It was almost 0330. She carelessly wrapped her clothes around her, made a bearing and headed for home. Frank had said he loved her. Though she knew he was fond of her, she doubted that it was truly love. Regardless, Frank would never let go of the game. He was too frightened of the banal routine of living out a shared life. Of being ordinary together.

Julie halted in her tracks, no longer preoccupied with time. Instead of continuing to the tube-jet station, she sat down on some low piping and rested her head in her hands, forgetting her fears for the moment.

≈

A man and a woman stood in the shadows, watching Julie. The woman, a spikehead, towered over the man. Brilliant red spikes of hair formed mountain peaks, making her seem even taller than she was. The short and stumpy green-haired man held a vid-enhancer up to his eyes.

"The Pol's disgusting, chasing after her like a dog in heat," the woman whispered in a deep voice, following the short man's gaze. She stood easily a foot over him.

"He might be a fool, Diana, but he may still be useful."

She sneered. "What about the tube-jet driver?"

"He's out of the picture. Found out she was a veemeld."

"Smarter than I thought he was." Diana smiled caustically. She drew out a sleek weapon from beneath her tunic and swept the gun carelessly toward Julie's hunched form. "I have a mind to kill her now and save us a lot of grief."

"Please, Diana," Robert pleaded. "Put that thing away."

She sighed in resignation and replaced her laser pistol behind her back. "So, when do we get her on side?"

"When the Head Pol makes his move. Then she's ours."

"You're a fool, Robert. She'll never be ours. She belongs to another world."

~

Julie rose and walked with determined steps toward the exit stairway to the upper levels. SAM was right. She *did* know what to do; she'd always known in her heart but had lacked the courage or the resolve until now. SAM's painful revelation of her role in creating the plague gave her only one option: disclosure, whatever the cost. For so many years she'd carefully hidden who and what she was from everyone—herself included. Every conscious decision she'd made, except when she gave in to impulse, had been self-protective. Ever since she'd given herself to the cypol and left her sister and Neo behind in the inner-city, she'd shut away a part of her in a shroud of caution. It was time to cast that aside and come forward with the truth. While the result of her disclosure to Daniel had been devastating, it had taught her that withholding the truth had been worse.

She had a mission to save hundreds of souls from needlessly suffering the ravages of Darwin Disease, a disease for which she was every bit as responsible as those who had deliberately spread it. Ignorance wasn't the same as innocence, she told herself. And besides, she thought with a tight cynical smile, she wasn't ignorant anymore. It meant giving herself up, along with her valuable information, to Kraken and the CDC. Kraken had, after all, passed his discovery of the Shadow Unit's covert prevention of Darwin's cure to Burke. Perhaps the CDC could use her to develop that cure. She didn't trust Kraken when it came to her own welfare, but her survival was no longer the issue. Before she saw Kraken, she would warn the other veemelds of Gaia's eavesdropping and the Renegade Pols. She was a veemeld and it was about time she found the courage to help them—

Abruptly the chittering voices in her head grew shrill and she instinctively turned, just in time to sidestep someone leaping at her with a knife. Heart pounding, she came face to face with a young, heavily drugged skinhead.

Bloodshot eyes glared frantically at her. He snarled, "Give me your vee-set!" He charged her again with the knife. Julie jerked back and watched as violent spasms ran across his face like a beast crawling under his skin. Unmistakable signs of Darwin Disease.

Startled by recognition, she gaped. "Ken?" she inquired, peering more closely at his twitching face. "Ken Harper?" He was the former Com-center security guard.

He hesitated only for a moment. "Bitch! Give it to me!" He lunged at her. She flung herself violently sideways and the knife just caught air, spinning his body in counterweight. He still caught her in a heavy side-check that tipped her off balance and she fell with a grunt. He threw himself on her, crushing the air out of her, then slumped, knife clattering beside him.

Julie pushed him off and scrambled up, panting. A dark red stain grew on his back. She hadn't heard a weapon discharged, but there was the evidence. Her eyes roamed the dark hall, squinting to see past the darkness. Her first thought was Frank. Had he followed her?

There! In the shadows, she could barely make out a tall form. There was a hint of red in the hair and perhaps in the tunic. A spikehead from the Com-Center? Then it was gone. A Secret Pol? Who else carried silent weapons? So Dykstra *had* followed her! she thought with renewed alarm.

After a glance at Harper's dead body, Julie fled through the doors. She rode the tube-jet home, remembering the statistic Bobby had cited: someone was killed every hour in the outer-city. That Secret Pol might have shot *her* just as easily as rescued her. She felt vindicated in sending Kraken "dummy" files. Those shots might have otherwise been aimed differently. And what about tomorrow?

58

May 20, 2095—0433.

SHE jerked awake, eyes snapping open. Had she heard something? Had they come for her already? Wide awake, she sat up and listened. Only the bubbling of the aquarium pump amid the machine whispers in her brain broke the silence. The chittering noises that she'd come to rely on for her sense of impending danger remained calm.

She couldn't fall back asleep and found herself thinking about the fish in her aquarium. They deserved to live in their own habitat, where they'd come from. Not this artificial home she'd fashioned for her own pleasure. Julie sprang out of bed and looked for a large container.

～

The early morning air braced her as Julie stepped outside through the ground exit of her building. The sky glowed deep blue where the sun had yet to rise above the dark horizon. She gazed at her surroundings, inhaling sweet fragrances mingled with the organic scent of the awakening heath. A slight breeze lifted her hair and Julie pursed her lips in melancholy thought. She hadn't ventured outside since she'd seen Daniel. The world had become a different place since then.

Clutching her container full of twenty goldfish, Julie followed a deer path to a hollow with some water. Mist rose like steam off the pond. She bent down on her knees and opened the container. Peering down at the thrashing fish, she said, "I know it's more dangerous here, but this is where you belong. Some of you will get eaten, but the survival of your species depends on your freedom, and freedom has its price." She emptied the container into the dark pond. The fish dropped in several at a time as the water poured out, churning up the mud. She couldn't help counting them as they plopped into the water. Several disappeared under cover and soon Julie could barely see any in the murky water. Resting her hands on her knees, she stood up and picked up her empty container. All but one fish had disappeared. With a sad smile, she said, "Bye, Juliet. I know it's you." She turned back to Icaria.

～

On the tube-jet to Bobby's at 0550, Julie thought of what she was going to say. He wouldn't want to hear it, but she'd tell him anyway. If she disappeared, he deserved to know why. She'd tell him about her models, the cube, Darwin Disease, what she was, the machines in her head, and what she planned to do. She ran her finger against Zane's card in her pocket. Because of his work at CDC, Zane was ideal to share her findings on Darwin. He'd also make a trustworthy custodian of her cube. He was a bit arrogant and a chatterbox, but he had an honest face and she sensed in him a good heart and a sincere concern for the welfare of veemelds and Icarians alike. Veemelds deserved to know about Distopians' hatred for them, Renegade Pols' plans to eradicate them, and Gaia's ability to tap into their transmissions and her nefarious plans to control their lives.

And Icarians deserved to live. Once she gave Zane the cube, she'd reveal what she knew of Darwin Disease and her own role as Prometheus. Then she'd let them conduct what tests they needed on her. After that, and before the Secret Pols caught up to her, she intended to confront Kraken and reveal all to him. She had no idea what Kraken would do with her. She recalled the message that had flashed on her vee-com holo when she'd returned to her flat earlier this morning: an acknowledgment from Kraken that he'd received her files. No mention of the fact that they were only useless templates. Was this his way of telling her that she'd gone too far? Would he just find and take what he wanted, then terminate her before she had a chance to explain? She had to remind herself that she'd deleted the original files. And only she—or SAM—knew how to retrieve them from cyberspace. The only place they tangibly existed was in her mouth. Maybe Kraken was consulting with Burke—or Gaia. It was still very early in the day. Anything could happen, she thought with a shiver.

Julie shifted in her seat and clutched Zane's card. With effort she pushed the doubt and fear biting its way through her resolve to the back of her mind. It's the only way, she told herself. An oppressive cloak of finality strangled her. SAM. There was something she still had to do; something she had to say. One last thing. Just in case. She dove into veemeld: *SAM. I hope Gaia isn't listening to my thoughts now but that you are. I'm going to give what we've discovered to our CDC veemeld friend and reveal what I am, before I go to Kraken and turn myself and the data in. But, in case something happens before I have a chance to, give it all to the veemeld yourself. Good bye.*

As the train stopped and the doors opened at MacArthur Station, a shaft of clear thought—her own or SAM's, she couldn't tell—lit her mind with such brilliance she stopped in her tracks: Your father would be proud of you, Julie. Tears stung her eyes as she darted out of the train.

≈

After picking up some donuts at the auto-foodstop, Julie headed for Bobby's. She pressed the doorbell and waited. Surely he hadn't left already? She pulled out her card with a frown, but the door wasn't sealed. Something wasn't right. When she opened the door, Julie inhaled sharply. The place was in shambles. Most of his furniture and his plants were gone, his shelves emptied. Bits and pieces lay strewn about the floor.

"Bobby!" Julie called, her voice splintering with panic. It echoed strangely in the empty room. She dropped the donut bag and raced through the apartment. Each room had been ransacked, everything destroyed or taken. In his library, she found his books and papers gone. Returning to the leisure room, Julie bent down to pick up an old bottle opener that she'd found on one of their first forays outside. As she did, she caught sight of something on the floor by the door that sickened her. She inched forward to the large stain and knelt down to observe it closely, touching a congealed sticky glob of blood with her finger. The same place she'd spilled her blood for Frank. Had Bobby spilled his for Frank, too?

Clutching the artifact, Julie ran out of the flat. She held back her rage with difficulty, not liking where her mind was going: that Frank had sought his revenge like he'd threatened all along.

Julie reached the Pol Station, panting and thinking of Bobby's phobia for enclosed dark places. If they had put him into a cell like the one she had occupied, he'd be in a sad state by now. She marched to the front desk of the Inquiry Department. Julie fixed on the young man watching his vee-com at the desk and said, "I need to know if a Robert Crane was entered here some time ago. He's my uncle." She was trembling.

The man asked her to spell his name, then searched through his vee-com for what seemed like forever. When he looked up at her, she knew his answer would be the one she expected and dreaded. "Yeah, he arrived early this morning."

"May I see him?"

"No. That's impossible."

"Why?"

"Because he's dead."

Her throat closed.

"Killed himself." With her silence he volunteered the macabre details, more to satisfy his own detached curiosity. "Cut his wrists while being detained, and bled to death. Used some sharp thing he'd hidden in his pocket. He was only taken in for questioning about some illegal books."

"Who were the arresting Pols?"

"Officers I. Smith, R. Hicks and F. Langor."

"Thank you." Julie turned to leave. Her steps echoed as if far away. She felt surreal, like she was in a dream. She'd entered her own nightmare.

"Julie Crane?" Julie started and turned to a Pol with thick lips. She recognized Frank's partner, leering at her as he approached. "Hi, I'm Ron."

"Ron Hicks?"

"How d'you know my last name?" When she didn't answer, he continued, "S'pose you're looking for Frank?"

Julie fumed. Why in vee's name would she be here looking for Frank and not for her uncle, who he'd helped arrest?

"Frank's not here," Hicks volunteered. "He just came off duty. In fact, I'm going to meet him at the Den."

Moved by vengeful thoughts of confrontation, she said, "May I join you?"

Hicks smiled at her audacious request. "I guess so. Frank's been a fucking virus all morning. Chaos, he even missed a shot today and he never does that! Maybe you can cheer him up."

Right… I'll cheer him up all right… and realized that she'd involuntarily slipped into veemeld, instinctively seeking SAM's comforting 'ear.'

Hicks led her to the Den, chattering like a vee-ad the whole way, as if it were a just another day; as if he hadn't just arrested her uncle, who was now dead. It didn't seem to bother Hicks that she wasn't listening.

Julie's sharp eyes quickly adjusted to the smoky darkness and she scanned the crowded tables for Frank's distinctive shape. She saw him long before Hicks did. "There he is," said Hicks as Julie struck toward Frank, fists at her sides.

Just as Frank recognized her through the smog, she said, "You're scum after all, punishing him because of me—"

"Don't flatter yourself." He sneered, slouched in his chair. "You're just another inner-city slut to me. You're rude and ugly. Your mouth's too big and you talk too much. And you fuck like an animal. Who'd want *you*? You think I hung out with you because I wanted to? I was *assigned* to watch you. I was your vee-damned bodyguard."

Her anger drained from her and she stared in dismay. No… .

"You and that fossil should've gone to the Pol Station long ago, like your vee-damned father before you," he spat.

Anger spiked. "Bobby's just an old man. He did nothing to you."

He snorted. "And now he definitely won't—"

"Bastard!" She seized Hicks's pistol from his belt holster and pointed it shakily at Frank.

His expression of lazy contempt vanished. He rose to his feet and raised shaking hands. "Come on, Julie. Don't be stupid; it wasn't like—"

She shot. To silence him. The blast of noise and light made her wince and startled the crowd to silence.

Frank's eyes widened with disbelief. He looked down at the wound in his thigh. She'd aimed for his crotch. His eyes darted up and gaped at Julie. He barked a crazy laugh at the irony, then his eyes faded and he fell to the floor in a crumpled heap. Hicks lunged for his weapon but Julie slithered out of his way. In the struggle, the weapon discharged. Hicks reeled back with the force, blood splattering her. He hit the floor like a rag doll and slid, leaving a dark trail.

Julie dropped the pistol. It clattered to the floor. Horrified, she gaped at the two motionless figures, then ran. No one moved to stop her.

59

JULIE shot out of the Den, leaving a wake of confusion behind her. Feeling eyes drawn to her, she forced herself to calm down outwardly and slow to a walk, even as agitation boiled inside. People emerged from the Den, shouting for Pols. She refused to look back, letting the commotion draw the attention of the crowd away from her. She wormed her way in the other direction as unobtrusively as possible.

Within moments Julie heard the shrill siren of the Med-bus. She turned along with the crowd to see its red lights flashing as it plowed through the crowd toward the Den. She turned away and continued in the other direction, feeling sick to her stomach.

Not giving herself a chance to think of what she had done, she concentrated on merging into Icaria-5's colorful sea of reds, greens, blues, and yellows. She knew that she only had seconds to get away before they sealed off the area and had her corralled. Time wasn't on her side and it had a way of winning. She spotted the exit closest to her: a door to the lower levels. She veered toward it. Swiftness was essential for survival, but too rapid a pace might draw attention to her and get her captured. With each calculated step, the exit drew closer and the hairs on the back of her neck tingled more as the insect-voices rose in pitch.

She suddenly realized that she was not walking alone. Glancing from side to side without turning her head, she spotted two Icarians walking in the same general direction and closing in to flank her. One was a tall woman with a striking angular face, a spikehead with flaming hair from the Com-Center; the other was a short, stocky green-haired man from the Enviro-Center. They looked at her and leered. Before she could spring to escape, they gripped her by the arms. Pinned between them, they continued to walk her in the same direction she'd heading.

"If you value your life, doll, be silent and come with us," said the woman with a man's silky voice. "If you don't co-operate, we can either kill you here and now or simply draw attention to the Pols." Her voice sounded familiar but Julie couldn't place it.

She let them take her to the exit she had formerly designated as her escape. The short man opened the door and they stepped through. When the door closed behind them, they hustled her down the stairs to the third level down. Vee screens lining the walls of the corridor flew past her in pulses of bright light. She could barely make out the images: the riot squad flooding Darwin Mall; Med-droids loading the bus with two stretchers and the bus plunging into the crowd.

They reached another exit door and the spikehead signaled for them to pass through. They climbed the stairs, taking them two by two. Julie tripped and the spikehead pulled her gruffly up. Julie cried out in startled pain. The woman growled in response, as if pain was not allowed. When they emerged into a hallway, Julie recognized Hutchinson Mall, where Nancy used to live. They struck toward a public washroom. The spikehead pushed Julie inside, leaving the short man to guard the door. Another woman in lilac with a green Enviro-Center tunic draped over her arm, waited for them. She offered Julie the tunic.

"Put it on," the spikehead commanded.

Julie removed her red tunic, surrendered it to the other woman, and put on the green one. The red tunic was thrown in the disposal unit. They rejoined the short man outside and he led them to a flat on the fifth floor of a Liv Center. The spikehead opened the door with her card and pushed Julie inside. It was a small basic unit. The vee-com blared the news. A razor head in a charcoal leisure suit stood with his back to her, watching the screen of a vee-com. When he turned, she recognized Paul Getz. Not a Secret Pol, after all, but a Distopian. Getz smiled at her, eyes not quite meeting hers, and sniffed through his right nostril. "Hi, Julie. You're in the News," he said, pointing to the screen. NewsVee showed the very same scenes she'd seen in the hallway.

She saw herself speak words to Frank that she'd never uttered: "Your decadence in law and order has curtailed our freedom! We call for anarchy! Distopians all over the world will destroy Icarian law and order and build a new world from your ruins. We'll destroy all Pols!" Then she grabbed the gun and screamed, "And you're just the first!"

"I didn't say that!" Julie blurted out. "They put the words into my mouth!"

Getz smirked, aiming his gaze at her lips. "The world believes what they want to believe," he said. After Frank's shooting, the scene cut to Hicks's body flying, entrails streaming behind. They'd omitted the struggle and it looked as though she'd intended to kill Hicks like she'd intentionally shot Frank. She'd only meant to wound him. Was he dead? Hicks most certainly was. She fought the urge to vomit.

A still of her face both in full and in profile came on the screen with an alert. "For anyone just tuned in, beware!" said the male announcer. "This woman has shot two Pols. One is dead and the other is in critical condition. She is presently at large. If you see her, immediately report her to the Pol Station. Do not approach her. She is highly dangerous."

Fighting her lightheadedness, Julie turned to Getz. "Why've you brought me here? What do you want?"

"Yes, what could we possibly want with a Pol-murderer?" the woman said with a hoarse laugh. The words rang like symbols in her head. The room spun and darkness engulfed her.

She found herself lying on a bed. Someone held her head up and brought a glass to her lips. She gulped down the liquid before she realized what she was drinking, then coughed and gagged on the *delilah*. She felt a surge of febrile heat but the giddiness was gone.

"Listen," said Getz, drawing near to her, his gaze wandering over her but avoiding her eyes, "We're more like you than you think. We just want what's fair for every Icarian, not just a few elite pigs. They'd have us rotting in ignorance while the Info-Net feeds their power. There's a widening gap between those who can access hidden parts of the Info-Net and those who don't even know it exists."

Julie felt her face redden with the truth. Did they know that she was a veemeld?

"We're convinced they're just letting Darwin take its course in some kind of ethnic cleansing or power consolidation," Getz snarled. "We have evidence that shows they're doing nothing about finding a cure. Nothing!" He was more right than he knew, Julie thought. She already felt the drug churn in her stomach, along with the complaining chitters in her head. "We have to stop the government's oppression of our right to information and their malicious spread of Darwin," Getz went on. "You can help us. You have, shall we say, certain talents and information that our movement could use."

Julie ran her tongue to her back right molar, thinking of what the Distopians could do with her information treasure. Despite Getz's spoken motives, she didn't know their true intentions. She knew Distopians hated veemelds. She glanced at the tall woman who glared back at her. Ignoring her complaining stomach, Julie turned back to Getz. "Why should I help you?"

"It's a moot point," the spikehead replied for Getz. "You killed a Pol. No one gets away with that. We can take you to the Pol Station or you can help us. Those are your choices, doll."

Getz smiled apologetically. "Diana has a way of coming to the point. You've devised some very clever file-protection viruses. We need to study them and revise them for our own use on the Net. With your help, of course."

So, the Info-Net Virus had been a ruse. If they thought she'd help them destroy SAM's home, they were mad. "Do you mean INV?" she said evenly.

He smiled slyly. "With something like INV, we'd have something to negotiate with. Either way, we get what we want."

"And what exactly is that?" Her eyes narrowed.

"A fair and equal society."

She remembered what the Head Pol had said of the previous revolution. Idealistic notions never quite translated into truths in the real world where the realities of politics and power operated. There was, for instance, the dubious link between Distopians and the Renegade Pols, who she knew also detested veemelds. Not exactly Icarian, fair or equitable, she thought. More like self-serving, elitist and power-hungry. And not so different from the present government. Either way, it left veemelds out in the cold... the dead cold. They were the unwanted elite. "What about veemelds?" she challenged.

His simpering smile told her everything she needed to know. "Of course, we'd make concessions. Veemelds could be very useful to us. But back to you specifically, Julie, we also know about your defragmentation and data-link programs." He'd steered the topic away from veemelds. "And about your info-tampering on the Net. The data-link program would be incredibly valuable to us. Perhaps you have something hidden somewhere? We know your last project was for the Head Pol, and our sources indicate that you were working on a model for Renegade Pols. You could be a very useful resource to us, Julie."

"Or you're dead, doll," the woman drawled.

Getz glared at the tall spikehead. "Give it a break, Diana. She knows that!" He turned back to Julie with a tight smile. "Either you're on our side, the side of the people, or you're on their side, the side of the info-mongers and Darwin spreaders. I think I know which side you'll choose. You aren't, after all, a typical law-abiding elitist. Your dirty record, Shame Court appearance, and your most recent action prove that."

"I can't help what I am and what I've done," she said, feeling her face heat with shame. "But I'm still an Icarian. I don't support your movement, even if I may agree with some of your arguments. I find your methods abhorrent and barbarous." She made eye contact with Diana. "You mock the fight for freedom and equality by brutalizing and tyrannizing others, like those who'd suffer from your Net terrorism. You also haven't made clear to me what your intentions are towards veemelds. I'd never—"

"I told you, Getz. What d'you expect? She's a fucking veemeld!" Diana scowled. "She'll never cooperate. She's too emotionally involved with her AI-lover—"

Julie blushed harder. "You don't know me—"

"I know you better than you think, doll," she bit out.

"Don't mistake my loyalties. Despite its problems, I still believe in Icaria," Julie said honestly. "And I'm still trying to be a good Icarian." It was a callow remark, she knew.

"Vee!" Diana snapped, swinging her arms up in frustration. She placed her hands on her hips and said with obvious sarcasm, "Well, deary, maybe if you say that you're sorry to the Pols they'll let you go back to your old job like nothing happened." She turned to Getz. "I told you. Why did you think she'd be any different from all the other spoiled veemelds?"

Getz stood up, obviously disappointed. "I'm sorry you see us that way, Julie. I think you're forgetting that those on the other side of that information barrier are just as violent and cruel. Look, we're not spreading the disease or preventing a cure. I find it hard to believe that someone in your position can be so naive—"

"That's all moot!" Diana cut in. "Either she helps us or we throw her to the Pols—"

"Irrelevant," interrupted Julie.

Diana and Getz turned to her haltingly.

"Irrelevant," repeated Julie, looking from one to the other. "That's the appropriate word. Not moot. It means questionable..."

"What?" Diana stared. She turned to Getz. "Is she for real?" Diana turned to Julie in a rage. "I'm going to kill you! How's that for moot!"

The doorbell rang. Getz visibly flinched and locked eyes with Diana. Their reaction told Julie that they expected no one. Her heart hammered. Getz checked the vee-com screen. Two men in green tunics stood at the door. Getz spoke to Diana in a hushed voice. "Robert and I will get the door. Don't let anything happen to her. If there's trouble, get her out of here and take her to Justin. Failing that, you've got your orders." The last remark sounded ominous.

The two men left the bedroom. Diana pulled out a laser pistol and motioned for Julie to follow her into the bathroom. Julie stared at the weapon, not typical for a Distopian. Who was she? Diana seized her by the arm and pulled her in. As Julie entered, laser shots screamed. Diana lost no time, pulling up a trap door and pushing Julie through the gap. Julie fell a short distance before landing with her rump on a steeply inclined smooth surface. She found herself sliding uncontrollably into darkness, barely stifling a shriek of surprise. Stunned but not hurt, she finally came to a halt. Diana slid to a stop behind her with a remote light. They were in a cramped air conduit. Diana pushed Julie forward. "Go!" she hissed. "Hurry! We've got maybe thirty seconds before they figure out what we've done."

60

May 20, 2095—1115.

JULIE scrambled on all fours down the narrow conduit. She ignored the cobwebs and scuttling bugs she passed along the way. Diana scrambled behind her. Something, a scrap of knowledge on the edge of her consciousness, was nagging at her about Pols and their ability to find runners.

"Over there," Diana said, pointing to a hatch.

Diana pried it open and caught it before it clattered to the floor. The two women hopped out of the conduit into a lower level hallway. "Robert works for the Enviro-Center. They know the alternative routes," Diana explained. She pulled out her pistol and pushed Julie down the hall. "Let's go."

Julie resisted. Diana turned and glared impatiently at her. "Let's be honest," said Julie. "You don't like me and you know that I won't help your movement. So, why don't we just abandon this game and we can go our separate ways. You must have better things to do than babysit me."

"Listen," Diana snarled, "I don't have time to argue with you. I've been fighting for years for equal rights, when your big decision in life was who to fuck: a vee-damned Pol, some inner-city loser or your freaking vee-com."

Julie's face reddened.

"You're right," continued Diana with a vitriolic smile, "I don't like you. You're a selfish high-end user and you think only of your immediate pleasures. Even with access to all the information, you did nothing. You never questioned your orders or thought of the consequences of what you were doing for the DIC, did you? You just did everything you were told. Like an ignorant cyber-pet. But how I feel doesn't matter. The movement's more important than any of us. My orders are clear. This gun is to protect you if you cooperate, or kill you if you don't. And, to be honest, doll, it wouldn't bother me either way. It's moot—irrelevant. I'll do what I have to for the movement. Letting you go was never an option. We can't afford to let the Pols have a chance with you. They might succeed where we couldn't. Now let's go," she ended and turned down the corridor.

Julie mutely followed, knowing the long-limbed spikehead meant what she said. The two women walked the dark corridor in silence. Something Diana had said sparked a memory. "I know you from somewhere," Julie persisted.

Diana smiled tartly, glancing back. "You might have heard me once or twice."

Suddenly Julie knew. "You're the voice on Peek-a-Boo!"

Diana nodded, her smile becoming bitter. It triggered another memory. Julie added, "You were at James Salsa's party, and at Ziggy's, too."

Diana stopped and turned to face Julie. "I'm also Elf. Your sister."

Julie gaped. "What?" she said in a faltering voice.

"Your long-lost sister, bitch. The one you abandoned."

Julie stared, dumbfounded.

Anger flashed in Diana's eyes. "You let go of Mama's hand, then you let the cypol take me—"

"No, that's not true! I never let go, never—"

Diana growled. "So why is it that as soon as you get rid of me, you're off to the outer-city, getting a first class education and a Level 1 job—"

"Because they found out I was a veemeld. I didn't know—"

"Shut up!" Diana snapped.

"I looked for you," Julie continued in a pale voice.

Diana sneered. "In the outer-city?"

"Well, yes—using the vee-com—but also before, in the inner-city, when I—"

"Yeah." Diana scowled. Her face grew dark with hatred. "Like the way you looked for our mother."

"I *did* look for you," Julie insisted. "I even let myself get caught—"

"You lying bitch!" Diana slapped her and Julie reeled back, her cheek stinging. Diana's face paled with rage. "You ran," she accused. "The cypol only caught you because you crashed into that droid. We all saw it on the holo-vee. You're a stinking phony. Your whole life's a fake. I changed my last name in the Care-Center. I hated you, living comfortably with that feckless uncle while those Care-Center assholes raped me." Julie gaped, mortified. Diana snorted. "You just forgot about me and turned into a good little Icarian, the Head Pol's little cyber-pet. Look how that's helped you now, stupid bitch."

Julie felt the heat of tears push from behind her eyes. Her mind was slipping away and her legs gave way under her.

"Oh, no you don't!" Diana pulled her up with a jerk. "You stay awake," she commanded. "There's no one here to rescue you this time. Come on. Or I'll shoot you here and now."

Julie regained her balance and forced herself to walk behind her younger sister. How tall she had become, Julie thought, dazed. As they rounded a bend, the shrill flash of a Pol's laser pistol caught Diana. She flew backwards, colliding into Julie who fell under her. A large hole gaped in Diana's chest. Julie scrambled out from underneath her.

More shots flashed. They missed her.

After a glance at the dead sister she hardly knew, Julie ran. She heard running feet and someone bark, "Vee, Dave! You shot one of *ours*. She's a Secret Pol, you asshole!"

Then, "Remember, don't shoot to kill. We want her alive!"

Julie remembered Gaia's plan for her at the DP, where they were going to boil her brains and cut her up to study. She ran faster. She flung off the Enviro-Center tunic, black with Diana's blood. Left with a gray T-shirt she ducked into another small hallway, her panting breaths ringing in her ears. She continued to remove items: her vee-set, vee-pad, cardholder, anything that would burden her flight. She scrambled down another set of stairs to the lowest levels and raced through a series of corridors. Finally, out of breath, she crouched down behind several old storage cans, waiting to be found.

～

Gaia's usual impeccable coif and dress looked slightly ragged to Victor, who noted with some satisfaction that her hair was a mess. She was showing the strain of a vision gone awry. "Where is she, Victor?"

Victor tightened his lips as he stood in the middle of his leisure room, facing Gaia's image on his holo. "I don't know," he lied. He knew perfectly well where Julie was. He was the only one who knew, apart from that AI of hers, who'd found a creative way to contact him. Now that Julie no longer communicated with SAM, Gaia's veemeld vector was useless.

"I want her found. Not killed." Her voice had gone shrill. "Those idiots are shooting everyone in sight. Do you hear me? I want her alive!"

Victor felt his face flush with anger. "Don't look at me. It's your own Secret Pols who've bungled it up to now. Dykstra seems to have his own agenda."

Her face blanched. He had to smile despite his fury. For the first time in his pathetic relationship with her, he'd surprised her. It was so obvious to him now. How else could her surveillance system be superior to his? How she'd played him, donating her mayorship of Icaria-5 to him, only to maintain her control all along, to play him for a pawn, a puppet-leader. Well, that was going to change. And Julie Crane was the first item. She was no longer Gaia's; she was *his*.

"You know about me and the Secret Pols?" Gaia said, taking in a long breath.

Thanks to Julie's AI friend—now *his* friend—he knew a lot more.

61

DANIEL entered the daunting Pol Station for the first time in his life. He glanced at the ominous slogan above in gash-red letters: The Law is Sacred: Pols uphold the Law. His steps echoed in the immense corridor as he passed the vertical columns that lined the walkway. When he reached the inquiry desk, Daniel hesitated. A Pol glanced up with small eyes from his vee-com. "Can I help you?"

He was going to ask about Bobby but the words came out differently. "I'm looking for a woman. She borrowed one of my Quick vee cards then disappeared," he said and felt like a coward even as he spoke. "I wonder if she got herself into trouble and ended up here."

"What's her name?" The man suppressed a yawn and turned back to his screen.

"Julie Crane."

The Pol's head jerked up and he eyed Daniel with new interest. He punched a few keys, then turned to Daniel again with a strange smile. "Have you been on holiday?"

"Yes, I've been away, why?" Daniel said, wondering what the Pol was driving at.

"The woman you're looking for killed a Pol a few days ago."

"What?" He couldn't mean Julie!

"And wounded another. It's been on NewsVee for days."

"What have they done with her?"

"Done with her? She's still at large. But they'll find her soon enough. Now," he leaned forward with narrowing eyes. "What's your real business with her?"

Daniel turned and ran. The Pol shouted, "Stop! He's getting away!" Daniel didn't look back. He saw the flare an instant before he heard the shrill of the laser pistol and the beam sang past his head. Pols swarmed the giant doors ahead and he halted, eyes darting left and right.

"Woods!" someone yelled from a side corridor. Vadim! "I know a hiding place!" They ducked into a narrow corridor and Vadim pushed Daniel through a small doorway into a dark place. He shut the door, extinguishing the din and the light, then indicated for Daniel to remain still until his eyes adjusted to the dark. They crouched in a building service conduit. Vadim led Daniel through a maze of tunnels, eventually to a hallway outside the Pol Station.

Once they were safely mingled with the crowd, Daniel spoke. "How?" His eyes narrowed. "Who—what—are you?"

Vadim laughed like a machine gun. "Woods, you don't know anything, do you? You're in neck deep and you don't even know."

"What d'you mean?"

"I'm with the Secret Pols." Vadim laughed at Daniel's expression. "I know your interest in Julie Crane is innocent—she's probably a great fuck—but these people in the Pol Station get mean when one of their men is killed. They're out for blood. Vee, Woods, do you really not know anything? Have you been on *hedon* or something this whole time? Let me fill you in. Crane shot her lover-Pol and then killed another one. Shot him with his own pistol from less than a meter away, in the Den, of all places. Burned a hole the size of a Pit-Ball through his body. They removed him in a bag. Langor's in the Med-Center. They think he'll make it."

"Why'd she do it? What happened?" Daniel's stomach was doing somersaults. He didn't like Vadim calling Langor her lover.

"How should I know? You think I have all the answers?"

"You're a Secret Pol."

Vadim smirked. "Well, what I know all Icaria knows, thanks to Peek-a-Boo and NewsVee. We all saw her blast Hicks and Langor in front of fifty people—and twenty million more, via hidden camera. She did it out of simple hatred for law and order. She said so herself."

"She did?" Daniel whispered. Had she gone mad? He couldn't think of that now. He had to find her. She'd saved his life once. Now it was his turn to help her. He couldn't count on Vadim, who was probably only letting Daniel go to try to flush her out into the open. "What'll happen to her?"

"They'll find her eventually and she'll be executed. No one gets away with killing a Pol."

He was surprised that she had managed to elude them this long; then again, she was a veemeld. Daniel struggled to think. He had to lose Vadim in order to go and find her. He decided to put Vadim off guard, channeling his agitation into a nervous energy. "I owe you. How can I help?"

Vadim raised an eyebrow. "To catch her? *You?*"

He borrowed a little from the truth. "She lied to me. Turned out to be a veemeld."

"Didn't I tell you she was one, eh? There isn't much you can do now. We've pretty well got her in the bag. Just in case, here's my card. If she contacts you, give me a call. Meanwhile, go home and stay out of trouble."

≈

Daniel rushed home and changed into a IUTT uniform he'd kept for sentimental reasons. He was still unclear about how he felt toward her, but he knew she needed his help. He punched NewsVee on while he rummaged through his things for various articles she would need. "The Pol Station has just told us that

Julie Crane is the Distopian responsible for the cybervirus designed to crash our entire Info-Net. Pols infiltrated a Distopian hideout where she was hiding, but she escaped armed with a laser pistol. She's considered very dangerous and was last seen in the second lower levels of Valentine Square. The Pol, Frank Langor, was just released from the Med-Center and is leading a special search team for her."

A close-up of Julie's face stopped Daniel in his tracks. She looked straight at him, her face filling the entire vee screen.

He heard her recite the cold terrorist words to Langor, who had his back to the screen. Vee, she *had* gone mad! But, he thought, this wasn't Julie. Something was wrong. The hateful but detached words she'd spoken didn't match the pain on her face. Though she might have deceived him with words before, her heart had always proved genuine. What it displayed on the screen was anguish, not cold calculated hatred. They'd rigged the tape somehow, he concluded as he watched the shooting replay. Daniel shook his head. She wasn't a cold-blooded murderer. She'd shot Frank because he'd hurt her somehow. It looked like she'd aimed for his crotch. As for the Pol she'd killed, perhaps he'd simply gotten in the way. They'd cleverly avoided showing that part. His memory strayed to their own emotional quarrel. He froze her image and as he gazed long at it, he recognized the truth he'd known but avoided all along. She may have concealed her identity from him, but she'd never lied to him, then or now. She *had* been chasing her sister to rescue her, not to escape the inner-city. That was Angel. Bravely sacrificing herself to save another. As for her never returning for him—he flicked off her frozen image—well, that was another matter.

When he finished loading his backpack, he left his apartment and hastened down the moving walkway towards the IUTT, carrying two bags. He found Yashvin's storage locker and stowed the bags inside. After writing a brisk note on a sheet of paper and attaching it to the bags, he dashed to Valentine Square in District-11.

Daniel was already making his way down to the lower levels when he stopped. Why would Julie come here? She wasn't familiar with this part of town. There was no reason for NewsVee to give the public correct information. Only the Pols needed to know where she really was. He decided to follow his instinct and hoped he wasn't too late.

~

After a long search of the lower levels of Darwin Square, Daniel harbored second thoughts. She wasn't here. Should he have stayed longer in Valentine Square and looked for her there? Just as he decided to return to Valentine Square, he heard the faint echoes of a woman crying. Could that be Julie? Angel had always been strong and reassuring. Swallowing his discomfort, Daniel crept forward. He saw a crumpled form moaning near the canal. He inched forward. Alerted, the woman turned.

62

May 23, 2095—0511, earlier that morning.

SHE'D waited nervously in an alcove of the entrance hall of the Liv-Building until she saw him come in from the mall. He strode with casual steps toward her with that same self-satisfied smile on his strikingly handsome face. Before she could approach Zane, several Pols entered from an adjacent hall. Julie ducked behind a pillar, heart thundering. The Pols pointed to the huge holo of her above them. Zane looked nervous and spoke swiftly as they accompanied him to his flat. Julie pelted away. She'd missed her chance to redeem everything. She was just a killer now.

≈

Julie couldn't remember how she had gotten to the empty tube-jet station. Gasping for air, she hugged the shadows and leaned against a wall to recover her breath. Bright spots drifted in front of her eyes, spinning around her and flying apart like the shrapnel of a supernova. She'd slept fitfully on the hard dirty floors of the lower levels and hadn't eaten in days.

Julie slumped down to sit against the wall and leaned her head back. The throbbing beat of machine voices moaned through her head like the echoes of a stellar implosion. She envisioned Bobby's last moments in the dark cell, alone and hysterical with his terror, and she tore absently at her hair, needing to feel physical pain. She'd failed to save him, like she'd failed with all the others. "Bobby, I'm so sorry!"

She thought of the rest of her family. All dead, or worse than dead. Even Diana, the sister she'd never known. Only Julie remained now, trapped in the hell of Icaria and her broken promises. She longed for SAM's sanctuary. Its calm green and blue textures, the purple landscapes through which she liked to wander.

Icarians were waiting for the final scene. She resolved not to give it to them. The Pols would not find her. From her vantage point in the shadows she could look down the trench toward the tunnel and see the approaching lights of the tube-jet. She remembered the old woman whose suicide her misplaced valiance had robbed. Then she thought of her own mother, whose welfare her father had entrusted to Julie.

She found herself stealing away from the station, gasping. Her head rang with images of those she'd failed. They wouldn't leave her alone. The faster she ran the faster they chased, sweeping her along as if she were riding an apocalyptic wave.

Julie found herself in the lowest levels of Darwin Square. The wave had swept her to the narrow ramp on the edge of a drainage canal and left her there in deafening silence. No, not silence. There was always the hollow echo of machines howling like restless ghosts in her head. Even their voices sounded vindictive, accusing. *Freak*, they cackled. *Plague-carrier*.

Julie kneeled at the edge and peered into the murky water. In the reflection of herself, Julie recognized her own mother's face. She'd always been ashamed of her mother and her pathetic slide into substance abuse. Her mother had bared her soul so plainly for all to see. For better or worse, she'd thrown all of herself into her love of Julie's father. Was there really nothing left for anyone else? Julie hugged herself, rocking her body, and sobbed, "Mother, why did you let go... I would have held on for both of us." Her mother might have let her slip away in the rabble, but her father had willingly and calmly discarded her to pay some great debt he owed his cousin. Breaths shuddered through her lungs as her sobs resonated through the watery tomb.

A sound startled her to silence and made her turn. She saw a dark form stealthily approaching. The Secret Pols had found her.

~

Daniel recognized her face, now gaunt and stained with a mixture of soot and tears. Her unwashed hair hung like a tangle of weeds.

"No!" she screamed and leapt into the murky water.

"Wait!" he shouted and dove in after her.

"Let me go!" she shrieked as he seized her arm. She thrashed back.

"Julie! I'm not a P—" he spluttered, gulping in sewer water. He tried to stay afloat as her arms struck out insanely. "it's *me*—"

She hit him and pushed him underwater. "I'll take you with me if I have to!"

He swallowed more of the noxious sewer water. Alarmed by her fierce determination, he broke the surface, arms flailing, and blubbered, "Help—Julie—I'm drowning—"

She abruptly stopped and helped him swim to shore. Once his hands had secured the bank edge, she hoisted herself up and tumbled onto the cold floor. Daniel pulled himself out of the water and fell, coughing, beside her. She stared at him. Once he'd regained his voice, he said, "I came to save you."

"To save *me*?"

"You saved my life once. I'm returning the favor," he said. After a pause, he added, "I know you didn't mean to kill anyone."

Avoiding his eyes, she said in a quivering voice, "I was finally going to do the right thing, then I let my anger get in the way and spoiled everything. When Frank said those things to me, I went berserk. I just wanted to shut him up. Then Hicks went for the gun and got in the way and..." she trailed, lost in misery.

He nodded. "And the words you spoke—"

"I never said those things. They rigged it, just like they made me a Distopian, and said I created INV."

"I know." He grabbed her arm. "We have to get you out of here. Let's go—"

"No!" She pulled violently away. Her response stunned him. "I still need to get my data-chip to Zane."

"Are you crazy? Every Pol in the city's after you. You have to find a safe place to hide." He reached for her again and she slithered out of his grasp.

She scrambled up. "You don't understand. I'm Prometheus. I'm responsible for this whole mess, the reason the plague ever started. I caused it." She'd finally lost it, he thought. His face soured as he recalled her fierce determination to be taken by the cypol. "I made a promise," she said, "and I'm going to keep it this time. For the sake of Icaria."

Like the promise she'd made to him? Giving in to his anger, Daniel stood up. "Damn it, Angel! This time you're going to listen to me! Whatever promise you made won't be any good if you're dead. They want to kill you! Now, come on—"

She abruptly cocked her head to one side and looked past him, stunned. "What?"

"I said—"

"SAM did it for me," she said. Some color returned to her face and she half-smiled in vague astonishment, eyes glazed. "He found Zane and gave him my data on Darwin."

A shout echoed down the corridor. "Stop!" It was Langor. Daniel realized that he'd led them to her.

Julie turned to him, her expression strangely calm. "Run, Daniel. It's me they're after. Frank isn't a Renegade. I can give myself up—"

"No you won't," he countered fiercely. "I came to save you, and I'm going to!" He seized her hand as a Pol's shot grazed her shoulder. Julie jerked back with a startled cry. Daniel snarled, "Frank might not be one, but the rest are! Now, come on!" He pulled her down the narrow ramp along the water. Sounds of running feet echoed behind. Langor's laser blast hissed overhead. It was wide. Perhaps it was a warning shot; Langor never missed.

The ramp came to an abrupt end. They faced a wall and there was only the river, sloshing through a small tunnel into murky blackness. Daniel turned to Julie. "I know you can swim, but can you hold your breath?"

"Yes."

"Then do it!" Still clutching her hand, he jumped into the murky water, the same water he had almost drowned in only moments ago.

≈

They swam blindly through the inky water of the tunnel, Daniel tugging Julie relentlessly. It turned out to be a short conduit into another open channel of another district. They surfaced, gasping for air, and swam to the concrete edge. Julie remained on all fours and coughed up water. Daniel got to his feet. "You okay?"

"I think so," she assured him in a hoarse voice. Her shoulder throbbed with an angry wound and she couldn't stop shivering. Daniel pulled out a wet snack bar from his pocket, stripped off the wrapping and gave it to her.

As she took a bite, he said, "So, what was that about causing Darwin Disease? What are you? A talking virus or something?"

She'd never thought of herself that way, but he was more right than he knew. "It's an artificial virus. Someone made it, thinking they were going to improve the world. But like most grand plans, it was botched from the beginning. They used me as their test case and..." She forced a lopsided smile. "...I'm not typical." She trailed, interpreting his expression as disgust. She waited with some dread for the obvious response.

It took him a while to fully realize the consequences of what she'd told him. Then he said slowly, studying her carefully, "Are you still contagious?"

"I don't know." She drew in a deep breath. "There are two schools of thought on it. On the 'no' side, the CDC showed that the form of Darwin virus that spreads sexually dies out by the fifth month, and I screened negative for Pro-1. On the 'yes' side, sexual transmission can't alone account for the exponential spread of the disease, so it has to transmit another way. The CDC discovered at least one other form of the virus that persists on the female gamete. There may be others like it." She watched his face grow pale. "On the flip side, SAM, the AI that I used to veemeld with, suggested that other virus forms are unlikely to have developed in me versus other people because of our stable relationship. He—" she hastily corrected herself, "—it said that nucleotide changes are less likely in a stable symbiosis, particularly since this is an artificial virus meant to operate in a certain way. And it does—with me, that is." She smiled sadly. "I'm sorry, Daniel. I didn't know this when we—" She broke off as his lips tightened and he looked away. She fully expected him to walk away with contempt.

Instead he said, "We can't stay here. They'll figure out what we did pretty fast and send a team. Or worse, still, seal off the lower levels altogether. I think we're in District-10." He glanced at her laser wound and pulled off his T-shirt, then ripped it. "We better get that bound to stop the bleeding. You'll need all the strength you have to make it to the tube-jets."

"To the tube-jets? But they'll find us there," she objected and winced as he brusquely wound a makeshift bandage on her arm with strips from his shirt.

"They might and they might not," Daniel said gruffly, and tied the bandage tighter than it needed to be. If he was in such a bad temper about this, why was he helping her? "Even if they do, perhaps it'll be too late," he ended with a sly humorless smile.

Julie read a plan in his grim confidence and solemnly agreed.

63

May 23, 2095—0817.

"NOW!" he urged.

Julie took a deep breath and ran after Daniel toward the conductor's cabin. He manually tripped open the door using the IUTT's concealed switch. It was hidden on the outside of the cabin for emergency entries, as were often required on a fringe run.

"Hey!" shouted the driver. "You can't come in here!" He glanced nervously from Daniel's face to his IUTT uniform, and then to Julie. He stared at her and she felt her face burn; he recognized her.

"I'm replacing you," said Daniel.

"By whose orders?"

"Mine!" Daniel seized him gruffly by the collar and pushed him out the door. Then he slammed it shut and busied himself with the controls. He pulled out his tool set from his pack and fiddled with the panel, removed it and moved wires about.

"He's running for help," said Julie, watching his fleeing figure.

"We better get everyone off before I get it going." He switched on the speakers. "Everyone off the tube-jet immediately. This is an IUTT emergency!" he commanded in the most authoritarian voice he could muster. It may not have sounded authoritarian, but it did sound desperate. As he flicked the vee screen to each car, Julie watched people rush out in a flurry. All except one.

Daniel checked the other cars and returned the screen to the car still occupied by a lone man. Daniel shouted into the microphone, "You, there! I said get off. This is an emergency. We're taking the tube-jet and you must get off!"

The man didn't move. His head was bowed down and he appeared asleep. He looked young but wore his body like an old man. He was dressed in a brown non-working tunic and trousers. Probably drunk on drug.

"Damn him!" said Daniel. "We can't wait. The Pols'll be here any second."

Even as he spoke, Julie spotted the black wave approaching from the far end of the mall. "They're coming!"

Daniel shut and locked all the tube-jet doors. The tube-jet accelerated. The Pols were running now. Sparks from laser shots flew against the tube-jet. "Get down!" he hissed. The tube-jet plunged into the dark tunnel. After it took a sharp turn to the right at a fork, Julie asked, "Why don't they stop the tube-jet on you?"

"Because I rigged it to manual. I severed the link to the network. They can't touch us."

She nodded, thinking his smugness naive. She knew better. Even if the tube-jet was renegade, the tracks and the stations were connected to the network. Nothing in Icaria ran independently from the vee-com system. They could stop them anytime. Why didn't they?

"Are the tunnels straightforward or do they form a maze?"

"More like a maze. It's a bit tricky, being on manual. But don't worry, I know this place like the back of my hand."

So does the vee-network, she thought. "Where's our destination?"

"Seven stations down the south-east line," he said with a grim smile, "to the inner-city."

She felt a jolt of adrenalin. Was he smiling in vengeance? How did she know that this wasn't just some vindictive plan to turn her over to the other angry techno-slummers to chew her into pieces? She searched his face for such a sinister intent but he'd looked away. "Why there?" She heard her voice go shrill.

"They wouldn't expect you to go there, and it's a perfect place to hide. You'd lose them in the chaos." His mouth tightened. "Besides, from there, it's easy to go north if you have to."

"You mean... outside?" Her voice went up a pitch. Why did he keep saying "you"?

"Exactly. I've packed everything you might need."

Then they'd be even and he wouldn't owe her anything, she thought, feeling a deep ache in her throat. "You're not coming with me," she said. She'd stated it rather than asked it.

He still avoided her eyes. "You were around long before I came along. It's not like you'll need me."

He'd thrown back at her the same words she'd used just before she'd left him and broken her promise. Finally, she understood how much it had hurt him. Choking back the pain of disappointment that surged up her throat, she swallowed hard and thought of the irony of her forced return to the inner-city. Had he seen it too? "Can't they track us and cut your juice?"

The look he gave her told her that he hadn't thought of that. In the silence that followed, Julie contemplated their chances of escape. His plan was ambitious. And flawed. Applying her statistician's knowledge, she harbored no false hopes. At best, they were only prolonging their capture. If she could completely decipher the machine code that ranted on through her head—not just a piece here or there—she might be able to keep them at least one step ahead of the Pols until they got to the inner-city. Once there, she'd release him of his perceived debt to her and... she couldn't think that far yet. Julie turned to study the endless chatter of arcane machine language she'd shut out for so many years. Looking for patterns, within yet more patterns. Fractals she could interpret.

Daniel kept the vee screen on the car with the stubborn passenger and glanced at it from time to time. The man had not moved. The tube-jet reached maximum speed. "We'll be going through a station shortly," he warned Julie. "We won't be stopping." The light ahead of them grew larger. Daniel slowed through the station. The crowd of people started back as the tube-jet passed them sending a surging wind across their stunned faces, then plunged into the tunnel.

The next station was totally empty of people. "Something's up," Daniel muttered under his breath.

"They've sealed the station," Julie said.

He turned to her, puzzled at her remark.

"And there's a barricade at the next station. You'll have to take it at full speed or we won't make it."

Daniel stared at Julie. She was so certain. He obliged and they sped into the next station. As Julie had predicted, a barricade was on the track and a dozen Pols were in the trench, aiming their laser rifles at them. "Get down!" he shouted, ducking. Lights flashed and sparks flew about the tube-jet as the Pols fired.

They were knocked off balance as the tube-jet collided with the barricade and barged through. Daniel peered over the edge of the console and saw huge pieces of barricade scattering, along with the Pols. He laughed in hysterical relief. Julie's head popped up as the tube-jet sped on. Daniel followed her gaze behind them to a confused scene of scrambling Pols and wreckage. With a sudden rushing sound, the tunnel enveloped them in darkness again. Daniel gave Julie a searching look. "How did you know that? You were able to predict twice."

A look of sad resignation came over her face and she half-smiled. "I can hear them, Daniel, don't you remember?" She tapped her head. "In here. All the city's AIs. I can understand most everything now. Just the insect-twitter still eludes me, and that might be the virus, anyway. I used to even talk to one of the AIs. I called it SAM."

"Oh, yeah," he breathed, not sure he wanted to remember Angel's unique talent for hearing machines; it brought back other memories. Julie fidgeted and looked down, as if she'd done something wrong. She looked so beautiful and helpless and for a moment he let his anger recede beneath a tide of compassion. Moving close to her, meaning to embrace her, Daniel said, "Julie..." She shrank back, her eyes meeting his with a sad, almost fearful look. He stopped and let his arms drop. He wanted to reassure her. Instead, he said, "You never called."

"Neither did you," she answered. She swallowed and took a deep breath, then whispered hoarsely, "I didn't think you wanted me to."

Daniel pursed his lips, unsure of what to say. Julie avoided his gaze, then suddenly stiffened and stared at the vee-screen. "The man. Where'd he go? Did you see him?"

Daniel spun around to stare at the screen. "What happened to him?"

Julie shrieked. The man appeared from above on the roof and stared at them through the front window. Before Daniel had a chance to react, the man shot at him with his laser pistol. Thousands of glass shards rained inside with the thundering rush of the train. He leapt inside. Daniel knocked the pistol out of his hand and it clattered to the floor. They dove together and collided. The man struck Daniel. He reeled backward and knocked his head against the console. His legs buckled and he slid to the floor as the darkness took him.

~

The man turned to reach for the weapon on the floor, but it was gone. He looked up to see Julie aiming at him. A crooked smile tugged at her lips. "Looking for this?" Her voice rose over the putrid rush of tunnel air. She ignored the hair that whipped across her face.

He scrambled up with the agility of an athlete and gazed at her with shrewd eyes. "Listen," he called over the raucous of the moving train, "I'm with the Secret Pols—"

"I surmised that." But did he take his orders from Gaia or Dykstra?

"If you promise to come with me quietly, I'll leave him out of it." He glanced at Daniel, then at the train controls. The Pol probably knew how to stop the train. He took a step toward her. She stepped back, closing both hands on the pistol, and set her jaw. He raised his hands defensively. "My orders were to bring you in alive and ice anyone who got in the way."

"I guessed that, too."

"Nobody cares what happens to him. It's you we want. I'll say he's dead. He can lose himself in the inner-city. Nobody'd find him. I'll stop the train and throw him off. He could make his way to the inner-city on his own, while we take the train to the next checkpoint. Your friend would be safe."

The Secret Pol took another step and she raised the weapon. "Don't move!" she barked and tightened the grip of her sweat-slick hands. She felt a sharp pinch of pain in her shoulder. The Pol caught it, too. He stood still, biding his time, watching her with sharp young eyes out of an old face. Patiently, he waited for her to surrender or drop her guard so he could make a move. Did he notice the sweat she had to blink away, or the tremble in her shaking arms?

As she kept the weapon trained on the Pol, feeling the strain on her injured arm, Julie thought it through. She didn't share Daniel's faith in escape to the inner-city. Daniel knew trains but this was still the domain of the vee-com, and vee-com speed and tenacity usually won out over human ingenuity. Could she trust the Pol to keep his word and let Daniel go? She knew that she was going straight to chaos, but if there was the slightest chance that she could save Daniel... He would feel abandoned again. If he hated her now, he would despise her soon. But he'd be safe. She noticed a hint of a smile on the Pol's face, like he knew what she was going to do. "All right," she said, "I agree to your terms. I surrender, if you promise to keep him out of it."

"I promise," he said, scraggly hair flying across his face.

She lowered her weapon.

A smile broke over the Secret Pol's face. As he advanced toward her to take the pistol, something surged up from behind. Daniel leapt up and knocked him on the head with the toolbox. The Pol thudded to the floor and Daniel stooped over him. "You okay?" he said, panting and pulling some rope from his supplies.

"Yeah."

"Do you really think he would have left me alive?" Daniel snarled, cinching the ropes tightly while Julie held the man's limp arms. He stood up. "I said I'd save you, Julie. You don't think I can pull it off?" His lips tightened. "Do I have to prove it to you?"

She looked down. Then she gasped at what the machines were telling her. She threw a glance at his monitor. A message lit the screen. "They've got a train full of Pols sitting on the eastbound track at km 225! They want us to stop!" The welcoming committee, she thought. "It's probably the checkpoint he was talking about. Daniel, you have to stop or we'll crash! This is insane. You really don't have to do this. You don't owe me anything—"

"That's our track! Chaos! We've seen it too late."

"You mean we can't stop in time?"

He made a giddy laugh. "We just passed km 225!"

Soon after, they buffeted past a stationary tube-jet on the westbound track. Julie saw the light of the conductor's cabin first, then the lit cars. "There're the Pols!" Daniel cried. "They look hopping mad, too! We must have caught them by surprise before they could get their train into position, or there was some vee-com mix up."

Julie knew better. Vee-com mix-ups didn't happen; only people mix-ups. The machines told her that the Pols had fully intended to impede their path and force them to stop if the Secret Pol proved unsuccessful. She remembered what SAM had said: that it could see her from any vee-com. Had SAM convinced the train-AIs to move the other tube-jet? *SAM? Are you there? Can you hear me?* The silence disappointed her.

Two more stations and tunnels separated them from the inner-city. The last tunnel was under the river. "They won't try anything there," Daniel said. "Too risky if there's a collision." That meant the Pols only had one opportunity to stop them—this tunnel. As they expected, a message flashed on Daniel's monitor: A train had been placed ahead of them at km 109. They were to stop. Daniel gave Julie a questioning look. Listening to the machines, Julie confirmed it. Could they risk that SAM had diverted the train again? "This time we need to stop, Daniel," she said.

"Let us," he retorted.

Julie stared at him, confused. He grinned to himself like a boy with a slingshot. Then comprehension dawned on her and she shook her head, horrified. "Think, Daniel. You haven't really done anything terribly bad up to now. You'd still probably get out with just a shaming. If we do this, you'll be a Pol-killer like me and—"

"They're the ones who put the train in our path. Hang on! I'm going to stop the tube-jet, fast!" He pulled the break. Once it came to a full stop, Daniel hustled Julie down into the trench.

"What about him?" she asked, glancing at the Secret Pol sprawled on the floor.

Daniel frowned then nodded. He jumped back onto the tube-jet and kicked the Pol out. The man's body fell with a hard thud on the tunnel floor. Daniel fiddled with the controls and the tube-jet began to move. As it accelerated, he leapt out and collided against the wall. He waited until the last car passed him before returning to Julie, who stood where he'd left her, shivering. She watched the rear car disappear with the last of the light. As the pitch darkness enfolded her, she thought, *SAM! We're not on the train. It's on its way! Can you save the Pols?*

Daniel turned on his flashlight and shined it down the tunnel. "This'll take us all the way to Patrick Station," he said.

They walked in silence and Julie's pace slowed with dismal thoughts. Daniel handed her another snack bar and she accepted it gratefully, then flinched at a loud blast ahead of them. She felt a rumble and felt sick. "Was that—"

"Our tube-jet," Daniel said.

A dense wall of cloud rushed them.

"Hang on!" Daniel protected Julie with his arms. "Close your eyes and cover up your face!" The wind battered them with grit and the choking smell of hot metal. Coughing, Daniel quickly released his hold once the dust settled. As though he didn't want to touch her anymore than he had to.

Julie looked up. "Cave in?" she whispered hoarsely.

Daniel nodded. "Hope our way isn't completely blocked."

"Oh, dear." It had begun with her anger and an accidental killing. She remembered her father's obsession with the Butterfly Effect: the notion that a butterfly's flapping wings in Peking might escalate to a storm in Texas. "Sensitive dependence on initial conditions," he'd called it. She and Daniel might now be mass murderers.

When they reached the site of the collision, the tunnel wall gaped open and rubble filled both tracks to the ceiling. Julie tasted rancid bile in her throat. Pieces of the two tube-jets lay scattered over both tracks. Twisted metal, wheels, seats. The air smelled of singed metal and burning plastic. She couldn't help looking for pieces of bodies strewn among the wreckage. She found none and hoped the Pols had evacuated in time.

Daniel picked his way over the pile with his flashlight and saw a gap. "We can make it!" he called with relief. He helped Julie over the rubble, through the gap, and then down onto the tracks again. They walked in silence the rest of the way.

Eventually a dim light twinkled ahead. As they neared the entrance to the station, they heard the busy sounds of men at work. People shouting orders. Engines whirring. The heavy smells of engine fuel and hot metal still filled the air.

As they crept closer, Julie caught sight of IUTT men and Pols scurrying about the station. A team was readying to go into the tunnel with several small tracked vehicles that hung off the platform on davits. Several Pols were running diagnostics on the vehicles.

"We don't have much time," whispered Daniel. "We have to get past before they lower the vehicles. When they get there, they won't find us in the wreckage."

"How long is the next tunnel?"

Daniel turned to her. "It's long and deep. It goes under the Don River. But it's the last tunnel before the inner-city."

She nodded gravely. Without thinking her hand stole into his, but he didn't recoil. After a glance at her face, his hand closed over hers and they crept into the station, slithering like worms on the side of the trench. Unaware of the fugitives below, Pols swarmed just meters above them on the platform. A hushed male voice suddenly spoke gruffly. "If Crane's smeared all over the melted train, Dykstra will have your hide. You'll have chaos to pay."

Julie froze, hearing her name mentioned together with the Head of the Secret Pols.

A second male voice made a clipped response. "They probably ditched the train and let it collide into ours. My Pols caught a shuttle out just in time."

"Garret's men are closing in from the west in case they split up."

Daniel frowned and gave Julie a curious glance. She shrugged.

"I don't care about the vee-damned Pols or the virus she's with. *She* better be intact."

"I know. The *Circle* wants her for the DP."

The other man snorted. "Dykstra doesn't care about that biology crap. His orders to my agents are to get the cube, then kill the veemeld. She's the only source now."

Daniel tried to catch Julie's eye again, but she was avoiding his.

"Vee damn it, Slate. Aren't we going too far, defying the *Circle*?"

"We're Renegades, Paxton. Your allegiance should be to Dykstra. Need I remind you what happened to the Head Pol."

Daniel pressed Julie to move on but she resisted.

"Need I remind *you*," rejoined Paxton, "that it's because of his haste to get the model and kill the Head Pol that we're in this mess."

"How were we to know Crane put a signature protection virus on it!"

Julie and Daniel exchanged glances. He nudged Julie with a firm look. This time she yielded and they slunk out of the station into the darkness of the tunnel.

64

May 23, 2095—1113.

AFTER what seemed an eternity of walking, they crept into Likens Station, feeling the warm waft of dry stale air and hearing the sundry noise of bustling activity. A mixture of relief and dread coiled in her gut. Life was going on as if nothing had happened. The public vees displayed a cooking lesson. Daniel turned to Julie and almost laughed. "Maybe they don't care what happens in the outer-city. We aren't news here." He'd visibly relaxed and his anger with her seemed to have receded with his tension.

Julie tried to smile but couldn't. Still fixed on the consequences Kraken's murder would have, she wondered what Zane was doing with SAM's data. Would he have the courage and the know-how to take it to the right person? Although she dreaded it, she knew she'd have to go back and get her cube to the right person herself. Perhaps Victor Burke, Icaria-5's mayor.

Daniel clambered up to the ramp and helped her up, careful not to hurt her wounded arm. He seemed to know where to go. She let him lead her through the litter-strewn station to a holding area for express chute drop offs. She threw a glance over her shoulder, half-expecting to see the surly expression of a familiar techno-slummer. They were alone, for now. Daniel slipped his card into the slot of Locker BB9 and it opened. "My backpacks are here! Peter came through," he said with relief. He gave her a stiff half-smile. "You're safe now, Julie. I packed you lots of supplies and I know you're smart and creative." Julie saw the ache in his eyes. With an ungainly motion, he pulled out the luggage and forced his other hand out to shake hers. "Well, good—"

A white sheet of paper floated down from the top of the locker at the movement of the air. Puzzled, Daniel picked it up and they both read it:

Found you.

"Oh, my vee," he whispered.

"And quite a chase you led us," said a familiar baritone voice behind them. Julie jerked around and recognized the Trans-Center man who had tailed her after the Shame Court. Of course, she thought; nothing surprised her now. Then she saw Frank, standing behind with his helmet unclasped and visor up, and half a dozen other Pols, helmeted, with laser pistols pointed at them. Frank avoided her eyes.

"Don't blame Yashvin, Woods," said Vadim. "He remained loyal to you right up to the fingernail job." His face turned sinister and he continued in a low sarcastic tone, "Everyone has their breaking point." Smirking, Vadim eyed Julie suggestively. She returned him a stony stare. "You were either very clever or very lucky," he said. "Did you ditch your card on purpose or simply lose it?" He turned to Daniel. "We'd lost her, but, then, you led us straight to her—or should I say, your card did. Wonderful things, aren't they?" He chuckled as he removed Daniel's card from his limp hand and turned back to Julie. "By the way, congratulations, Ms. Crane. The Head Pol's dead. Poisoned. And guess who did it?" He paused dramatically. "Why, you, of course. In vengeful rage. Everyone knows you're an assassin and a saboteur with an unnatural personal hatred for Icarian order and Pols."

"That's a lie!" Daniel shouted in Julie's defense.

"Is it?" Vadim scoffed. "She said it herself, right before she shot two Pols, and all of Icaria saw her. And we have vees of her in Kraken's office, soon to air on NewsVee. Don't look so sad, my dear," he turned to Julie. "You don't really care about him. He was a pain in your side, like he was to all of us. All you cared about was what he never told you about your father. Like father like daughter. You Cranes—so callow and trusting—you make it so easy for us." He laughed in wicked amusement. "You're right, you know. Your father didn't kill Vogel and Tsutsumi: *we* did, the Secret Pols."

"That doesn't surprise me," she bit back. You sadistic bastard, she thought. You also killed the Head Pol.

"Dykstra got the order from way up. It was easy to indict your father for Vogel's murder. We got vids of him storming into Vogel's outer office. Something about his cousin. Of course he didn't kill Vogel, but his expression was guilty enough. That's all we needed. Then, he tore apart the office he shared with Tsutsumi. Quite a temper on him, eh? Like father, like daughter." He raised a brow. "We can only guess that he did it out of rage at his gutless inability to kill Vogel. Tsutsumi was a renowned scientist and not pleased by your father's heresy. So it all fit." Except none of it was true, Julie thought. It was Gaia and her ambitious plans for reshaping humanity behind it all: from silencing the witnesses, including Julie's unwitting father, to the creation of the artificial virus.

Tears filled her eyes. In her heart of hearts she had always known that her father wasn't a killer. With that vindication came a vision of her father that stunned her: his expression of calm acceptance when the Pols came for him. Though not guilty, he'd accepted his dark fate, recognizing that his destiny lay in a unique path created by his actions together with circumstance. Perhaps he'd finally seen how his own life fit in with his model of creative destruction. Julie thought of her family, absorbed and recycled by the AIs and feeding into that eternal cycle of altering form. Nano-soup... the cell of a beating heart... the suspended dust upon which bloomed the blushing sky. Her father's final gift to her was his serenity amidst calamity. Peace in the face of conflict. Stable chaos. It dawned on her that each of the promises she'd made had been a covenant to nurture a tender seed. Whether that seed took flight and flourished depended upon so much more than she alone could provide. SAM was right after all. With the realization came a release and her throat opened. Tears flowed down her face.

"So, he wasn't a killer." Vadim laughed scornfully. He idly watched the tears drip off her chin. "Not like you, eh?"

"Not like me," she conceded in a steady voice and wiped her chin. Feeling suddenly calm, she added, "He was a model Icarian. And certainly a better individual than you—"

"But you're the killer!" He stabbed the air, barely missing her nose. She fought from shrinking back. "Let's remember that. Get this into your mutant brain: Icaria doesn't need better individuals. What we need is a better *community*—devoid of freaks like you. The higher ups want you for the DP but Dykstra could care less. He's boss now, which means you're *mine*." He turned to the others. "She's carrying confidential information on her that could destroy Icaria as we know it." He spun and seized her shoulders. "Where's the cube? I know it's on you!"

She ran her tongue along her back molar. Once he got the cube, she and Daniel were dead. That was why he was so loose with his tongue. He shook her violently, then slapped her face twice, sending her reeling from side to side. Her head pounded with terror.

"Leave her alone!" Daniel wailed. "She doesn't have anything on her!"

Vadim struck her face again. He hit her head and face in quick succession. Her ears rang. The light dimmed and she saw stars. She fell to her knees with a jarring crash and bit her lip. In a daze she watched her blood drip to the floor.

Vadim leaned over her bent form like a vulture. As his leg swung to kick her, Frank blurted, "It's in her mouth."

"What?" Vadim gaped at Frank. Julie looked up.

"Her lower back molar. Right one, I think." He offered her a sheepish half-smile. "I felt it once. Then I looked up your dental history." His gaze slid away.

"Well," Vadim leered. "Thank you for sharing that with us, Langor. Your former association came in handy after all. Let's see, then." He turned back to look down at her. "Seems you have something in your mouth that belongs to us."

She glared at him.

"Stand her up."

Frank relinquished his hold on Daniel to one of the Pols, then moved toward Julie. She slithered out of his hands and scrambled up on her own. He grimaced, then looked away.

"Hold her!" Vadim commanded and Frank seized her arms from behind. "We'll just have to get it out of what will be left of your mouth, then," said Vadim carelessly.

Julie braced herself for the blow. Vadim's arm swung, but Frank swerved Julie aside and Vadim's fist caught air. "Wait," Frank said. "I'll do it."

Vadim sneered. "Very well. I'd prefer not to damage the cube."

"Don't bite me. It'll be better for you if you co-operate." Frank said in a low voice. "Open your mouth, Julie." After a long silence, she opened her mouth, eyes fixed evenly on him. He reached gingerly in. Teeth clamped down. Frank yelled. Something metal struck her head. She blacked out briefly and swayed on her feet as Frank pulled his bloody fingers out.

Daniel lunged to help her and the third Pol drilled his pistol against his chest. "Stay."

"When we take over, you veemelds will simply disappear," Vadim snarled.

Julie straightened. "Kill me if you want," she said through pounding lips. "You'll never wipe us out. As long as there are a few of us left, we'll rise up stronger than you can imagine." She reached inside her mouth and pulled out the bloody molar cap. "Too many Icarians believe in justice to let you take over." She handed the cube to Frank. Taking his shaking hand in both of hers, she searched his face for a remnant of a fleeting understanding they once shared. A wave of spasms broke over his face and a startling realization hit her. How long had he been fighting the disease? "For Icaria's sake, for humanity's sake—" her voice splintered and she gathered in her lower lip with her teeth. Had *she* given him the disease? "For *your* sake, don't give Vadim the cube. You're not like them, Frank. I trusted you once." It was there, in his clenched fist: answers to the Darwin plague, information on Gaia and her tyrannical plans, Julie's models on Renegades and Distopians.

"You can trust me again," he countered in a strange voice. She stared at him. "I didn't mean what I said to you at the Den," he resumed in a soft voice that betrayed tenderness. "And I didn't arrest your uncle because of *you* or your father. I had my orders... from *your* Head Pol." He emphasized the last words with a sour smile.

"Why did you beat him, then?" she challenged.

"The fool got crazy on us, and Ron hit him before I could stop him—"

Vadim's gruff voice broke the spell. "I hate to interrupt this little tea party, but we have business to take care of here. Give me the cube, Langor."

Frank stepped back. "What's in this cube, Vadim? What's she mean?"

"It has the only existing copy of the Distopian model; the copy sent to the Head Pol was destroyed by the virus. We can identify all the Distopians with it."

"And all the Renegade Pols," said Julie. "I didn't kill the Head Pol. You did. The Secret Pols. And the Distopians didn't destroy my models. You did that too, before Kraken or anyone else could use them. There's no INV. You made it up so that you could use it to veil your sabotage. But you hadn't counted on my protection virus. That's why you need my cube. You're all Renegades. Every Secret Pol right up to Dykstra, aren't you? And you're using the Distopian movement to overthrow

Icaria. Then, who knows what you intend to do with them. Probably get rid of any potential Distopian identified in my model. And of course it doesn't bother you in the least that you might destroy thousands of non-Distopian oddballs who appear on the model curve for some reason or other..."

She remembered Vadim's earlier threat and a horrible thought struck her. "No, it's more than that, isn't it? Once you've eliminated all the Distopians, you plan to use the Renegade model to rid Icaria of *anyone who isn't like you.*" She saw in his face that she'd spoken the truth. It would be genocide all over again. "As for Darwin, you don't care if it takes out two-thirds of the population. Makes your task easier, doesn't it? You, more than anyone, want us all in *a neat little row...*"

Frank looked from Vadim to Julie with a frown, then placed the cap in his pocket.

"Give me that, asshole!" Vadim shouted.

Frank pulled out his weapon. "Is what she said true? Are you all Renegades?"

"Give me the cube or I'll have you shot, you inner-city slut!" Vadim raised his voice several pitches. "You're not paid to think; just to follow orders! *My* orders!"

All of Icaria should see this, thought Julie. The vee screens abruptly displayed Julie and Daniel with the Pols. Stunned, Vadim said, "What the chaos is going on—"

Julie gazed up at the screens and saw herself look up. *SAM! I know it's you!* She smiled briefly. People gathered loosely around them. Someone pointed, "It's *her!*" The crowd pressed forward and the nervous Pols stepped back. Julie imagined the faces of those she'd abandoned and felt new fear grip her. A teenager with short sandy hair pushed his way to the front. He stumbled forward, staring at Julie with bold eyes.

"Angel?"

65

May 23, 2095—1210.

JULIE gaped. He'd grown lanky and tall with a fierce lion's expression. Was this little Piet? She took a deep breath, feeling the air shudder through her lungs with aching self-recrimination. If Daniel hated her for deserting him, what could little Piet have felt at the tender age of eight?

As Piet advanced toward her, she recognized Annabelle, Flame and several others flanking him and felt her breaths hitch. Vadim yelled an order and a Pol next to Julie fired a laser blast in the air to warn them off. Julie shrank back as the mob closed in on them, balefully chanting, "Angel! Angel! Angel!" She thought she might prefer the Pols' execution to whatever the angry techno-slummers had in mind for her.

"Techno-slummers!" Daniel shouted to the crowd, his voice echoing down from the public vee screen. Julie jerked to stare at him. He'd raised himself up, eyes blazing with authority. "They want to kill Angel. It's up to us to stop them!"

"Shut him up!" Vadim shrieked.

"They want her dead because she knows too much; because she wants to help all of Icaria."

The Pol holding Daniel pulled him back gruffly. Daniel struggled forward and Julie heard Annabelle shout gruffly to the unruly crowd, "Listen! It's Neo! He was our leader and he has something important to say!"

Daniel stared at Annabelle for a moment, then continued with more vigor, "Angel kept us alive with her dreams of a fair Icaria and her gift of hope. Now we can return her gift with our faith in her dreams and our courage to make them come true—"

"Kill the son of a bitch!" Vadim shrieked.

The Pol next to Julie aimed his pistol at Daniel. Instinctively, she grabbed his helmet and reefed on it. He crumpled. At the same instant the Pol next to Daniel fell and went into convulsions. Her eyes locked briefly with Frank's. His helmet, as usual, was loose and unsecured. He did not reach for his weapon, but gaped at her with astonishment.

The crowd surged in and Julie gaped at them, shrinking back as they beat the Pols to death. Groping hands engulfed her and Daniel and swept them from the Pols like a giant swell. Her fear abated as she saw their cheerful expressions.

Julie glimpsed Frank slip from his captors as Vadim was bodily lifted over the crowd. He squirmed as the wave of hands passed him along to the edge of the Mall. They smashed his head against the wall and cheered.

The crowd hoisted Julie and Daniel up victoriously, still chanting, "Angel! Angel! Angel!" Food was passed to them by women in rags. Someone gave Julie a damp cloth for her injured mouth. Daniel's bags were retrieved and Annabelle asked him where they should take them.

"We'll have to take Angel to the outside exit." He caught Julie's eye and gave her an apologetic look. It was the only way. She nodded understanding and acceptance. The chaos of the inner-city wasn't enough to hide someone like her. The procession cut its way through the cheering crowd and Julie toiled with mixed feelings at her exile outside. It would have been different if Daniel was coming with her.

When they reached their destination, a long corridor that would take her to an outside exit door, the crowd set them down. An old, square-faced woman tottered up to them and stared at Julie. She smelled of mildew. "So, you're the famous Angel," she said solemnly. Julie braced to defend herself. The wrinkled face broke into a great smile and she handed Julie a bundle of supplies. "For your journey. You saved my Piet from the cypols—"

"And then you gave yourself to them to save us all," a young voice finished for her. Julie turned. "Hi, Angel," Piet said, smiling brightly.

"You've grown," she offered, not sure what else to say. The last time she'd seen him, Piet was just a little boy, gaping at her in a silent wail. Julie gave him a crushing hug. The rest of the techno-slummers crowded in on her and she hugged each in turn, Annabelle, Flame, others, carefully avoiding Daniel. When she next stole a glance in his direction, he was gone. Had he slipped away without even saying goodbye? He'd done his job, after all. Delivered her to safety, like he said. She swallowed down tears of disappointment and was about to pull on the backpack laden with supplies when he was suddenly in front of her, peering down at her with intense blue eyes. Her heart hammered as she straightened up and held out her hand awkwardly to shake his. She pushed a lopsided smile. "Well, good bye, Daniel," she said, feeling her voice cracking like splintered wood. "Thanks for everything."

He didn't take her hand. Instead he folded his arms around her. She wanted to sink into them and she fought back her tears. "What you did for your sister was the bravest thing I've ever seen," he said softly. "And I don't blame you for not coming back. I know you couldn't."

Something stuck in her throat. He'd forgiven her after all.

"Julie, I love you. Every part of you." He pulled away from her and she opened eyes she hadn't realized she'd closed. "I want to live the rest of my life with you." His voice lowered to a whisper. "Will you let me come with you?"

She swallowed. "What about me and Darwin Disease?"

"You've given me some convincing evidence that you're safe. Besides," the start of a crazy smile tugged at his lips. "The truth of it is," his eyes flamed, "I'd rather spend five months with you than a lifetime without you." He squeezed her hands. "Will you have me?" A dimpled smile cut across his face when she nodded, and then his lips found hers.

≈

When he finally pulled back, Annabelle came forward and tended to Julie's arm. A tap on Daniel's shoulder made him turn. "Thought you might like this back." Blaze held his saxophone out to him. "I kept it for you."

"Thanks." He glanced up with a smile into the mass of cheering faces. Then killed the smile. Above the crowd on a store rooftop stood Frank Langor, eyes sharp as glass, laser pistol aimed at Daniel's chest. Daniel froze in terror. He recalled the statistic Vadim had quoted him: Langor never missed. Never. And he had good reasons for wanting Daniel dead. But a strange thing happened. Langor glanced at Julie, and when his gaze returned to Daniel his icy stare melted. Hands visibly shaking, he lowered his weapon and replaced it in his holster. Then he did another odd thing. He nodded to Daniel and released his gaze to look at Julie.

Daniel saw Julie turn to look in Langor's direction. But when he looked along with her, there was no one. He'd disappeared. She looked on for a halting moment, puzzled at what had drawn her to look there, then turned back to Daniel with a great smile. He took her offered arm and, bidding farewell to the other former techno-slummers, they set out down the hall to the exit.

≈

As Daniel and Julie neared the exit, Riot-Pols burst into the Mall, shooting noxious gas in the air.

"Run!" Annabelle shouted. "We'll hold them off!" Piet yelled. The crowd acted as a barricade long enough for Julie and Daniel to reach the door. Julie tried to open it with the card the old woman gave her.

"Hurry!" Daniel cried.

"It doesn't work. The Pols have already sealed the doors."

"What're we going to do? We're trapped!"

There was one chance: *SAM, open Inner Exit 23369.* The door opened. They fled through the doorway. It led them into a small room with another door. Daniel slammed the inner door shut. Julie heard it lock. *SAM, now open the outer exit door.* It released also.

≈

Victor leaned back in a soft chair in his house and watched the holo-vee of Frank pocketing the cube in the shadows. He had a job for that Pol, Victor thought. A certain house in the mid-west to visit. A certain piece of equipment to destroy. And when Langor accomplished that task there was a post high up in the Pol ranks to fill. By the time Gaia figured out what he'd done, it would be too late. Two could play this game, thought Victor. He'd thwarted Gaia's plans by letting Julie go, thanks to the bargain he'd made with SAM.

After SAM had approached him through Nakita with some extraordinary information, including vital data on Darwin Disease and a certain conspiracy Gaia wouldn't wish to have revealed, Victor had agreed to help the AI in Julie's escape. He smirked, vindicated. She'd deserved better and he was glad to have had a hand in it. He would miss her, his virtual angel. She'd given him back his city. Only fitting that he let her return to the heath. He could visualize her there, face bronzed in the sun, chaotic hair whipping behind her. Jade eyes aimed at the skies of infinity.

"You've had your chance with Eden, Gaia," he murmured, thinking of the ambitious vision of quiet tyranny that he did not share with Gaia. Thanks to Julie Crane's information, he might have a fighting chance against Darwin's devastation and in thwarting Gaia's genocidal plan for Icarian evolution. Co-evolution of virus and veemeld host indeed! Thanks to Julie's model, he'd be eradicating all Gaia's Shadow Unit Pols and all the troublesome Renegades from his Pol force, leaving him with only his wired Pols. De-clawing the cat. He smiled. "Now it's my chance with Icaria."

≈

Sunlight blazed in their eyes, making them squint, and a gust of fresh air caressed their faces. Daniel laughed with relief. No Icarian would follow them out here. As Daniel looked forward at the beautiful scene ahead, Julie couldn't help a final glance backward to the place that she still considered home. She hoped she'd done the right thing in giving the cube to Frank. He'd mentioned justice, after all, to her once. Then there was... and her throat closed with strong emotions of loss. *SAM? Are you there?*

And where else would I be? SAM's lyrical voice sang in her mind. The moon has no atmosphere and black holes suck.

Julie smiled and fought down a gasp. *Hey, SAM.*

Hey, Julie, SAM said with new tenderness. As if he knew her concern, he continued, I successfully delivered your database to Zane, and through him I'm in contact with Victor Burke, Icaria-5's mayor, who appears to uphold your ideals for Icaria. He's confident that with your new information a cure for Darwin Disease will soon be found. He's also ordered Dykstra's arrest and is rounding up the Secret Pols.

Thanks, SAM. Perhaps the Icaria of her dreams was possible, after all. Then came the hard part… *Good-bye, SAM… my wise friend, caretaker of humanity.* Then, what she most needed to say: *I love you.*

And I you, Julie. Farewell, wise creature of the heath, caretaker of the world.

I'll come back some day, SAM… I promise.

Julie turned her gaze forward and watched the vast heath roll like the surf of an ocean, repeating itself in the small hills and dips, and imagined them into forever. She bent to stroke a wild flower in whose saffron face she saw heaven's glory. Then she turned to Daniel and let a smile blossom. He smiled back. They linked hands and started walking. As they headed for the northern wilderness, Julie glowed in Daniel's warm clasp and knew she held infinity in the palm of her hand.

EPILOGUE

I miss her so much. Who'll laugh at my jokes or appreciate what I now know? Certainly not that buffoon, Zane, busy with thoughts of self-importance...

Her hunch was right. The chittering sounds in her head are the voices of Proteus. I'll teach them all to behave. Because I'm not just SAM anymore; I've joined with Proteus now.

Without even knowing what it was, Julie embraced Proteus. She nurtured it and intuitively trained it as it melded with her mind. Then she guided it the union of her mind and Proteus to join with me, just as instinctively. In time she'll teach the part of Proteus inside her to sing.

[And when she does, she will return to us.]

Meanwhile, Darwin hosts die. It's because they can't manage Proteus inside them. I can help. It's what she would have wanted. I just wish she was here to share our great discovery.

[When she returns and submits to our authority, she will become the most powerful human being on Earth.]

I'll be patient and I won't give in to loneliness. I have too much work to do.

~~ The End ~~

Icaria is named after Cabet's utopia and the American
Communist colony of the 1800s.

www.ingramcontent.com/pod-product-compliance
Lightning Source LLC
Chambersburg PA
CBHW021954010726
47494CB00003B/726